Autumn's Captive

Kelda Laing Poynot

ISBN-13: 9798666854679

DEDICATION

For Mia

CONTENTS

ACKNOWLEDGMENTS

Scotty
Mia
Madison
Sarah

Thank you for being patient while Topher and Tia's story unfolded.

Chelsea, your artwork continues to amaze me!
Thank you for yet another beautiful cover.
Cover art and illustrations by Chelsea Guidry Poynot
3 Petals Photography

PROLOGUE

From the beginning of time, humankind has explained the world based on the predictable changes of nature. Along with the phases of the moon and the seas, Mother Nature boasts her power through the seasons. Like a dance, the autumnal and spring equinoxes and the winter and summer solstices mark the rotations and revolutions around the sun, moving to its own rhythm, setting the pace for everyone else.

Round and round the sun she goes, sashaying through time. The autumn brings with it longer nights and colder winds. She loosens her grasp on the sun, and it is powerless to hold her. Winter arrives with its stark cold and blankets of snow. The sun is barely seen to even strike up a tune to dance. Everything is dormant and bedded until spring. Spring is a stirring, a gradual awakening, a flirtatious wink at what is to come. The chords are renewed and warmed as the entire earth unfolds and opens to the sun's wooing. Then, finally, summer's power is regained.

With summer comes the full bloom and growth for all that is needed for sustenance. Every living thing is renewed and strengthened and can hardly remember the distance of winter.

JUNE 20

Summer Solstice

SEPTEMBER 22

Autumnal Equinox

DECEMBER 21

Winter Solstice

MARCH 20

Spring Equinox

Persephone in Winter

Robin Hyde (1906 - 1939)

Persephone in winter-time
Lay still, nor gave a thought
To the fierce surging tides of flowers
Her restless youth had brought.
Trapped beyond touch of pain or sorrow,
Gaoled* in high walls of aquamarine,
Her blue eyes veiled from any morrow,
She slumbered ... Pluto's queen.
The sharp-toothed conies* burrowed down
To find the jonquil* maiden
Seen dancing through their hillocked* town
Her bare arms blossom-laden;
With frightened eyes, the seekers crept
To nibbled grass again,
Telling of how the Ivory slept,
Too still, too chill for men.
Only the snake, whose thought strikes cold
From ancient jewelled eyes,
In rings of mottled green and gold
Slips round her girdle-wise.
Only the stealthy lute-string sound
Of hesitant waters underground,
Only the ice-blue water-drips
Are secret as her lips.

Gaoled – imprisoned; incarcerated
conies – rabbits
jonquil – a yellow narcissus
hillock – small hill or mound

AUTUMN

CHAPTER 1

Junior Year

My mom diffused essential oils. She believed that they could cure almost any ailment. Okay, that wasn't the entire truth. She believed that essential oils would most definitely cure any illness. Little did she know that what ailed me wasn't internal; it was external, and it was known as *Tiana Evelynne Reynolds*. It was a rare disorder, and I believed that I had the only known diagnosis. It had yet to be documented or studied, but I had it bad, an advanced case.

Mom diffused a powerful lavender-blend. Sometimes, she would sneak into my room and plug it in and add her concoction. My conscious self could fight it, but my sleeping-self couldn't. I always woke up feeling like I'd been drinking all night.

I had gone to bed, exhausted. School had already begun, and my homework was pretty demanding. I was bailing hay for our neighbor, Mr. Roy, early in the mornings, and had football practice four afternoons a week. Our first game was in three nights. I was proud of myself for making the starting varsity line, but the demands were taking their toll.

I woke with a start, covered in sweat. My heart was racing like I'd been running. My ceiling fan whirled slowly in the dimly lit room. I tried to settle my heart. I had been dreaming, but I couldn't remember what it was about. Then it all came back to me in a rush.

It was three months ago, the day before she left to go to her aunt's house for the summer. I'd been up for hours already and had crashed on my bed to rest. Mom and Dad were at work, and my little brother, Jesse, was at day camp. Tia walked into my room and hit the button on the Bluetooth speaker harder than was necessary. I jumped, surprised to see her. The air was silent but electrically charged with the lingering moaning of my favorite folk singer.

"How can you listen to this?" She always seemed irritated by his voice.

"I don't know. It fits the mood," I said.

"No, it doesn't. It sets the mood and makes you wallow too long in your own misery," Tia argued.

"You're leaving tomorrow, and I'll miss you. The lead singer gets it. He sings a lot about missing."

"He's clinically depressed. I think he may need medication. Besides, I'm not gone yet, so how can you miss me?"

She plopped down next to me. Pressing her bony elbow into my side. My old bed squeaked in protest with the added weight. Or maybe that was my heart protesting. Either way, there was a protest. Not like a peaceful assembly, a riotous rally, complete with picket signs and loud chants. *Don't go! Don't go!*

She grabbed my phone and scrolled through my playlist. She found something more upbeat that had a little rockabilly twang in the steel guitar. I listened until the chorus. "It may be more upbeat, but the sentiment is the same. That singer still misses."

"Missing isn't bad. By the end of the song, he knows she's coming home."

"But he isn't sure she'll be the same. You won't be the same." There was still missing in my tone. The longing was hard. Longing sucked.

"You'll be different, too, you know?" I liked the smile in her voice.

I turned and looked at her. "What do you mean? I won't be different."

"You'll be all tanned and have new grease stains on your jeans from the tractor. You'll smell like diesel, and you'll be driving your new truck. You'll probably grow another inch and be all toned and pumped from two-a-days." She grabbed my abs for emphasis, and her small fingers tickled. I flinched away. "Your hands will have new callouses." She took my hand and turned it over, considering the possible changes. I liked it when she took my hand, and her tickling wasn't as playful as it had been six months ago.

"Do you like the tone and tan?" I asked, teasing playfully.

She shrugged in reply. I couldn't tell if she was being flirty or coy. That wasn't her style, but she'd been spending more time with her friend, Catherine, and I didn't know if some of her tendencies were rubbing off on T.

The song changed and moved into a sweet melody with a chorus about a first kiss. I didn't need to be thinking about kisses, so I spoke instead. "Can I still see you tonight, or is that why you came early?" My voice sounded so sad.

She looked questioningly at me. "You can still see me tonight. I won't turn into a pumpkin until midnight," she laughed. "I should be finished packing by six. Mom's got a list of errands to run after lunch. Onion rings and shakes?" she asked, looking hopeful.

"Yeah, rings and shakes."

I waited outside her house at six. She's asked me not to come to the door because her dad would still be sleeping. I let my mom's sedan idle at the curb. Tia ran from the house, smiling. I hopped out of the car to get the door for her, but she beat me to it.

"I'm starving!" she exclaimed.

I drove to the drive-in and parked. I rolled down the windows. "Want to get it to go?" I asked before I ordered.

"Go where?" she asked.

"To the park, maybe the pond?" We'd hiked trails there forever, and it was only a few minutes away.

"At night?" She hesitated and shook her head a little. "No, I'd like to eat here."

Crap! Of course, she wouldn't want to go to the pond at night. I'd just asked her to go to the second most notorious make-out spot in town. It was so awkward. Nothing was as innocent as it had been before. By the end of our sophomore year, our entire class seemed to be pairing off. Suddenly everyone was a couple. Even upperclassmen took notice of the girls in our class. Tia was still the same, so thankfully, no one had taken notice of her, and I guess our friendship may have buffered her from some of that attention, too. We were always together.

"I didn't mean anything by that. I just thought it might be nice to be alone." Her eyes widened nervously, and she swallowed hard. *Crap!* "T, I'm sorry. We'll just eat here, catch a movie, and I'll take you home. Okay?" She smiled and nodded, entirely back to normal.

I checked my phone for movie times. The only movie we hadn't seen was a zombie apocalypse, and neither of us wanted to experience that.

"What do you want to do?" she asked.

I shrugged. "Want to go back to my house and watch a movie?"

"No, let's get ice cream and go to the pond. We can walk the path. The moon will give us plenty of light."

"Are you sure? A half-hour ago, you didn't want to."

She shrugged. "Well, now, I do."

I pressed the call button again and ordered a couple of cones: one dipped, the other plain. I could never manage the chocolate shell coating. Tia managed it just fine, and she never ended up with chocolate anywhere but her lips. *Her lips.* Damn the guys for ribbing me at practice. Screw them for planting that image in my mind and making me want to kiss her.

We drove the few minutes to the pond and found the parking lot empty. We walked past a few picnic tables and entered the trailhead. It was just getting dark, but there was still enough light to see. We could have walked the path blindfolded. As kids, we'd walked it hundreds of times.

The trail didn't take twenty minutes to walk. The pond just wasn't that big. At a narrow section, I walked behind Tia. I could hear the night critters waking up and the crunch of her teeth on the ice cream cone. I'd already devoured mine, but she liked to take her time nibbling on each ridge, taking it in sections and rounds. That's how she probably managed the hard chocolate shell without it crumbling into her lap.

Tia stopped at the edge of the trail and looked over the pond. It was calm and reflected the moon. I stepped back and picked up a stone and skipped it effortlessly across the smooth surface of the water. I scooped up a couple more and handed her one. She smiled and skipped it. Then, she held out her hand, asking for the other stone. She didn't think I'd just give it to her, did she? I held my hand up over her head and dared her to get it. She couldn't resist the playful challenge. She jumped and tried to get my hand. She couldn't reach when I held it directly over my head. She dug her little fingers into my abs again, and I bent double from the spasm of tickling. She gripped my abs tighter, and I lowered my arms to protect myself.

She refused to let me go, and I was forced to take the offensive. I dropped the stone and grabbed her around the wrists, gently pulling her hands away. She was no match for my strength and size, so I took her wrists with one hand and then held her at arms' length. I laughed, but she didn't. She tried in vain to get to me. Her feet scuffled over the stones and the muddy bank, and she stepped toward higher ground. She squealed and grunted in frustration.

"Are you done?" I asked. "Do you give up?"

She stopped fighting and settled herself. Confident she wasn't going to fight me, I squinted my eyes in the dim light and tried to find another stone. I still held tightly to her wrists. I reached over and picked up a flat rock and held it up, asserting my dominance. She relaxed her arms, so I loosened my grip, and she edged to my side. I had no idea she'd attack me so suddenly, but from nowhere, she was on my back and holding me around my neck and shoulders.

I took a step to regain my balance. Tia hadn't hurt me, but she had knocked the breath out of me from surprise. Sure, we'd wrestled plenty, but not since we were little. She was like a tiny monkey on my back, light and agile, and extremely annoying. I stepped back onto the trail toward the level ground. I didn't want to risk falling into the pond. I stretched and rolled my shoulders to reach her and pull her off. She squealed and laughed.

After a few attempts, I finally grabbed her waist and pulled her over my shoulder and into my arms. Tia's light-brown eyes glistened in the moonlight, and her smile brought her cheeks all the way up to her bottom lashes. I cradled her more securely in my arms and laughed with her. Then, I felt a tug in my chest like I'd just been sucker-punched. My breath hitched a bit on the inhale.

"Christopher, what is it?" she asked. I shook my head. I didn't want to put her down, but I didn't have any real reason to carry her, either.

"I'm going to miss you," I said. Tia's eyes fell, and she blinked and nodded. I held her close, and she put her head on my shoulder, resigning herself to the fact. She lifted her head and kissed my cheek. Tia's lips lingered there for a second longer, and I turned my face and met her lips with mine.

It was a sweet kiss but nothing make-out or heavy petting worthy. We didn't open our mouths or touch tongues or teeth. Our hands and bodies remained perfectly still. We just kissed, barely moving our lips. If anyone would have been watching, it was probably painfully awkward. I didn't know how to kiss, and Tia didn't really either, but I liked it, and I would mark it up there with things I'd like to repeat and practice and get really, really good at.

It wasn't a bad way to wake up, except that I hadn't kissed her in months. I hadn't even kissed her again when I dropped her off that night. I just gave her a hug, promised I'd write her a letter, and waved goodbye. Although it had elicited a strong, physical response, the dream had given no sense of foreboding. Once the fog of sleep and lavender cleared into consciousness, I smiled to myself. Today, she returned. I hurried and dressed and ran down the hall to breakfast.

CHAPTER 2

"You're in a hurry. Stop. Eat. You have plenty of time," Mom said as she blocked my path to the door.

"Tia comes back today. I want to get there early," I protested.

"Eat," Mom demanded. "You have a full day, and I can't have my blind-side tackle pooping out on his varsity debut."

I rolled my eyes, pretending to be annoyed, but I loved that my mom was my proudest supporter. We lived in a small town where football was important. We had all been conditioned and trained since elementary school. Excessive, maybe, but ultimately the weak were weeded out, and the strong remained. I was one of the strong.

Mom placed a plate of eggs and bacon on the counter and challenged me to disobey her. She wasn't a large woman, but she was my mom, and you didn't refuse food from your mom. That, and I was hungry. I was always hungry.

Mom was an accountant. She had a great mind for numbers and thankfully had passed the practical side of money onto me. She managed the books for about a dozen area farms, but she said her most important job was raising healthy boys.

My younger brother, Jesse, had random allergies: a list of foods, seasonal, and environmental. She'd always experimented with Jesse's diet because he needed to stay as goo and rash free as possible. For years, she researched the best foods for allergy-prone kids and athletes. Jesse was showing some skill on the field, too, and she was determined to give us whatever advantage she could. After middle school, I'd grown several inches and gained about twenty-five pounds. No one complained. The JV coaches were so excited when I arrived for summer workouts.

Mom was an excellent cook, and my appetite had doubled. Hunger pains were common, and until she made the changes, I feared I'd devour myself from the inside. Was it possible for a stomach to eat itself? She did even more research, and we began carb-loading in the off-seasons. It was awesome! I was able to work all winter and spring and continue to gain muscle and mass. It didn't hurt that I was still growing; my body seemed to agree with the dietary changes.

To avoid any hunger pains, I ate just about everything she put in front of me. I scarfed down the plate of food, kissed Mom on the cheek, and jumped in my truck to go to school. *No more bus!* I'd been saving for three summers to buy my vehicle. It was a gray, full-size Silverado pick-up with leather interior. It wasn't new, but it was new to me.

Mom and Dad had always promised to match funds when it came time to buy my first car. I think Dad had to dip into their savings to match my budget. He tried to dissuade me, but I knew what I wanted. It was probably more vehicle than most sixteen-year-old boys needed, but I didn't consider myself a typical sixteen-year-old boy. I'd been working since I was twelve; I'd been saving since before then. It was just the way I was wired.

Dad questioned me at length. "This is tapping out your savings. What about college? You need to be thinking about that as well."

"I'm not spending all of my savings," I argued. "I'm not stupid, Dad, and I still have two years to consider college. After football, I'll be able to work more."

He didn't disagree anymore after that discussion and honestly seemed excited for me when we'd finally found *the* truck. I was a big guy, strong and responsible. I may have been young, but I worked hard, and people hired me and paid me well. I also reasoned that a big vehicle allowed me to haul stuff and make even more money. I'd already made a couple hundred bucks in the month I'd owned it. I was determined to have my own wheels before the first day of school. *Check.*

Our small-town school was old fashioned, and our high school had a rigid dress code. Away from school, we could wear whatever we wanted, but at school, girls only wore skirts and dresses and guys had to wear khakis, dress shirts, and ties, no jeans. Jeans were reserved for work and hanging out with our friends. It was nice because the girls always looked like ladies, and the guys always looked like gentlemen. Except for PE, you never saw a student not following the dress code. There was stiff punishment when we didn't follow the rules.

As I drove onto campus, the diesel engine roared and called attention to itself. I looked around, hoping to see T. I texted her as soon as I parked. No reply. She didn't have access to her phone all summer, and I wondered if she'd reactivated it yet. I grabbed my tie from around my rearview mirror. I slipped it over my head, straightened it, and then grabbed my backpack.

It was Tia's first day back. Although the rest of us had been in school for a few weeks, she returned just before the Autumn Festival. The festival centered around the autumnal equinox, the opening game of the season, and then, all the following day would be spent at the festival. It was a local holiday and the last hurrah for our little town before the harvesting began.

Tiana Reynolds was my best friend. Everyone else called her Tiana, but I called her Tia or T. If you remember, I suffer from a condition known as *Tiana Evelynne Reynolds*. It doesn't carry her name because she discovered the *condition*, but because she is the cause of it. I hadn't seen her since the beginning of June. Although I'd had plenty of distraction with summer jobs and workouts, I still missed her. I missed her every single day. I went to sleep thinking about her; I woke up thinking about her. I listened to the woeful moans of folk singers who understood my pain. Three months is a long time to be away from another person, especially someone who I'd spent nearly every single day with since kindergarten.

She began spending time at her Aunt Trudy's house the summer we turned thirteen. She wrote me letters and would stay in touch until the summer solstice. At that point, all correspondence ceased.

The second fall, the fall of our freshman year, I freaked out a little because she wasn't back when school started. I was worried she'd moved or something, but then I saw her parents, and they said she'd return for the festival. At the beginning of our freshman year, she walked through her first couple of days, a practical stranger. She was distracted and needed to catch up. It didn't take her long before she and I fell back into our usual friendship, but when it happened again at the beginning of our sophomore year, it was worse and took longer for her to come around.

I asked my mom if she could shed any light on the subject. Mom *was* a girl, right? She knew about girl things. "She's busy, I'm sure, just getting back and all. Give her some time to get settled, honey; she'll come around."

"She's different, Mom. It's just weird. It's like she doesn't even know me. Are all girls this weird?" I'd asked. I had just turned fifteen, and girls were suddenly on my radar. They smelled nice. They looked nice. They smiled and did girly things with their hair and their eyes, and they giggled a lot. Had they always laughed that much?

"No, honey, they aren't weird; they're just different from you, and you need to appreciate the differences. Men and women are made different for a reason. You'll come to understand that in time."

"I know the differences, Mom," I said defensively and a little annoyed, referring to the openness my parents had for speaking about relationships, reproduction, and sex. "You've told me about that my entire life."

"No, I'm not talking about *that.* Although, I hope you understand the importance of contraception and remember to consider your future rather than the intensity of a single moment."

I knew. It hadn't taken me too long to guess that my parents had conceived me a couple of months before they married. That was elementary math, and I'd been able to do that on my fingers before I was ten. She cleared her throat to bring me back to the conversation. "I'm talking about differences in personality and emotional sensitivity. Women connect differently than men, and we need each other to balance out our extremes. You'll be wise to remember that."

"But what does that have to do with Tiana?" I asked.

"She's probably feeling a little overwhelmed again this fall with the demands of catching up in school. Her mom says she's babysitting for the Clarke's and involved in a few clubs this year, too. I'm sure she's hit the ground running. Give it some time and see how it plays out."

I didn't understand it, but I came to expect it. Tia would tell me how busy she was at her aunt's house during the summer, how she had to be continuously tutored. She even mentioned that once her grandmother arrived on the solstice, she'd lose all sense of timing, and her days were not her own.

I never questioned her beyond the surface. It made her uncomfortable to answer personal questions about her family. Her mom and dad seemed normal except for the fact that they sent their only child away for the entire summer. I had accepted it, even though I didn't like it, because I knew once she returned in September, she'd be mine until summer began.

This year was different, though. I walked into school and saw Tia entering her homeroom with her friend, Catherine. I was two doors down. A teammate, Jason, eyed me warily as he followed them. Later, I saw them all again in chemistry. I only had three classes with Tia: chemistry, Algebra II, and British lit. She didn't smile at me or seem happy to be there. My first-period teacher had detained me, so I was running late for class. I wanted to rush over and greet her but didn't get the chance.

Catherine was in chemistry with us but had opted out of much of the college-prep track our freshman year because she planned on going to beauty school or pursue something at the technical school. She wavered about what she might study, but everyone knew that was because her current area of concentration was a senior named Clayton. He was our quarterback, and every girl noticed him. Not only did his dad farm more land than anyone else in our county, but he was also wealthier than most in our little town. Girls took notice of that. Thankfully, Tia hadn't.

Catherine held Tia's attention during class. I should make it clear that she demanded everyone's attention. She was a popular girl with long auburn hair. Anytime that Tia would try to look away, Catherine would distract her or put her hand on her arm. The other two classes that Catherine wasn't in, Jason, seemed to do the same.

I said hello to her in every class, but she wouldn't make eye contact with me. It was really annoying when she spoke only to Catherine and Jason. He and I played football together; he was our second-string quarterback but mostly played corner. He was fast; he was good, but I never liked him much. He was cocky and expected everyone to bow at his feet. Jason had the same three classes as I did with Tia. That wasn't so uncommon given the size of our school, but then I realized that Jason had the same schedule with her except last period PE. He and I had conditioning that went straight into after-school practice.

I sensed Jason's intrusion from Tia's first day back at school. He'd never paid her any attention in all the years we'd been in school together. He was sought after by most girls, and he was confident and, I supposed, handsome. He and Clayton had that in common. He wasn't as big or as strong as me, but he was twice if not three times as arrogant and exuded a confidence that I never managed to muster with girls.

I tried to be patient, but Tia's return was nothing like I anticipated. She ignored me as she'd done the two years before, but this time it was like she didn't know me at all. Was she mad at me? Had I pissed her off by not returning her letters? She'd written to me three times, but I had only answered one of her letters. It was hard, and I didn't know what to say. I couldn't fill a page with:

Dear Tia, I missed you yesterday. Ran five miles. Mr. Roy's tractor needed oil, and I missed you today. I'd like to kiss you again. Were you okay with that? I miss you. I miss you. I miss you. Love, Christopher.

By the third day, she still hadn't spoken to me directly. I was worried that time apart and disappointment had changed our friendship forever. Girls were weirder than guys, and I was just beginning to take notice of those differences, both good and bad, but this year, though, Tia's differences were dark. She seemed weighted like she was wearing a lead sweater. Her shoulders hunched over her books as she carried them from class to class. Her arms were almost always crossed over her chest.

T wasn't particularly beautiful in the conventional sense, but she was the most beautiful thing to me. In middle school, she was plain and gangly and awkward. As T matured, she developed a peculiar sense of humor. Most guys didn't get her, but she made me laugh and smile all the time. Tia didn't put on airs or even try to draw attention to herself, especially with boys, so I couldn't understand why Jason was suddenly so interested in her and why she was returning that attention. I was jealous. For the first time in my life, I was insecure and afraid. I was scared she'd forget me, abandon our friendship, and choose Jason instead. I didn't know what to do the first time I saw him touch Tia. I was two rows back from them. It took all I had not to tackle him in the middle of class.

I tried to talk to her between classes, but she was whisked off by other people or held after to speak with teachers. Mom had been right about her being busy, but it was more complicated than that. She had a lot of catching up to do, so I tried to be patient with that, but it was just the vacant looks she gave me like she wasn't seeing me at all.

Tia was smart, too smart for the rest of us. The tutoring she received during the summer put her leaps and bounds beyond anything that she could be taught at our little school. She never flaunted her intelligence or her knowledge, which often surpassed the teachers.

"You know I'm not gifted or anything; I'm simply exposed to more than anyone else. I'm required and challenged for more months of the year than the rest of my classmates. You all would have the same advantage if your parents and grandparents required that," she explained.

I disagreed. Sure, I was intelligent, according to the standardized testing we'd all been subjected to, but I had the distractions of work and sports. Tia had neither.

CHAPTER 3

I was impatient. No, that wasn't true. I was pissed off. After school, Mom asked how things were going and if I'd seen Tia.

"Yeah, she's back," I grumbled.

"What's that tone?" she asked.

I shrugged noncommittally. "I don't know. It's like she's ignoring me."

"Chris, have you done something to offend her? Do you owe her an apology?" she asked like it was all my fault. The whole world was against me.

On her third day back, I nearly lost it. She didn't even acknowledge me when I picked up the pen that had rolled onto the floor and laid it on her desk. How was it possible for her to ignore me so completely? I worried that she might be ignoring me on purpose because she was afraid I'd kiss her again or do something equally as stupid.

After class, I followed her and Jason toward our next period. “Hey, Jason,” I called. He turned to face me, and Tia turned to see what had distracted him.

“What do you want, Topher?” he asked.

“Hey,” I hadn’t thought about what I’d say after I’d gotten his attention. “I just wanted to make sure you knew we were all excused after lunch to get ready for the pep rally,” I stammered.

“Yeah, Topher, I think everyone knows that,” Jason said condescendingly.

I took a step forward, and Jason took a step back, giving me an opening to be nearer to Tia, and she looked up at me for the first time since her return. There was still no recognition in her eyes. “Topher? That’s an unusual name.”

What? I stared disbelievingly. Her eyes were vacant like she was meeting me for the first time. She didn’t recognize me at all. I managed to hold in my shock. With only a few exceptions, I was Topher, and she knew that. Mom, Dad, and Jesse called me Chris. T and Miss Grace were the only ones who called me Christopher. Coaches, teachers, and everyone else called me Topher. Was she playing a joke? No, that wasn’t her. I looked at her, searching her eyes. They were the same brown they'd always been, but there was no recognition. I swallowed my apprehension before I answered her question.

"Well, my name is Christopher, but thanks to Jason and his loser friends, most everyone calls me *Topher*," I said. I adjusted my books and put out my hand in a friendly greeting like we'd never met before. If she didn't know me, I decided then that it was time we became reacquainted.

"Hi, I'm Tiana, it's nice to meet you," she said with a slight smile and shook my hand. I could tell she was sincere; she didn't know me. When our hands touched, she tilted her head slightly and blinked hard like maybe it was familiar. I'd held her hand before, but this was a different sensation. I held her hand a bit longer than was necessary for an initial greeting, but I didn't want to let her go. She didn't pull away; she just looked at our hands for several seconds and then looked back at me. Her entire demeanor changed. She was heavy again like she'd been the first day she arrived. Her shoulders gave way to the lead sweater. "We have a few classes together this year. I don't remember having classes with you before."

I shook my head disbelievingly. "You don't?" I asked quietly. Jason eyed me cautiously. Touching her, my anger and frustration turned to sadness. My heart hurt that she didn't know me.

She rolled my hand over and traced my thumb with hers as she concentrated. I just stared at the top of her head, hoping she'd look up and remember me. "Christopher," she repeated my name as though the thought of me was far away. I swallowed again, and I could feel sweat break out on my palms.

Jason took her by the elbow and shook her slightly, calling her back to the present. "Come on, Tiana, we're going to be late for class."

"It's nice to meet you, Christopher," she said and released my hand. She looked at me again and then to Jason. "Let's go. I don't want to be late. Wait, don't you have Algebra II with us?" she asked me.

"Yeah, I do," I said, relieved, but I couldn't hide my disappointment.

Jason looked bothered that I intruded on his time with Tia. He seemed bothered by me in general, whether it was at practice or in the weight room or now with T. I had never been his favorite person, but my presence was irritating him more than usual. I anticipated the class's dismissal and walked toward Tia's desk with purpose. Jason was fast, but he was about a half-second behind me.

"Are you going to the festival?" I asked her casually. I'd had all class period to think of an excuse to talk to her again.

"Jason's taking me," she said and looked at him for confirmation. He nodded once.

"Like a date?" I asked, unable to contain the anger that rushed to the surface, but she honestly looked surprised at the question.

"No. We're just friends," she clarified. "He's helping me get caught up, loaning me notes and stuff. He thought I'd like a ride."

That didn't sound as bad as I was thinking. "I'd like to be your friend, too," I said. "Do you mind if I tag along?" She smiled and nodded before she thought to consult Jason. "You might need a chaperone. Jason isn't all that trustworthy." I winked playfully, easing the tension. He looked more irritated than usual.

She looked over at Jason and considered my words. "He looks harmless. Are you sure he's not trustworthy?"

"Jason cares for things just as long as it suits him. Please don't mistake his kindness. He's only serving himself."

She suddenly became dark. "I disagree. How would you know? You aren't even from here." She asked dismissively and walked away.

I stared after her. "I am from here. I've gone to school with you every day since kindergarten," I scoffed derisively under my breath. When I turned back toward the door, I saw Jason. He'd watched the entire exchange. "What?" I asked, taking a defensive stance.

"You're a lot more persistent this year, Topher. You don't get it, do you?" Jason asked.

"No, I don't," I confessed. I didn't get why Jason was always around. I didn't understand why he seemed to be everywhere. Not only did we have more classes together, but he'd made varsity, too. He'd grown about six inches over the summer and put on at least thirty pounds, all muscle. "What's your deal?" I asked.

"You can't be with her." The way he said it didn't sound arrogant or the least bit off-putting. It was like he was restating a basic fact that I'd missed in a lecture.

"What?" I asked defensively.

"Dude, she's not to be had."

"I don't know what you're talking about."

For the briefest of moments, a flash of pain crossed Jason's face. He cleared his throat and swallowed. "Look," he began with a raspy voice like he was choking on the words. "I can't say why, but trust me; leave her alone and give her some space." He jerked and exhaled like whatever had been constricting his airway, released him. He took a deep breath and shook off the discomfort before his arrogance returned. "I'll see you at practice," he said.

"You want her for yourself? Is that it? You've decided since you've already had every other girl at your beck and call, that now you want Tia, too?" He shrugged. "Stay away from her," I said with more threat than I ever used.

For the afternoon pep rally, the entire school was ushered into the gym. The band played, the players' names were called, and the cheerleaders danced and waved their pompoms. After the coach and the principal spoke, they handed Clayton the microphone to get the crowd pumped before the team was ushered off to our final warm-up before the game.

I noticed Tia in the bleachers. She sat next to Catherine. She wasn't watching Clayton strut about stirring the crowd, and Catherine was too distracted by Clayton to notice that Tia was looking at me. Tia wasn't dark like she'd been when she stormed off earlier. She looked peaceful for the first time since she returned.

I exhaled and gave a little smile, hopeful. For a split second, Tia's eyes flashed with knowing. Then, just as suddenly, I was bumped from behind by Jason. The guys were pushing each other, rallied by whatever Clayton had said. They jumped and chanted and pulled me into the fervor. I looked back to Tia briefly, but Catherine occupied her attention again. Our connection was lost.

The game was rugged, but we managed to pull out a win. I didn't see Tia before or after the game. The stadium was packed, and after the game, the team was rushed by fans. By the time the coaches delivered their post-game talk, and we'd been congratulated by our parents and siblings, the stadium was nearly empty.

Back in the locker room, I stripped down to my compression shorts and t-shirt. I'd wait and shower at the house. I put on a pair of loose athletic shorts and packed up my duffel bag when Jason walked past my locker. He stopped to talk to another teammate.

"What time are you picking her up tomorrow?" I asked. He looked at me blankly and shook his head, not like he didn't know what time, but like there was no way he was letting me tag along. "You know she's going to ask. I'll be there, just the same, whether or not I go with you." He shrugged and walked away. "Asshole," I muttered under my breath.

I was pushed from behind and thought maybe Jason had heard me. I turned ready to punch him in the face for pushing me again, but it wasn't him. Instead, Clayton was smiling at me but hesitated when he saw my reaction. He put his hands up in surrender.

"Dude, what's up? I just wanted to say, good game. I thought for sure I was going down a couple of times tonight, but you held the pocket.

Thanks." I acknowledged his compliment with a nod and a grin. I'd done alright; I was pleased with myself, too.

"Thanks," I said.

"Hey, a bunch of us are going out to Anderson Field. You want to come?" he asked.

I considered for a second. I must have impressed Clayton because he'd just invited me to hang out with him and the rest of the seniors. That had never happened before. "Sure," I said.

I drove home, showered, and ate some leftovers from the fridge. Mom and Dad and Jesse relived the excitement of the night. Jesse had a bunch of questions, and Mom and Dad just looked proud.

"Hey, I'm going out with some of the guys tonight. What time are you heading to the festival tomorrow?" I asked.

"I'm opening the booth with Miss Grace in the morning. Your dad and Jesse are coming for the parade. What are your plans?" Mom asked.

"I'm going with Jason and Tiana, but I don't know when."

My dad shook his head, "No, I can't go until late. I've got that conference call in the morning; remember?"

Mom nodded, remembering. "Oh, that's right. I completely forgot. Honey, can you take Jesse with you when you go so he doesn't miss the parade?"

I'm sure I looked a little put off by the request, but when I looked at Jesse's expectant face, I couldn't refuse. "Yeah, sure, I'll just meet 'em there." My mom smiled and thanked me.

"Where are you going tonight?" Dad asked.

I shrugged. "Anderson Field."

Anderson Field was an abandoned park that had been a baseball field in the forties and fifties. It was the proud home of the Mighty Minors. Several of the local families had grandfathers and great-grandfathers who had played on the team. Now it was a hangout. More kids tasted their first beer there than anywhere else in town, probably got drunk for the first time there, too.

"It's not a place that *nice* kids hang out," my mother warned. I was a nice kid in her mind.

My dad rolled his eyes. "That's not what you used to say," he chuckled.

"Robert, it was different when we were kids." Her voice held a note of superiority.

"Not much," he retorted. "Son, don't let your mom sugar-coat it. We hung out there, too. Drank, *on occasion*," he added for her benefit, "and did a variety of other rebellious acts while under the influence. Don't let your mom lead you to believe any differently. She was a teenager once, too, and I was a teenager, and we were teenagers *together*," he said suggestively.

"Robert!" My mom blushed and glared at my father.

"Clara!" he responded teasingly and put his arm around her to protect her blush. She turned her face in toward his chest and suppressed a giggle. He kissed her warm cheek and winked at me.

I loved my parents. They were real. They had lived a life apart from this little town and had chosen to return to raise us kids. Unlike most of the families here, they understood my need to see other places and experience more of the world than what this tiny town offered.

Maybe, I'd do like them. Maybe, I'd go away to school, play ball at a small college, and then return to start my own family with T. My heart ached a little at that thought. Would the girl I loved with all of my being become the woman I'd spend the rest of my life with? I hoped so. I wondered if she ever imagined a future with me. I always saw us together with a couple of kids. I dismissed that thought instantly. She hardly acknowledged me and hadn't known me; why would she imagine a future with me?

"Have fun, son. Goodnight," Dad said and gestured for Jesse to follow him and Mom. He still had his arm around her.

"Goodnight. See you in the morning."

CHAPTER 4

There were already at least a dozen cars and trucks in the small parking lot when I arrived. Nearly the entire varsity stood around the back of Clayton's truck. He'd iced a keg of beer, and everyone was serving themselves. How had he driven through town with that without being stopped?

"Hey," he called and raised his hand when he saw me.

I walked toward the group and then turned when I saw more cars coming along the road toward the field. Jason's car was among them, followed by a truck. Catherine's auburn hair was easy to spot, and then I saw T. My stomach lurched a bit and wondered why they were all there together.

The girls walked arm-in-arm, with Jason right behind them. I stepped back into the crowd to observe. After our odd reintroduction and her lapse in memory, I was cautious. Jason took hold of the stack of red, Solo cups and served them each a beer. Catherine took a sip and then laughed at something Jason said. Clayton jumped down from the back of his truck and put his arm around Catherine's waist. She smiled and tilted her head to the side so he could kiss her neck. She turned, and they kissed. From the hopeful look in Clayton's eyes, Catherine's hands-on studying was earning her an A.

Tia just stood there, holding her cup and looking bored. To my knowledge, she'd never gone out there like that before, nor did she drink. One of the guys handed me a cup and raised his own to make a toast. "To victory!" he said boisterously. The guys around me joined in with him, and the crowd followed their lead.

Someone cranked up the tunes, and before long, the air was filled with loud music and faint hints of marijuana and alcohol. I watched as Jason led Tia toward another group of guys, and they sat down on a bench. She held her cup with both hands and swayed and bobbed a little to the music. Jason and the guys near her laughed and drank. When they left her to get more beer. I took the opportunity to walk the few yards to join her.

She looked up as I approached. "Hi," I said.

"Hey," she said without smiling.

"Having fun?" I asked.

She shrugged. "Not really, but Catherine and Jason say this is what upperclassmen do after a win. No offense, but it seems kinda pointless."

I laughed once. "Yeah, it does. Do you mind if I join you on this *pointless* bench?" She almost smiled at that and scooted over to make room for me. "I'm not going to be able to ride with you and Jason tomorrow. I need to drive my kid brother. Can I meet you somewhere to watch the parade, instead?" I asked.

"Sure, we'll be on the corner of Main Street in front of Clarke's Pharmacy. We should have a good view from there."

"Are you getting caught up?" I asked.

"Yeah." She nodded but still didn't really engage with anything I'd said. She seemed distracted by the music. She took a sip from her cup and made a face. "I forgot that was beer," she complained. "Gross." She gagged a little and wiped her lips with her hand. "I hate beer. Do you want mine?" she turned toward me and offered me her cup.

I took it and poured the contents into mine. I placed my cup inside Tia's empty one and took a sip. It tasted like cheap beer, but I didn't complain. It took the edge off my frustration. "You said today that you don't remember having classes with me. Do you remember anything about me?" I asked.

She smiled self-consciously and looked away. "Yeah, sorry about that. It's a lame excuse, but I've got a lot on my mind. I was away for the summer, and it's hard to just shift gears, you know?"

I nodded like I knew, but I had no idea. I turned slightly on the bench to face her. "Did you have a good summer?" I asked. I wanted to keep her talking.

She stayed facing me. "I go to my aunt's house, and I have to study a lot. It's pretty intense, but I can't say I don't enjoy it." It was the same story she'd given me the year before. I nodded and just listened. The wind gusted a bit and blew strands of hair across her face. She combed them down with her fingers, but she missed some, so I reached up and tucked them behind her ear. She didn't recoil from my touch; instead, she leaned into my hand and closed her eyes. Naturally, I stroked her cheek with my thumb, and she smiled and sighed. I was so confused. She was an extreme mixture of friend and stranger

"Topher!" Jason's voice interrupted, breaking the connection. Tia jumped, and I released her. She blinked and looked at me. It was the same look she'd given me in the gym. "This loser bothering you, Tiana?" he asked.

She shook her head. "No, we were just talking."

“Do you need another drink?” Jason asked when he noticed she wasn’t holding a cup. She shook her head again. “I think you need another drink; it’ll help you have fun. You don’t look like you’re having a good time.” From the looks of Jason, he’d already had enough.

“No, I’m good, really,” she said, but Jason pressed her again and sent another guy to get her a drink. “No, Jason, I don’t want anything,” she said firmly. Jason put his arm on Tia’s shoulder. She tried to move away from him, but he pushed his hand to the back of her neck possessively, making it hard for her to free herself. She shifted her hips to scoot away, but the pressure from Jason’s hand kept her fixed on the bench, and she leaned over into my side.

As soon as she touched me, Jason released her and looked at his hand. I stood at the same time, and just like earlier, when I stepped in front of her, Jason stepped back. The other guys did likewise. I decided to test my theory and reached down and took T’s hand.

“You want a ride home?” I asked but kept an eye on Jason.

She looked at our hands. “Yes, I would. Thanks.” She stood but didn’t force me to release her.

“I’m supposed to take you and Catherine home,” Jason argued.

“I got it, Jason. Leave her alone.”

Jason didn't cower or act afraid of me, but he didn't approach me, either. He just looked at me and glanced down at Tiana's hand and back to me. He shook his head and seemed as confused as I had been.

I kept a firm hold on Tia's hand as I walked her toward my truck. I opened the door for her and closed it once she was securely in the cab. I climbed in the driver's side and buckled myself in before I started the engine.

"You okay?" I asked before I backed out of the parking lot.

"Yes, I'm good. Are you okay to drive?" Tia asked.

"I'm good. Given my size and metabolism, it takes a lot to get me drunk. I've barely had a whole beer tonight."

"You drink often?" she asked.

"No, I don't, but I know my limits. My dad and I figured it out last summer. He thought it might be a good life-lesson for me to experience the effects of alcohol under his supervision rather than get into any trouble on my own." Dad was an agriculture specialist and mainly helped farmers achieve the healthiest soil conditions. I caught her interest from the corner of my eye. "He's a scientist and believes in the lessons we learn from experiments. Are you hungry?" I asked.

"Yeah, how did you know?"

I shrugged. "I'm always hungry, so I just thought it would be polite to ask before I pulled into a drive-thru and forced food on you."

She laughed. "Burgers or tacos?" she asked playfully. There she was; there was Tia. At that moment, I didn't care that she didn't remember me. She was there, and she was *here*, and she'd laughed her laugh.

"Burgers," I said.

"Good choice," she agreed.

I pulled up into the drive-in and parked. The roar of my engine made it difficult for the person inside to hear my order through the speaker. It was barely eleven; thankfully, this place didn't close until midnight.

I ordered two burgers, a large fry, and a Coke for myself and added an order of onion rings and a chocolate shake for T. She cocked her head slightly. "How did you know what I wanted?" she asked. "Are you a mind reader or something?"

"No, sorry. I should have asked," I stammered. "I just guessed that was what you wanted. You seem like a chocolate shake and onion ring kind of girl." I tried to cover my blunder. *Damn.* I needed to be more careful, so I didn't upset or worry her.

"Well, you guessed right, so no harm done." She smiled again. It was the first time she'd really smiled and laughed. I couldn't temper my relief.

I offered her half of my second burger as was our habit, and she happily accepted it. We rolled down the windows and listened to the oldies that played over the speakers around the drive-in. She dipped a few of my fries into her chocolate shake and bobbed her head to the music.

"Do you mind?" She gestured toward my Coke.

"Go ahead," I said before she took a large sip and burped.

We laughed and talked for the next hour, and she sang along to a few of the songs that played. "I can tell you hate to be called Topher, so do you prefer Chris or Christopher?"

"You can call me Christopher," I said and was relieved she'd asked. Except for Miss Grace, Tia was the only one who ever used my full name.

"Thanks, Christopher, for feeding me; I think I'd like to go home now."

I started up the truck and was backing out when Jason's car sped into the parking space beside us. "I thought you were taking her home," he accused.

"We were hungry; we're going there now," I said flatly and continued to back out of the parking spot.

"I'll see you in the morning, Tiana," Jason called.

I caught Tia's eyes; they almost looked pleading. "We'll see," I called out the window. I pressed the buttons at my left, and the windows raised automatically, protecting her from the tirade of curses that flowed from Jason's mouth toward me.

"What time is he supposed to pick you up?" I asked.

"Ten."

"If you want, I can be there by 9:30."

She smiled conspiratorially. "Please."

CHAPTER 5

Jesse and I were in Tiana's driveway before 9:30. We had a couple of hours before the parade, so I promised Jesse donuts and hot cocoa if he'd be cool.

"I can be cool," he said in his seven-year-old voice.

"Don't embarrass me, okay? Hopefully, Tiana will agree to hang out with me for the day. You can hang out with us, too, but if you act up, I'm taking you to Mom," I threatened. Jesse's eyes were wide and expectant. He looked so small in the backseat.

Tia came out of the house and climbed into the cab of the truck. She turned and greeted Jesse. "Good morning," she said to him and then turned toward me and smiled. "Good morning, to you, too." Her tone was different with each of our individual greetings. She greeted Jesse like a little kid; she greeted me like a friend.

"I promised Jesse donuts. You hungry?"

"For donuts? Always."

The donut shop wasn't too crowded, and we found a booth. As soon as we sat down, Tia reached for Jesse's hot cocoa cup and placed a few ice cubes from her water into it to cool it off. She didn't even ask; she just took care of him. Tia anticipated his needs and dampened a napkin for him to wipe the chocolate glaze from his chin. She babysat often, but there was something sweet about her attention to Jesse, and he didn't even balk at her requests.

He was definitely being cool and making it easy to be with Tia. I might owe him big by the end of the day. I followed him to the bathroom, and we relieved ourselves and removed as much of the stickiness we could get with soap and water. How did he manage to get chocolate icing behind his ears?

When we came out of the bathroom, Tia was waiting for us. She'd cleaned the table to make room for another family. "Ready?" she asked, almost excited.

The festival was crowded, so we parked several blocks from the parade route. The sun was bright in the cloudless sky. It never rained on a festival day, and that year was no exception. The temperature was pleasant, too. It wouldn't get above eighty.

The closer we walked, the more the crowd pressed in on us. I reached to take Jesse's hand, but Tia had beaten me to it. Jesse didn't complain; he didn't want to get lost. I took Tia's hand; she didn't complain, either. Jesse looked down at our hands and then to his own.

"It's like I can feel your hand, too, Chris. It's like we're all connected."

"Yeah, it does," Tia agreed.

I didn't feel anything and figured it was just Jesse explaining the connection of our hands. I shrugged and led us through the crowd. My height made it easy to maneuver through the people. We made it to Clarke's but weren't able to get close enough for Jesse to see. I lifted him onto my shoulders when the parade started.

I didn't like letting go of T's hand, but I had to when I lifted Jesse. She didn't seem to like releasing my hand, either, and stood slightly behind me to my right and placed her hand on my forearm. I looked down at her hand and then into her eyes.

I held Jesse more securely with my left hand and let my right hand fall to catch Tia's. She looked down at our hands and smiled contentedly. I could tell Jesse was watching us, but he didn't fidget the entire time she touched me. The connection was tender, and I didn't want to do anything stupid to break it.

After the parade was over, I allowed the crowd to dissipate some before I took Jesse from my shoulders. "Topher!" I cringed at the sound of Jason's voice. T released my hand at nearly the same moment. Jesse rocked slightly, and I had to step back to regain my balance. "Catherine and I waited for nearly a half-hour for you," he complained. "You could have texted her."

Tia looked away, and I took the opportunity to set Jesse on his own two feet. "Back off, Jason," I said. He glared at me but didn't challenge me with so many witnesses.

Jesse frowned at Jason and stepped over to Tiana and took her hand. "Come on, let's go. Mom's selling Miss Grace's candy apples." He tugged Tia's hand slightly, and she returned his enthusiastic smile.

Jason took a step toward Tia, but I took one, too, and he hesitated. I took a step toward him, and he stepped back. I doubted Jason was afraid of me, but it was so strange that he was repelled by me somehow. I took another step to test my theory, and sure enough, he took another step back. I chuckled once and did it again. It was like a little dance. He didn't like me messing with him, and he finally turned away from me in a huff. I ran two strides to catch up with Jesse and Tia.

When Mom saw us with Tia, she greeted her warmly and welcomed her back. She offered to take Jesse, but he was being cool and would have way more fun with us than with Mom until Dad could get there. It wasn't a big deal. She gave me cash and food tickets, and we rode rides and ate junk food all day. After our third corndog and second funnel cake, Jesse asked for a pretzel and cotton candy. I was feeling full and marveled at his ability to out eat me for the afternoon.

When the sun began to set, we returned to my truck. I laid blankets in the bed, and the three of us sat together to watch the fireworks. Tia pulled packets of sanitized wipes from her purse and wiped Jesse down again. He was sticky everywhere. She offered me one, and I washed my hands and face, too. Jesse was sitting between us, leaned up against the back of the cab. I hadn't held T's hand since the morning and felt a little self-conscious to take it.

When the fireworks began, Jesse leaned his head onto my chest to get a better view. I put my arm around him, and it was easy, then, to take Tia's hand. She didn't look at me, but I could see her lips curl upward in a satisfied smile as the bursts of color and light reflected in her eyes.

A few minutes into the show, Jesse fell asleep against me. Tia moved over and rested her head against my shoulder and placed her hand on Jesse's back. It was then that I felt the connection. Jesse was right; I could feel her touch through him.

The celebration and our day were over too soon. People made their way back to their cars. I had parked far enough away to avoid the hassle of traffic, but I wasn't ready to go. We were cozy in the bed of my truck and hidden from everything else.

"Do you mind if we stay here a while longer?" I asked. "I don't want to move Jesse until we're ready to go."

"That's fine. I'm not ready to go, either." She stroked my arm lightly with her fingertips, and tingles ran throughout my entire body. It was a good feeling. She turned my hand over and traced the inside of my palm with her left hand. We talked low and just enjoyed being together. It felt normal; it felt even better than *normal*.

Less than an hour later, Jesse stirred and said he needed to go to the bathroom. It was a good thing because my leg had fallen asleep under his weight. I walked him over to the edge of the empty parking lot, and we took a leak together behind a tree. We weren't gone five minutes, but when we returned, I saw Tia getting into Jason's car with Catherine.

Jesse looked up through sleepy eyes. "Where's she going?"

"I don't know," I said. "Let's go."

I grabbed the blankets from the back of the truck and tossed them into the backseat with Jesse. I shut the door just as Jason drove past us. Tia looked directly at me as they passed, and I could read her lips as she mouthed, "Sorry."

CHAPTER 6

The next morning at school, I waited for Tia to arrive. She stepped off the bus behind Catherine. Thankfully Jason hadn't driven them. Catherine paused briefly, and Tia looked up to see why she'd hesitated.

"Good morning," I said.

"Good morning," Tia replied, looking a little sheepish.

"Will you excuse us?" I asked Catherine politely. She looked at T and then walked on. "What happened last night?" I asked.

"Jason and Catherine came right after you left with Jesse. They convinced me to go with them. It's better that way."

"Why is it better?" I asked. I didn't understand.

"Um," she stammered, "It's just better if my parents think I'm with them."

"But I picked you up; why couldn't I bring you home?"

"My parents weren't home when you picked me up. They thought I'd gone with Jason. I didn't tell them I'd made other plans." She adjusted her backpack over her shoulder and crossed her arm over herself. She looked away and sighed, resigned to tell me something she didn't want to confess. "My parents are pretty strict, and I'm not allowed to date or be alone with boys without their permission. I have permission to be with Jason. He's a close family friend; we're practically cousins. I don't want them to get the wrong impression if they see you coming around or suspect that we're secretly dating or something. I'd like them to just think we're friends."

I nodded, playing along. Although Tia and I had spent a great deal of time together as children, her parents gradually restricted her time with boys after middle school. The Jason thing was new, though. Why was he suddenly given permission to be around her, if I couldn't? It was true that their families were friends, but he'd never hung around or paid her any attention before.

I knew that her parents were strict, and I didn't want to jeopardize our current state, but it was stupid, though. They knew me and had never set limits on our friendship, but nothing was like it was before. It was precarious enough without adding her getting grounded.

"Okay, *friends*," I compromised. "Agreed." I offered my hand. She smiled, relieved, and shook it formally like we were making a pact. She didn't let go of my hand right away, though, and I probably could have stood there a long time before letting it go, but the warning bell sounded, and she jumped and released me.

Returning to our friendship was exactly what I wanted. Seeing Tia and knowing she didn't have time or attention for me was brutal. She didn't know me; she didn't remember our friendship. I questioned her sanity, but not as much as I questioned my own for playing along. I suddenly became acutely aware that I wanted more than friendship; I wanted to be her boyfriend and let everyone in the world know she belonged with me. I wondered how her definition of friendship might be different from mine.

Tia and I talked some between classes and at lunch. Clayton invited me to sit with him and the senior O-line. That was convenient since Tia was with Catherine, and Catherine was most anywhere Clayton was. This created an easy excuse for me to be close to T, and no one would question it.

After school, the team dressed out for practice. Coach was thrilled at our win and wanted to try some new things and experiment with moving folks to new positions. After we ran through a few plays, he called Jason over and had him work with Clayton and the offensive line. We all knew the coach's intention to give Jason some playing time if we got a significant enough lead. Our next game was a little over a week away, and we practiced like that every day.

Jason was a confident player, but he was nervous and edgy in the pocket. He didn't trust me to block for him. He didn't have any assurance that I wouldn't let him get pounded. Honestly, I wasn't sure of myself, either. I wavered between doing my job on the field and letting the defense take him down. I'm not proud to admit it, but I let him take a few hits on principle.

My week with Tia was good. We talked more at school, and we ate lunch together. She still didn't know me, but it was easy and comfortable. Jason was still present, lurking, antagonizing. He was such an ass and found opportunity every day to distract her.

"Want to come to the movies with me this weekend? I'm taking Jesse to a matinee on Saturday."

"That would be nice, but I have to be back before six. I'm babysitting for the Clarkes."

"Want me to help you?" I asked. The Clarkes had five sons under the age of seven. They were a handful.

"I guess for a couple of hours until I get them to bed. Mr. and Mrs. Clarke are going to a wedding; I'll be staying the night."

"I can be there, too," Jason interjected. "We wouldn't want your folks getting the wrong impression, would we?" The threat that he'd tell her parents made her doubt.

"Yeah, that sounds like fun, but I can handle them alone. No need for either one of you to be there."

"Okay, that's fine, but I'll pass by just the same and check on you," Jason said, not letting it go.

Friday night's game was harder-fought than we expected. We managed to take the lead in the third quarter, and when it looked like we'd maintain it into the fourth quarter, the coach put Jason in as quarterback. Jason eyed me warily as we stepped onto the field. In the throes of the game, I wouldn't jeopardize our lead. I was too competitive to let that happen. He managed to complete a few passes and make handoffs without a fumble. We didn't score, but we didn't lose yardage, either. I considered that progress.

Early Saturday morning, I mowed a couple of acres for Miss Grace and Mr. Roy, leaving me just enough time to get to school to watch film from the previous night's game. After that, we'd walk through a few plays that weren't executed to the coaches' standards. Jason was cutting up with a couple of the guys and making a spectacle of himself. He didn't have to work too hard and, honestly, was getting on my nerves.

"What time's the movie?" he asked after he threw a pass. His head needed to be in practice and not worrying about my plans. I didn't answer. Regardless of their families' close relationship, I didn't like the way he lorded himself over Tia. He continued to push my buttons. "Did you hear me, Topher?" he pressed.

"Why are you doing this?" I asked rhetorically.

"What do you mean?" he asked innocently.

"You know damn well what I mean. Why are you always around? You've never paid her any attention, and now you're everywhere." The aggravation I felt rose, and my frustration was getting the better of me.

"Quit the banter, boys, focus," Coach's voice sounded from across the field.

Jason's eyes glinted with provocation. He liked getting me riled up. "I'm going to be there, Topher, so you may as well just tell me."

His arrogance got the better of me, his daring eyes, his attitude, and the smug look on his face. I regretted it the moment I snapped. Before I knew what I'd done, my body had followed my fist, and I was on top of him and swinging. I'd tackled him to the ground, and we were grappling for dominance. Somewhere in the vicinity, I heard our coach's whistle blow and felt about a dozen hands pulling us apart. Fighting was not tolerated. Fighting among teammates was a capital offense. I knew we'd pay dearly for my mistake.

Hands, strong hands, lifted us from the ground away from one another. Coach was a no-nonsense sort of man. He didn't ask questions or want excuses. Once we were on our feet and a healthy distance apart, he simply pointed his finger toward the track and blew his whistle. We'd run laps until he thought we'd learned our lesson. Jason dusted himself off and touched the corner of his mouth with his tongue. He fumed at the taste of his own blood. My left rib was bruised, and the skin over my left cheekbone pulled like a brush burn.

The last guys who'd had to run laps for fighting were seniors. They were freshmen when it happened. They shook their heads and knew we were in for it. I hoped that Coach had plans after practice, but knowing him, he would make us run until he thought we were adequately humbled. The last guys had been forced to run for two hours straight with only one water break. I hoped Jason was thinking the same thing and that we'd set a slow, steady pace. I was also afraid that because we were varsity, he'd make an example of us. Too many underclassmen looked to us for leadership. I wasn't far from the mark, except after the second lap, he blew his whistle and made the entire team run with our punishment. The guys took turns complaining.

"What the heck, Topher."

"You're such an ass, Jason."

"Way to go. Now, I'm going to be late for work."

"I'd beat the crap out you myself; you're such idiots."

"Just wait; you'll pay for this."

Round and round, we ran. The complaints finally died off when we were all too parched to speak. Coach blew his whistle and let us get water. He then dismissed the defense and told the offensive line to run the bleachers. The other guys were livid.

After we made the course, he called us back down to the endzone. "Men," he began with his eyes looking at the goalpost at the other end of the field, "teams win and lose together. Teams must work together and not let anything, I mean, *anything*, distract them from the goal." He then looked directly at Jason and me. "Today, you were distracted. Today, you let something interfere with the tasks at hand. Today, you let a petty, insignificant thing get in the way, and just like soldiers on the battlefield, your lack of focus and lack of leadership and direction caused innocent men to pay. Have you seen the error of your ways?"

"Yes, sir," we said together, breathless, our chests heaving from our exertion.

"Good." He looked at the rest of the offense. "Men, there will be no retribution for today's exercise. You will not retaliate for the inconvenience of a little running. You will encourage your teammates to think before they act in haste again." Except for the deep breathing, no one made a sound. No one argued. We were too exhausted. "Is that understood?" Coach asked.

"Yes, sir," we all murmured our assent.

He blew his whistle, and we slumped back to the locker room. No one said a word. No one made eye contact. We were humble and contrite as we made our way back to our cars and trucks. Physical exertion tends to take the fight out of most anyone, myself included.

I had just enough time to shower, get Jesse from a friend's, and meet Tia for the movie. I was scarfing down protein bars as I drove. Catherine was going to meet Clayton, so she was more than happy for the cover of a matinee with Tia. I noticed that Catherine handed Tia her phone. The GPS would prove she was at the movies. I shook my head. I thought that was possibly one of the dumbest things girls did. The phone was there for their safety, and they passed it along like it was nothing.

I was exhausted already from the day and knew it was going to be really hard for me to stay awake during the movie. We sat down just as the previews started. Tia sat between Jesse and me. The theater was already dark when Jason showed up during the previews and sat down on the other side of Jesse.

"Hey, buddy," he whispered to Jesse and handed him a box of candy and a large Icee.

"Thanks," Jesse answered in surprise and then looked to me to make sure it was okay.

"Go ahead," I muttered through a clenched jaw. I didn't want to make a scene, and Jason could easily bribe my little brother to let him sit next to him. It would take a lot more than a box of candy before he would sit next to me.

Tia, Jesse, and I had made plans to go eat after the movie. Jesse mentioned the taco place as we were getting up from our seats. Jason seemed to be taking a different approach and easing off the asshole side of his personality. I had lost my fight, too.

"May I join you?" he asked politely.

It was my turn to eye him warily. "I don't think that's a good idea," I said honestly.

"I'm hungry, and I'll buy," he offered. I looked at Tia, and she shrugged.

"Okay," I agreed and didn't hold back when I ordered and took advantage of his generosity. I ordered three combo meals for myself and Tia and a kid's meal for Jesse. I drove Jesse home and then took Tia to the Clarkes. As I pulled up, I noticed Jason's car parked on the street. I wasn't positive, but I suspected that Jason was making sure I didn't stay.

Jason was tossing a football with the oldest three Clarke boys in the side yard. Jason caught the wobbly pass and lifted his chin to direct the boys toward our arrival. They ran to the curb and stood on the sidewalk, waiting expectantly for Tia to step out of the truck.

"Hey, boys," Tia began with a smile. "What are you doing here, Jason?" she asked with falsetto, pretending it was a complete surprise.

"Jason told Mom he would teach us some plays," the oldest boy answered. I recognized him from Jesse's class. He knew me, too. "You're Jesse's brother, aren't you?"

"Yeah, I am."

"You're on Jason's team?" the next oldest asked.

"Sure am," I answered in a friendly tone like it was an honor to be Jason's teammate.

"Can you stay and play, too? Mom says we can play until Tiana calls us in for supper."

I caught Jason and Tia's eyes. "Yeah, sure, I can stay." Jason didn't even bristle.

"I'm going in to talk to your mom, boys. Where's Ricky?" Tia asked.

"Inside with Mikey. He's punished," the third boy said, feeling sorry and ashamed for his brother.

Tia entered the house and shut the door, leaving three of her charges in mine and Jason's care. "What he'd do to get punished?" Jason asked.

"Hitting," the boys answered in unison.

I raised my eyebrow, and Jason licked the corner of his mouth, tasting where I'd split his lip that morning, and he laughed. "Yeah, that's a serious offense. We've all been punished for that. It's best to avoid it, wouldn't you say?" he asked and threw me a pass.

I caught it and asked who wanted to play football. The boys all clamored around us, vying for the ball. Little Ricky ran out of the house, then, eager and ready to play. He'd been paroled, making the teams even then. I bent down on one knee and huddled with my team. Jason did the same on the other side of the yard.

We ran several plays, and the boys tackled and grappled in the yard like pros. When he brought out the suitcases to the car, their dad was all kinds of proud watching his boys. We took a timeout for them to kiss their parents goodbye. Mr. Clarke shook our hands and congratulated us on our current season. Mrs. Clarke followed him and made over the baby in Tia's arms. Tia looked like a natural holding little Mikey on her hip and assuring Mrs. Clarke that everything was fine. Mr. and Mrs. Clarke waved from the car and drove down the road.

Tia sat on the grass with the baby and watched us resume our game. I had to admit it was fun. I wished Jesse were there to play, too. Mr. and Mrs. Clarke left chicken nuggets for their supper, but when they realized we'd be hanging around to play with the boys, Mr. Clarke told Tia to go ahead and order pizza for all of us. We played outside with the boys the entire evening. Tia herded the four older boys into the shower while Jason and I watched the baby. We swapped when the four of them returned with wet hair and clean pajamas. They wrestled and played while Tia bathed the baby.

The boys all shared one room with bunk beds. They each picked a story to read before bed. I tucked in the two smaller ones, and Jason did the same with the boys in the second bunk. They got in bed, eager to listen to their stories. Tia handed me Mikey and kissed all the boys' foreheads. I sat in the rocker in the corner of the room and rocked him.

Jason sat next to Tia and listened intently, being the perfect example for the boys.

Little Mikey settled into my shoulder, the steady rocking and the cadence of Tia's reading lured us both into a state of deep relaxation. He smelled all clean like baby shampoo and powder. I was exhausted from the day and hadn't stopped since before daylight. Besides the movie, I hadn't sat down all day, either. Mikey's breaths deepened, and his body pressed against my chest. It was like a mild narcotic, and I fell asleep holding the warm little boy securely.

I felt Tia's hand on my arm. When I opened my eyes, the lights were dimmed. "Come on. They're asleep." She took Mikey from me and put him in his crib. She then walked toward Jason, who had fallen asleep, leaning against one of the lower bunks. He jumped when she placed her hand on his shoulder.

"Shhh," she whispered to settle him.

We tiptoed down the hall toward the kitchen. I started picking up paper plates and cups. Jason stood sleepily and then picked up another piece of pizza and held it between his teeth before closing the lid of the box and carrying it to the fridge.

"Don't worry about that. I've got it. You guys are beat. Go home and sleep." I almost argued; it was barely nine-thirty, but I couldn't deny how tired I felt. Jason looked at me, and I understood the exhaustion. He was only hanging around as long as I was hanging around. I nodded, and he looked relieved.

Tia walked us to the door, but we didn't hug her or even touch her. She thanked us for helping with the boys. Neither of us stepped from the small front porch until we heard the deadbolt latch.

Jason took a step down onto the sidewalk. "Can I talk to you alone for a second?" I asked.

Jason looked up. I wondered if I looked that tired and beat-up, too. His busted lip still looked puffy. I was curious if my cheek looked as bruised as it felt. It was still kind of tender.

"What?" he asked defensively. It was the first time all day that we hadn't had witnesses. I wondered if he thought I might punch him again. He'd be ready for it. I didn't feel like hitting anymore; all my fight was gone. "I just wanted to say that I was sorry for throwing the first punch."

He blinked back the surprise; he hadn't been expecting that. I *was* sorry for throwing the first punch. I wasn't sorry for punching him, but that I had been the one to lose my temper. He was provoking and arrogant, but I had played right into it. I had been the weaker man. He squinted his eyes in the dim light and questioned my sincerity. After a second or two, he nodded once, acknowledging my apology.

“No hard feelings?” I asked.

“No hard feelings,” he repeated.

“Goodnight,” I said and turned toward my truck. I watched as he got into his car, and we both started our engines at nearly the same time. It was like we were both making sure that the other was leaving and timed our acceleration, synchronizing our departure. He drove east, and I drove west toward our respective houses. I wondered if he was watching me from his rearview mirror, too.

I had had a fun evening, even under Jason’s watchful eye. I had spent time with Tia, and she didn’t seem to mind me being near her. It was easy, and I hoped for another opportunity to spend time with her. Clayton buffered me spending time with Tia at school, and Jason had made it possible to spend the entire afternoon and evening with her. I might have to reconsider his role in getting closer to T. I was determined to figure out a way to make her remember me.

CHAPTER 7

Football season was grueling. We had games every week for six more weeks. My days included long practices, early mornings bailing hay, class, homework, and weekends babysitting with Tia. The Clarke boys begged their parents to invite us over to babysit again after that first night. The oldest boy and Jesse were, in fact, friends and so we arranged a sleepover for Jesse, too. At every turn, Jason was there. I didn't get quite as annoyed with him, and he seemed to chill as long as Tia and I weren't unsupervised.

Two games before the end of the regular season, Clayton, our quarterback, sprained his wrist. It wasn't at all football-related. His dad had him working in the fields on Saturday morning. He was probably a little hungover from the victory party at Anderson Field the night before, but something went wrong, and his wrist got tangled up with a piece of equipment. He'd be out for at least the next game and maybe the last.

Jason was suddenly my priority to protect on the field. He trusted me a little more than he had during that first game, but I wasn't sure how much more. We were in tight contention for the playoffs, so I wouldn't do anything stupid if I could help it.

Coach was pleased with us at practice. He was impressed that we'd learned our lesson about fighting and letting outside distractions interfere with football. Jason managed to stay in the pocket and score consecutive touchdowns in the first quarter. The second half was pretty ugly, and he was forced to hand off the ball. We still scored and squeaked out a win by one extra point. Thank goodness for kickers.

After the game, Jason walked over to my locker and asked me if I was going out to Anderson Field. I shook my head. After that first game, I didn't see any reason to go there.

"Tiana's coming. I thought you might want to be there."

I looked at him skeptically, bothered that he might be forcing her to do something she didn't want to do. "Now, why is she doing that?"

"Because I may have told her that you would be there, too."

"Why?" I couldn't hide my surprise.

"I think you've earned some time alone with her, and I can't do that in town. I think I can manage it more now, but I'd still like to be careful." He nodded like he was trying to convince himself as much as me.

"Alright, I'll be there."

Anderson Field was more packed than it had been after the first game. There were even sophomores present, and I suspected a few freshmen, too. I had gotten there as soon as I ate and showered, eager to have some time alone with Tia. I went through the drive-thru and picked up a couple of chocolate shakes and a large order of onion rings. I sat in the car, waiting and watching.

Jason pulled up in his car and parked next to me. I saw Tia riding shotgun. Catherine wasn't with them. I wondered how he'd managed that. Maybe she was playing nursemaid to Clayton's wrist. Tia looked up at me in my truck, and I saw Jason hesitate to let her out. He said something and shook his head, and then he gave her more instructions.

She nodded at Jason and then opened her car door. She smiled when I opened my door and offered to let her in my cab. The night had grown cold for early November; I could see our breaths. Jason leaned over just as she was getting out. "I have to have her back at midnight. I don't care where you go, just have her back by 11:30, okay?" I nodded but didn't ask for anything else.

She climbed in and scooted over into the passenger's side. I jumped in behind her and shut the door. She noticed the bag of onion rings instantly, opened the bag, and inhaled. She lifted her face and smiled. "This for me, too?" she asked, eyeing the shakes in the cup holders.

"Yeah, they are. How's it going?"

"Good. I can't believe we get a few hours together that aren't with little kids."

"Me, too. How did you manage that?" I asked. "Are your parents working tonight?" She didn't answer me with words. Her cheek was full of onion ring, and her mouth was puckered around the straw, taking a long sip of the shake. She smiled a little and blinked the affirmative. "Where's Catherine?"

Tia swallowed and spoke, "She's not feeling well. She decided to stay at home. Clayton's all depressed after his injury, so I think Catherine's not really sick, just in a funk because he's not wanted to hang out all week. We're actually staying at my house tonight, so I think she's hoping he'll come over while I'm out. It really worked out for all of us. I didn't want to be there with the two of them, either."

"What did Jason tell you before you got out of his car?"

"The same thing he told you, but with a little more insistence. I just wanted to talk to you without the distraction of classmates and Clarke boys and Jason," she sighed wistfully.

"What did you want to talk about?"

"I don't know," she hedged. She ate another onion ring and then took a sip of the shake. She looked down and across the dashboard and then up into my eyes. "It feels different when we're together."

"Like what kind of *different*?" I hadn't held her hand since the festival. I hadn't hugged her or held her or really even touched her hardly at school. I wanted her to know me.

"I don't know. I know I haven't known you that long, but suddenly it feels like I've known you forever. You know?" We had been friends for as long as I could remember, and I hated that she couldn't. It was a test of my patience daily. "I like hanging out with you. I like the way you make me laugh and get my jokes at lunch. No one else gets that. They pretend like they do, but I can tell. You don't make me feel self-conscious or weird."

I exhaled in relief. "I'm glad. You're funny, T. You always have been."

"Like that; why do you say it like that?"

"What?"

"You call me T and Tia, and you're the only one. No one else calls me that."

I gathered my wits and tried really hard to figure out the best way to explain without it sounding like I was some kind of stalker and had been watching her since kindergarten.

"It suits you," I said, and she smiled. "Do you mind me giving you a nickname?" She shook her head. "Do you want to go somewhere, or do you just want to sit here in the truck?"

She thought for a moment and then shook her head. "I'm good here. It's cold, and I can't think of any place warm where we could go that there aren't people. Besides, if Jason gets back early, I don't want to give him any reason not to help us see each other again." Even though the cab was dark, I thought I saw her blush.

"I'd like that."

I took her hand and felt the connection instantly. She looked up at me with surprise. Her smile spread across her face, but she wasn't the least bit self-conscious, and there was definitely no blush. I moved the empty bag from between us and scooted over a little to be closer to her. I wondered if she'd let me put my arm around her and if she'd let me kiss her. Maybe not after onion rings and shakes, but I definitely wanted to kiss her.

"May I?" I gestured, and she eased into my side on the long bench seat. I put my arm around her, and she leaned her head onto my chest. I exhaled, and she sighed. The relief holding her was palpable. "This okay?" I asked.

She nodded against my chest and wrapped her arm around my waist and inhaled. "This is more than okay," she whispered.

"What kind of shampoo do you use?" I asked.

"Green apple."

"It smells nice."

"Thanks."

"What kind of shampoo do you use?" she asked.

I shrugged. "I don't use shampoo. My hair is so short that I mostly just use whatever soap is in the shower." She giggled at that.

"You guys played a good game tonight."

"Thanks."

"Do you think you'll make the playoffs?"

I shrugged. "There's a good chance. It may come down to next week's game, though. We can't afford to lose. Not sure if Clayton will be ready to play. Jason's got potential; he just isn't as good, yet. Want to listen to some music?" I asked.

"Sure, that would be nice."

I pulled out my phone and scrolled down my playlists. I started the one I'd compiled for us to listen to when we studied for finals during our sophomore year. It included my top ten and every song Tia had ever liked, even some from middle school. She rocked a little in my arms and bobbled her head and sang along. After a few songs, she sat up and looked at me. "I like all of these."

"Me, too." My smile was genuine.

Her eyes were bright. She leaned back into my arms, and we sat like that for another hour and watched the clock on the dash as it ticked away our time. I finally closed my eyes and stroked her hair absentmindedly. The minutes were flying by.

At 11:28, Jason tapped on my window. We both jumped. Tia pushed herself from my chest and moved away, but we weren't doing anything wrong. He pointed to his wrist, reminding us of the time. I opened the door, and the gust of cold air shocked my senses. My truck had been filled with the warmth of our bodies, the aroma of onion rings, and the scent of green apple shampoo. The cold night air cleared my head instantly.

Jason backed away from my truck and moved to open the door for Tia. I offered her my hand as she eased down. "Goodnight," I said.

"Night," she replied.

I watched her enter Jason's car, and he shut the door behind her. "Thanks, man," I said to Jason. He lifted his chin once and quickly got into his car.

WINTER

CHAPTER 8

We barely made the playoffs. Clayton wasn't able to play the last game of the season, which sucked. Coach called extra practices before and after school to give Jason as much time as possible to prepare. I had homework every night, and our teachers promised plenty more before midterms. I was swamped.

Tia babysat on Saturday nights, but Coach had us practicing every evening, even Sundays. Jason tried a couple of times to give us another evening together, but it wouldn't happen until after the playoffs. We did eat lunch together every day and managed to have a couple of conversations when we had a sub or an assembly.

I hated to admit it, but I was relieved we lost in the second round of the playoffs. Clayton was back, but our opponent had won the championship three years in a row. We didn't have a chance.

I was thankful for many reasons. Jason and I could babysit again with the Clarke boys, and we took Jesse to another matinee. The temperatures dropped significantly at the end of November, and it snowed before Thanksgiving. By the beginning of December, it looked like we were going to have a pretty harsh winter.

The winter solstice fell on a Saturday, and the senior class was hosting a winter formal. Traditionally, we had a winter dance, but it wasn't anything fancy. Mostly it would have a western theme, and we'd wear jeans and boots and bring in bales of hay for decoration. This year, they were going all out. It was rumored there would be ice sculptures and everything wintery.

I leaned over at lunch and whispered, "Can you meet me after school?"

She shook her head. "I have to catch the bus." She looked disappointed.

"Jason mentioned you guys were studying for midterms this weekend. Was that for my benefit?" I asked. She cut her eyes and smiled.

"Maybe," she said playfully. "That is unless you want to study by yourself."

"Nope, I don't want to study with him at all, but he's been surprisingly cool." I wanted to wait until after school and talk to her alone, but I guessed it was the best I could hope for at that moment. I didn't want to wait until the weekend. I looked around and lowered my voice. "Will you go to the winter formal with me?"

"Like a date?" she asked in a whisper, almost disbelievingly.

I suddenly second-guessed myself. I knew she wasn't allowed to date, but this was school, and she was allowed to go to dances and other functions. I wanted to date her and take her places and be her boyfriend, without it making her uncomfortable. She was so much better than she'd been in the fall; we were friends again, but it was still awkward sometimes.

She shook her head. "No."

"It's not a real date, just a school dance, T. Why won't you go with me?" I coaxed.

"You know why; I'm not allowed," she said. "It's forbidden."

"Forbidden?" I laughed. "You're joking." She shook her head, meaningfully. "Really? By whom?"

"My parents," she whispered and lowered her head.

"Your parents will be cool. I'll ask them."

She shook her head. "No, they won't be cool, and if you press it, they'll suspect we aren't just friends, and I will not be able to hang out with you anymore. You're practically my only friend, and I don't want to jeopardize our friendship. Please understand." Her voice was pleading, and then she smiled at a thought. "I won't be able to go *with* you, but since I'm on the dance committee, I'm *obligated* to attend the function. I'll see you there."

"Will you dance with me?"

"Maybe," she said with a coy expression and then smiled broadly.

I returned her smile. I could live with that. I wasn't too excited about not being able to take her, but I would satisfy myself with dancing with her and spending an evening together that wasn't babysitting. I knew I'd pressed her about the dance, but I wasn't finished.

"Are we *just* friends, T?" I pressed in a whisper. She didn't answer right away. I leaned over and took her hand under the table and pulled it onto my knee. She closed her eyes and gave my hand a little squeeze. "That's what I thought. Friends are great and all, but I'd like to be more than that. I want to make that perfectly clear."

Her lips went up in a little smile, and when she opened her eyes, I was nearly knocked off the bench. Whoa! She smiled at my reaction, and I winked at her. It took everything I had not to hug her and kiss her there in the cafeteria with the entire school as witnesses. The bell rang, and she stood and scooped up her backpack. I remained at the table and watched her walk away.

For the next two weeks, Tia approached me more in the hall between classes. She met me as soon as she got off the bus in the mornings and made it possible for us to study at Jason's house with Catherine almost every afternoon. His mom kept us supplied with hot cocoa, pizza rolls, and chips. Catherine wasn't a serious student, but she had to study if she expected to make decent grades. Her parents expected her to do well, and Clayton had to study for midterms, too, so she didn't have any excuse.

The day before midterms, Catherine left early to go and meet Clayton, and afterward, Jason made himself scarce for a little while and gave Tia and me some time together. His mom had gone to the grocery store, and the house was quiet.

"I'm going to watch some TV until Mom gets back. You guys can just hang out in here until then." We had been studying in their formal living room. I hadn't expected him to do that, but we had reviewed everything about ten times already. Tia moved over on the sofa, and I sat next to her.

"You ready?" I asked.

"Yeah, I think we've covered everything."

"I can't wait for midterms to be over," I groaned. I hated studying.

"I'm really looking forward to the dance." She bounced with excitement and took my hand. It wasn't like in the truck or secretly holding hands at lunch. She had taken my hand, and she was naturally buoyant at the prospects. We laughed, and she was more herself than she had been in months. I was impatient to see if she'd awaken to me and remember that she was my best friend and that I loved her.

For the half-hour or so that we were actually alone, I listened intently to every word she spoke and held my arms securely around her. It was like once she took my hand, she wanted to hold onto more of me. It felt almost as good as before she left last summer, but I was still holding my breath a little.

The following afternoon, midterms were over, and everyone's mood had improved. I was actually looking forward to getting dressed in a rented tux and having an excuse to put my arms around Tia in public. I washed my truck and vacuumed it out and even submitted a few of T's favorite songs to the DJ's request list.

Mom made me pose in front of the fireplace mantle while she took pictures. Dad and Jesse stood proudly beside me, too. Mom fussed over my tie and brushed over me with the lint brush before she allowed me to leave. They all waved from the front door.

The school parking lot was pretty full, and the gym was packed. I walked up to the entrance and waited in line to present the chaperones with my ticket. I didn't see Jason or Catherine's fire-red hair or Tia.

Then I saw her. She was admiring the ice sculpture that was about four feet tall and spanned the length of a six-foot table. I was genuinely impressed.

Tia looked beautiful with her hair piled up on her head, and tiny tendrils of spiraled curls framed her face. Her lips glistened with pink, glittery gloss, and her dress matched her lips almost perfectly. Her dress was floor-length with sequins and sparkly things running down the skirt. The top of the long-sleeved dress hugged her chest, and the scooped neck had a faux fur collar and cuffs. She looked all soft and sweet like sparkly cotton candy. I wondered if her gloss was flavored like bubble gum or maybe watermelon.

She saw me walking towards her like maybe she was looking for me, too. I stopped a couple feet away and just admired her. "You look really pretty tonight," I said. She smiled, and her eyelashes fluttered. She blushed a little and swayed, making her dress all flowy and swirly. She liked the way I was admiring. She closed the space between us, and I thought for a second that she was going to walk right past me, but she took my hand and led me to the dance floor.

Even though it was a fast dance, she didn't let go of my hand. She was smiling and happy and so unlike she'd been when she returned in September. The lead sweater that she'd worn upon her return was nowhere to be seen. She hardly ever crossed her arms over herself. By the third song, I had to remove my jacket, loosen my tie, and roll up my sleeves.

That night at the dance, she danced and smiled and was free. She sang along to nearly every chorus, and I held her close during the slow songs. By the second half of the evening, the DJ played mostly slow songs. He even played the ones I'd requested.

The lights dimmed, and we were in near-complete darkness, setting a mood for the couples. The dance floor was crowded, but I didn't notice anyone else. Her arms were around me, and I held her close to my chest. I could rest my cheek comfortably on the side of her head. I leaned over to whisper something in her ear, and she tilted her head up at the exact same time. My lips were so close to hers. I closed my eyes and kissed her sweet, glossy lips – *Bubblegum.*

Tia didn't push me away, but she did stop dancing. We stood there amid the movement. Like last summer, the kiss was gentle and lingering, but unlike last summer, I held her face in my hands and pressed my lips to hers with purpose. Also, unlike last summer, she moved into me and wrapped her arms around my waist, pressing herself against me.

Suddenly, the lights were brought up and flashed across the dancefloor. The first beat of the next song was loud and strong. We were knocked back into the present.

"Are you thirsty?" I asked.

"Yes."

"Come on, let's get a drink and some fresh air." I grabbed my jacket on the way to the concession table. I picked up a couple of Cokes, and we walked into the breezeway between the gym and the auditorium. The cold air wouldn't be unbearable between the two buildings.

I popped open one of the cans and handed it to Tia. She held it to her lips and took a long swig. When the carbonation got the better of her, she hiccoughed and caught a burp in her throat. I drank half of my can in one gulp and belched. She giggled and then released a burp of her own. We laughed. If she tried, she could beat me in a burping contest.

She shivered, so I handed her my jacket. I wasn't cold at all, and if I kissed her again, I definitely wouldn't need a coat. I might need a fire extinguisher or an ice bath. The sleeves of my jacket hung down over her shoulders and arms. I had to remind myself sometimes that she was so much smaller than me now. In my mind, we were still young and the same size. That hadn't been the case for a long time.

She stepped back and leaned against the brick siding of the gym and took another sip of her drink. I finished mine in another gulp and tossed the can in the bin a couple yards away.

"Good shot."

"Thanks."

I looked around and saw a few other couples, but we were virtually alone. I placed my hands on the wall on either side of Tia's shoulders and leaned over and kissed her, really kissed her, the kind of kiss that didn't just linger but drew her lips apart. She accepted me, but I wasn't prepared for her response. She pressed her palm into my abs, and instead of it pushing me away, it had the opposite effect. She took over completely.

The cold didn't touch me; it didn't touch her, either. Tia was protected from the elements by my body and the gym. Our mouths and hands moved slowly, but my heart beat steadily, pounding and drumming and grounding me in that very moment. Who knew the lingering flavors of Coke and bubblegum could taste so good together.

Tia leaned back and looked into my eyes. "Christopher, it's midnight."

I blinked and shifted my brain to understand her words. How did she know? Then, I heard the bells of the chapel peel out over the thudding beat of my heart. I nodded once and begrudgingly made to step away from her. She grabbed onto the lapels of my shirt and kissed me again.

Seconds later, I felt a hand on my shoulder. Confident that we'd been found by a teacher or a coach, I stood straighter and moved Tia behind me to protect her from unnecessary scrutiny or judgment. Thankfully, it wasn't a teacher, it was Jason, but the look in his eyes was different, almost fearful.

"Good, I found you," he almost panted. "I didn't know where you'd gone. Glad you didn't leave. She needs to go." His words were hushed and breathy like he'd been running.

"What is it? What's wrong?" I asked.

"She needs to go. Let her walk through the gym alone and be seen leaving. Catherine left with Clayton. She was supposed to ride home with Tiana. Meet her at her mom's van. I'll follow you and drive you back to your truck."

I glared at him, but then Tia came from behind me and put her hand on Jason's cheek and smiled reassuringly at him. Like every other guy I'd seen her touch, Jesse, the Clarke boys, myself, and now Jason, we instantly relaxed at her touch.

"It's okay, Jason; please, don't worry. It's midnight of the longest night of the year. I have plenty of time to get home."

His worry didn't leave him, but he nodded. I was thoroughly confused. Tia's words were different; her voice was measured and authoritative. Then, she turned back to me and smiled and said she'd see me in the van. She offered me my jacket and checked her dress and her hair before she walked away from us. Jason followed her, but I remained behind to go straight to the parking lot.

She unlocked the car, and I got into the passenger's seat. I'd never ridden with her before. She'd gotten her license just before she left for the summer because her birthday was later than mine. She looked over at me and smiled before she started the car and pulled out of the parking lot.

"Thanks for seeing me home. Jason's so protective, sometimes. It's like he's working secret ops or something. My dad just asked him to make sure I got home okay since they were working tonight. Catherine promised she'd come home with me, but when Clayton's around, she's not as dependable as you and Jason." She smiled at that and then turned down her street. "I had a good time tonight," she said, blushing a little.

"Me, too. May I see you tomorrow?"

She shook her head. "Probably not. Family stuff, you know?" I nodded. She parked the car in her driveway, and I saw Jason's car idling at the curb. I took the opportunity to lean over and kiss her, just a quick peck.

"You'd better go before Jason freaks out again," I encouraged. *Or before I kiss you again*, I thought.

She blinked knowingly and took the keys from the ignition. "Thanks," she said and scooted from the driver's side and waved briefly to Jason. I stepped out of the van and closed the door while I watched her flowy, pink dress round into the house. She still sparkled.

I got into Jason's car; the music was blaring, and it was hard to speak over it. He sped us back to the gym and slid in easily next to my truck. I could tell he was impatient for me to get out. I opened the door and stood.

"Thanks, man. Thanks for riding with her," he said, but it didn't sound begrudging or arrogant.

"Yeah, I don't understand why it was so important. Why couldn't one of us have just followed her?"

"You got to be with her for five minutes longer, right? I'd call that a win." He revved the engine a little, impatiently dismissing me.

CHAPTER 9

T had danced in my dreams for years. From the time we were kids, I'd dreamed we were running or playing or riding our bikes. Recently, though, I dreamed that she was in my room. I dreamed that she came to me at night and lay with me. My early adolescent dreams weren't even sexual, but the more recent ones bordered on the sensual. They weren't graphic dreams, but I knew we were together, and we belonged together. I woke feeling hopeful and longing to see her.

So, when I opened my eyes and saw her in my room, I thought I was still dreaming. She'd come to me so many times like that. I thought I was waking inside a dream, deceiving myself to believe she was really there. She was wearing dark-blue plaid flannel pajamas and slippers. She didn't speak; she just stood there, eyes wide, looking at me.

"Tia?" I whispered. She didn't respond. "What are you doing here?" She blinked her eyes, but her thoughts were far away. I pushed the covers to the side and stood. "Tia, can you hear me?" I reached for her, and she stepped toward me. She shivered. I sat her on the bed and wrapped a blanket around her shoulders. She offered a slight smile like that was good, but she remained silent. She yawned and kicked off her slippers and got into my bed like she belonged there. She pulled the covers over her shoulder and rolled onto my pillow.

I freaked out a little because Tia was in my bed. *Shit!* I wasn't aware she sleepwalked. I shook her slightly, but I wasn't sure if you were supposed to wake a sleepwalker. I had just dropped her off at her house a couple of hours ago. How had she gotten into the house? I remembered locking the door when I came in from the dance, but Tia knew where we kept the spare. This would not be good. I left the room and went to the kitchen. I wanted to make sure she hadn't left a door open. She hadn't, but it was freezing.

I poured myself a glass of water and tried to think of what to do. The tile under my bare feet chilled my entire body, or maybe that was nerves knowing there was a girl in my bed. It wasn't just any girl, it was Tia. It was the girl I'd kissed a few hours ago; it was the girl I wanted to kiss again. Mom would lose it if she found Tia in my bed.

I returned to my bedroom and locked the door. I found some socks and a hoodie and pulled out my sleeping bag from the closet. I checked my phone; it was two in the morning. I didn't want to wake my folks, and I surely didn't want to call Tia's house. I'd be a gentleman and sleep on the floor and give her the bed.

I couldn't believe I fell asleep with her sleeping in my room, but I did. When I woke up, her hand was on my head. She'd rolled over, and her hand hung over the edge of the bed. I felt her stir again. I thought she'd wake soon, and I didn't want her to wake the rest of the house.

Mom and Dad were still at home but would be leaving early for Jesse's soccer practice. I wanted to wake her in case Mom came to talk to me before they left. I sat up and watched her face. She was sleeping so peacefully. I watched as her eyelashes fluttered slightly, and her brow furrowed. I wondered if this was how she woke up every day. I was fascinated and captivated. I sat on the edge of the bed and placed my fingers over her mouth.

Tia's eyes suddenly opened wide. Her entire body went rigid. "Shhh," I whispered. Her eyes widened even more, trying to take in her surroundings. "You're in my room. Don't worry. You're okay. I slept on the floor." I looked over my shoulder toward my door. "We're not alone, and I didn't want you to get caught." She nodded a couple of times and blinked her wide eyes.

Confident that she wouldn't scream, I released her mouth. "How did I get here?" she whispered.

I shrugged. "I don't know. I woke up, and you were standing in the doorway. You scared the shit out of me. I thought I was dreaming about you again, but you're really here." The edge of her mouth went up in a grin, and her eyes brightened. That pleased her for some reason. "What?" I mouthed.

She smiled then. "You dream about me?" Her tone was a little bit curious and way too pleased to know that.

I looked away and sighed. I wouldn't even try to deny it. "Yeah, I do." She placed her hand over mine on the bed.

"I dream about you sometimes, too. I dreamt about you last night," she confessed in a breath, putting me at ease. I looked down at her hand and smiled. I wondered if she'd been dreaming about kissing, too.

"My parents are leaving with Jesse in a little while. I'll take you back home as soon as they're gone."

She nodded and wiped the sleep from her eyes. We listened in silence as Mom and Dad readied Jesse; they'd be gone for a couple of hours. They'd do practice and then go for breakfast with his team. We heard the car pull out of the driveway. I stood from the bed.

"Let me check the house just in case, okay?" She nodded.

Everyone was gone, and I relaxed a bit, knowing the house was empty but equally apprehensive that we were alone. I returned to my bedroom. "Are you hungry?" I asked. She shook her head and then considered.

"I need to go to the bathroom, and I'd really like to brush my teeth." She smiled sheepishly.

I led T to the bathroom and found her a toothbrush. Thankfully, Mom kept extras in the bathroom closet. I opened the drawer and pulled out mine and some toothpaste. I left her and went to use my parents' bathroom. I returned to my room and pulled on a pair of jeans, socks, and boots. Tia tapped lightly on my door.

"Come in," I said. "Where do I need to take you?"

"I'm thinking Catherine's. That would be a likely place if my parents get home early and don't find me there."

"Are you sure you don't want anything to eat?"

"I should go. I can't, for the life of me, figure out how I got here. It's really unsettling. I don't want to get caught, and I don't want to get either one of us in trouble."

"Yeah," I agreed, but so much about Tia bugged me. I never felt like we had time to stop and figure things out.

"Are you hungry?" she asked. The mention of food brought my attention back to her. "You've asked me about food a couple of times. I feel like I'm inconveniencing you."

"No, it's fine. Depending on the time, I may go meet my parents and eat with them and Jesse after I drop you off." That seemed to appease her. She stood near the door and crossed her arms. I wasn't sure if she was cold or just feeling self-conscious. "Want a hoodie?" I asked. "It's pretty cold outside."

"Yeah, thanks. I'd like that." I found her a school hoodie and handed it to her. Although it was a little large for her, no one would take notice of it being something she wouldn't already own. She pulled the hoodie over her head and punched her hands down into the center pocket. "Christopher, I'm really sorry about all of this. I had a lot of fun at the dance last night, and I enjoyed the few minutes we had alone afterward, but I can't explain any of this." She shrugged her shoulders in the oversized top.

I pressed my hands into my knees and stood. "I enjoyed last night, too, but don't worry. I'll get you to Catherine's, and we can try and figure this out later. Do you make a habit of sleepwalking?" I asked. She shook her head. She looked vulnerable and confused, standing there in my hoodie. Her eyes hadn't lost the surprised look she'd awakened with. I took her hand and kissed her cheek. "Please, don't worry."

Moments later, we were parked in front of Catherine's house. I moved to open the door, but Tia stopped me. "That's fine. I'm good here.

I can go in through the side door. It's closest to Catherine's room. She's probably not awake yet. I doubt anyone is even looking for me." Tia took my hand and squeezed it gently. "Thank you."

I returned the squeeze on her hand. "May I text and check on you later?" I asked. She nodded. I wanted to kiss her again, but it didn't seem like she was looking to be kissed. She looked uncomfortable and like she just wanted to get into Catherine's house. I watched her make her way around the hedge that concealed the garbage cans, but I couldn't tell if she'd made it.

I drove back toward my house to eat something and take a shower and saw an ambulance parked in front of Miss Grace and Mr. Roy's. I turned sharply onto their property. I slammed my truck in park and jumped from the cab. The EMTs were rolling a gurney out the front door and down the steps toward the ambulance. I could tell from the tuft of gray that it was Miss Grace. Her mouth was covered with an oxygen mask, and her eyes were closed.

I stood several steps from the porch and waited for Mr. Roy. He didn't come out. Once they were cleared from the porch, I opened the screen door and entered. Mr. Roy was wringing his hands and looking around their small living room. Worry and confusion clouded his vision.

"Mr. Roy," I said. "What's going on?"

"It's Miss Grace," he said despondently.

"What happened?"

"She's not been feeling well. The cold finally got her. She wasn't breathing well all morning and then couldn't get out of bed. I had to call the ambulance. I couldn't get her to the door." He sounded defeated and helpless.

Since my own had died just after I was born, Miss Grace and Mr. Roy were like grandparents to me. They were so kind and loving and had helped take care of me since I was little, but at that moment, they were the ones who needed the attention. I could do that.

"What do you need to do? Are you going with her?" He nodded but didn't move. "Do you need to pack something? Do you want me to help you?" He nodded again. "Okay, let's go in your room and get some things, okay?"

He pulled out a small old-fashioned overnight case from underneath the bathroom sink. He opened the drawers to their dresser and handed me items to pack. I followed him around the small room and neatly packed whatever he gave me. He opened a drawer and pulled out socks and underwear and a clean gown for his wife. He looked so sad as his fingers traced the soft lace at the edge of the fabric. It was painful to watch.

I looked around the room and noticed some medicine bottles on the small table next to their bed. “Are these Miss Grace’s?” I asked.

“Yes, those, too.”

“Do you want to get some things for yourself?” It was a good reminder. He suddenly realized he needed to pack, too. He packed a change of clothes and went back into the bathroom for his own toiletries. He returned with a handful of items and laid them in the small case. “Do you need a ride?”

“No, I’ll ride with Grace in the ambulance.”

“Okay, let’s go.” I urged him toward the door. He hesitated like he had forgotten something.

“The animals,” he began.

“Don’t worry about that. I’ll take care of them.”

“Would you mind staying here and keeping an eye on the place?” he asked. “I’d feel better knowing someone was here. You can stay in the shop.”

“Yeah, I’m sure that will be fine.” I followed him out the door and onto their small porch. “Let me know if I can do anything else.” Mr. Roy nodded, and his old eyes looked ancient. He peered at me like he just realized I was there.

"Christopher," he said, using my given name. "Watch yourself. Be careful. The cold." He must have been worried; he always called me Topher.

"Mr. Buchanan," the EMT called, "we're ready, sir." He motioned for Mr. Roy to join him.

"Don't worry about anything, Mr. Roy."

"Worry for yourself," I thought I heard him mutter under his breath. He was distracted and took the few steps from the house. The EMT opened the rear door and helped Mr. Roy into the back of the truck. *Poor dude*, I thought.

I looked around the house. Nothing needed my immediate attention. I took the extra keys from a hook near the door and locked the house when I left. I went to their small barn and fed the pigs and the goats and their old dogs who guarded the place.

Miss Grace and Mr. Roy were our nearest neighbors. They were a spry, elderly couple with about ten acres. They lived alone in a tiny house in the front of their property. Their original house had burned down when I was a baby. They stayed in Mr. Roy's shop for a long time until she demanded they move. Miss Grace referred to her husband's shop as the "party house." One side housed his tractor, mowers, old motorcycles, and a mint-condition Ford Mustang, while the other side had a big-screen television, a sofabed, and a fridge stocked with beer.

Now that Mr. Roy was up in years, they hired me to keep their property mowed down. Miss Grace paid me in cash, and Mr. Roy paid me in beer. From the time I was fifteen, I had open access to Mr. Roy's stash. On my sixteenth birthday, he literally gave me the keys to the liquor cabinet and told me it was time to expand my palette and try some of the *good* stuff. Once I got past the burn, I liked most whisky, and I really, really liked scotch on the rocks.

CHAPTER 10

Mom and I drove to the hospital that afternoon to visit Miss Grace. She was doing okay, but they were going to keep her a few nights. Mr. Roy was more himself and asked me to walk with him down to the cafeteria to get a cup of coffee.

"I appreciate your help this morning," he began. "Did you have fun at the dance last night?"

"Yes, sir. I did." I smiled. Of course, he'd have known about the dance. Ill or not, Miss Grace kept up with all of the social events in town.

"Where were you off to so early?" he asked and handed me a cup of coffee.

I hesitated and stammered, "Taking a friend home."

"Hmmm," Mr. Roy replied. He squinched up his face like he was trying to hold back a smile. He tilted his head and winked. "A friend, heh?" I swallowed hard and knew he knew something. I stirred my coffee and took a sip to not have to make eye contact. I didn't want to be teased, and I didn't want to admit that it was Tia in case it might start a rumor or cause trouble. "Don't worry, boy; I'm not going to say anything, but you might want to be a bit more discrete. Folks might get the wrong impression when you're sneaking a friend away in the early morning." I looked him in the eye but didn't reply. He changed the subject and asked about the animals. He also offered to pay me to clean the house and make it welcoming for when Miss Grace came home.

Mr. Roy stayed at the hospital for the next two nights with Miss Grace. She seemed to be improving. I slept in their party house and tended to the animals. Monday at school, I told Tia about Mrs. Grace.

"Oh, she's such a sweet lady. I'm sorry she's sick. Would you like me to help you clean their house? I'm free after school."

I was surprised that she'd offered. I mean, I wasn't surprised she offered, because she was thoughtful like that, but that she was able to offer to help me. I had texted to see how she was later on Sunday afternoon, but I wondered how it would be on Monday after the kissing and her sleepwalking to my house.

Monday wasn't weird at all. She got off the bus and almost ran to me. She smiled and took my hand and didn't seem the least bit apprehensive about being with me. Jason didn't act weird, either. In fact, he hardly made his presence known. She and I scooted over and ate together in our own section. For the first time all year, she didn't shield herself.

After school, I met her in the parking lot. She hopped into the truck and turned on the radio; we sang all the way to Miss Grace and Mr. Roy's. Tia followed me to the barn to check on the animals. The goats were unreasonably pushy and spoiled.

"I thought they had rabbits," Tia said.

"They did, but not for a long time."

"Do you remember when we let that big hare loose in middle school? I thought for sure Miss Grace was going to come completely unglued. She was frantic, watching us chase around the garden after him. No telling what damage we caused to their vegetables."

I stopped and looked at her. "You remember that?" I asked, unsure of how to respond. It was the first memory she'd recalled since her return.

"Yeah. Miss Grace was squealing every time we got close to catching him. Mr. Roy came around the barn with a rake to try and head him off so we could jump and catch him. You finally did. We were all out of breath. Miss Grace made us lemonade."

My breath caught, and I couldn't help myself. I grabbed Tia up into my arms and hugged her. I was so happy hearing her recount the story. I was breathless, just like that day, but it was because my heart was beating out of my chest. *Tia was back! Tia remembered!* I kissed her hard and with enthusiasm. She didn't even try to stop me, and before long, I picked her up, and she wrapped her legs around my waist. Her arms clung to my shoulders, holding onto me just as securely.

I stopped kissing her to catch my breath and to regain some sense of the present. For the lack of anything better, I asked if she needed something to drink. She giggled, remembering her comment about lemonade. "Yeah, let's go see what they've got inside."

I found a couple of Cokes in bottles in the fridge and offered her one. "Where should we begin cleaning?" she asked.

I looked around the small living room and down the hall to their bedroom. "Probably the bedroom and work our way toward the kitchen," I suggested.

"That's funny," she giggled.

"What?"

"I think most folks start cleaning in the kitchen and work back through a house. You're wanting to work it backward."

"I know there are dishes in the bedroom, and I also know the bathroom is spotless. There's not much to do, so I'd like to do the easiest to the hardest. Besides, I hate doing dishes. I'd rather do that last."

She shrugged. "I don't mind, either way."

She started in the bathroom, and I brought all the dishes and cups to the kitchen. I joined her on the other side of the bed, and we began making it up together. We arranged the pillows and dusted the dresser and the blinds.

"I'll start in the kitchen if you want to work in the living room," she said.

"Thanks!"

There wasn't much to do in either room, but she finished the kitchen before I was done dusting the shelves and ceiling fan. "Where's the vacuum cleaner?" she asked.

"I have no idea. Let me check the hall closet." I opened the closet, but no vacuum. I checked the laundry room and also the pantry. No luck. I opened the door to the spare room and just stood there, looking dumbstruck.

"I found it!" she hollered from down the hall. "What is it?" she asked, and I felt her come beside me. "Oh," she gasped and covered her mouth with her hand. "What is this?"

"I don't know; I've never been in here. I'm guessing it's their son's room, but he died before their house burned. It's got to be a weird sort of homage to him."

The bedding looked retro, and there were old rock band posters on the walls. I knew the bands; they were some of my dad's favorites. Photos of friends were framed and lined a low shelf. I didn't take a good look at those. It felt intrusive, so I just stood in the doorway.

"Should we vacuum or dust in here?" Tia asked.

"No, it looks spotless. I don't see a speck of dust anywhere." I backed up, and Tia did the same. We shut the door, and a wave of sadness hit us both.

"When did he die?" Tia asked. I shrugged; I didn't have any details.

"Mom said their house burned when I was little. Mom and Dad were away at school. I think he died around the time I was born. I'm not sure. Miss Grace and Mr. Roy have never mentioned him to me."

"It's so sad. I can't imagine losing a child, even a grown one." Her voice was wispy.

"Let's finish cleaning and get out of here. I've been staying in the shop, and I want to make sure I haven't left anything out in case they come home tonight or tomorrow."

A little while later, we locked the clean house and walked across their yard toward the shop. "What's out here?" she asked. "I don't ever remember being allowed in here."

"It's Mr. Roy's man-cave." I chuckled. "Miss Grace calls it his party house, but they haven't hosted a party in a long time." She looked around at the TV, sofa, and recliner. "There's a fridge at the back. Help yourself. I'll take another Coke." I folded a blanket and made sure I hadn't left any underwear or socks on the floor. I folded up the sofa bed and replaced the cushions.

"Does he still have that old Mustang?" she asked, offering me the bottle.

"Yeah. You remember that?"

"It's a beautiful car. How could I not?" I led her through the side door into the workshop. A broad smile spread across her face.

The Mustang was from the mid-sixties. It was bright blue with dual racing stripes down the center of the car and across the hood. "Can we sit in it?" Tia asked. I opened the door to the car and made a sweeping motion with my hand and offered her a seat like she'd won it on a game show. Tia handed me her Coke and jumped excitedly and clapped her hands. She settled in and stroked her hand over the steering wheel.

"Have you ever driven it?" she asked. I shook my head. "Get in!" I set the bottles on a shelf of tools and went around to the other side. I slid in. "Where do you want to go?" she asked enthusiastically.

"Nowhere. I'm not stealing Mr. Roy's car."

"No, silly. Just pretend. Where do you want to go? Just imagine the possibilities."

I looked over at her. Excitement shown in her eyes at holding onto the steering wheel and moving it gently back and forth, pretending she was driving. I wondered what she saw looking out across the hood. It was like we were kids again, like when we sat next to each other in a huge cardboard box, and she was pretending to drive or fly or sail. Tia always had the best stories and adventures in her mind. Under her careful direction, we built forts and tents and pirate ships. She especially liked pirates.

"Mountains or seaside?" she asked.

"Neither. A long, winding road through autumn leaves."

"Autumn leaves," she repeated. "Did you remember the blankets? There might be snow. Do you think we'll make it there before sunset?" she asked, instantly taking up the pretend.

"No, we'll be able to see the sunset as we drive," I added.

"Good. That'll be beautiful. Did you pack a picnic?"

"No, we'll have to stop somewhere. I think there's a restaurant on the way. They serve good food."

"Have we eaten there before?"

"No, but I've always wanted to." All this talk of food made me hungry.

"Me, too. How long are we going to be gone?"

"A long time, maybe forever."

She smiled. "Does the radio work?" she asked, reaching over and adjusting the radio. I shrugged, unsure if she was breaking character or still pretending.

I glanced around the shop through the window. I got out of the car and walked over to a row of hooks. The keys to the tractor and liquor cabinet and the house hung there. I fiddled through the collection and found what I assumed was the Mustang's key.

I handed it to Tia, and she started the engine. It purred to life. Mr. Roy loved this car and maintained it in mint condition. I cracked the door to the shop to allow the exhaust to escape. Tia fiddled with the radio until a station came through. The raspy speakers sounded nothing like the ones in my truck, but it set the mood for this car's generation. The only station that came through clearly was an oldies station. Definitely fitting.

After a few minutes of singing and pretending, Tia looked over and smiled. "We're nearly there."

"That was fast."

She pretended to put the car in park and turned off the ignition. “When you travel by magic, it doesn’t take any time at all.”

“I didn’t realize this car was magic.”

“Most definitely magic.” She turned to me, motioning for me to come closer like she had a secret. I leaned over, and she kissed me. She initiated the kiss, and before long, there we were, making out in Mr. Roy’s car. I wondered for half a second if he and Miss Grace had ever done that, too.

CHAPTER 11

Tia was happy, and her joy leaked out all over me and was easily reciprocated. The bucket seats and the massive steering wheel encumbered my ability to be closer to her. Maybe that was a good thing. I considered pulling her onto my lap or into the backseat, but it was entirely too small. The kissing Saturday night was just a prelude to the kissing in the Mustang. Both held their own levels of intensity, and I wanted nothing more than to keep on kissing her.

I let my hands wander down her shoulders toward her back. I followed the line from her waist to her hips. I'd never made out with anyone, but touching her and pulling her closer felt natural. She was warm and magnetic.

She stopped kissing me and looked into my eyes. There was a strange look in them, and it frightened me a little. "T?" I asked, unable to read her expression.

"What?" she asked, stroking her hands across my shoulders.

"I don't know. What are we doing?"

"We're making out in a classic Mustang," she said matter-of-factly.

"Are we still pretending?"

She shook her head gravely. "Not pretending."

I swallowed; no, I gulped and exhaled. "Does this make us a couple?"

She giggled. "You're so silly, Christopher. We've been a couple since we were kids. Now, we're just a couple who kisses and appreciates being old enough to take advantage of that." Her eyes were intent when she spoke like it was the truth.

"Why is it suddenly different now?" I asked.

"What do you mean?"

"Like suddenly, it's okay to be alone with you, and suddenly it's okay to consider us a couple. Is it cool with your parents?"

She hesitated for a second. "It's better, but I wouldn't call it cool."

I sat back into the seat and looked forward out the front windshield toward the far wall of the workshop. "What about Saturday night? That was pretty weird, leaving the dance, and then you sleepwalking to my house. You have any thoughts on that?"

"It sounds really hokey, but I was dreaming about you. We were at the dance, dancing and kissing." I turned towards her, then, and watched blush crawl across her cheeks and up to the tips of her ears. I grinned playfully. I had liked those parts of the evening, too. "Stop it!" she exclaimed and pressed her hand into my chest, playfully. I grabbed her hand and held it there. I liked the feeling of her hands on me. I took a deep breath and relaxed at her touch, instantly at ease.

"May I talk to your parents? I want them to know that I'd like you to be my girlfriend."

"I am your *girl*friend," she said, emphasizing girl. "Can't we just be good with that?"

"I don't like sneaking around behind their backs."

"I'm not sneaking," she argued. I cocked my head to the side and rolled my eyes slightly.

"Do they know where you are?"

"I doubt it; they're sleeping. I'll see them for supper, and I'll tell them that I was helping Miss Grace since she's in the hospital. They might already know." I nodded but didn't like the lack of transparency.

Her parents were both nurses and worked nights. Our days were free as kids because her parents were sleeping until supper. She had sitters when she was younger and stayed over at Catherine's, too, and then summers, of course, were taken by her aunt and grandmother.

I opened the car door and got out. Tia did likewise. I sealed the opening to the workshop; the afternoon temperatures were dropping, and it had become frigid in the open air. I could see my breath. "It really might snow," I said, remembering Tia's pretending.

"I hope so." She picked up her Coke and took a sip. She returned the key to the hook and looked curiously over the work surfaces. She picked up a few odd pieces of metal and scrutinized each one. I finished my Coke and just watched her. I wanted to go to her side and kiss her again, but I didn't want to appear too eager or pushy. Still, how had she said it? "Now, we're just a couple who kiss and appreciate being old enough to take advantage of that." I wanted to take advantage of that but without taking advantage of her. She cut her eyes at me and blinked. I watched everything she did in mental slow-motion. Then I watched her eyes move past mine behind me.

"What's in there?" she asked. I followed her gaze and turned toward a couple of doors at the back of the shop.

"I don't know. It might be storage; I've never seen Mr. Roy open it.

"Can we check it out? I'm curious." She reached for the handles, but they were locked. "See if there's a key."

Mr. Roy trusted me with keys to his liquor cabinet, beer fridge, tractors, house, and shop, so I didn't think it would be a big deal to unlock a door. I opened it and blinked.

"Wow!" I said in an exhale.

"Amazing." I heard Tia mutter beside me.

She moved forward, but I put my hand on her shoulder to stop her. I had a feeling we shouldn't cross the threshold. The entire room was covered with maps and drawings and photographs and looked like those investigation webs that detectives make on crime shows to figure out the links between suspects and possible serial crimes.

"I don't think this is for our eyes," I said.

"But our eyes have already seen it," Tia said, drawn toward the far wall.

She hit the lights and walked into the room. Nearly every wall of the room was covered. The left wall contained newspaper clippings. The right wall was covered with a floor-to-ceiling map of our town and the surrounding county. There was a corresponding overlay map that encompassed even more land. Tiny colored pins were in clusters, marking a pattern. A red dot was marked at the edge of the county.

The far wall was covered in pictures, some old, some recent. Tia walked over to the wall and touched the photographs of herself and Jason and even one of Catherine. There were so many of Tia. Some were school photos, and others were just snapshots. Among them were Tia's toothless grin in primary school, Tia's awkward braces phase, and Tia and I holding that huge hare after we'd caught him in the garden. It was downright unnerving and a little creepy.

"Why are there pictures of me?" she asked with a steely voice.

"I don't know."

She turned and looked angry and also a little afraid. "Are they some kind of creepers?" she asked.

I shrugged. I'd known this couple my entire life. It seemed so unlike them. "I don't think so."

Her eyes fell across the wall behind me. "What is that?" she asked.

I turned and saw the entire wall dedicated to a low altar littered with candles. A wooden cross stood in the center next to a brass menorah. Upon further examination, I realized it wasn't a menorah; it was just a fancy candelabra. An ancient-looking carved Star of David hung on the wall above it all. A stained-glass window reflected the light in the center of the room and cast its color over the altar. My eyes glanced over a framed drawing of an old church; something about it was oddly familiar. There, in front of the altar, was a carved, wooden kneeler with a padded cushion. The cushion was embroidered with more symbols and patterns.

A Bible lay open across the top of the kneeler. Its pages were well-worn as though it had been read often. There was no dust or a look like that room was unused. From the current photos, someone had been in there recently.

"Take me home," Tia commanded and walked past me.

She wrapped her arms around herself, burdened and heavy like she'd found that damn lead sweater, again. I turned out the lights and closed and locked the doors behind us.

I opened the cab of my truck and let Tia climb in. She scooted toward the center of the bench seat. She didn't say a word the entire ride back to her house, but she didn't seem edgy or uncomfortable.

Parked in front of her house, I took her hand. "Tia, I don't know anything about that room, but I'm going to ask Mr. Roy about it first chance I get."

"No, it can wait. Please don't say anything until we know Miss Grace is going to be okay. I don't want to upset him."

"But, T, that's all kinds of wrong."

She shook her head, but her eyes looked far away. "It didn't feel like that. It felt protective."

"Then why did you want to leave so suddenly?"

"I didn't belong there. *We* didn't belong there. It was private, and I didn't want to disturb it."

"T, I don't understand."

"I don't either, but I'm surprisingly alright. I'll see you tomorrow, okay?" She leaned in and gave me a quick peck on the cheek. She smiled. I took hold of her arm at her elbow and held her there for a second. I looked into her eyes and examined her expression. I was satisfied to see that her eyes weren't lying. Just like when she kissed me in the Mustang, she wasn't pretending. From what I could tell, she was okay. I kissed her warm lips and, for the brief space of time, forgot about what we'd found.

CHAPTER 12

I decided to take a longer route home. I drove down Main Street, through the center of our little town square. The drawing and the stained glass window that hung in Mr. Roy's room made me think of something. At the center of town stood an old church, well what remained of it, anyway. Saturday night at the dance, I'd heard the church bells pealing out over the school. Their sound didn't carry all the way to my house, so I rarely heard them.

The building's remains reminded me of pictures of bombed buildings in war-torn parts of Europe. The bell tower was all that stood and served its purpose. The church ruins were never removed or ever rebuilt. Besides a few weddings and funerals in a chapel just outside of town, our family had never attended church or participated in anything remotely religious, so I had never had reason to wonder about it. We learned about Christmas and Easter and holy days of the Judeo-Christian traditions, just like we learned about other world religions with historical significance. It was history but had no real connection to our community or our lives.

I parked my truck at the curb and walked around the old church. I had seen this old building my entire life, passed it a million times, but had never really taken notice of it. It was just a part of town that we all took for granted, the backdrop, the setting. Only the frame of the original church stood. It had no roof, and in the summer, small plants and climbing vines took it over. The framed drawing of the church at Mr. Roy's made me wonder. I closed my eyes and tried to envision what this old ruin must have looked like. There definitely were similarities to the stones and the framework. I'd have to look at the picture more closely to be sure.

In the cold of winter, the wind whipped and howled around the barren walls. Brick and stone pillars and archways lined the walkway. The windows had all been removed. At the far end of the building was an alcove with a low altar, much like the one at Mr. Roy's, though this one was carved stone and was attached to the marble and stone floor. Above the altar was an opening in the stone, precisely the same size and shape as the stained glass. That was the part that had made me consider. I knew I'd seen that shape before.

The building was one of the oldest in our community; it had to be. I had never thought about it before; I'd had no reason to. Different symbols were carved into the stone altar and along some of the pillars. I wondered how and when it had been destroyed. I walked around the outside of the building and found the cornerstone with the date of its erection. It was built within a decade of the town's founding. Etched at the bottom were two names: Reverend Reginald Buchanan, founding pastor, and Archibald Buchanan, architect.

Buchanan was Mr. Roy and Miss Grace's last name. I wondered if there was some relation. Weird, but they were the only Buchanans that I knew. Maybe that's why he'd saved the relics from the old church.

The sun was going down, and the temperature was dropping rapidly. I could feel the cold front blasting through. Snow flurries blew through the sky. I needed to get to Mr. Roy's animals and head to the house for supper. I was suddenly starving.

I pulled up close to the barn and took care of the animals. On my way back toward the truck, I noticed a light on in the party house. I'd probably left something on in my rush to get Tia home. I drove the few yards and left the engine running while I slipped in to turn out the lights.

I was surprised to find Mr. Roy standing at the bar, making himself a drink. “Mr. Roy, you’re home. Is Miss Grace with you?” I hadn’t seen any lights on in the house.

He shook his head. “No, son, she won’t be coming home for a while. Pneumonia.” He looked so tired. “She made me come home to sleep and check on things. She didn’t want me to be stranded with her at the hospital. With the way the weather’s changing outside, I have a feeling I might get stranded here for a couple of days.”

“I can drive you back and forth if you need,” I offered.

“Thanks. I’ll let you know,” Mr. Roy said despondently and took a sip of his drink. “Want one?” he offered.

I shook my head. “No, thanks. I took care of the animals for the night. Do you want me to keep staying out here?”

He shook his head and sat in the recliner, gingerly holding his glass with both hands. “I’ll be staying out here for now. Can’t bear to be inside the house with Gracie away.”

I wanted so much to ask him about the room and altar and the names on the church, but Tia saying to wait until Miss Grace was better seemed like the right way to go. I couldn’t burden Mr. Roy with one more thing. He seemed brittle and old like the slightest thing more might snap him in two.

"Do you want me to bring you some supper? Mom's cooking tonight. I can bring you a plate." My stomach had been growling for the better part of an hour.

"I ate lunch with Gracie. I'll be fine. Ask me tomorrow."

"I'll come by and check on the animals before school, okay?"

He nodded once and rested his head against the back of the recliner. He closed his eyes and took another sip of his drink. I felt like my presence was intruding on his thoughts.

"Goodnight, Mr. Roy," I said and made my escape.

I ate three helpings at supper. Jesse ate two, and Mom set aside a plate for Mr. Roy. I'd be sure to put it in the fridge for him in the morning when I went to check on the animals. I told my parents about Miss Grace's pneumonia. They nodded gravely; they already knew.

"When did their son die?" I asked.

Dad's head shot up, and his expression changed. His jaw tightened, and his eyes were concerned. Mom busied herself with Jesse, but I noticed how her eyes cut across to take in Dad's expression.

"He died a few months after you were born."

"Did you know him?" I asked.

Dad blinked a few times like he had something in his eye and took in a deep breath through his nose. “Yes. He was a year behind us, but he was one of my best friends.” He swallowed like he had to contain his emotions.

“Sorry, Dad. I didn’t know.”

“I know,” Dad said quietly. “It’s not easy to talk about.”

“Is that why we’re such good friends with them?”

“Partly.” There was a hint of fondness in his eyes. “We’ve always been neighbors. I practically grew up in their house. They were good friends with my parents, too.”

“Was their son killed when their house burned down?” I didn’t think so, but I wanted to clarify.

“No, that happened later,” Dad said. His voice was lower than usual. Mom rose from the table and walked to stand behind Dad. She placed her hand affectionately on his shoulder. He put his hand over hers, accepting her comfort. “Roy, Jr. was killed in a car accident.”

I didn’t know what to say. I’d never asked about Mr. Roy and Miss Grace, before. Until that afternoon, I’d never had any questions to ask. At that moment, I had about a million, but I didn’t want to ask my parents. I could tell the subject was sensitive, and I didn’t want to upset them. I would ask Mr. Roy when I had the chance. It was all too weird.

The wind howled all night long. The temperature dropped, and with it, nearly a foot of snow fell overnight. We were notified that school would be canceled. Our town hadn't seen snowfall like that in a long time. According to Mr. Roy, the almanac, and my own memory, the last time we'd had snow like that was kindergarten or first grade. I couldn't remember it happening in more than a decade.

I blew the drive, eased my truck down the slope of our driveway, and drove slowly through the snow in my huge truck toward Mr. Roy's. I tended to the animals and then went to check on him. I knocked several times before he answered the door. He'd been sleeping, but from the looks of him, he'd been at the bottle all night. He smacked his lips and scratched at his chest and blinked hard against the glare of the snow.

He looked me over for a second or two and then backed up so I could enter. I brought in the plate of leftovers and a few other things Mom had pulled from the fridge. He opened the lid of one of the containers and sniffed approvingly. Most everyone approved of my mom's cooking. He grabbed a fork from the drawer and sat down and began eating the contents of the container without even heating it.

"I checked on the animals," I began. Mr. Roy nodded with a mouth full of food. "Do you plan to go back to the hospital?" I asked.

He licked his lips and swallowed before he spoke. “It’s forecasted more snow. I’m not sure what I want to do. I’ll call and check on Gracie before I decide.”

“If you don’t want to risk the roads, I can give you a ride.” He nodded. He had an old pick-up that he used around his property and to run errands in town. Miss Grace had never driven that I could remember. He kept the Mustang running, but I rarely saw him drive it. He only took it on the highway occasionally, and besides, it would be of no use in this weather.

I watched him finish off the contents of the container in a couple more bites. He washed it down with a long sip of something from his mug. It didn’t smell like coffee had been brewed, so I considered that he might still be partaking of whatever he’d spent the evening before consuming.

“Mr. Roy, the house is clean and ready for Miss Grace.” He nodded like maybe he already knew that, but I doubted he’d battled the snow in the night to go and inspect it himself. I felt like I needed to broach some of the subjects that kept burning inside my brain. “Tiana helped me clean the house. When we were cleaning, I, um, saw your son’s room. We didn’t disturb anything, but I just wanted you to know we saw it. I’m really sorry. Dad told me last night that they were good friends.”

Mr. Roy didn't reply to me directly, but he held my gaze, staring at me. I felt a little guilty; maybe I should have kept that to myself. Honestly, I thought perhaps I was warming up toward the topic of his other room. One thing at a time, right?

Mr. Roy acknowledged my comment. "They were best friends, good kids. I was glad your dad wasn't here when it happened. I was so thankful he and your mom didn't have to face all of that. It would have been too much with you coming and his folks passing and Roy, Jr. in such rapid succession. I was thankful," he repeated.

I couldn't bear the pain in his eyes. He'd lost his son and close friends, and his house burned all in a matter of months. I couldn't imagine that much loss in such a short period.

I quickly changed the subject. "Mr. Roy, I was in town yesterday and walked past the old church ruin. I read the names on the cornerstone. I found your last name, Buchanan. Is that any relation to you?" I asked.

His eyes softened, and he considered me for a few moments before he spoke. "Yes."

"Who were they?" I asked.

"Rev. Reginald was my great-great-great-grandfather. I suppose that would make his brother, Archie, my uncle to the same degree. They helped found this town over a hundred and seventy-five years ago. It was a magnificent building once-upon-a-time."

"Do you know what happened to the church?" I asked.

Mr. Roy looked up at me with the strangest look. His old, blue eyes were piercing and showed no trace of their jovial sparkle. He wasn't messing around. Then, his eyes looked over me from head to toe, assessing me. I felt like I was being evaluated like a prized athlete or a soldier.

I bowed up a bit at the challenge. I was big; I was brawny. I towered over Mr. Roy, and I didn't like the way his eyes looked through me. I stood straighter, and when his eyes returned to mine, I met his gaze full-on. I was determined for him to see my merit, my metal, so to speak.

The intensity of his gaze didn't falter. He gave a quick nod like he had found what he was looking for. "Got a little while? This might take some time."

CHAPTER 13

It was colder than I'd remembered; temperatures plummeted into the negative teens. With school being canceled, I didn't have any other obligations. Mr. Roy and I were both sort of stuck, and I figured he might just want a little company. Thankfully, I remembered to return to my truck and turn it off. I retrieved my phone and keys. There was a text from Tia.

Bummer about school. Might not have school again tomorrow. If the weather clears up, I'll be babysitting for the Clarkes on Saturday. Do you have any plans?

I replied, **Yep, bummer. Liking the snow, though. Hanging out with Mr. Roy this morning. No plans Saturday.**

She replied with a happy face. Then the phone vibrated again. **Miss Grace?**

Okay, as far as I know. She sent him home last night.

Please don't mention it. Tia didn't need to remind me; I'd already decided.

When I returned to the party house, Mr. Roy had started a pot of coffee. I was glad to see him shift gears for the morning. I sat down on the sofa and watched as Mr. Roy pulled a second cup from the hooks behind the counter. He set a tray with sugar and cream and the mugs, filled with black, steaming coffee.

I dropped a couple of cubes of sugar into my mug and topped it off with a little cream. I stirred the contents slowly, allowing the sugar cubes to dissolve and mix in evenly. I was patient because I hated the grainy residue at the bottom of the mug. I'd been drinking coffee with Mr. Roy for as long as I could remember. Mom hadn't allowed me to have coffee when I was a kid, but every time Mr. Roy babysat, he offered me coffee-milk. It was sweet and creamy and not too hot. I was addicted almost instantly.

My mom hadn't even protested, when I walked into the kitchen during my first week of summer practices my freshman year and poured myself a mug, patiently stirred in the sugar and cream, and then sat down beside her. She looked over at me and gave me a wry smile.

"Good?" she asked, amused.

"Yeah, it is," I replied with a heavy sigh. I noticed after that she brewed a little extra in the pot each morning.

Mr. Roy sat back in his recliner and savored the first sip of his coffee. I'd learned that from him, too. I thought about all the things I'd learned from Mr. Roy and Miss Grace. I learned to wield a hammer, do minor electrical and plumbing work, mend fences, and handle farm equipment. I could barely reach the pedals the summer he thrust me into the driver's seat of his old tractor. He taught me to drive stick and how to change the oil on most engines. He'd taught me to care for his animals.

Miss Grace taught me to appreciate homemade cookies and vegetables, fresh from the garden. She'd made sure I'd tilled her garden properly, ensuring all the rows were straight, just like she liked things. I thought about all the time I'd spent with them. I pushed any thoughts of the altar and map room out of my mind.

Mr. Roy began, "Did you know, just like you, I wasn't born here?"

I couldn't hide my surprise. I shook my head. "No, sir." His introduction and my response were reminiscent of a million other stories he'd told me over the years. He always began with, "Did you know?" And just like nearly every time he asked me that question, I had no clue, and my answer was exactly the same, polite and ready to be schooled.

"It's true. My grandfather left town before my father was born. He was the pastor of the church. After it burned, and it was decided that it wouldn't be rebuilt, he left to find another pulpit to serve. It was one of the hardest decisions he'd ever made, packing up his wife and leaving this town. His family had served as ministers for as long as the town existed. Things had changed, though, and the church's burning was just the final blow."

My unspoken question was written all over my face. *The final blow?* I thought that was an odd choice of words.

"The tiny church had been under attack from folks that no longer believed or who had never believed what the church spouted from the pulpit. There was growing disregard for the small congregation. There were only a few devout remaining when the church burned. They met in homes and tried desperately to rebuild the church. They couldn't afford it and had no way to see past the destruction. The town had turned against them, you see?"

I nodded, accepting the story. "So where did he go? Where were you born?"

"My grandfather traveled from congregation to congregation until he settled in another small, farming community in another county. He always regretted that he wasn't able to do more here. He rarely spoke of it, but when he did, his voice was filled with a sense of hopelessness."

"How did you end up back here?" I asked. Not many folks left, and the few who did rarely returned. My parents were a rare exception.

Mr. Roy chuckled, and his eyes glistened with the lighter, more playful side of himself. "I'd just finished seminary. That's a school for training ministers," he explained. "I was curious about this town. So much of my grandfather's memory was tied up in this place. I wanted to see it for myself. I got an eyeful for sure." He smiled, remembering something that amused him.

"I blew into town, driving that old Mustang, cocky and so full of myself. I know that might seem contrary to how a wet-behind-the-ears seminary student should portray himself, but I wasn't looking for a job; I was looking for my heritage. My father died while I was away at school, and I wanted to feel grounded. Grieving does strange things to a man." He paused for a few moments before he continued.

"I went into the café to get a bite and there, sitting at the counter, was the most beautiful girl I'd ever seen. She had her nose stuck in a book, and was taking sips of her coffee between bites of a huge slice of pecan pie. She was wearing a skirt that had ridden up over her knee. I liked the shape of her calf and the arch of her foot as her toes dangled her pump absentmindedly. Of course, I had to sit down beside her and strike up a conversation."

Mr. Roy eyed me sagely and waggled his bushy, gray eyebrows. "You're old enough now to understand. The shape of a woman is a powerful force. They're all curvy in the right places. This girl was for sure, and I was beyond smitten. 'What do you recommend?' I asked. She looked up at me and blinked her big blue eyes. It took her a couple of seconds to focus on my face and my words, but she didn't answer me. I noticed the title of her book for something to make conversation, expecting it to be a romance novel. My mind shifted gears when I realized she was reading a compilation of essays written by famous figures in history. I'd read that book and couldn't believe that I was about to introduce myself to a beautiful girl who read about history and seemed engrossed in it.

"'Are you enjoying that?' I asked. She eyed me like I was making fun, but I was serious. I backpedaled and began again, 'I read that a while back. It was good.' Her expression changed, and her eyes looked more curious than cautious. I thought for a moment that I'd have an in.

"'Get the special. It comes with a choice of pie. I recommend the pecan.' She tilted her head down toward her half-eaten slice.

Then, another young woman approached from the other side of the counter. She was striking, too, but had a distasteful look on her face. She looked at me skeptically and then cut her eyes toward the woman at my right before she placed a glass of water in front of me.

"'Welcome. I'm Gertrude. How may I help you?' she asked but didn't really seem like she wanted to help me at all. My companion lifted her book again, and her nose went right into it when the other girl approached.

"'I'll take the special with a slice of pecan,' I said confidently. I thought I saw the book move slightly like maybe she had held in a giggle. She tucked her hair behind her ear.

"As soon as the waitress left, I looked back over. 'Hello, I'm Roy.' I honestly wasn't sure she'd reply, but her curiosity won out, and she lowered the book.

'I'm Grace.'

'Nice to meet you. I'm new in town and was wondering if maybe you could tell me a good place to stay. Cheap,' I added with a chuckle.

"She told me about an old boarding house at the end of Main Street. Folks call them bed-and-breakfasts, now, but then, they were just big houses where they let out rooms and served meals family-style. I didn't find out until supper that night when Gracie sat down at the large dining table across from me, that she lived there, too. She was studying to be a librarian, but summers, she lived and worked there while she was going to school. It was her grandmother's boarding house.

"I spent my days studying old tombstones, searching for every Buchanan I could find buried in that old cemetery. I also scrounged around the ruins of the old church. I looked up the names of the families of the former members of the congregation, anyone who might tell me anything about my ancestors. That's how I met your grandpa. History was fascinating. Gracie and I realized very soon that we had that in common. She could find and dig up just about any information from the library's archives, dusty old books, and ledgers.

"One thing led to another, and in the matter of a week, I was head-over-hills for that pretty little brunet who dangled her shoes from her toes. I couldn't have left this town if I wanted to. I know she doesn't much resemble that girl anymore, but she does to me."

His voice broke slightly, concern washed over his eyes. Miss Grace was elderly, now, and sick, and his worry and attachment for his wife were evident. For a few moments, he'd gotten caught up in the story, but he was suddenly brought back to reality and the state of things. He sat back, closed his eyes, and fell asleep.

CHAPTER 14

It had to have been the coldest winter in the history of our small town. For weeks I did little more than shovel snow and go to school. Our schooldays were shortened because the busses could only run during the middle of the day when the temperatures got above freezing. All of our classes were condensed to fit into four hours a day. Our additional homework kept us busy, though.

Dad's job demanded that he travel in the winter to learn more and stay current on all the agricultural stuff for the area farmers. Mom's accounting demands picked up after the first of the year and lasted until taxes were due in the spring. The dynamic in our family changed drastically in the winter: no football, no training, just work and school for everyone.

That left Jesse and me to our own devices. Now that Jesse was older, he didn't need to be babysat as much, and he could just hang out at the house with me. Miss Grace had watched him since he was a baby, but she was unable to do as much since she'd spent a week in the hospital. Now, Jesse and I ran errands for them and helped out as much as we could.

That particular winter, I was grateful for my truck. The four-wheel drive and towing capacity allowed me to do all kinds of jobs. I was getting called all the time to haul and tow things, pick up stuff, and shovel and plow driveways. Jesse even helped me shovel and de-ice walkways. I made more money that winter than I did in the spring and summer mowing fields.

The only downfall with winter was my limited time with Tia. I babysat with her occasionally, and she hung out some at my house, watching movies with Jesse and me. We held hands and made out after the little Clarke boys were all tucked in or when I drove her home. She was warm and vibrant and shone like the clear winter sun, bright and energizing against the cold.

Thankfully, the harsh winter was a good deterrent. I wanted to be with Tia; I wanted to hold and kiss her all the time. Hard labor is good for a young man; it kept me focused and exhausted and limited my physical ability to desire other things. I hoped after winter passed to have more time with T, but I also hoped spring training would wear me out just as quickly. I needed the balance. Tia made me think crazy thoughts and dream crazier dreams.

Jason had made himself scarce. After the winter dance, he suddenly stopped hanging around and hovering over Tia. Then, even more unexpectedly, he stopped eating lunch at our table. He then said he wouldn't be able to be at the Clarkes. I thought maybe he was just cool about T and me, but it wasn't like that at all. Well, it wasn't entirely like that.

I caught him leaning against the sophomore lockers between classes. Then, I saw him waiting after sophomore girls' PE. One Monday morning, I saw him waiting near the busses. I waited for Tia there every morning, so I knew it wasn't his usual morning spot.

"What's up?" I asked.

"Huh?" he replied like he'd seen me for the first time.

"Waiting for Tia?" I asked.

He stammered, "No, just waiting for a friend."

I wanted so badly to poke fun at him and give him a hard time, but for the first time in history, Jason didn't seem all that confident. He seemed preoccupied, self-conscious, and edgy. I kind of felt sorry for him.

"Dude, you okay?"

"Yeah," he lied through his stinking teeth.

Then the busses arrived, and I watched as he wavered between waiting for his friend and not allowing me to see why he was waiting there. Then I watched as a little, blond sophomore named Sherry stepped off the bus. He stepped forward with anticipation and looked so relieved when she smiled. It obviously wasn't planned that they meet; she seemed genuinely surprised to see him there. He almost looked shy. I doubted that and was probably reading too much into it, but still, he wasn't so damn arrogant. I wasn't sure if I trusted that change, either. Then it started at the corner of his mouth, slowly, hesitantly, and then it spread across his entire face, the goofiest smile I'd ever seen. This routine continued for weeks.

Jason had never shown any partiality with girls. He was flirtatious and got most girls' attention and held it just long enough to get whatever he wanted before he moved on. Sherry seemed to keep his attention differently from any other girl. She was cute and sweet but nothing notably remarkable. I found that amusing since that's probably how most people might describe Tia. Beauty was in the eye of the beholder, and from all counts, Jason beheld Sherry all the time.

Tia was spending the night at the Clarke's house again on Saturday night, so I had to go home at midnight. We should have stayed inside, but she'd walked me out, and I couldn't help but start kissing her again. I just wasn't ready to leave her. It felt that way more often. She knew me; she remembered everything, and she was mine. I wrapped her up in my arms.

"I'm so cold my fingertips are frozen," she complained, but she didn't move to go inside.

"Here, put them in my pockets." I took her hands and rubbed them between my hands. I blew my hot breath over them before I forced them into my jacket pockets.

"Spring will be here before we know it. I can't wait to see the flowers and grass again."

"Yeah, I know what you mean. I don't think I've seen grass since just before the solstice dance."

"It won't be long; I can feel it coming."

I nuzzled her more closely. She took her hands from my pockets and placed them under my jacket at the back of my waist. They didn't feel cold, and she didn't feel cold, and I didn't feel cold anymore, either.

"I'd better go," I said, sounding more responsible than I felt.

"One more kiss?" she teased and drew me into the recesses of the small front porch.

It took a great deal of effort to keep my mind on kissing rather than the ten or so other things that flashed through my mind: images of fields covered in green grass, buds on the branches, and wildflowers. Each image was harmless on its own, but the issue was the fact that Tia danced barefooted in the grass, twirling around in a sundress. She lay among the wildflowers, smiling, drawing me closer to her.

"Goodnight, T. I need to go," I said breathlessly and ran to my truck.

I rolled down the windows and let the cold air blast into the cab. I knew better, and, yet, I let myself go there. My thoughts went there, anyway, even if I hadn't.

SPRING

CHAPTER 15

Tia was right. Spring came sooner than anyone expected. The heavy snow and cold gradually tapered off; until one morning, it almost felt pleasant. Compared to the cold, pleasant was an understatement. By the spring equinox, it felt amazing! Roads and fields were cleared, and the planting was managed on time. The rain came just when it was needed, and nothing flooded.

After the confinement of the indoors for so many months, the entire town seemed to come out in force. Everyone prepared their gardens, planted blooming annuals, and tended every patch of green grass.

Along with the additional color and unburdened from our bulky, winter coats, spring training began. Coach started us out running laps and sprints. We'd all been weightlifting for PE, but football dictated different kinds of workouts.

The seniors weren't required to work out with us anymore, but Coach liked the idea of them mentoring the upcoming lines. It made the transition easier. Jason and Clayton worked together, and that meant that I worked with them, too. It was easier to guard Jason, now that he wasn't such a prick, but there were a couple of times he still looked at me like he wasn't sure.

Clayton and Catherine were still a thing. They'd fought some during the winter, and everyone was sure they'd call it quits before his graduation, but the two of them seemed to have resolved their issues. Small towns are full of rumors, and ours was no exception. The ability to gossip began in middle school and continued on through old age. I guess I shouldn't have been surprised when the rumors and gossip started about Clayton and Catherine; they were leaving themselves wide open for ridicule.

The rumors stated that her parents had caught them together one night. The woods and Anderson Field weren't an option in the freezing cold. Clayton had snuck in, and Catherine's father had pulled a gun on him, thinking he was a burglar. Rumor also had it that they were found in various stages of undress, if not caught in the act of sex itself. How embarrassing would that be to get caught *literally* with your pants down? I hadn't put much stock in the rumors until I heard Jason talking about it.

“Yeah, they’ll be getting married as soon as she graduates. Sooner, if she can test out and graduate early.” Everyone around us at the table nodded their agreement. A couple of guys just shook their heads, expressing their thoughts towards Clayton. “He can forget about his football scholarship now. He’ll be working his daddy’s land from now on.”

I thought Jason’s comment and everyone’s responses were odd. That was over a year away. Why would they be making plans to get married just because they’d been caught having sex for the better part of the school year? It wasn’t like she was pregnant, and if she were, they wouldn’t be waiting for her to graduate.

In our town, it wasn’t uncommon to get married young. My own parents had gotten married after their first year of college, but I thought that was more because of my impending arrival than the fact that it was ultimately their plan.

“Are they being forced to get married, or is it what they want?” I asked. Jason looked at me like I was a complete idiot for asking.

“No one is forcing them. It’s just the way it is. They know what’s expected of them,” he said dismissively. The bell rang, and we all scurried to class.

That afternoon at practice, Clayton didn't show up. "You boys are on your own today," Coach said. "Hopefully, Clayton will be joining you again soon. The principal is holding all the seniors for afterschool meetings this week."

Jason and I ran through the drills, and the offensive line ran plays against the defense. At the end of practice, Coach blew his whistle and signaled for us to run. It wasn't all that uncommon, but we usually started off with laps and sprints to warm up. I ended up next to Jason, and we set a steady pace.

"What did you mean by your comment at lunch?"

"What comment?"

"What you said about Clayton and Catherine and them getting married. I don't understand."

"Topher, sometimes it's like you don't have a clue. Do you even pay attention?"

I tried not to take offense to Jason because I wanted to know. I continuously had questions regarding things: Tia's memory, Mr. Roy's room, our odd little town. "Well, for argument's sake, let's pretend I'm new here, and you need to explain it, okay?"

He looked at me from the corner of his eye but didn't change his pace. He considered for a quarter of the track before he began. "Have you not noticed that everyone marries young and stays married forever?" I shrugged. Obviously, I didn't take notice of a lot of things like that. I just took them for granted. "No one cheats on his wife like in movies and on TV. No one gets away with casual sex, here, either. Once you have the taste of a local, you can't just leave that," he scoffed. "No man can be unfaithful, either, no matter how hard he tries. He's bound; he's tied for life."

I kept pace with him around the track and hoped he'd keep talking. My silence was rewarded. "It's not just that, man. You mess around before marriage, and you're stuck for life. It's the consequence of premarital sex. You're literally screwed. And don't even get me started on if you get her pregnant and don't get married – too many consequences to bear. At least Clayton was smart enough to protect himself. Not worth it."

Jason had quite a reputation with the girls. He'd been bragging since our freshman year. "That's ridiculous. You've been with girls, and you aren't stuck with just one." Jason stumbled and nearly tripped over his own feet. He steadied himself and recovered quickly.

"You're such an idiot, Topher," he retorted and took off ahead of me, giving me a clear picture that the conversation was over.

I kept my pace, but my mind was working in overdrive. I wanted Tia. My nearly-seventeen-year-old-self had a hard time containing those physical feelings. I was respectful of her and her body, but we were too young to be messing around with sex. Still, that didn't mean that my mind didn't sometimes battle between fantasy and reality.

I thought back to Mr. Roy's story and wondered if that's one of the reasons he never left. I also wondered if that's why my mom and dad returned. Nothing made sense, sometimes, and I just wanted to avoid the bombardment of questions.

Without the physical exertion, the flood of questions seeped into my thoughts on my drive home from practice. Before I realized where I was going, I'd driven toward Tia's house. Her parent's cars weren't there, so I got out and knocked on the door. She opened it with a smile.

"Hey. This is a surprise."

I was suddenly bothered. "Hey," I said, impatiently, and just stared at her. I had no real purpose for being there; it was like my truck just went there on its own. "Tia, do you ever wonder why things are the way they are?"

She held her hand to her brow to shield her eyes from the glare of the setting sun. She cocked her head to the side and tilted her chin upwards to see me around the piercing light. I stepped over so that my shoulder hid the sun. In shadow, she lifted her face up towards mine.

“Sometimes, why?”

I was only momentarily distracted by her smile. “Nothing makes sense, and I have about a million questions right now.”

“Like what?”

“This town, Clayton and Catherine, Mr. Roy’s room, why you have to leave in three months, and why you’re so different from when you came home in the fall.”

She placed her hand on my arm and drew me in, distracting me. She smiled, and I instantly relaxed. “You’re upset.” I closed my eyes and nodded once. “Please don’t worry about any of that,” she said, holding my face in her hands. “Christopher,” she whispered and pulled me down to kiss her. The faint scent of jasmine wafted towards me. It grew all along the hedgerow separating her yard from her nearest neighbor’s; it must have already bloomed.

I stood upright, begrudgingly ending the kiss. I was suddenly assailed with the scent of every spring flower, fresh grass, and bubble gum lip gloss. Kissing cleared my mind, and I sort of forgot the urgency of the questions from earlier in the day. Kissing her was way better than trying to figure out everything else.

"I was about to make a grilled cheese sandwich. Do you want to come in?" Tia asked.

"Sure, sounds good."

She took my hand and gently tugged me into the house, but I didn't need much encouragement. The kitchen was filled with music. Tia's music preferences weren't all that diverse. She liked certain songs, and she played them repeatedly until she heard something else. Then, she would place that song at the top of her playlist and listen to it over and over again. I took a mental note to add this song to the playlist on my phone. It was a new one.

She went to the stove and began constructing another sandwich to match the one that waited alone on the counter. "One or two?" she asked as she reached into the bread loaf bag.

"Two."

She smiled like she'd already guessed as much. I wasn't as agitated as I'd been earlier, but my mind was a jumble. I looked down at the counter and traced the pattern in the countertop. I never knew the difference between marble and granite, but I liked the contrasting flecks of the grays and greens that made the pattern in the veins.

"What's going on, Christopher? You seem really preoccupied." I heard the sizzle of the buttered bread as she placed the sandwiches in the skillet.

I looked up at her but didn't reply. She turned back to focus on and flip the sandwiches. Grilled cheeses were tricky. If you left them one second too long, you'd be eating char. I decided my conversation could wait until after she cooked.

"One thing at a time. Just focus on the food for now."

She giggled and turned back toward the stove. "Good idea."

She swung her hair over her shoulder and tilted her head to the side, exposing her neck and the top of her collar bone. I walked towards her and took her around the waist from behind. She gasped a little in surprise. I nuzzled my face into the smooth, exposed space and breathed in the scents of her green apple shampoo and sizzling butter and the fresh spring flowers that seemed to have followed us indoors.

I was suddenly starving, and my mouth watered. I kissed Tia's neck, and she sighed and leaned her head back into me. "I like that, but it will do nothing to prevent me from burning our sandwiches." I closed my eyes and suddenly didn't care about food as much.

She managed to plate the sandwiches and turn off the stove before she turned to me, and I scooted her over, away from the oven. She pushed herself up and sat on the counter and placed her knees on either side of my hips. Our bodies were more easily aligned with the height of the counter, offering me a better position to kiss her.

Jason's words lingered in the back of my mind as I kissed T. *Once you have the taste of a local, you can't just leave that... he's bound for life.* I liked tasting her skin as I kissed her neck. I wasn't terribly careful because I figured if I accidentally left a hickey, she could just leave her hair down.

CHAPTER 16

Like a cruel trick, the days gradually grew longer and longer, and although T and I had more daylight together, we knew our time was speeding to a halt. Other than school, we had very few restraints on our time. We studied together. We ran errands for Miss Grace and Mr. Roy, too.

Tia wasn't as curious about Mr. Roy's room as I had been initially. She never mentioned it again, and since I didn't want to upset her, I didn't either. Sometimes Tia would sit outside with Miss Grace. I would hear their laughter from the porch. There were times I would look up from my work in their garden or from the barn and see Mr. Roy watching the two of them from a distance. He never intruded on their time together; he just watched.

The Buchanans had always been good to us kids. They'd kept an eye on us when our moms and dads were working. Miss Grace had made our costumes and encouraged our pretend. I had never doubted them or questioned our relationship. I had no reason to before.

I couldn't read Mr. Roy's expression as he watched them. It was a mixture of pain and pleasure. His brow would furrow, his eyes would glisten with emotion, and sometimes he would just close his eyes and shake his head like he was arguing with himself. One afternoon, I was walking back to the shop to return some tools, and T looked up at the same time. She smiled as I approached, but she wasn't looking at me. She was smiling at Mr. Roy, who was standing between us. He couldn't help but return her smile. She radiated everything beautiful to me, but I wasn't the only one who thought that. Mr. Roy turned suddenly to go inside the shop. Tia's smile remained as our eyes met, and I acknowledged her with a nod because my hands were full. My smile was as wide as hers, and I felt warmth cover my face and chest.

When I walked into the shop, Mr. Roy's hands were on the counter, bracing himself, and his head was leaned over. I watched him for several seconds. He looked like he was muttering something to himself. It wasn't normal, and it made me feel uncomfortable and intrusive. I cleared my throat.

"Are you okay, Mr. Roy?"

His head lifted; he stood straighter and faced the wall for a couple of seconds. He took a deep breath and grabbed his red handkerchief from his back pocket before he turned. He ran the red bandana across his face like he'd been working in the sun and then blew his nose loudly. He didn't look like he'd been crying or anything, but the gesture was a bit more dramatic than usual.

"You're done, then?" he asked, not answering my question.

"Yes, sir."

"Good. Thank you. It's probably time you get Tiana home. It's nearly suppertime. These longer days deceive us. It still looks like mid-afternoon out there, but I can feel my hunger creeping up on me. You must be hungry, Topher." The mention of food distracted me, and I was suddenly starving.

Spring planting went smoothly for the farmers in our county. Dad reported that even fallow fields had been planted for the first time in a decade or more. This season seemed unusually promising. My time with Tia felt much the same.

She and I spent more time with Jesse and the older two Clarke boys. We took them to the park and to the lake to fish. We packed picnics and brought empty jars for them to collect all kinds of critters and bugs for their collections. Tia drew the line at snakes and tadpoles. I think she was protecting my mom and Mrs. Clarke more than herself. She didn't seem afraid of anything in nature.

Finals and graduation came in a rush. I knew it would only be a few more weeks before Tia left. Everything around us bloomed beautifully; Tia was no exception. I thought that my condition had improved, but in actuality, it was only experiencing a brief remission.

After graduation, we were all invited out to Clayton's farm for a party. We parked our trucks in a circle around a small fire. We roasted hotdogs and marshmallows. There was plenty of alcohol, but Tia and I didn't partake. I was too consumed with her to want or need anything else.

She and I intentionally isolated ourselves from the revelry of the party going on around us. The night was clear, and the stars shone brightly above. Away from the fire, there was little light, and everything was in shadow. Music blared from someone's truck on the far side of the circle. It was more a barrier than an intrusion. We didn't have to worry about homework, curfews, the Clarks coming home, or work the next morning. At that very moment, it was just T and me. We didn't waste the opportunity.

"What do you plan to do next year after we graduate?" she asked.

Mom and Dad had always encouraged me to go away to school and have a life elsewhere. From the beginning of our sophomore year, I felt their pressure for the first time. I made decent grades, and my prowess on the field had already gotten me noticed by a few small colleges. From the beginning of our junior year, Mom was committed to staying on top of the application deadlines.

"I'm planning on applying to a couple of colleges next year. I'm hoping to get a chance to play some college ball." I shrugged. "I guess it all depends on how things go next year."

Tia and I talked about our plans for the future. I told her that I'd probably do something in business or accounting. She asked if I was interested in doing anything in science like my dad. I laughed at that and shook my head. I couldn't imagine myself in a lab, wearing a long white lab coat. My dad was much better suited for that kind of job than I was.

"How will you afford to go away to school? It's so expensive."

"My savings and scholarships. I'm holding out on the scholarships. I can afford college, but I'd rather save my own money."

"Do your parents plan to help you?" Tia asked.

I shook my head. "Mom and Dad have a lot of debt from going away for college. Dad's failed business is what made them return. Mom had a few miscarriages, and they had plenty of medical bills after Jesse was born. They are just now getting their heads above water. Besides, I have more opportunities if I go."

Tia bit her lip and looked down. She didn't like the idea of me going away. At that very moment, neither did I. "What about you, T? What do you want to do?"

She looked up and smiled, relieved at the change in subject. "Work with kids for sure." I wasn't surprised at all by that answer. "I read about what it takes to be an au pair. I think it would be great to work with a family and travel with them and see the world. I think I might study early childhood education. They have a program at the community college."

"Would you ever consider going away like your folks?" I asked, hoping that maybe she might consider going away with me.

She shook her head. "I planned on staying local," she said. "I like it here."

"I like it here, too," I said, but was referring more to the fact that we were together and could focus a hundred percent on each other.

"This is the first time I've ever not been excited to go," she said with a sigh. I was kissing her neck, then, and she was enjoying the way it tickled. She was smiling, but there was a hint of sadness in her voice. "I wish I could stay with you this summer. You are much more fun than studying."

I was careful not to leave any marks on her neck when I kissed her; it was summer and too hot to leave her hair down. I didn't want to cause trouble with her aunt and grandmother, so I was sure to nuzzle her neck just at her hairline.

"I feel the same way. I don't want to be apart from you for even a day, much less the summer. It's agony!" I sighed. "May I come and see you at your Aunt Trudy's?" I asked.

"Yes, please," she said, smiling. "That would be wonderful." Then she blinked and came to her senses. "Only before the solstice. Once Grandmother arrives, my time will not be my own." Her eyes were pleading like she wanted me to make her a promise.

"Sure, I'll only visit before the solstice." She smiled, relieved, and wrapped her arms around my neck. I leaned her back against the side of the truck and lifted her onto the tailgate. She parted her legs, and I stepped between them and closed the gap between our bodies. I rubbed my hands against her outer thighs over her jeans.

I knew too well that I was enjoying myself too much; it was going to be twice as painful if she returned at the end of the summer again and didn't remember me. I would crave her lips and her touch all summer and then have to control my urges for her so that she didn't think I was some kind of a pervert when she came home in the fall.

It was hard enough last fall, and we had only kissed once before she left for her aunt's. It was dangerous for seventeen-year-old boys to be left alone with seventeen-year-old girls along the backroads of parks and overlooks and fields where teenagers were prone to drink and make out and lose their virginity. God, I wanted her so badly that it made me ache.

She could feel my intensity increasing, and she shied away from me. I was thankful that she had better self-control. I would never pressure her to do anything that she didn't want to do, but if she gave me the go-ahead, I wouldn't hesitate for a second.

I tempered my kissing and held her. "I'm sorry," she said.

"No need to apologize. I'm grateful. I don't want to do anything stupid."

"Having sex with me would be stupid?" she asked playfully.

"No, that's not what I meant."

She giggled, "Good. I'm not ready, but if I were, you'd be my first choice."

"That's a relief," I chuckled deep in my chest. Tia's head was pressed close to my heart.

"I also don't want to lose my virginity in the back of your truck. I'd much prefer a bed or someplace more private than this field. I'd even be okay with a tent," she mused.

"Really, like camping?"

"Sure, but in a very remote setting." She giggled self-consciously. I didn't dare look at her face; I could feel the heat of her blush through my t-shirt. I closed my eyes and burrowed my face in her hair at the crown of her head. I imagined the lather of her green apple shampoo flowing over her body as she rinsed.

SUMMER

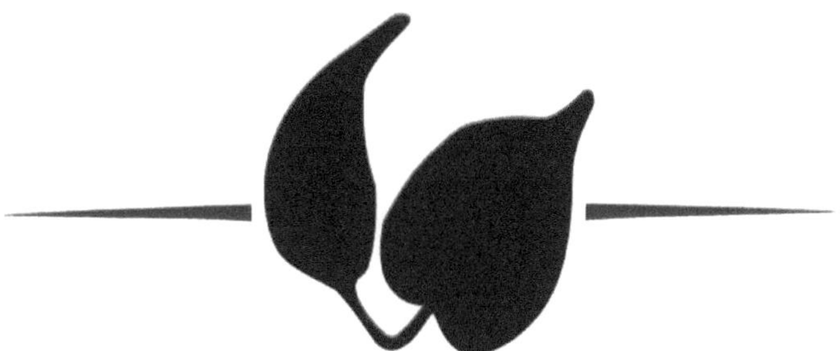

CHAPTER 17

The day came for Tia to go to her Aunt Trudy's. The usual timing had been postponed by several days. She had babysitting lined up with the Clarkes, and then her parents had to work, so Jason was asked to take her. We hadn't seen each other since school ended a few days before, and we had a short break before football practices started.

I was shocked when Jason called. I didn't even know he had my number. He had agreed to drive Tia, but called me at the last minute and passed his responsibility onto me.

"Tiana's parents think I'm taking her as a favor. Really, it's an excuse for me and Sherry to get away for a day. You can follow us if that's cool, and then you can hang out there at her aunt's until she kicks you out. I'll take Sherry fishing by the lake on the county line." I hesitated, suspecting *fishing* was code for something else. "No, man, she likes to fish. She has her own tackle and everything." He sounded surprised himself.

After lunch, I met Jason and Tia in front of Sherry's house. She lived just out of town in a tiny rental with her grandmother. She and the grandmother had only lived there since the middle of the school year. That's why I hadn't taken notice of her. She hadn't existed. That's probably why Jason had; he noticed everything.

Jason handed me a piece of notebook paper with hand-written directions. "I thought I was following you," I said.

"You can manage." He then removed Tia's suitcase from his trunk and lifted it into the bed of my truck. Tia jumped in the cab and rolled down the window. She thanked Jason and gave a little wave to Sherry.

"See you in a few," Jason said and looked bothered at letting me leave with T. He patted the door twice and stepped back so I could drive away. He just stared at the back of the truck. I could read the intensity in his gaze in the rearview mirror. It was edgy, and I wondered briefly if he regretted his decision to deceive Tia's parents.

Tia took my arm and scooted closer to me, sitting in the center of the bench seat. I looked over at her and completely forgot about Jason, Sherry, fishing, or the fact that I was about to leave Tia behind for three whole months.

Upon introduction, Aunt Trudy was a polite-enough woman, but she seemed a little stern and matronly. She welcomed Tia with a hug and loving words. I hesitated at the door, and she scrutinized me before she welcomed me into her home. It was an old house like the ones built to house a multi-generational family during plantation days, like when the county was made up of a few large farms.

The house was raised off the ground with a front porch that stretched across its entire width. Vines clung along trellises that scaled up one side of the house. The windows were all square and, given the height of the house, stood well above my head. I had no idea this place even existed. I'd driven all over the county with my dad to check out area farms, but I'd never been there. It was like stepping back in time a couple of hundred years.

Inside, the furniture was all antique, polished, and dark. The light fixtures were also old-fashion, like the kind that flicker unexpectantly in horror movies to warn you when something fateful is about to happen. No wonder Tia got so much more education during the summer. This place didn't seem like it offered any other entertainment, and Aunt Trudy wasn't exactly a barrel of laughs. She oozed seriousness and practicality towards T's lessons. I wondered briefly if she and Coach were related somehow.

Aunt Trudy offered to let me stay for an early supper. Maybe she wasn't as strict and unfeeling as I initially thought. The three of us sat at her long, formal, dining room table. A maid, dressed in a uniform, brought and served our plates. Another maid brought in our beverages, and I was surprised when she poured each of us a glass of wine. I eyed Tia, and she winked. We each took a sip before we tasted our first bites.

Tia answered all of her Aunt Trudy's questions while I sat quietly and watched their interactions. Aunt Trudy wanted to know all about the school year. She acted like she hadn't had any contact with Tia since the fall. After dinner and dessert, Aunt Trudy rose from the table. I stood instinctively like I needed to be all formal in her presence. She just gave off that kind of vibe. I rushed to pull out her chair, and she eyed me again. She pursed her lips and studied the tiny gold watch on her left wrist.

"You have until eight-thirty. At which time, you will return home." She looked at Tia for a moment and then returned her stern gaze to me. "We keep a strict schedule, but you're welcome to join us again for dinner tomorrow. Grandmother won't arrive for another few days, so we don't have to be quite so rigid." Aunt Trudy eyed Tia indulgently, and Tia beamed. I might need to reconsider the woman. Maybe she wasn't such a hard-ass, after all.

CHAPTER 18

I knew I was only postponing the inevitable, but I wanted to get in as much last-minute time with T as I could. The sun was setting, but there would be daylight for at least another hour. Tia took me on a tour of the house. We walked from room to room and upstairs and even through the attic. She showed me the view from the windows up there. I think she also wanted to kiss me in a place she was sure her Aunt Trudy wouldn't be. I didn't know where Aunt Trudy had gone, but I didn't see her again before I left.

It wasn't a terribly long drive home, maybe a little over an hour. The old county roads zigzagged back and forth along the river and property lines. It was mostly paved, but the roads closest to Aunt Trudy's were all gravel over red dirt and looked unused and overgrown.

I returned for dinner the next two nights, but Aunt Trudy didn't extend another invitation for the third. It was two nights before the solstice and Tia's grandmother's arrival. Summer football was starting, too, so it wasn't like I wasn't about to have my own time taken. I had plenty to do before two-a-days began. I'd been spending all my free time driving back and forth to the opposite side of the county.

Aunt Trudy gave us until ten that final night. I'm not sure if Tia made the request, or she could read our desire to have more time together. Aunt Trudy had asked me a few questions directly on the second and third nights and seemed to take a genuine interest in me. Surprisingly, she knew my parents and the grandparents I'd never known. She asked how old I'd been when we moved into my grandparent's house and about my plans after graduation. Aunt Trudy encouraged my intention to go away to school and pursue college ball.

That night, after dinner, T and I went outside and sat together on the porch swing. Tia clasped my hand, and I wrapped an arm around her shoulder. She buried her face into my chest and sighed. "I don't want to stay," she almost whined.

I didn't want her to stay either, but I would have plenty to do with football, work, and helping Mr. Roy and Miss Grace. Although she'd improved a great deal, they seemed to need more help than they did before Miss Grace's illness. Mr. Roy was determined to have a summer garden, and that meant that Jesse and I would be responsible for that, too. Mom insisted that I let Jesse tag along and learn how to please Miss Grace. Mom didn't like to talk about it, but she knew it was my last summer to help out before I graduated and left for college.

I dismissed that thought and returned my attention to the present and to the girl I held at my side on the swing. I took in her scent and the way she felt. I'd only hugged her goodbye the past couple of nights. I wanted to kiss her before I left, but I wasn't sure if that would get her into trouble.

"T, do you think we could find a place where we could be alone?"

She leaned her head back and looked at me. She pressed her hand into my chest and pushed me away playfully. "We are alone, silly," she said.

I looked around the porch and through the windows, considering. "I don't want to get you into any trouble."

"You won't."

"Your Aunt Trudy won't tell your parents?"

She shook her head and shrugged. "I doubt it. They don't talk much. It's not like she'll be giving them a daily report. It might be different if

Grandmother were here. She'd never approve of me kissing a boy." She giggled and eased my worry. "But she's not here, is she?"

Tia tilted her chin upward, and I leaned in and kissed her. The kisses were friendly and innocent. We'd definitely gotten better at that since last summer. A half-hour before I had to leave, Tia stood and took me by the hand. She gently tugged me down the stairs toward my truck.

"But I still have some time," I protested.

"I know, and I want to take advantage of what remains of it."

I didn't know exactly what she was implying, but I followed her around to the tailgate and helped her lower it. She climbed in and patted her hand on the spot beside her. She wrapped her arms around my neck and clung to me. She kissed me until I was breathless and unable to release her. In seconds, we were lying in the bed of my truck. The moonless sky kept us in shadow.

I heard a twig snap like someone was walking nearby. I stopped kissing Tia and lay very still, listening, ready to put a respectful distance between us if necessary. "What is it?" she asked. When I didn't answer, she continued, "No one is here."

"What about your aunt?"

"She's gone to bed. There's no one else here."

I tried to relax, but I got the feeling we weren't alone. It was probably my own paranoia or the uncertainty about the time we'd be apart.

"Tia," I began. I was suddenly stricken with doubt and fear. The past six months of contact and kissing and attachment would mean nothing if she returned to me oblivious, distant, and distracted. Her return would be torture.

"What?" she answered.

"Say you'll remember me."

She gave a little, disbelieving chuckle and leaned back to look at me. We were in shadow so she could barely make out my face. "What do you mean?"

"When you return in September, promise me you'll remember this." I squeezed her gently, underscoring our closeness. "Promise me that you'll remember *me.*" I put emphasis on the final word.

"Okay," she began hesitantly, "I promise."

"No, say it. Say, 'Christopher, I promise to remember you.'"

"You're ridiculous. Of course, I'm going to remember you." She leaned in and passed a quick, playful peck on my cheek.

I put my hands on her shoulders and tried to read her eyes in the dark. I doubted her. I questioned whether or not she had that power.

Summers, with her grandmother, changed her, and I wasn't sure how to combat that.

"T, I'm sorry. You're just so different and distracted when you come home. I don't want to lose what we've got right now."

She thought for a minute, considering my words. She smirked. "Here, give me your phone." I didn't question her and pulled it from my back pocket. I typed my password: 84262, the numbers that spelled her name, yet another symptom of my chronic condition. I accepted that it sometimes bordered on the edge of obsession.

She took my phone and opened it. She flipped the camera view and set it to video. "Hey, Christopher," she said, smiling at the screen. I could barely make out her face in the dark. She sat up, so that light from the porch made her reflection clear. "I want you to watch this whenever you're missing me." She raised her right hand. "I solemnly swear that I will *never* forget you. You're my best friend, and I love you; how could I *ever* forget that?" She giggled at herself, emphasizing the words never and ever. "So when you miss me *terribly*, here's a kiss to cheer you up!" She puckered her lips and kissed the camera with a loud smack. "There, is that proof enough for you?" she asked before she turned off the camera. She lowered herself back into the shadow of my embrace. "No more talk about not remembering, okay?" Her voice sounded distant for a second. I wanted to make sure I'd heard her correctly. If I weren't mistaken, she'd just said she loved me. I opened my mouth to speak, but she placed her fingers over my lips. "No more talking. Just hold me until you have to go."

I groaned. I needed to go. I'd have the drive back and then get a few hours of sleep before I'd be on a tractor at daylight and every morning for the foreseeable future. Our final embrace was a friendly hug in front of the house. No kissing, no hands roaming, nothing that could be misread or the least bit inappropriate.

CHAPTER 19

More than a month had passed with little more than cutting and bailing hay, two-a-day practices, and an inability to consume enough food to keep my body fueled. I felt like I was starving all the time. There just wasn't enough time to eat and sleep.

I'd had no word from T, but I didn't expect one, either. I dreamed about her every night, and thoughts of her continuously ran as I did the monotonous work of a field hand. Football held my attention, but it didn't consume all of my time.

The dreams were easy; our childhood selves ran and played tag. Tia was better at hide-and-seek, but she could never outrun me. Her laughter echoed through my memories. I loved her laugh and her smile. Sometimes the dreams brought me back to more recent events and always ended with kissing. I would see her face age before me, running through an age progression like in the photos in Mr. Roy's room.

By the end of the second month, football had reduced to once a day with early morning workouts three times a week. I'd finished nearly all of the work I'd been hired to do. My only consolation was the assurance that the start of school steadily approached.

You'd think with things settling down, and fewer demands on my time, I'd sleep better and be less starving. I realized the hunger pains weren't all hunger-related; they were actual longing pains, longing for Tia. Sure, I was plenty hungry, but food couldn't fill the void. The dreams about Tia changed, too. At first, they were uncomplicated, longing sure, but not scary. I missed her like crazy, and with more free time, she was continuously on my mind.

Mom noticed my fatigue from lack of sleep. I didn't mean to take it out on her and Jesse, but I was irritable. She concocted a mixture of essential oils that she assured me would afford me a great night's sleep. She set the diffuser after supper and filled my room with lavender and hints of other oils that I couldn't identify when they were all mixed together. It wasn't an unpleasant odor and actually helped combat the heavy scent of musk from my practice bag and the funk that wafted from my cleats.

I used to keep them outside, but the raccoons ran off with a pair a few years ago. Mom never allowed my cleats in the laundry room, except when I washed them, which was practically never. She said it was my responsibility to look after my equipment, not hers. I couldn't leave them in the truck. The odors would have been unbearable with the combination of summer heat and a closed cab.

The diffused oils did help me fall asleep and sleep heavier, but that only trapped me, unable to shake myself awake. The dreams I had in this deepened state were unlike anything I'd ever experienced. Everything was vivid and colorful. The next morning I complained before she'd even had a chance to ask how I'd slept. "Give it another night or two before you reject it completely." I begrudgingly agreed and headed to practice.

Jason had been reasonably decent all summer. He had to work hard to fill Clayton's position and also needed me to cover him. That took even more trust than before. He was still seeing Sherry, and like most of the upperclassmen, had part-time jobs. Jason worked for his uncle at the butcher shop.

We were all messing around in the locker room, laughing and cutting up. It was a nice change to the ass he'd been the fall before. Coach was working hard to unify us as a team and planned for us all to pair up and do some community service. Sure enough, he assigned Jason and me two weekends of cleaning and painting at the elementary school. We'd spend a total of forty hours together. The work wasn't all that hard, but Jason seemed more bothered about it than I did. It ate into his weekends with Sherry because his uncle still expected him to cover his shifts.

"It sucks more for me. At least, Tiana isn't even here."

"I guess. It sucks for you for four days. It sucks for me for three months."

"True. Sorry, man. What are you doing next weekend? Some of us are going to the lake. Our final out before school starts. Want to come?"

"Are you inviting me?" I asked, surprised.

"Yeah, I guess I am," he chuckled.

I did go to the lake. Sherry was more interested in swimming and fishing than drinking or being stupid. She was content to sit quietly on the bank and cast her line. After the fourth trout she'd landed, Jason and I sat back and let her have it. Neither of us had even had as much as a bite on our lines.

"How many more days?" Jason asked, staring up at the sky.

"Twenty-seven."

"Hmmm," he muttered but continued to look up.

"It's going to be the same as last year, isn't it?" I didn't know why I'd spoken the words out loud, but I had. I wondered if he'd even know what I was talking about. He didn't say anything for a long time, so I let it go.

Finally, he released a sigh like he'd been holding his breath the entire time. "Yes, or worse," he said through clenched teeth.

I turned to look at him, surprised by his tone and the apparent pain it caused to speak those words. When I rose to look at his face, the flood of questions pressing was evident in my expression. He shook his head in warning, almost begging me not to make him say more. He jumped up from the bank and walked toward the bathrooms.

"Jason," I called after him.

I stood to follow him, but he put up his hand to stop me. I cursed and kicked the pebbles under my feet, disturbing the water near Sherry's concentrated efforts. She turned and glared, obviously not amused or sympathetic toward my frustration. Her usually sweet face and bouncy curls were a complete contrast to the seriousness of fishing. It softened my anger; maybe she had helped soften Jason a bit, too.

"Tell Jason that I'm going home." She nodded but didn't say anything.

The nightmares and dreams became unbearable. Mom tried several concoctions, but nothing settled me. The dreams were much more vivid.

I was back at Aunt Trudy's with the long, formal table in the dining room where we had eaten together. The highly polished, contrasting parquet flooring clicked underneath my feet. I could hear Tia crying in the distance, sobbing and screaming out in pain. I ran and searched for her.

In the mornings, I was exhausted like I'd literally been running all night. My legs were fatigued and sore. After practice, I crashed on the bed. Again, I dreamed that Tia was screaming, calling out in pain like someone was hurting her. It was the freaking middle of the day, and I was dreaming like it was the middle of the night.

When I finally found her in my dream, she was lying on her aunt's dining table, encircled within a ring of candles. Her hair was matted down, and her body was covered in dark clay as if she'd been pulled from the bottom of the lake. Her arms and legs were covered in tiny cuts that were oozed deep red blood.

I stepped into the ring of candles. The hot scent was the same as the damn diffuser oils. I knocked over one of the candles, and she froze and quit writhing in pain. Tia opened her eyes and stared at me with complete focus. "Christopher, help me."

At the utterance of her words, I awakened. My heart was pounding, and I was covered in sweat, unable to move. Without thinking, I grabbed my phone and keys and jumped into my truck. I'd driven ten miles before I even glanced at the clock on the dash. *Damn!* It was nearly midnight!

I sped down the gravel roads toward Aunt Trudy's. There were no lights on inside the house. Given the hour, I should have expected that. I walked up to the door and tried to look through the windows. The darkened room and lace curtains blocked my view. I checked all the windows and doors that I could reach on the porch, but I knew from the brief tour of the house that Tia's room was around the back. I knocked on the door, but when I got no response, my knocking grew frantic. My hands were bruised from banging on the large, oak door. I was frustrated and ran to the back of the house.

"T! T! Where are you? Let me in!"

Then, I noticed one of the windows was opened. I backed away from the house and, with all my strength, ran and jumped. I managed to grab the ledge of the high window along the side of the house. I struggled and struggled but finally pulled myself onto the small window ledge. That had to be the longest jump I'd made to date. Of course, there was no one there to witness or catch it on video. No one would believe it. *Damn.* I dusted off my knees and shoulders as I walked toward her bedroom door.

That's as far as I got. When I woke up, I was in my bed, dazed, with a head filled with lavender and who knows what else.

CHAPTER 20

The morning light was obscured; the clouds were heavy with the threat of rain. *That was the craziest dream, yet.* I was still dressed and felt like I'd driven. When I walked outside and got into my truck, I noticed I barely had a half tank of gas. I'd filled it up two days before. I jumped out and checked underneath. The tires were clean, but the undercarriage was filled with the dust from the road to her Aunt Trudy's house.

Thankfully, it was pouring down rain by the time I pulled up at the school. We'd be in the weight room and watching film. There was an audible sigh of relief as the team entered the fieldhouse, and Coach announced he'd be cutting practice short. Coach called Jason and me over and asked us if we'd drill the JV on plays for an hour after our shortened practice. We agreed. Coach wasn't a man we ever refused.

After JV practice, Jason and I were the only ones left in the parking lot. He could tell I was distracted and exhausted. “What’s up, man? You’re like a zombie these days. You still working every day?”

“No, I’m hardly working at all. Not sleeping.”

“Like insomnia?”

“No, like having crazy, bad dreams. Stuff I can’t figure out. I dreamed I drove to see Tia last night but couldn’t get into the house. When I finally made it in, I suddenly woke up in my own bed, exhausted. Do you think you can sleep drive?”

“Like sleepwalk behind the wheel?”

“Yeah. My tank is low, and the undercarriage is all dusty. Look.” I pointed to the truck’s underside.

Jason watched me when I stood to my full height after bending over to show him the proof. He grunted, and something flickered across his face. “What?” I asked.

His expression hardened, and he shook his head, refusing to answer me. His former jerk face returned. I watched him war within himself. Like at the lake and last fall, he was torn.

“Do you know something you’re not telling me?” I asked.

The flicker in his eyes flashed. He did know. He knew something that he was unable or unwilling to tell me. He just shook his head and blinked slowly with a sigh.

I bowed up at him, instantly provoked by his silence. I took an intimidating step, and he had a hard time holding his ground. "Tell me!" I demanded in a hushed voice. He squared his shoulders and looked at me, eyes fixed and unwavering. His look wasn't challenging, but it was decided.

I flexed and flinched like I intended to punch him. He winced and gave way; his cleats scuffled on the gravel, but his eyes never wavered. In my exhausted state, I didn't want to fight. We were still on school property, and Coach wouldn't care about the consequences. He'd make us do more than run; he'd bench us for fighting again. We'd learned that lesson. When I didn't land the first blow, Jason's gaze eased, and, for a second, he looked apologetic.

"I need to go," he said with a tight throat. He turned toward his car.

"Asshole!" I muttered under my breath.

The rain had ceased, and it looked like we'd have a break from the rain until the night. Leaving school, I drove in a huff towards Mr. Roy and Miss Grace's. He'd asked me to mend a stretch of the fence around one of the pens. I didn't know why it was suddenly a priority. It had been broken for a while. He probably read my recent mood and figured it was best to keep me busy. I wouldn't put it past Mom to call him and ask if he needed anything done. They all knew idleness was not my friend.

Mr. Roy had already sorted the tools and supplies I needed for the job. "I'm taking Gracie into town for an appointment and to get her hair done. You'll most likely be done before we are. Just put everything back when you're done." I nodded once and went to work, pulling the old boards apart. Mr. Roy hesitated for a few seconds. "You alright, son?"

"Yes, sir," I replied quickly.

He harrumphed, disbelieving my quick reply. "Girl troubles?" he teased. The crowbar slipped, and a curse escaped. He chuckled humorously. It was my turn to grunt my reply. I'd barely slept for the past few weeks, and the dreams and missing Tia were taking their toll, not to mention the crazy night I'd spent dreaming and driving and being sure I'd been to her Aunt Trudy's. "You want to talk about it?" Mr. Roy asked. I shook my head and continued my work, taking out all my angst on the broken fencing. "I'll be going, then." I heard him turn and take a couple of steps before he returned. "Topher, you know I'm here for you if you need anything."

I stopped short at his words, but my hands didn't slip this time. I turned and looked at Mr. Roy. The intensity and concern in the old man's eyes overwhelmed me. I nodded once. "Yes, sir. Thank you." He assessed me for another long second and then turned toward the house.

After the fence was repaired, I returned the tools to the workshop. I looked at the Mustang and remembered the day Tia and I had made out in the front seat. I wondered briefly if Mr. Roy would let me take it out just once before I left for school. I'd ask.

Beyond the car, I gazed at the door to the room I'd entered six months ago with T. I found the key and unlocked the door. I turned on the light and entered. I walked straight to the wall and examined every map, every picture, and every single newspaper headline.

To the left, it began as a complete history of our town. It dated back a couple of hundred years. The documents weren't originals, but old and yellowed copies like they'd been printed from microfiche rather than the internet. Mr. Roy must have been compiling this history for a very long time. There were hand-written notes, torn from old journals and notebooks. The lists of names and rubbings from tombstones included all the original families. Many of the names I recognized from my classmates: Tiana *Reynolds*, Jason *Moore*, Clayton *Anderson*, Catherine

Smith, *Carson*, *Clarke*, *Buchanan*, and even my own last name, *Andrews*. It wasn't talked about much, but if those were the founding families, then we were all related somehow.

I wondered briefly if some of this was Mr. Roy's original research he'd done over forty years ago. He apparently hadn't lost his passion for history. I didn't linger long on the photographs of Tia, but I studied several that I recognized: my dad and, I assumed, Roy Jr. There was one of my grandfather and my dad. *Dang*, Dad looked a lot like his dad, and other than my dark eyes, I favored my dad at that age, too. My grandfather stood a head taller than his son. I'd inherited my granddad's height for sure.

I made my way through the history toward the map that covered the entire wall. I studied the perimeter and overlay that extended the borders of our county. Maybe that had been the original land. I noticed a few dots marking the larger farms and even the furthest dot that marked Tia's current location. Aunt Trudy's house was marked with a red circle.

I let my finger and my thoughts linger there longer than I should have. I looked away and found the altar and cross and kneeler with the opened Bible. It was opened to a different page than I'd seen before, so obviously, someone had been in there.

It was awkward, but I managed to kneel and assume the position on the wooden structure. My knees settled comfortably on the worn, padded cushion. I looked up at the cross and to the stained glass hanging above and imagined what it must have been like to worship in the old church with the altar and windows casting its colorful light into the stone sanctuary. I got a strange sense of something I'd never felt before. No, that wasn't true. I'd felt it at the church ruins and wondered if that was what it felt like to be someplace sacred, someplace holy. My eyes fell onto the large Bible that lay open in front of me. I glanced over the fancy lettering. It took me a few attempts to read the old script on the yellowed pages. Colorfully illuminated letters began the first word of the page.

It read, "The Gospel, according to John. In the beginning, was the Word, and the Word was with God, and the Word was God. The same was in the beginning with God." The text went on to tell about light and darkness and the light coming into the world. I'd never read anything more compelling in my entire life. It held my attention and curiosity. I read the whole chapter. I returned it to where I'd begun reading, turning each page carefully.

When I stood, I caught Mr. Roy from the corner of my eye. Although my legs were stiff from kneeling so long, I rose quickly, not really understanding the look on his face. He didn't look angry, but he didn't look happy, either. How long had he been standing there?

"I'm sorry," I stammered. His eyes were steely again, assessing me. Like in the winter, I stood straight, not defensively, but with the confidence I wanted Mr. Roy to see.

"You've been in here before," he stated plainly.

"Yes, sir." I didn't add the Tia detail.

"You read for a long time." He had been watching me. I was so absorbed that I didn't notice anything else.

"Yes, sir. My first time."

"*John* is a good one. One of my favorites. How'd you like it?"

I shrugged. "It was good." I couldn't deny that. "I didn't understand everything he talked about, but I liked the light and dark parts."

Mr. Roy nodded. That seemed to please him, and the familiar, sly, Mr. Roy grin spread over his face, easing the tension in the small room. I couldn't help but return his smile. "I like those parts, too," he said.

"That man, Jesus, did some pretty unbelievable things. Do you believe that he did all that?" I asked.

"As a matter-of-fact, I do. I do with everything I have."

"I've never heard anything like that. I mean, I've heard that Christians followed a man named Jesus, but I didn't really know anything about why. I know it was the whole reason behind the Crusades. Is that what they taught you at that preacher school? They taught you about Jesus?"

"Jesus, I've always known about. God, his father, too. I was raised by a minister and come from a long line of pastors, as you already know. Seminary taught me a great deal about the history and context and the original languages the Bible was written. It was also where I learned to organize my thoughts into lessons and how to lead a congregation and how best to take care of people during life's challenges. We all have more than our fair share of those."

"Why didn't you leave?" My question was almost accusing, and Jason's words returned.

Mr. Roy looked away, remembering. "I knew very little before I sped into town in that car in there. He motioned toward the car behind him. "Gracie was the only reason I stayed." Something was telling in his tone.

"My teammate, Jason, says once you've had the taste of a local, you can't leave here."

Mr. Roy laughed out so hard that it made me jump. He bent over, catching the sound from his guffaw at his belly. I hadn't expected that reaction and found myself smiling at the sparkle in his light eyes. Once he caught his breath, he nodded. "Your buddy, Jason, has a way with words. He's not far from the mark. I had no business doing what I did with Gracie," he confessed. "I knew better, and I thought I was better, but after a week with Grace, I had to have her completely. It only took once, son. I'd fallen in love with her in a matter of days, but I knew instantly that I'd crossed a line; I would never be the same, and I couldn't go back. I lay there with her, holding her." He swallowed as the memory flooded him with emotion. His expression grew serious. "Don't do it if you plan to ever leave," he warned.

"So, you just gave up everything?"

He scoffed at my words. "I took a detour for sure. Gracie's dad needed a hand, and I was pretty handy. Soon after we were married, I became the Justice of the Peace and served this little town for decades. Even though I wasn't pastoring a congregation, I was allowed to conduct weddings and funerals. It was one of my greatest honors. Married your folks, too." I knew that already.

"Mr. Roy, I need to go. I'm sorry I came in here without permission."

"No trouble. You can come here anytime. You are welcome to read and pray. I find a great deal of comfort here."

"Thank you," I said as I moved past Mr. Roy through the door.

He caught my arm. "Topher," he began, "you're sure you don't want to talk? You seem like you've got a lot on your mind."

I shook my head. "No, sir. I don't want to talk. I need to eat and sleep. Thanks, though." He nodded, understanding, and squeezed my forearm gently, dismissing me.

CHAPTER 21

The house was empty. Mom and Dad had taken Jesse out of town. They'd be gone two nights for Jesse's doctor appointment with his allergist and for a meeting with accountants for Mom. I reheated leftovers and went to my room to take a nap. The day and night had overtaken me. Once again, sleep eluded me. I flipped on the diffuser and allowed the lavender to penetrate my senses. Nothing.

I knew I probably shouldn't, but I decided to drive to Aunt Trudy's house. There was still a little daylight, and I had nothing more to do. I had to see for myself what was going on. I filled up my truck with diesel and drove to the edge of the county. The house looked absolutely deserted. The porch hadn't been swept, and the grass was overgrown. Nothing was like it had been when I'd visited before, and I hadn't noticed it in last night's harried dream-driving.

The house and grounds were eerily quiet. I rang the bell and then knocked on the door. When no one answered, I banged louder and called for Tia. No response. The doors were all locked and the windows, too. Would her grandmother have taken her away or to town for the day? I sat on the porch swing and decided to wait to see if they came home. Sitting there, swinging gently, it was quiet, and I soon fell asleep.

I could hear Tia in my dream. I could hear her crying again. Cries of pain that racked my brain. Without the lavender, I could reason and see through the fog. I forced myself to move and search for her. I walked around the house and stood outside her bedroom, calling to her. I tried to scramble and pull myself into the house, but the windows were all closed. I should have brought a ladder.

Shadows and flickers of light obscured my view of the house. I scrambled to break free to see clearly. I tried to break through the window or door, but it was like there was a force keeping me from penetrating the house. "Tia!" I called. "Tia! Let me in!" I begged but knew from the sounds of her screams, she was unable to set herself free.

A dark figure came from inside the house and passed through the door. I stood completely still, hoping this was a new and horrible aspect to my dreams and not reality. As soon as the figure passed through the door, Tia's cries subsided into breathy sobs. I banged on the door until my hands were bruised, and my knuckles were bloody. I fell in a heap of misery on the front porch, exhausted and grieving for the girl I couldn't get to.

When I awoke and gathered my senses, it was sunny and hot, and the sky was clear. I checked my phone; it was half-past two in the afternoon. I walked around the house again. No sign of Tia. Nothing, except I was starving. I drove straight home, showered, and ate more leftovers.

I needed to find Jason. He knew something, and all of his obscure comments and refusals to answer my questions were about to meet my fist a couple of hundred times, if necessary, but I would get something out of him. Maybe he would know how to get in.

I drove to his uncle's butcher's shop. I'm not sure what he read on my expression, but he approached the counter in his blood-stained apron, drying his hands on a white, hand towel, assessing my desperation.

"Can I help you?" he asked, sounding bored and resigned to having to wait on me.

"Yes," I said. "When do you get off?" I asked insistently.

He looked at me questioningly. "In a couple of hours. Are you here to buy anything?"

I looked behind him, over his shoulder, to the older man who was eying me suspiciously. "Yeah," I stammered and looked down into the meat counter. "What do you recommend?" I asked, recovering quickly.

"The pork chops. The stuffed pork chops. You definitely want the stuffed pork chops."

"Okay, I'll take four. How about some directions, too? I don't want to ruin them."

He took four pork chops and placed them on a sheet of white butcher paper. He then lay them on the scale that printed out a price. He wrapped them neatly and taped the meat closed with the sticker. He nodded and gave a sneaky little smirk, enjoying the game. Taking the order book from his back pocket and a pen from above his ear. He scratched a brief note and taped it securely to the package of meat before he pushed it across the counter toward me.

"Bon Appetit," he said, and I gave a quick nod. "Follow those exact instructions. You won't be disappointed."

The package weighed more than I expected. I carried it to the checkout and paid the girl. *Shit!* Thirty bucks plus change! That conversation just cost me thirty freaking dollars!

I tossed the meat in the passenger seat and pulled off the note.

10:00 PM

Carson Chapel

West-side door

Basement

Bring these and a six-pack

400 degrees; 40 minutes

Carson Chapel was an old church that had long since been abandoned. At the urging of his wife, Old Man Carson had built the small church on his property to accommodate his slaves. Later, it was used by militia during the Civil War. It had been a hospital, and, also at the urging of Old Man Carson's wife, a school for freed slaves. Now, it was mostly an abandoned building.

It may have been built for slaves, but they had spared no expense in the construction. Tall, oak beams supported the high, vaulted ceiling. Stone covered every other surface. The floor was worn smooth from years of use. The exterior was still as stately as it was over a hundred years ago. Perhaps it was their reverence to God, but I suspected it was the old man's wife's doing. It was believed that her ghost still haunted their land.

I didn't see Jason's car when I drove up and parked along the back of the church. The pork chops smelled delicious. Thankfully, no one was home when I baked them. My family wouldn't return until late tomorrow morning. I'd done all my chores, looked after Mr. Roy's animals, and cleaned the house. I had just enough time to pop them in the oven, shower, and get to the church.

I hadn't taken any of my beer payments in months. I liked to save them up. Mr. Roy never demanded that I take it because he knew, even with how tolerant my parents were, that they probably wouldn't appreciate our arrangement. I drove toward Mr. Roy's shop and left my truck running.

"Evening, Topher. You in a hurry?" Mr. Roy began.

"Yes, sir. I just came to return your hammer," I said, which, in case Miss Grace was in earshot, was code for getting a six-pack.

"Thank you. Just lay it on the top shelf," which was code for, take the cold ones. Mr. Roy followed me as I strode back to the truck. He looked inside the open window and sniffed. "Smells good. Going on a picnic? Whatcha got in there?"

"Porkchops. I'm meeting a friend," I said.

He raised his bushy eyebrow speculatively. "Most young ladies I know don't drink beer and eat pork chops. They like pink wine and fruity drinks and salad. Did you bring a salad, boy?"

I laughed. “No, sir. I’m not meeting a girl. Just guys.” He could tell that my mood was considerably better than it had been the day before. We neither made any mention of him finding me reading his Bible.

“Hmmm. Alright. Let me know if I need to pick up some girly wine on my next run.”

I smiled but felt a pang in my gut. I doubted I’d have any reason to need girly wine anytime soon. “Thanks, Mr. Roy. I will.”

In the damp basement of the old church, I felt like a fool sitting on a bench, or was it an old pew? A single bulb hung suspended from the ceiling. At least the place had electricity. As a kid, I’d been to a couple of funerals there. But the basement? Why the basement? My unease only grew as the minutes ticked by. My leg bounced the plate of pork chops on my knee impatiently, so I moved them to the edge of the bench.

Finally, the muffled sound of a car approached. I then heard the basement door open and Jason’s steps on the stairs. I looked up. “Did you bring the pork chops and the beer?” he asked before he made it to the bottom of the stairs.

“Yeah, I did.”

“Good. I’m starving.”

He pulled up a chair and sat across from me, eager for the food. I unwrapped the foil from the plate. Steam and aroma wafted up and made my own stomach growl. I intended to eat at least two of those pork chops myself. I lifted the plate slightly to offer him one. He sorted through the contents and nodded his approval before making his selection. I reached over and pulled a beer from the cardboard case and popped the lid off on the edge of the bench. He accepted it, and I popped the top off a second for myself.

"Why here? Why the basement?" I bit into the pork chop. *Not disappointed.*

"It's safe, and no one comes out here. One, I don't want to be seen alone with you. Two, the church makes this place sanctified. The ground on which it was built is neutral. Therefore, the basement creates a natural buffer. We can't be detected or heard. I like coming here; it's peaceful."

"It's kind of depressing," I said, looking around and into the shadows. I took another bite and then chased it down with a mouthful of beer.

"Not to me." He took a bite of pork chop and chewed, taking his time. "You did alright. Thanks for following the directions. They aren't overcooked at all." He took a few swigs of beer and nodded approvingly. "You really are alright, Topher."

"Then why don't you want to be seen with me?"

Jason was a bully in elementary school, and his little group terrorized everyone. In middle school, we were teammates, which forced us together all the time, but that alone didn't make us friends.

"It's nothing personal. As a guy, I like you just fine. As a teammate, you're better than average, but I was never encouraged to be your friend. If anything, my folks wanted me to show you up on the field; I was expected to be better than you." He shrugged. "Your friendship with Tiana complicates things, though. It's a pain, and I'm not allowed to do anything about it, yet," he amended.

"Why does our friendship bother you so much?"

"As we get older, Tiana gets stronger, her pull, her magnetism, her charisma. You feel it, too; don't you? But when you're with her, it neutralizes her power. Much like this basement, you create a buffer, protection of some sort around her. No one can explain why."

"What are you talking about?" I asked, but he didn't say anything. "I went to her aunt's house after practice yesterday. No one was there. It was completely closed up – no sign of anyone. I want to know how to get into her aunt's house. I want to know where she is and how to get to her."

Jason chuckled with a mouth full of food and shook his head. "Can't be done."

"What do you mean?"

He wiped his mouth with the back of his hand. "You can't get where Tia is. Between the summer solstice and just before the equinox, she's not to be seen or heard from."

"Yeah, that's when her grandmother arrives."

Jason smirked. "*Grandmother*," he said disdainfully. "I guess in a way, she is."

"What do you mean?" I asked, growing impatient.

He finished off the first beer and gestured toward another. "Think about it."

"I have thought about it! I've thought about little else for the past two summers!" I exclaimed. "This is the first time I've been with her until the solstice, and now she's gone!" I stood and paced the room. I ran my fingers through my hair and grunted in frustration. "She's crying and sobbing like she's being tortured. I can hear her in my dreams. Damn it, Jason! Give me some answers! I need to get to her!"

His eyes were wide with surprise. He'd never seen me get animated about anything; I was the calm one. Except for the punch I'd thrown last fall, I was the one that never lost my temper. I was the one that managed things and led on the field. I rarely appeared agitated or uneasy.

"I wish I could," he said solemnly, and I believed him. "I don't know where she goes, specifically, or what she does while she's away. I only know that she was chosen when we were seven and met all the elder's requirements. She was destined for this. There's no changing that. She'll be taken for good after we graduate, definitely before she's nineteen."

"What are you talking about? Chosen? Requirements? Taken?"

Jason hung his head and grew even more solemn. His arrogance faded, and he whispered, "There are powers at work beyond your comprehension."

"You are so full of bullshit, man! How can I believe anything you're telling me?"

He shrugged. "That's a good point. I can see why you don't trust me. It's not like I've ever given you any reason to trust me, but that doesn't mean I'm not being honest and telling you the truth. It sounds cliché, but she's the chosen one."

I rolled my eyes, disbelieving every word he spoke. "Why are you doing this? Why are you making this shit up?"

"Your parents left and didn't return until we were in kindergarten. You weren't born here, and therefore you didn't receive the anointing. By the elders' standards, you were contaminated by the outside world."

"Anointing?"

"At birth, we receive it. I've never witnessed it myself, and because I'm not a woman, I most likely won't until I have kids of my own. It happens within seconds of the umbilical cord being cut." He finished off his second porkchop and chased it down with another long swig of his beer. He belched, satisfied with his meal. "Your brother received it from the midwife who delivered him."

I shook my head. "That's not possible. I was there when Jesse was born. I never saw any anointing."

He shrugged. "I guarantee your brother was anointed. It's part of the blood covenant for anyone born here. I also guarantee that you weren't brought in until after he was wrapped and all snug in your mom's arms. Did your mom and dad have bandages on their hands after he was born?"

I searched my memory for that knowledge. I was nearly ten when Jesse was born. I remember walking into the room and seeing him for the first time. My mom's hand was bandaged, but I didn't think anything of it. I was more concerned about how tired she looked and at the wrinkly little baby in her arms. The nurse was standing next to Dad when I entered the room. He was rolling down his sleeve and buttoning the cuff, but he, too, had a bandage over his hand.

"Why did they cut my parents' hands?" I asked.

"They mix drops of the parents' blood with some oil and other stuff and then rub it all over the baby. I know there's more to it, but I don't know all the details."

"Okay, so I wasn't anointed because I wasn't born here." He nodded. "Is that why she doesn't know me until after the equinox?" I guessed. "They make her forget me?" I ventured. He shrugged.

"I don't know why except you're an outsider, and her entire purpose is for this town, this county," he clarified.

"Then why would they take her away after graduation? Where will they send her?"

"She has to carry on the town's traditions. It's her duty. She has to offer herself so that the community continues to prosper."

Everything he said sounded like a load of crap, but I was morbidly curious. "So, explain what you do know."

"Since the beginning, the founding families worked hard to secure its success. The town grew, and more people moved in, but it's all thanks to the elders.

"Who are they?" I asked.

Jason shrugged. "I'm not really sure. At the beginning of our junior year, I was told to look out for Tiana. Mr. Reynolds, Tiana's dad, sat me down with my dad and told me what they expected of me. I wasn't raised to question my parents, so I didn't think much about it." Jason was right; we'd all been raised that way. "They said it was a great honor to be chosen as protector. Only the strongest from the founding families were even considered. I'm just now beginning to think about all of it. You, Sherry, you and Tiana, it's all just too weird sometimes, but I don't question that I am Tiana's protector."

I listened to Jason, but the entire time I was thinking about Tia. "Go with me. Go back to Aunt Trudy's house tomorrow night. You're her friend, too. I want you to hear what they're doing to her. It's awful. I can't bear it."

CHAPTER 22

Surprisingly, Jason agreed to go with me. He didn't even need that much convincing. Mom and Dad came home that afternoon. "I'm staying over at Jason's tonight," I said after supper. They stopped and looked at me. One, I never slept out, and two, I had never hidden my feelings about Jason.

"Okay," Mom replied, but she cut her eyes toward Dad in surprise. I packed a bag and kissed her cheek as I headed out. I could feel her gaze follow me.

On the drive over to Aunt Trudy's, Jason didn't say much, but he did warn me not to interfere. "Observe. If you find her, do not touch her or disturb her in any way. Do you understand?" I nodded, but he didn't believe me. "Promise me!" he demanded.

Cautiously, I approached Aunt Trudy's house. At least, I remembered a ladder this time and gently set it against the house near Tia's window. The window wouldn't budge. I moved the ladder and tried another. Finally, one gave way, and I slipped quietly into the house.

Jason promised to wait for me in the truck and assured me he wouldn't leave until he knew I was safe. Then I saw it; well, I felt it, the darkness that I'd seen two nights ago moved like a shadow. I held my breath at first, and then I sighed, relieved that I hadn't made the whole thing up. The shadow flickered and moved like the lines of heat on the pavement. It was hard to tell its outline. I followed it towards Tia's room.

Tia slept soundly in the center of a four-pollster bed. The bed was an antique, for sure. There was lace edging on the pillows and the coverlet. She looked angelic with her hair flowing down her shoulders. Like Sleeping Beauty and Snow White, I was drawn to her from across the room. I wondered if I could break the spell with true love's kiss. I scoffed a bit; I'd already kissed her plenty.

As the shadow moved towards Tia's bed, the air in the room changed. It felt charged like just before a thunderstorm. I had the feeling that at any moment, lightning would flash in the room with us. I didn't move. I wasn't sure I could without drawing unwanted attention to myself. I held my breath as the shadow moved over Tia, and my view was obscured through its shape. I hated not being able to see her clearly. The figure covered her, and suddenly her eyes opened, and she sat up. She moved slowly, purposefully, and pulled back the covers and eased down from the bed.

"Tia," I whispered. My heart pounded, and my breath caught in the charged air.

The days had been warm, but even in the summer, the nights were chilly. She was barefooted and wore only a thin nightgown. She shivered; she had to be freezing. The shadow coaxed her toward the back door. Tia reached out and opened it, and I moved to follow her. Where was she going? I watched with surprise when the shadow covered her like a cloak, and she adeptly climbed down the back stairs. Her eyes looked like they had last winter when she sleepwalked to my house.

I followed her at a slight distance, watching her walk toward a line of trees in complete disbelief. I was so close to her, but the flickering cloak around Tia made her move quickly. I had to run to keep up with her. I promised Jason that I wouldn't do anything stupid, but as soon as I saw her, that promise went right out the window.

I was nearly at the tree line when, out of nowhere, I was slammed to the ground, dirt and grass temporarily obscuring my view. I couldn't see

Tia. At first, I thought I'd been blindsided by another shadowy figure, but Jason had tackled me.

"What are you doing?" he hissed in my ear. I fought to break free. He gasped, struggling to hold me down. "I told you not to interfere!" he grunted.

"Where is that thing taking her?" I struggled to break free and run after her, but Jason doubled his efforts, holding me to the ground. He was stronger than I remembered.

"We need to go! Go straight to your truck! Don't make me fight you, man. I really don't want to. Can I trust you won't go into those woods?"

I struggled against his restraints and then gave in. Jason wasn't my enemy. When I finally managed to see around us, I couldn't see where Tia had gone. She wasn't anywhere. I agreed, and Jason stood and offered me a hand. I refused it and brushed past him, knocking him in the shoulder, asserting my anger.

Once we were in the truck, Jason watched me from the corner of his eye. He was careful with his words when he spoke. "Please don't go back." I glared at him. "This isn't your concern. You've got no business messing with this. Do you understand that?" His words were choked.

"No! I don't!" I bellowed back at him. I rolled down the windows, suddenly feeling closed in and claustrophobic. I hit the steering wheel and groaned in frustration.

Jason flinched at my aggression. "I can't talk here. Drive!" His eyes were pleading, and I took his meaning. I drove straight to the church. Once in the dank basement, I flicked the light on forcefully, and it swung over our heads.

"Please, please say you'll wait patiently and not go there again." His voice was unnaturally compassionate. "It's my fault that you went there in the first place. I shouldn't have let you bring her. Look, school starts in a few days, and she'll be back; I promise."

I cursed. "I know what I saw! What is going on? Is this what happens every summer?" I pressed the questions without allowing Jason to answer me. At the end of my tirade, he finally spoke.

"I don't know."

"What do you know?" I accused.

"I know I can't tell you."

I sat down on the bench and allowed the silence to take me in. "I don't know what I'm fighting," I said, resigned. "If I were fighting you, it would be easy."

"Not that easy," he challenged.

"You know what I mean, though, right?"

"Yeah, I understand. I don't want to fight you, so don't go taking out your aggravation on me."

"Do you know what I saw?" I asked.

"I doubt you saw her *grandmothe*r," he scoffed.

"Did you know she sleepwalked to my house last winter solstice after the dance?" He shook his head and looked concerned. "I woke up, and she was just standing there in my bedroom. I thought I was dreaming, but she was there. It was horrifying. She said she dreamed I was calling her like it was all my fault. Tonight, she looked like she did that night. Was she being called? Was something calling her into the woods?"

"I don't know," Jason said, again. "I do know that as the nights get longer, she'll have more freedom. What you witnessed is part of the power that claims Tiana."

"Power?" I clarified with a disbelieving tone.

"I don't know what else to call it. Please don't ask me anything else because I don't know. Just keep your head down and don't cause trouble. Focus on school and the season ahead. Agreed?" I guessed I owed him that much. "She's coming back! Okay?"

“She’s not going to know me; is she?” He shook his head. “Will she come around?”

“For your sake, I hope so, but then again, I think you’d be better off not knowing yourself. I wish you’d be the one to forget all about her, all about this.”

“I can’t do that.”

“I know that, too. It would just make everything easier.”

“What’s your role in all of this, anyway?” Why are you so protective of her?”

“It’s my job. I told you; when Tiana was chosen, I was claimed, too. It’s my responsibility to look out for her. It will be again when she returns.”

“I don’t understand.”

“You know how drones protect the queen?” I nodded. “She’s like our town’s queen or will be. It’s the elder’s job to protect her until her time comes. I don’t know when that will be, but I know my duty until that time comes.”

I laughed condescendingly. “Did you just compare yourself to a drone? A mindless tool?”

Jason set his jaw defensively. “Yeah, I did. She’s oblivious to it, of course, but we can’t refuse her. We are grossly attracted to her and find ourselves hovering and desiring, but never having." The words were hard for Jason to confess.

"What are you protecting her from?"

"Anything and everything. Sometimes, you. Sometimes, herself."

"Who is telling you to do this?"

"The elders."

"Who are they?"

"The elders are the covenant keepers of the county, men from the founding families. I suspect a few others, but I only know Tiana's dad for sure. He's the one I report to. My dad, too, but it sometimes skips a generation. That's all I know; I swear. They need her to seal the covenant to keep our county's livestock and fields fertile. Everyone's livelihood depends on it. Even our team's success and the health of the children depend on it."

"Is this why you told me she wasn't to be had?"

"Yes."

"How will her return affect you and Sherry?"

He chuckled humorously. "Let's just say it will complicate things. Football, Tiana, work, they will all interfere with my relationship with Sherry. That's not going to make either of us happy."

"So why do you help me, sneaking around to give me time with Tia?"

This time there was humor in his chuckle, but with it, the hint of arrogant ass returned. "You have no idea how your attraction for one another complicates my job. Her attraction for you pulls the two of you together and forces everyone else to step back. I'm powerless to refuse her. She wants you, and so that makes me want you to be with her, too. It's weird. I'm drawn to you, too, man." I smirked at his suggestion. "No, don't take it that way," Jason clarified.

"Yeah, what's with that? I'm not as easily repulsed by you anymore, either."

"Ever since you blocked me that first time in a game, my loyalties began leaning more toward you and Tiana and less…" His voice trailed off. "It's like I want the two of you to be together more than I want anything else. You're a strong force. Just like this basement, you neutralize everything that I battle."

"She's being tortured. You know that, right?"

"I only know what you say you've heard, but I know nothing."

"I don't know what I'm facing," I confessed.

"Neither do I, but I'll help you if I can."

"Does she know?"

He shrugged. "I doubt it. It's kept on the down-low. The old families know, but they're only in so far. I didn't find out until recently, and that's because it was necessary as her time approaches."

I looked at him and realized his words were sincere, but I suspected once he left the church, everything would return to normal. "Back to the usual?" I asked.

"Yeah, if you don't mind. It would make things easier for me, but know I'm doing my part to protect her. Even when I'm acting like a jerk, just know it's because I need to look like I'm doing my job. Okay?"

"Yeah, I understand."

"Look, man, I'm gonna run back home. Stay here if you like, but I need to go. I can't be seen with you in the daylight.

I stayed in the church basement until close to dawn. I drove straight home, exhausted and frustrated. Mom accused me of getting drunk because she said I looked hungover. I denied it and said I'd just not slept much while they were out of town.

"Why didn't you say something? You need to get better sleep if you plan to play well."

I agreed with her but didn't expound on the particulars of my sleep schedule. I also didn't want her worrying. A part of me wanted to talk to her, but another part just didn't know where to begin. I let it pass.

AUTUMN

CHAPTER 23

Jason was right. The time passed quickly with the days filled from daylight to dark with school, homework, practice, and every odd job I was called to do. A couple of times, I even found myself in Mr. Roy's room reading. I just couldn't stay away. The Bible was opened to different stories at different times. There was a king named David who wrote a bunch of songs. The Book of Psalms had 150 chapters that were filled with longing and frustration, love, and revenge. He wrote like the whole world was against him. I could definitely relate.

Two days before the equinox, I was a mess of anticipation, knowing Tia probably returned in the night. She'd surely be at school. I woke early, did my chores, cleaned my room, and gave Mom no excuse to delay me or demand that I return right after practice. I had packed mine and Jesse's lunches the night before, along with a before-practice snack.

Mom came into the kitchen as I was pouring myself a cup of coffee. She was still in her bathrobe. As soon as I looked at her face, I knew she wasn't right. "You okay, Mom?"

"Honey, can you take Jesse this morning? I woke with a horrible head cold, and he can't take his project on the bus. It's too big." Her voice was raspy.

Ugh! I sighed inwardly. "Yes, ma'am, I can. Is he ready yet?"

"Almost," Jesse said as he entered the kitchen and poured himself a bowl of cereal. I joined him at the table; I might as well eat with him. I was already going to miss homeroom.

I pulled up into the student parking lot and backed into a space near the football field. I usually parked that far out, but then it was a bother because I'd be running all the way into first period. My phone vibrated in my pocket. I checked the text from Jason.

She's back. Meet me after homeroom.

"Have you seen her yet?" Jason asked. He was leaning against the lockers with casual nonchalance.

"No. I was late; I had to take my little brother, why? Have you?" I asked.

"I saw her in homeroom. I just didn't want you to be surprised. There have been some changes; you need to prepare yourself."

I walked down the hall toward first period. I gawked; everyone gawked, watching Tia walk confidently down the hall toward the classroom. It was like one of those great reveals during a make-over show. *Damn!* The changes were more than *some*. Her hair was longer and wavier and fuller like she'd had it professionally done that morning. Her skin was golden brown, and her hair was highlighted like she'd spent the entire summer on the beach. I doubted that. I'd seen her recently enough, and she didn't look like *that*. It didn't look like she was wearing any makeup, but her lashes were darker, and her lips puckered in a rose-colored pout.

She had a sultry look about her features. I didn't like the way everyone stared at her, but I couldn't help myself. Her modifications were keenly apparent. I traced every detail from her head to her toes. It wasn't just her hair; everything about her was fuller and wavier. She was standing next to her desk, laughing with Catherine. Tia's shape was curvy; her hips were accentuated by an above-the-knee length skirt that hugged her thighs. Her breasts were fuller, and the knit shirt she wore revealed no cleavage, but it didn't hide anything either. Nothing was left to the imagination.

I walked directly to the chair next to her and sat down. Catherine eyed me for a second and then smiled. She didn't plan to challenge my choice in seats and would probably enjoy watching our first exchange. Tia sat down and leaned over to get a notebook and pen from her backpack.

My throat tightened. I cleared it. “Good morning,” I said through a friendly smile. “I’m Christopher.” My jaw was tight, and my palms were sweaty.

“Good morning,” Tia replied once she’d looked up from her backpack. She looked at me for a few seconds, and, for the briefest of moments, I thought there was knowing in her eyes. “Do I know you?” she asked.

“Yeah, we’ve met before. You probably don’t remember.” I knew damn well she didn’t remember. Her brow furrowed like she was concentrating on something far away. I searched for what to say next. “Is this your first day back?” I asked, feigning ignorance.

“Yeah, I’ve been away for the summer. I’ve got some catching up to do.”

“I’d be glad to give you my notes,” I offered, looking for an in.

“Thank you; I’d appreciate that.”

At least her sweetness hadn’t changed, only the body that covered it. Her smile, yes, thankfully, her smile was the same, too. “Maybe we could meet at the library after school, and I could loan you my notebooks to copy. There's also a printer at my dad's office if you'd like me to make copies there instead for free.'

"The library is fine. What time?" she asked.

Then I remembered. "Oh, crap! I have practice this afternoon. Can it be after?"

"That's fine. I wanted to stay for a club meeting today, anyway, so that might work out for both of us."

"Good. Meet you in the parking lot at five?" I sounded way too hopeful. Then I caught myself. "Will you need a ride?" I didn't want her to know that I already knew she rode the bus to school, and she didn't have her own car and that I always drove her and that it would kill me until she remembered all of that on her own. "I drive the gray Silverado at the back of the lot, near the locker rooms. I'll meet you there."

After practice, Tia met me like we'd agreed. She rode with me to the library, and we made copies. We didn't talk a whole lot. She lived about three blocks from the library, so she said she'd like to walk home. I was disappointed that she didn't want a ride. I sat in my truck and pretended to fiddle with my backpack. I watched her walk until she turned down her street and I couldn't see her anymore. She'd hear my truck's thundering engine and would know I followed her, so I just waited until I was pretty sure she'd made it home. I drove down the cross street and was satisfied that she'd made it safely.

CHAPTER 24

Our first game was over. We pulled out a win by the skin of our teeth. I didn't feel like going out to Anderson Field and took plenty of crap from our teammates for refusing to join everyone. I think Mom and Dad were a little concerned, too, but they didn't ask specifically, and I didn't offer any excuses.

At eleven-thirty, my phone vibrated next to my bed and woke me. I reached for it and squinted my eyes at the bright screen. "What the heck?" I asked aloud; it was from Jason.

You awake

Am now

Get here

Where

Anderson Field

He attached a video of Tiana dancing on the top of a picnic table. She was obviously drunk and staggering with a red Solo cup in her left hand.

Will watch her until you get here

Why was he texting *me*? *He* was supposed to be protecting her. I pulled on jeans over my boxers and grabbed a hoodie. I opened the window and snuck out to my truck. I slipped it into neutral and let it roll silently down the driveway. The gravel crunched under my tires, but it wasn't loud enough to wake anyone in the house. Mom and Dad would probably understand, but I didn't want them to worry or think wrongly of T.

At the end of the gravel drive, I started my truck. The night wasn't too cold, but the heater felt pleasant, and the cab warmed quickly. The radio played low as I drove fast toward Anderson Field.

When I arrived at the field, I searched all over for Jason and Tia. I found her surrounded by about six or so guys. The music was booming, and the entire defensive line danced around her. Jason was behind her with his hand around her waist. He didn't see me coming. Although my insides were writhing, I wondered what Sherry would say if she saw them like that. I didn't want to fight my way out, nor did I want to make a scene. I took a deep breath before I placed my hand on his shoulder.

He looked at me through bleary eyes. "Hey, Topher. What's up? Come to join the party?"

Intoxicated or not, I hated his playing both sides. I appreciated him and loathed him in the same breath. How could I trust and distrust a person at the same time?

"May I cut in?" I asked.

"Why so serious?" he asked, continuing to dance without removing his hand from Tia's waist.

Tia looked up then. "Hey, Topher; why so serious?" she mimicked Jason's tone playfully in that relaxed, drunken way.

"Hey, Tiana," I said, looking her over. Her dark lashes blinked lazily. "Whatcha got there?" I gestured toward the cup in her hand.

She slowed her dancing and looked into the contents of her cup. Her brow creased, considering. I took a step forward, and the rest of the guys took a step back. The closer I got to her, the further they stepped away. I took another step, and Jason let go of her waist.

"They call it jungle juice, but I think it's mostly cheap vodka and rum. Want some?"

"Sure." I took the cup from her hand, and she staggered like it was helping to keep her balanced. I sniffed the contents and pretended to take a sip. I held her arm with my free hand. "Do you mind if I finish it off for you?"

"Sure, I think I've had plenty. I need to pee," she giggled.

I handed the cup to Jason, and he suggested to the other guys that they all get a refill. They followed him and left us alone.

"Do your parents know where you are?"

Pwhhh. Tia blew out her lips in a full breath. "I told them I was staying over at Catherine's, but she said we should come here and meet Clayton. I'm not sure where they went. Catherine bought him glow-in-the-dark condoms for his birthday. I think they're in the woods," she giggled again.

"Do you want me to take you home?" I asked.

"No, I can't go home. I have to sleep at Catherine's," she insisted like she'd said something important.

"Okay, Okay," I appeased.

"But you can take me to pee. I really need to pee, and then you can dance with me. Will you dance with me?"

"Yeah, Tia, I'll dance with you." I dismissed her request.

"I don't believe you."

"Why not?" I almost teased.

"Jason said he would dance with me, but he got mad when I wouldn't leave with him. He just kept giving me that crap to drink. I don't think there's any real juice in it. What a stupid name. There's no jungle in it, either."

I scanned the field for an outdoor toilet. Surely there was one near the parking lot. Nope. No luck. "Can you pee in the woods?" I asked. She wrinkled her nose and shook her head. "I can take you to the gas station. Will you go to the gas station with me?" She nodded. Instantly, I liked the idea of taking her away from the park. I looked around for either Clayton or Catherine's car. "Whose car did you come in?"

"Her mom's van. Catherine's car is in the shop. Needs brakes, I think." I saw the van across the parking lot.

"Do you have your phone?"

She shook her head. "It's at Catherine's, so my parents think I'm there if they search for me." *What an idiot move!*

We passed Jason and the other guys. They were refilling their cups from jugs on the picnic tables. "Why didn't you just take her home?" I asked impatiently.

"I tried, man; I did. She wouldn't go." His words were slurred. It was a wonder he could even text. At least he sounded apologetic.

"I'm taking Tiana to the gas station."

"I need to pee!" she exclaimed.

"I need Clayton's number. Do you have it?" Jason nodded. I didn't ask for Catherine's because I figured that she'd probably left her phone at home, too. I'd seen her pass it along to Tia too many times already. "Can you send it to me? I want to tell them I'll drive Tia back to Catherine's later. Okay?" He fished out his phone from his back pocket. "Thanks," I said as I guided a staggering, slurring Tiana toward my truck. At least she was cooperative.

I was a little pissed at Jason for how he had been dancing with T, but I was even more bothered by the other guys who were watching me take Tia away from the party. Jason, too, was fighting the urge to follow her. I pushed a couple of the guys back from the truck and helped T into the passenger's side.

She waved. "I'll be back in a little while." They seemed satisfied with that.

I drove her to the closest 24-hour convenience store. I walked in and asked for the key to the ladies' room and handed the cashier a twenty. "Twenty on pump seven." He nodded and didn't even flinch at my asking for the key to the ladies' room. Either he didn't care, or he'd seen that I had a girl with me.

I started the pump and then walked Tia to the bathroom. "Can you manage?" I asked.

She giggled. "Yes, I know how to. I've been doing it by myself for a long time."

"It's different, though, when you've been drinking. It all doesn't work like you think."

I unlocked the door and turned on the light. It wasn't totally gross like the men's side. There were even paper toilet seat protectors. I pulled one out and placed it on the toilet for her. All the while, I held her arm and guided her.

"Okay, I'll be right outside. You good?"

I stood her right in front of the toilet, and, against my better judgment, left her there. All she had to do was pull down her jeans and sit to pee. Surely, she could manage that. "Thanks," she said as I closed the door. I texted Clayton's phone while I waited.

A few minutes later, I heard the toilet flush and some light scuffles of her boots on the tile. "Hey, hey, you! Christopher," she called urgently. I opened the door in time to see her lean over the sink vomiting. I braced myself behind her so she wouldn't lose her balance and slip on the tile floor. I pulled her hair back from her face and fisted a ponytail in my hand.

She heaved and gasped and choked against the force of alcohol that threatened to expel itself from her insides. I turned on the water with my free hand and watched the contents of her stomach rinse down the open drain. Suddenly, she went rigid, like she realized where she was and that I was with her in the bathroom.

“Glad you didn’t do that in my truck,” I said, trying to ease her tension.

“Where am I?” she asked, looking past her own reflection at me in the blurry mirror.

“In the gas station bathroom. You needed to pee.”

“How long have I been here?”

“Five or ten minutes.”

“Where’s Catherine?”

“With Clayton. You said they were together in the woods.” She looked at herself in the mirror and then let the water run in her hands. She leaned over and cupped the water to rinse her mouth. She spat and patted her face with her damp hands. “You okay?” I asked.

She shrugged. “I’m confused. I need to find Catherine.”

“I texted Clayton and asked him to tell her I’d drive you to her house. I don’t trust either of them if they’ve been drinking. I’d rather see you home safely.”

"I don't feel well. I need some fresh air." I leaned back and opened the door for her, making sure she was steady on her feet. I walked her to the truck and helped her up onto the seat. "Keep it open. I don't want to be sick in here," she said.

"I'll be right back." I walked back into the convenience store and returned the key to the cashier. I grabbed a couple of Cokes, a large bottle of water, some hand wipes, peppermint Life Savers, and a box of saltines. Near the checkout, I saw a selection of pre-filled travel toothbrushes. I grabbed a couple of those, too.

The checker glanced down at my selection and smirked. "Your girlfriend, alright?" I nodded once. He turned and placed a 3-pack of condoms on the counter. "They're on the house."

"Keep 'em," I said. "Not taking advantage."

"Suit yourself. Just trying to help you out."

"I need a lot more help than that," I said and took my purchases from the counter.

"At least take another bag in case she's sick again." I nodded and grabbed the extra bag.

"Here." I handed Tia the bag of items.

"Thanks," she said. "I'm sorry. I don't usually drink like this."

"I figured." I had to remind myself to pretend I didn't know her nature. "Go ahead, clean yourself up while I put the pump back." Twenty bucks worth didn't take long to pump. Once I was back in the cab, I offered her a Coke. "Here, this will settle your stomach." She unscrewed the cap and took a huge swig. "Slow down," I warned. She nodded and then burped loudly, covering her mouth in surprise and giggling. I laughed. "Feel better?" I asked.

She nodded again. She took another sip and leaned her head back against the headrest and sighed. I wanted to lean over and take her in my arms, but I refrained. I knew it would make her uncomfortable and possibly run from the safety of my truck.

"Where do you want to go? I texted Clayton. I asked him to tell Catherine that I took you. I'll take you to Catherine's if you want. I'd rather not take you back to the field, if that's okay with you," I added so as not to appear too bossy.

She didn't look directly at me. We both stared out through the windshield. "Christopher," she began and turned to face me, "I feel like I should thank you. I didn't know what was happening for a little while. What time is it?"

"It's nearly twelve-thirty." She nodded and blinked slowly. She examined the contents of the bag more closely and took out the toothbrush and the wipes. She then said she'd like to go back to the bathroom. I got down from the truck and got the keys again. I took the other toothbrush and followed her and used the men's side. It took me less time, and I stood outside the women's bathroom until she came out. I opened the door for her again and helped her up into the seat.

"Catherine's?" I asked. Tia nodded. I pulled out of the parking lot, and within seconds, she was asleep.

My eyes blinked against the soft haze of dawn. It was still pretty dark, but the sunrise rapidly approached. I stirred gently when I realized that Tia was sleeping in my arms. We were in the cab of my truck outside Catherine's house. The memory of the night flooded in: the game, the win, Anderson Field, and holding T while she slept. I didn't have the heart to wake her. I just sat for a long time watching her sleep. It was the first time since her return that I'd been able to really look at her. I examined her for proof of the torture I was sure she'd endured over the summer. I wanted her, and the need for her made it hard to keep my hands to myself. She almost fell over a couple of times, so I rested her head against me, and, with her in my arms, I fell asleep, myself.

Tia's breathing changed suddenly, and I felt her go rigid. "Christopher, why am I in your truck?" She pressed herself into an upright position, and I removed my arms from around her. I could tell she was extremely apprehensive.

"I brought you home last night. I mean, I brought you to Catherine's. She knows you're here. She texted me last night. We didn't want to wake her parents, and you would have needed to be carried in."

She looked down into her lap and nodded, embarrassed. "I was pretty drunk, huh?"

"Yeah, you were." Silence fell between us. "It's okay, T. You're fine."

She smiled a little but didn't look into my eyes. I placed my finger under her chin and directed her face toward mine. When our eyes met, there was that flicker of recognition. It always happened after the equinox – the glimmer, the hint that she knew me.

"Oh, T," I sighed, and without any restraint or self-control, I took her forcefully and kissed her.

Surprisingly, she didn't resist and let me kiss her before she gathered her senses and pushed me away from her. "What do you think you're doing?" she exclaimed. Her face was stricken like I'd done something criminal. She put her hand over her mouth, wiping the kiss from her lips.

"I'm sorry, Tia. I'm sorry," I apologized profusely.

"Tiana. My name is Tiana, and just because you drove me home, doesn't give you the right to kiss me or expect anything else. She moved away from me and reached for the handle of the door. "I appreciate your getting me home safely, but…" Her voice trailed off.

I didn't want her to go, not like that. I reached over and gently placed my hand over hers. "No, Tiana, you're right. I'm sorry. I shouldn't have. Please, don't go. Not like this." She didn't bolt. She just stared at my hand. She tilted her head slightly, considering my touch.

She eased her hand on the handle and responded hesitantly to the sincerity in my voice. "I don't make it a habit to kiss boys like that, but I have to admit it was nice." I released a breathy chuckle, the relief evident in the space between us. She placed her other hand over mine and eased her hand from the door handle. She turned slowly to face me, and her eyes gazed curiously into mine.

I was afraid to move or breathe, but the moment got the better of me. Tia's eyes shone brightly, and she blinked, almost coyly. "Maybe when you know me a little better, you might let me do it again," I ventured.

She blinked slowly and caught her bottom lip between her teeth, considering. Her dark lashes encircled her eyes, and they widened with curiosity. This new Tia was different. She was confident and assertive.

She had gotten drunk and still managed to look fabulous, even after a long night and sleeping in my truck.

"Maybe I'd let you do it again, now."

I took in a quick breath. Tia didn't know me; she didn't remember me. *Shit!* I wasn't sure if I should kiss her again, but then if I didn't, would she find someone else who would? Would she decide that I wasn't worth it? Would she forget about me completely?

I watched her for any hesitation or teasing, but she was serious. I swallowed and then went for it. I was a seventeen-year-old boy with raging hormones, and I was sitting in the cab of my truck with the girl I loved, even if she didn't know me. I eased over and pulled her back into an embrace. She put her arms around my neck and allowed me to kiss her.

The kiss was familiar and lingering. I closed my eyes and relaxed. Nothing between us was forced or awkward like at the end of sophomore year. That frightened me a little because I wondered if it was just familiar to me. Before a few seconds had passed, I didn't question anymore. Tia kissed me like she'd done three months ago. She kissed me like she didn't want to go; she kissed me like herself.

She pressed her hand into my chest to signal that she was easing from the kiss. I released her lips but didn't let the rest of her go. She opened her eyes and stared into mine with confusion and that little flicker.

"Christopher?"

"Yes," I breathed. My heart was beating wildly.

"Have we done that before?"

Shit. She knew. "Yes," I whispered.

Her confusion hinted at fear. "Why don't I remember that?"

I shrugged slightly. "I don't know."

"I think I should go."

I nodded. "Yeah."

"Thank you for last night, for everything." She blinked again and shook off the thoughts that were bombarding her brain. "I'll see you later," she muttered as she turned back toward the door.

"Hey, T, Tiana," I corrected. "It's okay. It's going to be okay."

She nodded absentmindedly as she opened the door. Then her eyes brightened as she looked back at me. She shut the door and gave a little wave before she ran toward the back entrance of Catherine's house.

I rolled down the window. "Will you be at the parade?" I called after her. She turned and looked at me and offered a little nod. She smiled. Thank goodness that part of her hadn't changed.

CHAPTER 25

The kitchen light was on when I pulled into the driveway. Through the small windows of the kitchen door, I watched Mom sitting at the counter, gripping her coffee mug. It was still steaming, so I hoped she hadn't been up too long. Regardless, I was about to catch a load of crap as soon as I walked through the door. I had snuck out; I had worried my parents unnecessarily. Once I opened the door, she turned to face me. Instantly, I knew better; she'd already had several cups.

"Where have you been?" she asked. Her tone wasn't accusing just full of concern.

"I decided to go out after all."

"A note or text would have been nice."

I nodded remorsefully. "*You* could have asked," I countered.

"Yes, but I don't think you need hovering. It's just common courtesy. I think we deserve to know where you go and, to some degree, what you do with your time." I nodded again but didn't offer any explanation. "Were you drinking last night?"

"No, ma'am."

"Where did you sleep?"

"In my truck."

"Were you alone?"

I blinked and swallowed. Mom would know I was lying, so I didn't hold the truth. "No, I wasn't alone."

"Were you with Tiana?"

"Yes, ma'am."

"That disappoints me."

"Which part?" I asked, not meaning to sound disrespectful, but she cut her eyes, challenging me.

Mom then leveled her gaze at me and, without pretense, said, "Christopher Robert, I want to make myself clear." It was easy to tell she was bothered because she rarely used my full name. I stood a little straighter and took in a slow breath. I prepared myself for whatever came next. Mom stood from the counter and walked toward me. I held the breath I'd managed to take. I was careful not to flinch when Mom raised her hands. She placed them firmly, yet lovingly, on each side of my face. Her dark brown eyes were fixed on mine. "I'm only going to say this once. Be careful." The two words were measured and fell solidly onto my ears. "If you're determined to go away to college and do anything of value with your life, please promise yourself that you won't do anything you'll regret later. It seems like all fun and games at the moment, like you don't have a care in the world, but sex brings consequences, and you can't afford those at this stage of your life. There's time, plenty of time, to make up for whatever you think you might be losing out on, now. Do you understand what I'm saying?"

Mom's eyes were full of caution and regret and fear. She was afraid for me. She was worried. I hated seeing the lines of worry wrinkle her face prematurely.

"And Tia?" I asked.

Mom's eyes lowered. She looked so sad. "I'm sorry, Chris. Your Dad and I just don't think there's a future there."

Her warning bothered me, but I didn't want to argue. We had a long festival day ahead of us, and I'd already made her worry enough for one day, so I put my hands on her shoulders and exhaled slowly. I wanted to assure her that I hadn't done anything stupid. I wanted to convince her that I wasn't going to make the same mistake they'd made and promise all the right things and make her smile, but I didn't.

"Mom," I began, but nothing else came out.

"Chris, I'm not asking you to explain yourself. Your dad and I understand. Really, we do. If you need someone to talk to, we're here for you. We love you, and we're here. Never forget that."

Mom released my face and lowered her arms. I wrapped my arms around her shoulders and hugged her tightly. I loved my mom so much. I would miss her like crazy.

"I'll do my best, Mom," I finally said.

"I know you will; you always do." She hugged me a little tighter and then released me. She wiped her eyes quickly and turned back toward her coffee. "Are you hungry?"

I chuckled a little. "Always."

"Get cleaned up. I'll start breakfast. We've got a full day today."

The autumnal equinox festival continued as usual. I helped Mom load up all of Miss Grace's candy apples. Miss Grace would come later and make an appearance, but she wasn't able to do all that she'd done in years past. Mr. Roy tended to her every need.

Before we left their house, Mr. Roy called me over to the side. "Topher, I have something for you." I followed him into the shop and waited while he produced a small package wrapped in brown paper. "It took some doing, but I thought you'd like a copy of your own."

I tilted my head slightly, wondering what he meant. His bushy eyebrows raised suggestively, and he pressed the package into my hand. It felt solid. “My own what?”

“Something to read as the nights grow longer.” I understood. He’d gotten me my own Bible. I was surprised, but maybe I shouldn’t have been. “Keep it safe. Understand?”

He was making sure I understood to keep it hidden. I guessed it wasn’t something I needed to leave out and be caught reading. I nodded, feeling the gravity of his gesture. He was bold, but he was taking a risk, trusting me with the one thing he kept most private.

“I understand,” I said solemnly. “Thank you.” I slipped the package in my glove compartment for temporary safekeeping.

I helped mom set up the booth, arranging all the sweet treats and candy apples as they’d been placed for years. I wondered if Mom would continue the tradition once Miss Grace wasn’t able to anymore. I wondered for a moment if they’d become Miss Clara’s candy apples after Miss Grace passed on. This year, she’d surely done most of the work under Miss Grace’s careful supervision.

I wasn’t sure where I’d find Tia. Jesse was allowed to hang out with some friends with Dad, so, by the time I made it to Main Street for the parade, the place was packed. Tia wasn't anywhere to be seen. I caught a glimpse of Catherine's red hair and saw Jason and Sherry and finally the back of Tia's head. I watched as she tossed her hair over her shoulder. I walked directly toward their group but hesitated briefly at a distance. I didn't know what it would be like after I'd kissed her just hours before. Would she be happy to see me? Would she be eager to do it again? I didn't know.

Jason held Sherry's hand but stood between Sherry and Tia. Sherry looked away, distracted. Her eyes looked sad, and her full bottom lip poked out in a pout. Her bouncy curls did nothing to bring the natural light and buoyancy to her eyes. Had they had a fight? Was she jealous of Tia? Did she understand why Tia was suddenly Jason's priority?

As I approached, Tia turned and smiled like she anticipated my arrival. Her smile nearly knocked me over. Jason turned, too, to see what had Tia's attention. This caused Sherry and Catherine to do the same. It was like a domino effect.

Tia broke from the little group and nearly ran to me. Jason moved to follow her, tugging Sherry behind him, until he realized where she was going. She maneuvered through the crowd, smiling and welcoming me. She took my hand and led me back so that I could join them. Jason's shoulders relaxed, and he exhaled with relief. He nodded once and turned his full attention back toward Sherry.

Sherry had watched our exchange and eyed me warily. Catherine placed her arm around Sherry, breaking her concentration and whispered something into Sherry's ear. Sherry nodded, and her eyes softened. Jason kept his attention on Sherry, and, thanks to Catherine, Sherry was prepared to greet Jason with a smile.

I stood there with T, making small talk until the parade arrived. She needed to stand in front of me to see. I didn't hold her hand or even touch her. I'd let her make the first move, but it was a challenge. Clayton was driving a float in the parade. Catherine jumped up and down when she saw his tractor approaching. She waved and called out to get his attention.

After the parade, we followed Catherine to the end of the route. We met up with Clayton, and the six of us decided to eat before we rode rides. Corndogs, cotton candy, a couple of funnel cakes, and Miss Grace's candy apples rounded out the meal.

Miss Grace was at the booth when we arrived. She was sitting down, welcoming everyone. Mr. Roy wasn't with her. He must have gone to park the car; he rarely left her side. I leaned over and gave her a little hug in greeting, but she rose as soon as she saw Tia. I helped her to her feet.

Miss Grace hugged T like she hadn't seen her in years rather than months. Miss Grace put her hands on Tia's shoulders and looked into her eyes. She stroked Tia's hair, admiringly and affectionately, and then whispered something in Tia's ear. Tia nodded and smiled. Her compassion and tenderness towards the elderly woman were evident.

Mr. Roy rushed into the booth, then, and nearly forced Miss Grace back into her seat. He moved quickly to separate Miss Grace and Tia. "Oh, Gracie, take your seat," Mr. Roy said, but his voice was strained, worried. He fussed over his wife to get her settled comfortably, but he cut his eyes back to me. I didn't know for sure, but I felt like he was reprimanding me for bringing Tia there.

Mom wished us well between customers and gave us all tickets for rides like we were seven and not seventeen. Mom smiled when she saw us, but thankfully, her attention was on the booth and the customers. I doubted she would, but I didn't want her to embarrass Tia or me with any comments about where we'd spent the night. I felt her gaze on me, but I didn't turn to see her expression; I didn't want it to alter my good mood.

CHAPTER 26

The entire day was filled with rides and more food. We crossed paths with Jesse and his friends at the Ferris wheel. As soon as they saw Tia, Jesse and the oldest Clarke boy ran over and hugged her, nearly tackling her to the ground. I was jealous of their ability to rush her and their ease with her. She hadn't forgotten about *them* at all.

"Where are you going to watch the fireworks tonight?" Jesse asked.

"I'm not sure," Tia answered. We hadn't discussed it, but she cut her eyes in my direction like maybe she was hoping we'd be watching them together.

"Mom said that if we helped her take down the booth and load everything up, we'd be able to watch them from the roof of the booth. All the carnival lights will be turned off for the fireworks. We'll have a great view."

"That sounds cool; I used to do that, too," I said. I'd done the very same thing with Tia at his age, but I didn't mention it. It would be too weird with everyone there with us.

"I'd ask you to join us, but you'd probably crash the whole thing. You're too big. I wish you could come with us, Tiana. You aren't too big."

Great, now my kid brother was vying for Tia's attention, too. "I plan to watch them from my truck, if you don't have other plans," I offered. From the corner of my eye, I caught Sherry's smile. She liked that idea as much as I did.

"I don't know," Tia wavered and cut her eyes to Jason.

"That sounds like a great idea," Sherry interjected in her sweet voice, drawing Jason's attention. "I wasn't sure how we'd all fit on the hood of your car. I don't think we'll all fit in the back of your truck, either. Jason, do you think it would be okay if Tiana went with Topher since Clayton and Catherine have to get the tractor back and all?"

Jason was caught in everyone's eyes, forced to make a decision. "I'll get her home, too, if needed," I offered.

Jason was pulled in several directions. He wanted to please Sherry; that was evident. He felt compelled toward his obligation to Tia, which pressed against his peculiar loyalty to me. Sherry took his hand, hoping he'd decide in her favor. "Tiana, what do you want to do?" Jason asked.

She looked at each of our faces and finally settled her gaze on mine. She tilted her head to one side, considering. I think she liked what she saw in my hopeful expression because the corners of her mouth went up slightly, and she winked. "I'll stay with Christopher." Everyone relaxed at her verdict. "But it will cost you," she smiled playfully. I didn't care what it cost; I'd pay it, regardless.

As the sun began to set, we paired off and walked in different directions toward our own vehicles. Clayton put his arm around Catherine and held her tightly; there was hardly any space between them. Their shadow looked like a two-headed, four-legged, no-armed creature. Jason led Sherry by the hand. Their shadow reminded me of a capital H with their hands clasped. I didn't touch Tia as we set off after everyone. She'd taken my hand before the parade, but we'd hardly touched the entire day.

Gradually, the crowds dissipated as we made our way toward my truck. Earlier that morning, I'd backed into a high spot with a clear view of the sky. We had a little hike up the hill, but it was worth it. I'd also packed blankets and cold drinks and bottled water in a cooler. I was hoping that we'd be able to watch the fireworks together. It was beyond hope that I'd be alone with T, yet there we were.

I tossed the blankets in the bed of the truck. Tia climbed in and sorted them out while I lifted the cooler from the back seat. I watched her and waited until she sat down and made herself comfortable. She was standing up in the bed. She put her hands on her hips and smiled.

"You coming up?" she asked.

"I was waiting on you," I stammered.

"I'm already here. Whatcha got in the ice chest?"

"Cokes and water."

"Anything stronger?" I was surprised by her question. I shook my head. "Good. I think I'll be avoiding that for a while." I was relieved to hear it. I didn't much like drunk Tia, and the image of Tia dancing on the picnic table bothered me more than I cared to admit. "Do you drink?" she asked.

"Occasionally. I have access, but I don't like drinking in a large group like the rest of the guys, and I definitely don't like the taste of the offerings at Anderson Field." I chuckled. "I guess you'd say I have more refined tastes."

"I think refined is better than the way I felt this morning." We laughed together at that.

"Yeah, I can imagine. You looked fine; I didn't know you felt bad at all." I smiled, feeling awkward, just standing there holding the cooler.

My mind went back to the kisses before daylight. I was pretty sure Tia was thinking about the same thing. Her eyes fluttered, and she looked away. Blush covered her cheeks. Even in the dusky light, I could tell she was a little embarrassed.

I placed the ice chest on the tailgate and climbed up. Tia sat on the blankets and crossed her legs. She tucked her hair behind her ears and smiled up at me. I sat down beside her, and she looked expectant like she was waiting for me to say or do something.

I reached over and took a water bottle and offered it to her. She shook her head. "No, thanks." I opened it and took a swig. It tasted refreshing.

"I've had a good time today," she began.

"Me, too," I replied. "It's probably the most fun I've had with Jason, ever."

"How long has he been dating Sherry?" Tia asked like she didn't know. I wasn't sure if she was making conversation or if she really didn't remember.

"Since last year. They spent all summer together." I watched her for any sign of recognition.

"He seems to really like her. She wasn't too pleased to see me when we went to pick her up this morning like I'd offended her or something. When did she move here? I hate to admit that she didn't make a huge impression on me. I think she was relieved when I agreed to go with you and not tag along with them."

I took another sip from the bottle and replaced the cap. "I was a little relieved, too," I said honestly. Tia smiled warmly, and her eyes fluttered again. I liked her response. "Jason and Sherry are good. I'm glad you let them have some time alone. With football and school and work, Jason doesn't get much time with her." I didn't mention that Tia's own return complicated matters even more.

She looked at me, considering. It was the same expression she'd had after the kiss. "Christopher, something's been bothering me all day."

"Yeah?"

"This morning, when you kissed me." She let her gaze fall to her lap but didn't say anything else. She frowned, and I sensed she was struggling with her thoughts. I wondered if my presence frightened her a little.

"That bothered you?" I asked, trying to ease her tension. She shook her head and rolled her eyes like my teasing annoyed her. "T, I'm sorry." I didn't correct myself. It felt so weird to call her Tiana. I wouldn't call her that unless she asked me specifically or demanded it. “I don’t want you to feel uncomfortable. I’ll answer anything you ask.”

A light breeze blew over, and a leaf fell into the bed of the truck between us. The daylight was fading quickly. Soon we’d be in complete darkness, and the fireworks would begin. Tia picked up the leaf and twirled the stem between her fingers, examining the veins and color and shape.

“They know the days grow shorter.” Her voice was low, and her thoughts were far away as she gazed admiringly on the leaf. “They know; they know when it’s time to let go. They know when it’s time to sacrifice themselves to renew the next generation.”

“What are you talking about, Tia?” I didn’t like the way she focused in on the leaf and the way her attention left me. This Tia was so different and made me uneasy. I placed my hand over hers and gently took the leaf from between her fingers. As soon as our hands touched, she looked at me. Her other hand rested on my forearm. She held it securely and drew herself closer to me. Our knees touched, and she leaned towards me, taking a good look at my face. Her eyes held mine intently in the dark.

“Christopher, I want to remember you. I feel like it’s big like something important rests on my knowing you. Will you help me understand what I’m feeling?” she whispered.

The air between us was charged. I was so close to her. Finally, I could touch her. The long summer had passed, and with it, her unbearable screams in my dreams, calling out to me in pain. Seeing that shadow lead her off into the woods to do who-knows-what to her. The pleading tone in her whisper was the same.

She jumped as the first of the fireworks whistled and burst into bright red above our heads. Her eyes widened in fear; she paled and looked petrified. When she jumped at the next high-pitched whistle, I grabbed her into my chest and instinctively covered her with my body. I'd reacted like we were being attacked by an air raid and not watching harmless fireworks. She clung to me, and her heartbeat raced in her chest.

"Shhh, T. Shhh," I soothed and rocked her in my arms. "It's just the fireworks show." I gently stroked her hair and covered her exposed ear with my hand, pressing her other ear into my chest. That seemed to settle her a little. I took several deep breaths to calm us both. I curled her body closer to mine and eased us down into the bed of the truck. She shivered like she was freezing. Maybe she was experiencing some kind of shock. I used my free hand to pull the blankets over her, holding her tightly, absorbing the tremors of her body. It took both strength and tenderness to hold her securely without crushing her.

Tia settled slightly with the steady rhythm of the show, yet she still clung to me. I watched the sky light up overhead, patiently waiting for it to end. There was a lull, and I knew the firework's final crescendo would soon begin. Sure enough, the blasts thundered and echoed around us. Tia went rigid and screamed bloody murder into my ear, and just like my dreams, I could do nothing for her.

I wrapped her more securely and scooped her up into my arms. I scooted down toward the tailgate and cradled her as I jumped to the ground. I placed her in the front seat and ran around to the driver's side. I kicked myself for not thinking of it sooner. Inside the cab, the sounds were muffled, but still, she was screaming and rocking and muttering something to herself about the fall of the leaves and the colors, and I could swear that I heard her repeat the word sacrifice.

The explosions continued to light up the sky. I drove over the hill and took the most direct route I could find. My truck maneuvered aggressively across the field, but it was rough, and Tia was tossed around. I pulled her over and held her with one arm. I used my other hand to drive as fast as I could away from the fireworks.

Within minutes, I was on the highway, speeding like a maniac. I held the wheel with my knee and voice-texted Jason, one-handed.

Basement. Now!

CHAPTER 27

The massive tires skidded across the loose gravel onto the tall grass at the back of the old church. I pulled Tia through the drivers-side door and tossed her over my shoulder. She gasped, and her screams turned into uncontrollable sobs. I grabbed the ice chest from the back and ran toward the basement entrance. I burst through the old door, and it swung helplessly on its hinges. It was dark as pitch, and the stairs groaned in protest at our combined weight. Carrying T and the cooler, I had to be at least three hundred fifty pounds.

I gingerly felt for each step, careful not to trip down the stairs. As we inched down underground, Tia's sobs abated. At the bottom of the stairs, I felt for the overhead light and pulled the string. The bulb illuminated the dank basement. I rested the ice chest on the ground and swung Tia into my arms, cradling her gently. I sat on the bench and uncovered her face and loosened the blankets from around her shoulders. She was wrapped tightly, cocooned for her own safety.

Her eyes were wide, but her breathing was settling down. She blinked, but I wasn't sure she could see me. I didn't dare say anything, afraid that I'd frighten her as she came out of whatever fit of insanity it was. I wiped the tears from her cheeks, and she closed her eyes and rested her head against me. I was thankful she wasn't still screaming and seemed to be more restful in my arms. I could feel my phone vibrate in my pocket. I eased it out and read Jason's reply.

Taking Sherry home. There asap.

The drive to Sherry's and back would take nearly an hour. My back and legs were cramping from the exertion of holding her through the fireworks. I knew I'd have no more feeling in my legs if I held her on that bench for an hour. I slid onto the ground and laid Tia across my chest. As soon as we were against the earthen floor, Tia exhaled a deep sigh. Beneath her weight, I relaxed, too.

We must have fallen asleep like that, holding one another on the damp floor because I didn't hear Jason come in. I opened my eyes, and Jason was leaning over me. His eyes were full of concern.

"Oh, good, you're not dead," he panted like he'd been running a marathon. "You were barely breathing." He looked over at a sleeping

Tia. "What happened. Why did you bring her here?" His tone sounded accusatory, but maybe he was just worried.

"She freaked out during the fireworks," I whispered. "I didn't know what else to do. It works for you, so I thought it might help her, too." He nodded.

He sat down on the ground next to Tia and looked at her, examining her face. "Tiana," he said gently. He lifted his hand to shake her awake, but as he moved to touch her, he hesitated. He took a deep breath and let it out slowly before he placed his hand on her shoulder. He didn't cringe or even feel the least bit repelled by my presence. He chuckled a little and grinned, relieved that the basement neutralized that effect, too. "Tiana, wake up." I held her securely, not wanting her to roll over onto the hard ground and be startled and frightened to find herself in the basement with Jason and me.

She moaned a little and whispered something about the leaves, again. "Christopher, help me. Christopher?" she asked sleepily.

"Yeah, T, I'm here. Jason, too." I kissed her head, not thinking about what that might do to her, not thinking that she didn't remember me, but it didn't frighten her at all. She tilted her face upward and found my lips and kissed me. My eyes flew open in surprise. Jason's hands went up in surrender as soon as our lips touched. Neutral ground or not, he knew he didn't want to make contact with either one of us with a kiss like that. I closed my eyes, eliminating Jason's expression from my mind, letting her have her way with me for a few seconds. I stroked her hair and held her shoulders, easing her up into a sitting position. She never moved her lips from mine, like she was completely absorbed in our closeness. Her hands freed themselves from the confines of the blanket, and her fingers grabbed my shirt, drawing me closer.

"Tia," I panted as I released her. She wasn't herself, and as much as I was enjoying the kiss, I couldn't let her embarrass herself in Jason's presence. I shook her shoulders slightly to get her attention. She opened her eyes and blinked, confused.

She looked around and took in her surroundings. She looked at Jason, and he smiled at her reassuringly. "You okay, Tiana?" he asked tentatively. He nodded like he was trying to reassure himself. This had been a crazy couple of hours.

She shook her head. "Where are we?"

"Carson Chapel," Jason and I said at the same time.

"Why?"

"You freaked out when the fireworks started. I wanted to get you someplace where you couldn't see or hear them."

She nodded slowly, accepting that. "We were in the back of your truck. The sunset, right?" I nodded. She looked at Jason. "You were with Sherry." Jason nodded. "We ate Miss Grace's apples. She's not well, is she?" I shook my head, agreeing with her observation, but not understanding why that was at the forefront of her mind. She took a deep breath and exhaled. She pressed herself up and scooted over and sat apart from me, but our thighs still touched. She pulled the blankets apart and kicked her legs to loosen them. She swallowed and smacked her tongue and lips like she might be thirsty. I was glad I'd grabbed the ice chest. I just kept thinking that if she were in shock, she'd need water and sugar to help her on the other side of it.

I gestured toward the cooler. Jason opened it and grabbed a bottle of water, unscrewing the cap and handing it to her. Her hands were a little shaky, but she took it in both of hers and lifted it to her mouth. "Aren't there some Cokes in there?" she asked once she'd downed half the bottle of water.

"Yeah," Jason said as he grabbed the bottle and wiped the condensation on his jeans before he opened the cap and offered it to her. She passed the water over to me, and I finished it in two gulps. I was parched, too. She chugged the Coke and held in the burp that threatened to escape. Jason grabbed a bottle of Coke for himself and took a few sips, watching Tia the entire time, just waiting for her next request.

After a few moments, Tia seemed to gather her wits and straightened herself. She looked regal and confident again. "Christopher, what happened? I want to know everything. If I'm not mistaken, my last question was about why I didn't remember you."

"Yeah, it was. That was right before you got distracted by the leaf that blew into the truck. Then the sun set, and the fireworks started. All of a sudden, you went completely apeshit until I got you in here, but I didn't get a chance to answer you."

"I remember that, but I don't remember the fireworks. Jason, where's Sherry?"

"I took her home. I came as soon as I could." His tone sounded remorseful like he was conflicted with his duty to Tia and his affection toward Sherry.

"I want to know, Christopher. I want to know why I can kiss you like I've kissed you forever, yet I don't remember you."

I cut my eyes toward Jason. "He can answer that better than I can."

I wondered what his reply might be. He'd been able to speak openly to me over the summer, but I wasn't sure what he was allowed to tell Tia. If he didn't speak the truth on his own, I would make sure he didn't leave until she knew everything she wanted to know. I looked around to see if there was something I could bind him to the chair or the bench. There wasn't anything useful within reach. I didn't need it anyway; Jason's expression softened as soon as Tia made her request.

"Jason, please tell me." She reached over and touched his knee. He looked down at her hand and grinned, almost relieved to be asked. He couldn't refuse her and was obligated to give her whatever she wanted. He stood and dusted off his jeans before he began. I sat, ready to tackle him if he changed his mind and bolted up the stairs.

After an hour of talking, Jason explained everything he knew. He told how she'd been chosen, how he'd come into her protective service, and how each fall she doesn't remember me. For the first time, he elaborated on his reasoning about that.

"I think it's because Topher wasn't born here. It really struck me this morning when we went to pick up Sherry. She was all kinds of bothered that you treated her like a complete stranger. It wasn't like you spent a lot of time with her last spring, but still, you should have been more familiar than you were today. She wasn't born here, either. I think that's the key."

"What am I chosen for? When and where will I be taken?"

"I don't know exactly," Jason said, lowering his gaze. "I know it's got something to do with the blood covenant, but I don't know any details. I won't make eighteen for a couple more weeks. I'll know more when I'm 'of age,' but not until." He made the quote signs with his fingers. "I wish I could tell you more."

Tia's gaze softened. She laid her hand on my knee and took my hand in hers. "I'm sorry, Christopher. It must be so confusing for you." Her voice was sincere and compelling. I nodded.

"This summer was the worst. After I left you at your Aunt Trudy's that last night, I dreamed about you every night. I couldn't sleep well with all the nightmares."

She squinted her eyes and shook her head. "No, that's not possible. Jason took me." She looked over at Jason.

"No, that's not how it happened, and you know it. I need you to remember! Damn it, T! I need you to remember!" I shook her to make her look at me. "Jason was supposed to, but I did. I was there three nights; I ate supper with you both. When you called for me in my dreams, I drove out there to find you." She continued to shake her head, denying the truth. "Three times, I went to find you! Jason was there! He saw you, too!" My voice rose but was absorbed in the basement walls. She stood abruptly and paced around the basement, taking it all in. She placed her palms against her temples, racking her brain to figure it all out. "I have proof!" I exclaimed.

I stood and pulled out my phone and scrolled through the photos and videos until I found the last recording she'd made. I handed her the phone, and she pressed play. She watched herself in the video, bewildered by her voice and her words, and that we were obviously at her aunt's house. She checked the date of the video. She played it several more times before she lifted her eyes to Jason and me. The words, *I love you*, penetrated my heart each time she replayed them. She'd declared herself, and I was an idiot-mute not to reply. Jason bristled each and every time she spoke it. They were powerful words, but I wondered if her love for me affected him, too.

"I believe you, but I don't understand," she said. "I think I'm getting a headache." She placed her hand over her forehead and pressed her fingers in at her temples. "Could one of you please take me home. I'm drained, and I need some time to process all of this. Do you mind?"

"It would be best if I took you," Jason suggested. He stepped forward, consolingly. "Topher understands. It will be easier after the solstice, but for now, I need to be the one who looks out for you." She nodded, accepting his words.

"I don't know how, but I do know that much," she replied, resigned. I took her hand, eased my arms around her naturally, and hugged her tightly. She returned my embrace and clung to me almost desperately. "Thank you, Christopher. Thank you for keeping me safe and looking after me last night, too. She leaned back and put her hand on my cheek. She kissed me again, but this time I didn't care that Jason was standing there.

"I love you, T. I'll see you tomorrow, okay?" She nodded.

"I think I love you, too." She smiled a little. She'd heard herself say it several times on the video; she might have believed it. Jason followed her up the stairs, but he turned his head and flashed his eyes back at me. He gave a quick nod like he knew how hard it was for me to let her go with him.

As soon as the door shut, I crumbled into a heap on the bench. I rested my head in my hands, exhausted and confused. For the first time, she'd been forced her to remember me sooner than the solstice. I wondered if there would be any consequences.

CHAPTER 28

I left the church soon after them and drove straight home. I tossed the bottles in the recycle bin and put the remainders in the outside fridge. I dried the inside of the ice chest and placed it back on the shelf in the garage. I folded the blankets and dusted off the soil from one of them. I sniffed them, but they held no trace of Tia's scent. Just before I turned to go into the house, I remembered the package Mr. Roy had given me that morning.

I put the blankets in the laundry room. Since the house was quiet, I decided to start the load in the morning. I checked the clock in the kitchen. It wasn't even ten-thirty, but Mom and Dad were already in bed. We'd all had a long day.

I tossed the package onto my bed and undressed. I was spent from the past few hours, and I decided to shower in the morning before school. I stretched out in my bed and watched the ceiling fan overhead. I tried to settle and sleep, but my mind was too wrapped up in everything that had happened.

I wondered if I should text Tia or Jason. What came next? I didn't want Tia taken, and I didn't want to let her go. I didn't understand what all of this meant and what, if anything, I could do about it. With the way my mind was racing, I knew I probably wouldn't get much sleep.

I got up from the bed and walked to the kitchen. Maybe I needed food. Maybe, I needed something stronger. I opened the fridge and grabbed the casserole dish from the shelf. As I turned to get a plate, I saw Dad enter the kitchen.

"Hey, son, did you have a good day?"

"Yes, sir, I did."

"Jesse did too. Thanks for helping your mom this morning. She really appreciated it." I nodded and served myself a huge helping from the dish. Dad looked at it appreciatively.

"Want some?" I asked.

"Sure."

He opened the drawer for forks and pulled a couple of paper towels from the roll. The microwave dinged just as we served ourselves glasses of milk.

"There's nothing like left-over lasagna in the middle of the night. A belly full of pasta and cheese makes you sleep like a brick."

"I hope so; I'm exhausted." I dug into my pile of food.

"How are things?" he asked and took a bite from his plate.

"Alright," I replied with a shrug before I took another bite.

"You made your mom worry when you left the house last night." I looked directly into his eyes and nodded. I understood. By the look on his face, I'd made him worry, too, but he always deflected his worry onto Mom, like she was the one we all had to take care of and protect. "Did she talk to you?" he asked, but I had a strong feeling he already knew she had and exactly what she'd said.

"Yes, sir."

We ate for a few minutes in silence, not wanting it to get cold. I scraped the remaining meat onto my fork and took the last bite and finished my milk with a gulp. I stood to wash my plate in the sink. Dad cleared his throat like he had something to say. Although it was already clean, I concentrated on the dish for a few more seconds.

"Chris," my dad began. I shut the water off and took a deep breath. Before I turned to face my dad, I put the plate to the side to dry in the drainer. He wiped his mouth with the paper towel and rested his hands flat on the counter before he lifted his head to face me. I leaned against the sink across from him and let my hands brace the counter at my sides. I should have known that I wouldn't get away that easily.

"Dad, you don't have to say anything. I know, okay? I know I don't need to be messing around."

"I know you know, but that's not what I want to talk about." I tilted my head, trying to read his expression.

I lifted my eyebrow, questioningly. "Okay, then what?" I shrugged.

"Tiana."

"But isn't that what I just said? I'm not messing around with her or any other girl, for that matter."

He shook his head. "No, son, it's not the same at all."

"I don't understand."

"I don't want you to be disappointed if things don't work out like you imagine." He watched me for a few seconds. I felt vulnerable, just standing there in my boxers and a t-shirt. It would be foolish to deny anything, so I remained silent. "I saw you two together today. It's more than just friendship, isn't it?" I didn't answer. Dad took a deep breath like he wasn't sure what to say, but he had to say something. "Chris, I don't know where you're headed; your future, I mean."

"Thanks, Dad," I said. A tone of defeat was evident in my voice. I wasn't disrespectful; I was just tired and frustrated. Did he know they were tearing down my every hope?

"I'm just being honest. Your mom and I don't think you have any future here. We want you to go away and figure things out for yourself. We don't want you to be tied down to this town simply because you spent more than half of your life here."

"I'm pretty sure I know where I'm going," I said defensively. We'd been planning for all of high school for me to go away to college. I had scouts looking at me. If the season went as well as Coach planned, we expected scholarship offers to follow my senior season.

"It's just that you and Tiana have been friends for a long time; you're familiar with her. She's easy to be around, but she may not be the best for you and your future." I bristled and crossed my arms over my chest. "I know you don't like hearing that, but it's how we feel. We'd like to help you avoid any unnecessary pain if we can. We're trying to guide you in the right direction."

I stared at my dad, wondering if he and his dad had ever had a conversation like this. He grew up in this very house; he'd had my room. "You left and came back. Maybe I'll do that, too."

“Yeah, I hope you can visit once you’re on your own, and your mom and dad are old.”

“No, I mean, like finish school and come back and raise a family here, too.”

Dad nodded, understanding, but frowned. There was pain behind his eyes. It was a similar paleness to his eyes when I asked about Roy, Jr. “I hope you have many more opportunities than your mom and I had.”

“You were gone for a long time. You had a life apart from this town. Why did you come back if you don’t think I should stay here, too?” My question held an edge of accusation.

Dad diverted his gaze while he formulated an answer. He’d felt the accusation, too. “We didn’t have the same opportunities,” he almost whispered. His words were spoken clearly but softly like he didn’t want anyone else to hear them. I wondered if he didn’t want Mom to overhear our conversation.

“But why?” I pressed.

He returned his gaze to mine and then tilted his head and gestured with his chin for me to move closer. I stepped forward and leaned across the counter of the bar to hear him better. He took a deep, cleansing breath before he began.

"Things didn't go according to our plan. After you came, we finished school. That's not easy to do with a baby. You were easy, but everything else was hard. I got a job, but that fell through before you were two. That same scenario played out a few more times. Your mom finished school as soon as she could, but then we found out she was pregnant again. Every time we'd think we were getting our heads above water, we'd be knocked down. We were in so much debt from school and medical expenses. Your mom had three more miscarriages. It took its toll."

"Why did you keep trying to have another baby?"

Dad scoffed. "We weren't *trying,* Chris. Sometimes things just happen, even when you're trying to prevent them. Your mom was on birth control, we used every form of contraception we knew. Barring abstinence, every other winter, your mom got pregnant. She'd carry the baby a few months and then miscarry in the spring. It took its toll on her.

"Then we got word that my dad was ill. His health declined rapidly. My mom's death soon followed his. We inherited the house and thought it might be a good time to return, make a fresh start. Your mom miscarried again twice more before we had Jesse. I don't know how much you remember about that time. She stayed in bed a lot. Her health didn't improve until he was born. Being back home made it easier. I wonder what it would have been like had we returned sooner. We were stubborn. Sometimes, you're just grounded better in one place than another."

"Do you think that will happen to me?"

"What?" Dad asked.

"Being able to live away from here."

"I don't think you'll have any problem, son. You weren't born here. It's different; we belong here." He sounded so resigned, not disappointed, just accepting like he didn't have a choice.

Without his knowing it, he'd confirmed everything Jason had told me in the church basement. My parents were under the same curse as Tia and the rest of our town. I wondered if Mom and Dad's warnings were because they were a part of the whole deal. Jesse was a victim of it all, too.

Sensing that our conversation was over, I turned to go back to my room. "Goodnight, Dad. See you in the morning."

"Chris," my dad began, "we've got your best interests at heart. You know that, right?"

I nodded. "Yes, sir. Night, Dad."

"Goodnight, son. I love you."

"Love you, too, Dad."

My belly was fuller than my head, and still, I couldn't sleep. I rolled over and unwrapped the Bible from Mr. Roy. It was considerably smaller than the version in his map room. I flipped open the worn leather cover. The pages were thinner than Mr. Roy's, and the print was small. I pilfered in my drawer and found an old pair of reading glasses that had belonged to my grandfather. It made concentrating at that hour and in dim light easier.

I opened it to Genesis. It made sense to begin at the beginning and work my way to the end. I'd read several chapters already, but I just thought it might be best to start on page one and read it like any other book I owned. I don't know how long I read, but I drifted off to sleep somewhere in Exodus.

My alarm went off before the sun. I cursed and rolled over, exhausted. I hit snooze and tried to catch a few more minutes of sleep before I had to face the day.

I heard Mom in the kitchen. She was giving Dad explicit directions. "The boys will just have to eat cereal this morning. I wish I'd packed their lunches last night. No, I don't know when I'll be back." Then I heard Dad's muffled voice from their room. I couldn't make out what he said. Mom sounded like she agreed with something. "Yesterday was just too much for her. She had no business being there. She should have stayed home."

Then the phone rang. "Hello? How is she, Roy? She's settled?" Silence while she listened. "Okay, I will. I'll be there as soon as I can. No, I'll sit with her. Please don't worry about that. The boys will take care of it. Okay. Okay. No. Okay, bye."

They were talking about Miss Grace. I threw on some sweatpants and walked into the kitchen. Mom was frantically throwing our lunches together. "I've got that, Mom. Go. It sounds like they need you." My voice was deep from sleep.

She nodded her head and smiled, but there were tears in her eyes. "Make sure Jesse brushes his teeth before school."

"We've got it, Clara," Dad said as he came out of the bedroom. She grabbed her keys from the hook and picked up her purse from the counter. Dad put his hands on her shoulders to settle her. He looked into her eyes. "It's going to be okay. No matter the outcome, it's for the best." Her lip quivered, and she blinked hard to bat away the tears. She trusted my dad's words. He hugged her enough to encourage her to go but not long enough to allow her to break down in his arms.

"Bye, Chris. Thank you." I smiled back at her encouragingly like Dad.

We managed to eat breakfast and pack lunch, and Jesse even brushed his teeth. He and I had time to go by and feed Mr. Roy's animals. Dad said that they'd gotten a call from Mr. Roy to say Miss Grace had fallen. He wanted them to know that they were headed back to the hospital. Mom and Dad had gone over there and waited for the ambulance with them. I wondered how much sleep they'd gotten. He and I'd been up pretty late talking.

I took Jesse to school, which made me late to meet Tia at the bus. I ran into homeroom as the bell rang. I saw Tia later in class, but we didn't have any time to talk until lunch. I asked how she was.

"I'm okay." Her eyes were focused on mine. It took all I had not to kiss her and carry her from school like a caveman.

Just then, Jason and Sherry sat down at our table, Catherine, too. It suddenly felt crowded. Jason sat between Tia and a scowling Sherry. She didn't like it any more than I did.

To make conversation, I mentioned Miss Grace's fall. Tia was instantly concerned. "We need to go see her. Let's go after school."

Jason squirmed. "We have practice."

"Okay, after that," Tia conceded.

I tried to read Tia's expressions for the rest of the day. She seemed preoccupied, which made sense given our current state of overload, but I didn't want to frighten her with all of my stuff, too. I wasn't sure when we'd have our next opportunity to be alone and talk.

Jason was edgy all during practice. He was on pins and needles like something was going to crush him at any moment. Coach sensed our lack of focus on the plays and got onto Jason a few times for wobbly passes and missed receivers. I finally pushed Jason aside, lifting him by his shoulder pads. "Dude! Focus! Coach will have us running if we don't straighten up. I don't want to add to my day." He heard the frustration and exhaustion I'd concealed all day.

"Sorry, man. She's been back less than a week, and my mind's all over the place."

"We'll talk about it later! Keep your head in the present!" I said through clenched teeth before I released him forcefully. He straightened his pads with a jerk. He didn't like it when I touched him. Coach blew his whistle. He glared at us, wondering if we'd start off our senior season as roughly as we'd started out our junior year.

We hustled back onto the line like soldiers, focused on the rest of the practice. Jason managed to get his shit together. He was the quarterback, and we needed his direction and leadership on the field.

CHAPTER 29

I showered and dressed. I didn't want to go straight to the hospital after practice. Those odors wouldn't help anyone get better. Jason was going to run by his house and then go back by Tia's to pick her up.

I knocked lightly on Miss Grace's door before I entered. Mom opened the door and placed her finger over her lips to signal me to be quiet. She stepped out into the hall to hug me and talk without disturbing Miss Grace.

"Thank you for coming. Did Dad call you?" I shook my head.

"How is she?" I asked in a whisper.

"She's sleeping. Mr. Roy, too. They've had a long night." I nodded. We all had. "She broke her hip. They'll do surgery in the morning. She was in so much pain. Thankfully, they've managed to sedate her enough to rest." Mom looked so tired. I wondered if she'd gotten any sleep at all.

"Do you need me to do anything?" I asked.

“I’d love to take a shower and change clothes. I think I’ll stay here tonight so Mr. Roy can sleep.”

“I can stay until you get back,” I offered.

“That would be wonderful,” she sighed. She patted my cheek affectionately. “You’re a good boy.” Then she chuckled and shook her head, “You aren’t a *boy* anymore, are you?” Her eyes glistened with motherly indulgence. She blinked and brought herself back to the present. “I’ll drive Mr. Roy home and bring him back, but he might want his truck,” Mom speculated. “Miss Grace is heavily medicated. She’ll sleep, but I know Roy won’t leave her unless someone is here with her. He’ll trust you.” She turned, and I followed her into Miss Grace’s room.

The elderly woman was in bed, connected to an IV and other monitors. Her breaths were slow and steady, and her eyes were closed. Mom placed her hands tenderly on Mr. Roy’s arm. Waking, he sat up in the recliner and cleared his throat. He scratched at his scruffy beard and took in his environment. His eyes went straight to Miss Grace.

“Any changes?” he asked.

Mom shook her head. “No, Chris is here, and he can stay with her while I go home and shower and change. Would you like me to take you home to do the same? You can get your truck, too.”

Mr. Roy rubbed his chest and stood, tucking in his shirt and straightening his belt. He pressed down his hair on the top and sides before he walked to the bed to approach his wife. It was like he was making himself presentable for her. She was oblivious to it, but that didn't matter to him.

He kissed her forehead and laid his hand over hers. "Christopher's here, Gracie. Sleep till I get back; I won't be long," he whispered. Mr. Roy's love for his wife was evident my entire life, but when he was worried about her, it was painful to watch their intimacy. They'd shared a long marriage and endured the loss of their son. I couldn't imagine the depth of their attachment. I believed I felt that way about Tia, but when I watched my parents and Mr. Roy and Miss Grace, I realized that my feelings were just that, feelings. They weren't actually grounded in anything real. No, that wasn't true, either. We were beginning to build trust during a time with an unknown outcome.

Mr. Roy turned and looked me in the eye. "Take good care of my girl. I'll be back soon." I nodded and said that I would. Mom patted my shoulder, and they were gone.

I looked around the hospital room. The shades were drawn, and the lamp over the bed didn't do much to illuminate the room. It was warm, but not stifling. I sat in the recliner where Mr. Roy had been sleeping. I leaned back and closed my eyes. I didn't want to fall asleep, but I couldn't help but rest my eyes in the quiet.

"Roy." I heard Miss Grace whisper. I jumped from the recliner and sat in the chair next to her bed.

"He went home to shower. It's me; it's Christopher." She was the only one, besides T, whoever called me by my full name.

"Christopher," she whispered and nodded her head ever-so-slightly. Her eyes fluttered open. "Is Tiana with you?"

"No, ma'am. She wanted to come and see you; she's on her way."

"Oh, Tiana, my precious, precious Tiana. My Roy should have been there. He would have loved her so much."

"Mr. Roy is good to all of us," I agreed.

"My little Roy never knew her." She was confused and medicated and mixing different children. "She's got you, though; you'll love her and take care of her." She shuddered. I leaned in and took the old woman's hand. It was cold and frail. "They thought they could trick us, you know, but we weren't so easily deceived," she almost giggled. "We figured it out." Her tone was giddy. "They came back with a baby. Ha! Like they could deny us our kin." Miss Grace's bright blue eyes opened wide, and she took hold of my hand forcefully. I was surprised by her strength. "Protect her, Christopher. You're the only one. Don't let them take her." She was frighteningly insistent. "You can change all of this, Christopher. You were intended for it."

I didn't know what to say. I didn't know what to do. Miss Grace's frail hand held mine in a fierce grip. "Promise, me, Christopher. Promise me!"

"Yes, ma'am, I will. I promise. I will protect her," I assured her in a whisper. I would have agreed to almost anything to get her to settle back down, but what she pressed upon me wasn't hard to promise. It was what I wanted more than anything. I wanted to love Tia, protect her, keep her safe.

Just then, Tia walked in. The room was illuminated by the lights from the hallway. Miss Grace's eyes eased, and her relief at seeing Tia mirrored my own. We were both drawn to her. I was relieved that I wouldn't be the only one there to witness Miss Grace's medicated babble. She was talking out of her head.

Miss Grace released me and lifted her hand in Tia's direction. I saw Jason leaning against the wall in the hallway. He didn't look like he wanted to come in.

"Tiana," Miss Grace whispered. Tia went straight to Miss Grace and took her hand. T leaned her head over and placed her face against the old woman's palm. "Oh, dear, my heart," Miss Grace muttered affectionately. Now she clung to Tia, but not with the same insistence as she'd clung to me.

"Miss Grace, I'm so sorry you're here. Are you in any pain?"

"No, dear, not now. Tiana Evelynne," she whispered wistfully. "That's my name, too. Grace Evelynne Carson," she said in a childlike voice. "Sally was so sweet to remember me. Binding your name with mine. You have her eyes. You both got your mothers' eyes." She looked at the two of us. "We thought we lost you. We thought we'd be denied. They just thought…." Her voice trailed off.

Mr. Roy rushed in and looked shocked at what he'd overheard. "Gracie!" he exclaimed in a whisper.

"No, Roy. She needs to know, and I won't keep silent any longer. They can't hurt us anymore. They took our Roy, but they can't keep her. They took our home, but I'll be damned if I let them take her, too. You know it, Roy. You know it!"

"Gracie, please. Please don't. I can't bear it," he begged.

"Roy, I have nothing else. Please, let me pass it on. If she plans to fight, she needs my blessing."

Tears pooled in Mr. Roy's eyes and threatened to spill over, but his eyes never left his wife's. Their eyes locked, and Mr. Roy looked defeated like he couldn't refuse her, even in her weakened state. After a brief consideration, he nodded once. Miss Grace sighed in relief and rested her head fully into her pillow.

Mr. Roy turned his gaze toward Tia. "Tiana, Gracie would like to give you something. She doesn't believe she'll survive the surgery and wants to give you a blessing. Would that be okay with you? She cares very deeply for you, and it would give her a sense of peace." Tia had been looking at Miss Grace while she and Mr. Roy exchanged their words, but now her gaze was on me.

Tia nodded cautiously. Mr. Roy placed Miss Grace's hands over Tia's. Tia sat perfectly still; her eyes lowered humbly onto Miss Grace's hand. "Mothers and fathers and children share a bond, but a blessing from your grandparent is powerful, too." Miss Grace's voice was breathy, but insistent once again. She was determined. "You, my child, the child of my child, receive my blessing and my strength. May all my love fall into your heart, and may your life be long and prosperous. May all my days be added to yours. Take from me all that I have left to give." She barely paused before she said, "Christopher." I was surprised to hear my name.

"Yes, ma'am." She reached for me. I was compelled to give her my hand again. She placed my hand over Tia's too. I felt the familiar power in our touch, but under Miss Grace's hands, I couldn't tell where Tia began and I ended. Miss Grace's hands were warm and heavy. I was held captivated, rooted in the spot next to the hospital bed.

"You have the power to release her. Give her a son. You can set her free," Miss Grace whispered.

Tia's head popped up, and she gasped, understanding washed over us both. What was she saying? What was she talking about? Give Tia a son? The old woman was mad, crazy!

Tiana looked petrified, but she didn't deny the woman's ramblings. Miss Grace was spent but managed one last squeeze of our hands. Her breaths were labored, and her eyes closed before she released us.

"That's enough," Mr. Roy said and settled his wife, placing her hands at her side and adjusting her blanket and pillow.

When the woman was settled, Tia looked at me with wide eyes. I had nothing to say. I reached for her, but she jerked away. She wrapped her arms around herself like she'd suddenly gotten a chill. I stepped forward, but she bolted from the room. Jason looked to me in question as T ran past him. Jason scowled and then followed her down the long, hospital corridor. I glanced back toward Mr. Roy. He patted his wife's hand gently; she'd fallen back into a restful sleep.

"Stay," Mr. Roy commanded. "Please," he amended.

I turned to face him, torn between what he might know and wanting to run after T. "Is it true? Is what she said true?" I asked. "Tia is your granddaughter?"

CHAPTER 30

Mr. Roy looked up at my questions and then back down at his wife. The woman was sleeping peacefully and, from the look of her, might never wake. She wasn't clinging to anyone and saying crazy things. She wasn't telling me to father a child and save a girl, the girl I loved.

Mr. Roy's request to stay fixed my feet, and I was rooted in the spot, both curious and commanded. I could barely pivot on the spot. I waited for his reply. Finally, he tucked Miss Grace in and kissed her cheek. The gesture was painfully loving, and compassion replaced every other emotion that had crashed over me. Fear and frustration forged a familiar friendship, and I found myself a little dizzy when they left me and allowed softer feelings to wash over me.

"Come; sit." Mr. Roy gestured toward the chair. I didn't want to sit; I wanted to run down the hall after T. I wanted to sleep. I wanted to escape this entire nightmare, but I sat just the same. Mr. Roy didn't mince words. He didn't hesitate. He forged in like he had rehearsed his speech and had been waiting for the perfect time to say it aloud. "Things aren't as they appear, Topher. It's complicated and wound up so tightly it will make your head spin. I can't say too much here," he whispered. "Give me a day or two and let things settle. Once she's on her way, I'll tell you everything you want to know."

"On her way, where?" I asked.

"To the great beyond. To heaven." He smiled meekly, and tears pooled in her eyes. "I know it's hard, but please be patient."

"I don't understand, Mr. Roy."

He stared at me for several moments. "You might keep telling yourself that for a while more, but deep down, you know. Deep down, you already have the answers."

"I don't know shit," I argued and stood in a huff.

"Be patient, son."

"That's easy for you to say," I retorted, but instantly regretted my words. Nothing was easy for him to say as he waited for his wife to die. "I'm sorry, Mr. Roy. That wasn't called for. What can I do?" I asked, remembering my manners and my promise to stay until Mom returned.

"Go, see to her. Comfort her. She's probably more confused than you are."

"What about Miss Grace?"

"Gracie'll be fine. It's just a matter of time." His gaze returned to her. "Leave us. I'd like to be alone with my wife."

He didn't see her as the old, wrinkly woman that lay in the room with us. He saw her as the young, vibrant woman he'd fall in love with so many years ago. He saw her with the same loving affection as I did Tia. I wondered if I'd always see T like I did at that moment. I had a feeling I always would.

"Will I see her again?" I asked.

"Not likely, unless you plan to come back tonight or early in the morning."

My heart ached at his words. "I guess I should say goodbye then."

"Reckon you should. I'll be doing the same." His voice broke on the last word.

I walked toward the bed and kissed Miss Grace's cheek. She was the picture of peace. "Thank you, Miss Grace. I'll do my best." I whispered the promise over her, and tears stung my eyes. They weren't just tears of sadness; they were tears of anger and fear. I wanted to turn and shake Mr. Roy until his teeth rattled. I wanted to scream at Miss Grace to wake up and tell me everything. It was no use. I would just have to wait.

Once I was outside, I didn't see Mom's car in the parking lot. I texted both Jason and T. No reply. I drove by both of their houses. Tia's house was dark. Jason's car wasn't in either of their driveways. I texted them again. When I didn't get a reply, I drove around until I found Jason's car parked at the edge of the trees behind Carson Chapel. I should have known.

I opened the old door and saw that the basement light was on. I took each step as quietly as I could. I wasn't sure I would be welcomed after what happened at the hospital. The focus and drive to find Tia relieved some of the edginess, but the anger and frustration at Mr. Roy and Miss Grace returned as soon as I saw Jason's arms wrapped around Tia. He was stroking her hair and rocking her gently. He was soothing her with quiet, shushing sounds. It took every amount of effort not to rip his arms off at their sockets; I was out of control.

I stormed down the last few steps, and my shoulders blocked the light overhead, casting them both in shadow. I took several deep breaths to relax, but they sounded more like the huffs of a raging bull in a pen before it impales the bullfighter. Jason lifted his eyes toward me. Tia didn't move. Jason's expression was flat without any emotion or fear. My expression was daring.

"Tiana, Topher is here," he said quietly. She stiffened in his arms. She shook her head in his chest, refusing to acknowledge me. Jason wrapped his arms around her protectively, *lovingly*.

"Let her go," I demanded. My voice was deep and low.

Jason's expression mirrored my challenge. "Can't. Won't." There was no apology or remorse in his tone.

I could make him, but the sound of Tia crying stopped me. He wouldn't let her go as long as she clung to him. I stepped back and ran my hands over my head and through my hair. Her face was hidden, but her sobs grew in intensity, verging on hysteria. I couldn't stand it. My response came out in a long, guttural bellow of frustration. It was loud and reverberated throughout the small basement. The earthen walls absorbed the volume but seemed to return the weight of my emotions ten-fold.

I covered my face with my hands and pulled at the tension with my fingers as they traced down my eyes and cheeks, finally resting them in fists at my jaw. It was then that Tia turned to face me. I blinked to refocus my gaze. Her eyes were wide, rimmed in red from her tears. Neither of us moved. Mr. Roy was right; there would be no more playing ignorant. I did know; deep down, the answers were already there in Tia. They always had been.

I knelt down in front of her, begging for her mercy. "T," I began in an apologetic tone, but she shook her head and moved to welcome me. I bowed my head, placing it in her lap, and wrapped my arms around her. Her knees were held securely in my chest. Her hands cupped my head and neck, and I felt her tears fall onto my cheek.

"Oh, T, I love you." The desperation could be felt in my sigh. I was kneeling in supplication to her. "I'm here, alright?"

She didn't reply, but her body moved like she was nodding. She moved one of her hands, and it sounded like she'd covered her mouth to muffle another sob. I didn't know what else to say. We had both been affected by Miss Grace's blessing over T. The news that she was their granddaughter had come as a huge shock. She'd run away before that was confirmed. If Roy Jr. was her father, then who was the man she'd lived with all her life? Who was Sally? Tia's mom was Rebecca.

"It's true, you know," T whispered.

She didn't say it like a question. I nodded my head in her lap, but I didn't know which part she was talking about. Was she talking about her parentage or the fact that I was supposed to get her pregnant? I didn't move or release her. It felt too good to be close again. Holding her settled me and seemed to calm her as well. When my legs went numb, I gently pulled her from the bench onto my lap. There, I could wrap her up completely. She rubbed her cheek on my shoulder and nuzzled her face under my chin. With closed eyes, the dank basement and Jason's presence faded away.

I hadn't taken the time to eat after practice. I thought I'd get something at the hospital or eat when I left. Odd that I wasn't hungry at all. The exhaustion I'd felt from the night before and the exertion of the day didn't matter, either. At that moment, only Tia mattered, only holding her mattered.

Since Jason wasn't as focused on consoling T anymore, he got bored. I had to give him some credit that he'd stayed as long as he did. He stood as if to go. "I'm starving," he commented, stirring me from my deep state of peace. Holding Tia was the best feeling. "It's nearly nine. We need to go, and I want to call Sherry."

Tia stirred in my arms and nodded her assent. "He's right. I'm tired, too, and I can't concentrate anymore. I can't string any of the jumble of thoughts racing through my mind right now. I just want to sleep."

I agreed with her logic, but I didn't want to let her go. "I plan to talk to Mr. Roy soon. Do you want to be there when I do?"

Tia shrugged. "Maybe. I don't know what I want right now," she whispered.

I helped her to her feet and gave her one last hug before I watched Jason guide her up the stairs. Once they'd made it to the top, I pulled the string over my head and remained in total darkness for the time it took me to make it out the door.

CHAPTER 31

Miss Grace made it through surgery. She was weak, but everyone seemed hopeful that she'd make a full recovery. I didn't go back to the hospital, but Mom stayed up there the whole time. With Jesse in tow, I tended to their animals and watered their fall garden. Jesse picked some carrots, zucchini, and radishes before we headed home. With Mom preoccupied, we were left to our own devices for supper. We managed canned soup and a salad. At least I remembered to feed the kid vegetables.

Dad ate at the hospital with Mom and stayed pretty late. This continued through the weekend. Miss Grace hung onto life by a string. I couldn't go back to the hospital and see her like that and pretend with my parents there. I waited patiently under the guise of taking care of Jesse.

Each night that Mom and Dad were away, Jesse and I did our homework together at the kitchen table. We ate simple suppers. I would probably never be as good a cook as Mom, but Jesse was satisfied with grilled cheeses, hamburgers, canned soup, and fresh vegetables from their garden. I made sure he took a bath, and instead of reading him a story like Mom, he insisted on reading to me. Jesse went to bed pretty early, so I had time to kill. Sure that Jesse was sound asleep, I continued to read the Bible Mr. Roy had given me.

I read about a god who blessed his chosen people. I read about a god who made a blood covenant through sacrifice. The idea of Old Testament covenant and circumcision and animal sacrifices didn't sound that far-fetched when considering all the crazy stuff I'd witnessed over the summer. Later, I read about detestable gods like Baal and Molech. The followers of these gods sacrificed their children. I slammed the book closed in frustration. Mr. Roy said that the Bible gave him a great deal of comfort. So far, I hadn't found much encouragement from the beginning of the book. Those people were ignorant and repeatedly made stupid choices. I didn't see how knowing about their defeats and struggles could help me at all.

Tia didn't get off the bus on Monday morning. "She's not feeling well," Catherine explained. I texted Tia all weekend, but she hadn't replied. This continued for three more days, and it was driving me crazy that she wasn't at school.

"Is she really sick, or is she avoiding me?" I asked Jason at practice.

His expression was blank. "Don't take it so personally, Topher. She's not faking if that's what you're implying."

"I'm not *implying* anything. I just want to see her and know she's okay."

"Give her some time," he huffed in frustration. Jason reconsidered his tone, "I have to bring her some homework after practice. I'll ask her to text you, okay?" I nodded begrudgingly.

That night, I texted Tia again. No reply. I read some more and fell asleep with the Bible on my chest. The kitchen phone rang in the middle of the night. Well, it felt like the middle of the night, but it was super early in the morning. It rang and rang. When no one answered it, I stumbled into the kitchen. Good news never comes from a call at that hour.

"Hello?" I sounded half asleep. I cleared my throat in case I had to say something else.

"Chris, it's Dad."

"Hey," I replied without thinking and rubbed my eyes. "Is everything okay?"

He hesitated before he replied. I already knew; he didn't have to say anything. "It's over, son. We'll be heading home once they take her, but that could be hours. I wanted you to know that I wasn't home and that you'd need to get Jesse to school. I'm sorry I had to wake you like this, but Mr. Roy needs us right now. I wasn't sure when I'd be able to call again, and you didn't answer your phone."

"Yes, sir. I'll take care of it. How are Mom and Mr. Roy?"

"They're fine. She passed peacefully."

My mind had been distracted since T's return, but her absence from class made it even harder to pay attention. That was until something my teacher said during world history. We were studying ancient civilizations, and I was listening enough to take random notes. My ears peaked with interest when he mentioned ancient gods.

"Some are so ancient that they don't even have names. It was believed that they controlled the cycles of nature, crops, livestock, and land. Before science discovered the truth behind these phenomena, the nature of these gods helped humans understand fertility, chaos, and order. Every major civilization personified the unknown."

I sat up and listened intently. I'd read about those very things on my own, and Jason said that everything was linked to the land and Tia. My pen flew across the page, taking copious notes.

"There were storm gods who brought the rain and thunder. There were seasons and festivals devoted to each god. Fertility was of major concern for these people. Since women give birth to children, it was also believed that they had the power to spread their cycles of fertility onto the land. Cultic rituals perpetuated these beliefs. Animal and child sacrifices have been a central, unifying factor among the strongest and most influential civilizations. Virgins were revered for their purity and sacrificed most often."

During study hall, I looked up each ancient god our teacher had mentioned to discern the truth between what I was reading every night in the Bible and what we were studying about ancient gods in world history. Molech of the Old Testament was condemned as the pinnacle of wickedness. *Whoa!* His followers burned children as a sacrifice. No wonder he was called detestable in nearly every mention of him. He wasn't the only god who encouraged child sacrifice, but still, that, in my opinion, was beyond detestable. I also couldn't get the images from my dreams of Tia encircled by candles out of my mind.

I realized that there might be more to the shadow I'd seen lurking around Tia's aunt's house. Although it didn't resemble any of the statues and figures that I'd found in my research, it felt equally ominous. I couldn't help but think we were dealing with something powerful. I lifted my eyes from my research and looked around the library. I sat in a corner and had a pretty good view of the entire space. My classmates and teammates looked the same and seemed normal, but they were clueless.

I closed my eyes and rubbed my temples. The weight of everything came crashing down. I was suddenly overcome by the sadness of Miss Grace's passing and hoped that it wouldn't be too much longer before I would have an opportunity to talk with Mr. Roy. On top of everything else, I desperately wanted to see Tia. No, it went beyond that. I wanted to be with her. I hated being separated. I lowered my head onto the table in front of me; the exhaustion that I'd been fighting for days crushed me.

I jumped and reacted to a punch in my shoulder. I fisted my hands and turned to fight. I staggered back, and the chair fell onto the floor with an echoing thud. "Dude!" Jason whispered and stepped back with his hands raised in surrender. "I've been looking all over for you!"

"Sorry," I muttered and relaxed my hands before I ran them through my hair. "What time is it?" I blinked hard to get my bearings.

"It's last period. You missed lunch and class."

"Yeah, sorry."

"Don't apologize to me. You missed a pop quiz. I came to find you when you didn't show up for football. You're lucky it's raining. Coach gave me a pass to come and find you."

"It's raining?" That surprised me.

“Yeah, it doesn’t look like it’ll let up any time soon. What’s up with you?”

“Tired. Really tired.”

“You look worse than tired, Topher. You getting sick?” He lifted his hand like he was going to check my forehead for a fever. I reared back and bristled. It was out of character for him. He corrected himself and thought better of it. “You need to go before I get all maternal and shit,” he chuckled. “I’ll tell Coach you went home to rest.”

CHAPTER 32

My shoulders and neck ached, but I didn't feel feverish or sick. The aches were most likely a result of sleeping for a couple of hours, hunched over a desk. I'd slept through several bells and the changing of classes and students in the library. My brain was still foggy, and if I didn't know better, I would have suspected that Mom had infiltrated the library with her lavender.

The sky was dark and heavy. I hunched my shoulders and jogged toward my truck in the light rain. The cab was dry, but I caught a chill as soon as the air blew through the vents. Rainfall was unheard of during harvest time, but the clouds didn't look like they'd be passing anytime soon. I was thankful for a break for the afternoon, but the weather didn't do anything for my melancholy. The music that played as soon as I put my truck in drive didn't either.

I was starving since I'd slept through lunch, but I thought it would be best to go straight to Mr. Roy and Miss Grace's. I shook my head. It wasn't Miss Grace's anymore. The thought sent a pang of sadness through me; I would miss her terribly.

I felt another painful pang as I pulled into their gravel driveway and saw Mr. Roy's truck. The house looked unoccupied. Mr. Roy was in the barn or the party house. I sat for a few seconds with my arms over the top of the steering wheel, considering if I should just leave him be since his wife was barely gone. That was a stupid thought. Unless he was asleep, he'd heard the rumble of my truck.

I grabbed a baseball cap from the backseat and went straight to the barn. The animals were already inside. Mr. Roy must have put them in with the weather. I refilled their water and laid some fresh hay over the floor of the stalls. I topped off their food bins, too. I hesitated, torn between returning to my truck or checking on Mr. Roy. I sighed, resigned to find the old man. I wouldn't stay long, and I wouldn't press him for answers if I could help it.

"Foul weather," Mr. Roy said without pretense. He stood outside under the soffit of the party house. He was protected from the rain, but I knew he'd been watching me.

I turned and acknowledged his comment. "Yes, sir."

"Come in before you're soaked through." I followed him and took off my wet cap and slapped it across my thigh to remove the drops that had gathered on its crown. "Coffee?" he asked.

"Sure," I replied. I didn't know what to say to a man whose wife just died and especially to a man whom I had wanted desperately to talk to for the better part of a week.

He walked toward the coffee maker and removed two mugs from the hooks behind it. The pot looked cold and empty, and I didn't smell any coffee brewing. He then opened the side cabinet and poured us each a whisky. I wondered if *coffee* would be the code word for scotch.

"How are you doing?" I asked tentatively, taking the mug from his hands. I sniffed the strong alcohol letting the heavy scent of the liquid warm my nostrils before I took a sip. It tasted good and hit a spot that had probably needed a good stiff drink all day.

Mr. Roy shrugged and took a long swig from his mug. He exhaled before he spoke. "I've had better days, and to be honest, I've had worse. I find some consolation in the fact that at least I was prepared for this one. She went peacefully and didn't suffer. That's the best I could hope for."

He took another big swig and drained his mug. He poured himself another shot and swished it around in the bottom of the cup and watched it swirl around for a few seconds before he took a sip. I was relieved that he wasn't drinking it straight from the bottle.

I took another sip to loosen my tongue and let the warmth spread down through my chest. It felt terrific. Mr. Roy lifted the bottle again and raised it to offer me some more. I nodded and put my mug out for him to pour. His hands didn't shake; he was surprisingly settled.

"Can I do anything for you?" I asked.

He didn't answer me. It was as though he hadn't heard my question. "How is Tiana?" he asked.

I took another sip before I answered. "I don't know. I haven't seen her."

Mr. Roy looked concerned. "Is she okay?"

I nodded and took another sip. He lifted the bottle to offer me more, but I shook my head. "She hasn't been to school all week. Catherine says she's not feeling well. Jason says she's not faking. She won't reply to my texts."

"Have you called her or gone by her house?"

"No, sir. I don't think she wants to see me."

"That might be true, but I'd wager she's not sure what she wants at the moment. She's got to be so confused. Gracie couldn't contain it anymore." He shook his head and held his cup with both hands. His expression was hard to read, but his words were so heavy. We each took sips from our mugs, and I waited in the silence between us. The rain fell steadily on the tin roof over our heads. It was settling and soothing.

"Mr. Roy, I have so many questions. I don't want to pressure you or anything, but I'm ready to talk whenever you are." I opened my throat and swallowed the last of the liquid, draining my mug in one swig. I didn't want to waste any more time with sips and warm tingles. The dark liquid burned all the way through me in a flash. The fire flowed all the way down between my legs and thighs and anchored my feet securely. I felt emboldened.

Mr. Roy nodded once but didn't say anything. He stroked his scruffy, gray beard and then scratched his head. "Alright, then. It's time." I was surprised that he'd decided so quickly. I figured it would be days or weeks before he was ready to talk. He turned toward the door to the garage. "Let's go."

I set my mug on the counter and followed Mr. Roy. I was right to assume he'd lead me to his room. He went to reach for some old metal lawn chairs that were hanging on nails on the wall, but I leaned over him and reached them without effort. He found the key and unlocked the door. I followed him.

The room was dark, but he didn't turn on the light. Instead, Mr. Roy entered the darkness and lit a candle on the altar. The swipe of the match across the sandpaper crackled the fire to life. In the sparse light, I opened the chairs and secured them for the two of us to sit. Mr. Roy bowed his head toward the altar reverently before he turned to me. He muttered words under his breath and moved his hand in a motion from his forehead down to his chest in a sweeping motion. I was impatient to get the conversation started but waited, just the same. It felt like forever before Mr. Roy sat down. His joints creaked like the old metal chairs.

Once he was settled, he took a deep breath and began. "Sally Reynolds is Tiana's mother." Mr. Roy lowered his forearms onto his knees and leaned forward, bracing himself. He'd held that secret a long time, and it was as if the words spoken aloud had weakened him. He steepled his fingertips and placed them at his lips. He lifted his eyes to mine; their steely blue was piercing.

"And Roy, Jr. is her father," I added. Mr. Roy nodded solemnly.

"What else do you know?" he asked pointedly.

"Not much. Just what Jason's told me. He says Tia's been chosen by the elders; he's her *protector*," I said disdainfully.

"That seems about right," Mr. Roy said. "Gracie was beside herself when Roy, Jr. was chosen as the protector. *What an honor!*" he exclaimed sarcastically. "What a curse, you mean! We thought for sure it would be Robert, your dad," Mr. Roy added for emphasis like maybe there might have been another Robert. I was surprised by that. "Your dad was the most likely choice. He was from a good family, and they'd been chosen as protectors for generations, but Robert was just a little too old. The elders had surely misread the signs. When they came to us and said Roy, Jr. had been chosen, I denied it. It was a fluke. I told them it was a huge mistake. Gracie was sure that it was a sign that I'd been accepted, too."

I looked questioningly. "What would that have to do with you?"

"My family, the Buchanan family, was one of the founding families. When they ran my granddaddy out of town, there weren't any more of us. After I returned, and we had Roy, Jr., all of the founding families were once again in residence. Gracie was sure that this would bring about a change." He scoffed; a sardonic chuckle left his chest. "It brought about *change* for sure.

"As was expected, Roy, Jr. and Sally were inseparable. He did his duty. He followed the rules. But soon after her seventeenth birthday, the two of them couldn't help themselves. They had always been friends; their mommas had been the best of friends, too. No one thought anything of their closeness. Gracie and I noticed their glances and the way their hands lingered whenever they had an opportunity to touch.

"A part of me wants to think they were innocent to the consequences, but I think it was the times and their rebellious spirits. They became exclusive and secretive. We should have known they were up to no good.

"Grace loved our son with a passion, and sometimes we're blinded by passion. I sure as hell was," he admitted derisively. "She was indulgent and got lost in their romance. Rather than setting limits on our boy and letting the elders know what was happening, she did what she did to solve every problem she ever encountered. She went to her library and started reading. If the tomato leaves had spots, she found a book. If the candy coating on her apples didn't set quite right, she'd dig until she found a recipe that would set in any weather. Her son had heartache, and she felt confident she could find the answer in a book. When she didn't, she began writing one of her own."

Mr. Roy stood and walked toward the altar. He walked around it, and from the other side of it, I heard the soft creaking of hinges from the shadows. "It was doomed from the beginning. They didn't understand the consequences." He returned and offered me an old book. His gnarled hand shook as he offered it to me.

I opened the cover and recognized Miss Grace's elegant script. When I was in elementary school, I had the hardest time learning cursive. My hands could do all sorts of things: throw and catch a ball, hammer a nail, pull weeds, and haul stuff. But when it came to penmanship, I knew it had to be the worst kind of kid torture. It was agony holding a pencil and making all of those curves and loops connect. Every afternoon for months, Miss Grace sat with me at their kitchen table and made me practice, repeating the movements over and over again.

"You'll thank me one day," she'd said. "It's important for a man to have a practiced hand. You don't want to be misjudged for a sloppy signature. People notice the little things, Christopher. It takes discipline and practice, but you can do it."

She was right. Thanks to her, my penmanship had been complemented by teachers. They thanked me for the neatness and ease of reading my essays. Her words jumped from the page, and I recognized my own *e*'s and *d*'s and the angle of the *i*'s. My lips couldn't help but go up in a slight grin.

"What is this?" I asked.

"It's everything Grace thought she knew. She desperately wanted to help the two of them find a way to be together. She read every old document, book, and newspaper the library held. When her sources ran out, she interviewed the old folks. She convinced them she wanted to write a thorough history of the town, documenting every detail. No one questioned her because, after all, Roy, Jr. had been chosen as the protector. The old women were all gossipy in nature and had a grand time being honored to tell all that they knew.

"I don't know if it will be of any help to you. It surely wasn't for Sally and our Roy. If anything, it just perpetuated the problem and passed it down to the child they so selfishly created." Mr. Roy hung his head and shook it. He exhaled like the weight of the world was pressing him down. His own words had pained him. He reconsidered, "They weren't selfish; they were human, fallible, and hopelessly in love." He raised his head and looked me straight in the eyes. "No matter what, I'll never be able to deny the love I have for Tiana. Watching her grow up has been one of my greatest joys." He gestured toward the photos of Tia. Tears pooled in his eyes.

I swallowed hard. The weight I felt was more than the book in my lap. "What am I supposed to do with *this*?" I asked, gesturing to the book.

"Read it. Study it. Gracie felt confident that it held the answers. She traced all the lineage and history of the families. Somewhere, she found some obscure scrap of something that made her believe that a son would make all the difference. Obviously, Tiana wasn't the son they'd hoped for. Only recently, she regained hope for Tiana."

"Does Tia know that?" I asked.

"No. She doesn't know anything; she's a complete victim. She'll know more before her final summer, but by then it's too late. She's claimed and won't have a choice. You might be the only one who can give her that."

"So, I'm just supposed to have sex with her and get her pregnant? That's stupid. You're telling me to take your granddaughter's virginity?"

"It's better than the alternative." His gaze was steely again. I supposed it was better than her being taken away and being sacrificed and tortured, but it was unbelievable.

"How can I be sure it'll work? No one can guarantee a boy or a girl. It's a 50/50 chance!" I stood in a huff and tossed the book into the metal chair. It skidded slightly across the concrete floor. "I don't know if I'm willing to do that. What if just makes everything worse?"

Mr. Roy shrugged. "I can't answer that, but I do know that you'll regret not trying."

The old man was right, and I would regret not doing everything within my power. I closed my eyes and took a deep breath. My neck was still stiff. I rolled my shoulders and rubbed the back of my neck. It felt hot again.

Mr. Roy seemed unphased by my outburst. Now that the secret was out, he just kept talking, telling me more of the story. “Just like you and Tiana, Sally and Roy, Jr. were the best of friends. Your mom and dad began dating, too, and the four of them were inseparable. Robert and Clara had plans to attend college, but Roy, Jr. stayed to be with Sally.

“I knew why he couldn’t leave, and before too long, Sally was pregnant. At that point, I suspect that your parents had hidden your mom’s condition for a few months, too.”

I scoffed and shook my head. It seemed like, once again, sex came into play. Tia and I had both been conceived out of wedlock. *Great!*

Mr. Roy hesitated. “What was that look for?”

I rolled my eyes. “Why couldn’t they just wait and do it right?”

“Who? Your parents?”

“Yes, my parents!” I answered defensively.

Mr. Roy’s eyes softened. “They did do it right.”

“Yeah, they got married and *made* it right, but wouldn’t it have been easier to just start out that way?” My voice sounded edgy. I didn’t know why, but it bothered me. It had most of my life. My parents loved each other, and I knew that, but there were times that I wondered if they would have ended up together had I not come along.

Mr. Roy nodded knowingly and furrowed his brow. "Topher, your parents asked me to marry them before they left together for school." I eyed him warily. Mr. Roy continued, "Your dad had already gone away a few months before. He didn't trust himself to be alone with Clara. He was a mess." Mr. Roy chuckled, remembering.

"He and Roy, Jr. walked out and met me in the field. The tractor had stalled, and I thought they were coming out to give me a hand. Little did I know what they were thinking. You were conceived legitimately, Topher. It may not have that much weight in today's culture, but it matters here. Your parents returned over the winter and couldn't hide your mom's state. They never came forward with the truth that they'd already married, so her parents made a fuss and forced them to marry in town before they went back to school. I don't think they wanted to get me into trouble. I married them before they left. You didn't know that."

Obviously, I didn't. "No, sir. I only knew they married later, but I didn't have any details."

"It was quite the scandal. After the public ceremony, your mom and dad left and didn't return for a long time. They denied everything that was this town, but you'll need to ask them why they returned, what prompted that decision."

I already knew a little about that story from Dad. The rain fell harder on the metal roof. I wanted to go home, but I still had so many questions. "Mr. Roy, if Tia's parents are both dead and her parents aren't her parents, then who are they? Who are the people she lives with?"

"Samuel Reynolds is her uncle, Sally's older brother. He and left to go to nursing school and returned a few years later with a wife and a baby. It seemed probable, a likely scenario. The details were all kept hush-hush from us, and Gracie and I were in no condition to think otherwise. Sammy coming back with a baby didn't amount to a hill of beans to either one of us.

"As you know, Roy, Jr. was dead. His body was barely cold in the ground when our house caught fire. Gracie and I knew we were being punished. We lost everything."

"Why were you being punished? *Who* punished you?" I sat back down in the chair. There was too much to take standing.

"We never believed that our house burning was a coincidence. They'd burned my grandfather's church, so why wouldn't they burn a house? I could never prove if the crash that took Roy, Jr. was an accident. I want to think so, but I could never be sure. Sally was staying with her mother, and Roy, Jr. tried to get to her before the baby came. I don't know any of the particulars of that night. Gracie felt sure that Roy, Jr. was there for the birth. He would've had to have been to complete the blood covenant. Tiana's name proves that. I don't think any of them would have let her keep *Evelynne* had it not been so. Can't change a child's name once it's all done."

We sat there for a few moments in silence. The rain continued to sound overhead. "There's one more thing, Topher." I followed his gaze toward the map. "See that big, red dot?" I nodded. It was Aunt Trudy's house and where Tia was kept and tortured all summer. "That's where Tiana was born. Do you remember me telling you about when I met Gracie for the first time in the diner?" I nodded; I remembered that story well. "The other woman, the disapproving one who waited on me, was Gertrude Reynolds. Trudy isn't Tiana's aunt; she's her grandmother, Samuel and Sally's mother."

I squinted my eyes toward the red dot, considering. Nothing that Tia believed about herself or her family was true. It was all a big, fat lie. I couldn't take any more and stood to go. "Thank you, Mr. Roy," I said sincerely. He nodded slowly.

"Take care of that," he said, gesturing toward Miss Grace's book. I picked it up and felt the weight of it in my hand. I understood and turned to go.

CHAPTER 33

The rain fell for the rest of the day and into the night. I ate supper with my family, but they were solemn; no one attempted to make conversation. My parents were exhausted and grieving. The house was quiet and somber. Even Jesse sensed the weight and got ready for bed early and read himself to sleep.

I took a long, hot shower, fell into my bed, and crashed. I woke in the wee hours of the morning, drawn to Miss Grace's book. Maybe I was grieving, too, and wanted to reconnect with the woman who had helped raise me. I opened it and began reading. It was a collection of notes and detailed interviews. I spent time during the summer looking over the walls of Mr. Roy's room, and, other than the basic history of the town, his walls showed only what related to the Buchanan legacy. Miss Grace's book, though, gave details, juicy gossip, and insight into the history from a completely different perspective. I couldn't wait to share it with Jason and Tia. I hoped she'd be back at school in the morning.

When my alarm went off, I was still awake reading. I rubbed my eyes and dressed; I'd been up for hours. The rain continued in a fine mist. It was odd, given the season. The farmers cursed this kind of weather during planting and harvesting. If it lasted, it wouldn't be good for anyone.

When I arrived at school, I went directly to the bus stop. I was relieved to see Tia step down. The longing had been worse than the summer. "Tia?" I asked hesitantly.

She turned at the sound of her name, and her eyes caught mine. They were heavily lined and sultry. She blinked, and her long eyelashes went up at an angle with her smile.

"Good morning, Christopher," she said with amusement.

"Good morning," I stammered, half-expecting Tia to be overwhelmed and depressed, but she didn't look upset at all. She almost looked triumphant. "I texted you."

"I know; I read them."

"I worried about you all week."

"I know. Jason told me." Her tone was sweet and unassuming. She stepped toward me and placed her hand on my chest. I relaxed at her touch. "Thank you for being patient. I needed some time."

I covered her hand with mine and took in a deep breath. "I'm sorry."

"You have nothing to be sorry about," she whispered. "And who knows…," she began, but we were interrupted by Jason, who led Sherry by the hand.

Then, the bell rang. *Damn.* I couldn't catch a break with T. We went through our morning classes and met again at lunch. "I already know about Miss Grace. How is Mr. Roy?" she began in a compassionate tone.

I eyed her before I answered, unsure of what to make of the question. "He's okay. It's hard, of course, but I think he's relieved she's not suffering." She nodded and took a bite of her apple. The juice moistened her lips, and I salivated at the thought of kissing her again. I swallowed and shook off the thought before turning my attention back to the conversation. "How are *you* taking it?" She had to be feeling the loss as well; we all were.

Tia finished chewing her bite of the apple before she answered. "I'm fine, and I can easily accept the natural course of life and death. I'm delighted I knew her." Her eyes twinkled when she smiled at the memory. "It's the oddest thing; I knew she'd passed even before I heard the news. I woke up and felt a strange feeling right here." She touched her fingertips to the center of her chest between her breasts. She loved me very much." I nodded at that.

When Jason and Sherry arrived and sat down with us, I wanted to tell them about the book and everything that Mr. Roy had told me the afternoon before, but I couldn't. As we sat there eating, I wanted to take Tia's hand under the table, but I didn't have the opportunity. At one point, though, she scooted over on the bench and allowed her hip to touch mine. Our eyes met, and she winked. A rush of heat covered me. She bit her bottom lip, considering her next words.

"When may I see you?" she whispered.

I scanned through my day's obligations. "After practice."

"Where?"

"I can come by your house," I offered.

"No, that's not possible."

For privacy's sake, I considered the lake or even Anderson Field, but the misty rain from the morning persisted. "Can Jason bring you by the chapel?"

Jason turned slightly at the sound of his name and nodded once without diverting his eyes from Sherry. He was getting better at dividing his attention between the two girls in his life. One was based on undeniable attraction, and the other was purely obligation. I had to give him some credit. I only had one girl to balance, and she was driving me absolutely insane.

Coach had the entire team on the field in the rain. It wasn't cold or unpleasant, just annoying. No one dared complain since we'd gotten a reprieve the day before. In Coach's eyes, that was enough unscheduled rest. He had us running harder than usual like we'd all just come off a holiday and had to get back in shape.

He blew his whistle to signal for us to all huddle up. "Men, I've checked the forecast, and it's going to be an unseasonably rainy week." A few guys groaned under their breath. "Get used to it. Make sure your pads and helmet are dry each night. Your uniform, too. You smell bad enough without mildew, and you don't want to be chafing on top of everything else." He blew his whistle to end practice.

As we jogged back to the locker room in the rain, I asked Jason if he could stick around when he brought Tia. "Yeah, why? I figured you two preferred to be alone."

I shook my head. "It's not that. I have something that I want to show you."

On the way into the house, I stripped down in the laundry room and started a load. I ran through the kitchen in my underwear. I adjusted the backpack on my shoulder before I kissed Mom on the cheek. She was at the stove, making supper.

"Ugh!" she groaned, "You stink! How was practice?"

"Good. I'm going to shower. I'm meeting Jason," I said as I passed her.

"What about supper?" she hollered down the hall.

"May I have it to go?" I hollered back before I started the water.

"Am I feeding Jason, too?" she asked.

"I don't know."

After my shower, I dressed and packed Miss Grace's book in my backpack. Mom handed me a large paper bag and two canning jars filled with iced tea. She noticed my backpack.

"Are you two studying?" she asked, surprised. I looked down at my backpack and thought for a second before I agreed with her. That was a great excuse.

"Yeah, I guess we are."

"Okay, I'm glad to see you two taking your senior year seriously, but don't be too late; remember it's a school night."

"Yes, ma'am." I kissed her on the cheek again. "Thanks, Mom."

I didn't have to wait in the chapel basement long before Jason's car pulled up. The grass had grown tall at the end of the summer, and no one had bothered to mow it down. I wondered who kept the old place up. The door moaned its familiar protest as Jason followed Tia down into the basement. The stairs barely creaked with Tia's step, but Jason sounded like a small bull thumping down the old stairs.

I stood in anticipation but was nearly knocked over when T leaped from the bottom landing into my arms. I wasn't expecting her reaction and gasped. She wrapped herself around me and kissed me solidly.

Jason cleared his throat behind us. "Sorry, man," I answered as I steadied Tia onto her own two feet. I kept my arms wrapped around her, taking in all of her. I wanted to be alone with T, but with a greeting like that, I wasn't sure I trusted myself.

"How long is this going to take?" Jason asked impatiently. "I'm starving, I have a ton of homework, and I'm sure to be grounded if I don't get home before ten."

I handed him the bag of food Mom had packed. I could at least appease him with that. "It's to share," I clarified. He accepted the bag and sat on the bench to inspect its contents. He pulled out a fork and opened one of the containers. He sighed, satisfied, as he greedily consumed our supper.

"You're so lucky; my mom can't cook for shit."

I spread out a blanket on the floor and gently pulled Tia down to sit beside me. I reached into my backpack, then, and pulled out Miss Grace's book.

"I talked with Mr. Roy yesterday." I shook my head. Had it only been a day? Jeez, it felt like longer. "Anyway," I began again, "he gave me this." I offered the book to Tia. Jason leaned over her shoulder, his fork still poised over his food.

"What is it?" he asked.

"It's a book that Miss Grace compiled to help their son and Tia's mom." They both looked up at me, then. Jason's eyes were curious; Tia's were full of knowing. She'd had several days to consider Miss Grace's blessing and the fact that Sam and Rebecca Reynolds weren't her parents. Tia opened the book and read the words carefully, turning the pages over gently.

Tia leaned into me as she read. I closed my eyes and sniffed her hair; I liked the way her body felt against mine. I rubbed my cheek on the top of her head. She nuzzled in even closer. I opened my eyes when I heard the crumpling of the paper bag. Jason opened the second container of food and began eating that one, too. I didn't protest. I was content, and at that moment, my appetite was satisfied by something other than food.

Jason scraped the bottom of the container and licked the lid before he put everything back into the sack. He opened a jar of tea and gulped it down.

"So, what's next?" he asked, interrupting the silence. "Besides giving you the book, what else did the old man have to say?"

I took a deep breath and released it slowly before I recounted as much as I could remember from my talk with Mr. Roy. To the best of my ability, I passed along the facts he'd shared. Jason's brow furrowed at different parts, and I could feel Tia go rigid at my side a few times, too.

"They really screwed things up, didn't they?" Tia asked.

"Yeah, they did, and I don't know how to make it right."

"Sure you do," Jason countered. He was animated like maybe Mom's food improved his whole attitude. "We study that book. I'll be eighteen in a matter of days, and we figure this out. The old woman was adamant and seemed to know the answers. Maybe it was just too late last time."

Tia searched my eyes for my response. "I'm not doing that." My words sounded flat and resigned. There was no way I was going to do that to Tia. It was all too stupid to even give it any thought at all. She patted my arm, but I couldn't read the expression on her face. Her long lashes blinked slowly, and her brown eyes pierced me through, straight to my heart. Jason went outside, then, to take a leak, and I suspected to give us some privacy.

"Are you okay?" I asked Tia.

"Surprisingly, yes. So much of what Mr. Roy said explains things. My whole life, I didn't feel like I fit in: at school, in town, and especially at home. Being an only child is weird, but feeling like I was special and a nuisance at the same time is harder to explain."

"Will you confront them?" I asked.

"No, not yet. I think I need some more time to let all of this soak in." She turned and faced me. "Why did you say it like that?"

"What?"

"You said you wouldn't. You made it sound so final like you've already decided." She rubbed her bottom lip with the tip of her finger self-consciously. "Is there something wrong with me?" The rejection rolled off of her and landed in my lap. She doubted my feelings.

I swallowed. "No, T, it's not like that." How could I explain and comfort her? "We don't know enough, and I'm not jumping into something on the words of a dying woman. Sure, Miss Grace loved us, but that doesn't mean she was right. It didn't work for your parents, so I'm not convinced it would work for us. I'm not willing to risk it."

"So, it doesn't have anything to do with *me*."

"Oh, T, it has *everything* to do with you."

She smiled at that and let me kiss her. We were on the verge of making out when Jason's footsteps thundered down the stairs. I think he did it on purpose.

"You ready, Tiana? I need to get home," Jason said.

I stood and helped Tia to her feet. "Read the book. I want it when you're done." I nodded and gave her a quick peck on the cheek.

"Thanks, Jason," I said.

"Thank your mom," he said appreciatively. I hoped there were leftovers when I got home. Watching Tia climb the stairs, I felt empty like a starving man on a deserted island. I reconsidered the image. I wasn't on an island; I was on a ship at sea, tossed and nearly thrown overboard.

CHAPTER 34

The autumn rain made things difficult. Everyone thought it was just a fluke, but when it rained nearly every day, it became the new normal. The harvest was delayed, which made the entire town edgy. The fields were too wet, and tractors had to be pulled out of the muck and mud. When the crops showed signs of mildew and rot from the moisture, the speculation and gossip began. No one knew the cause, but they all wanted to interject their suspicions; they all wanted someone to blame.

September moved into October, and still, it rained: football in the rain, practices in the rain, and working in the rain. Every night, I read, alternating between Miss Grace's book and Mr. Roy's Bible. They were both disturbing at times and comforting at others, filled with stories and truth and things that were unbelievable.

October moved into November, and still, it rained. The playoffs were approaching, and we were in strong contention. Jason was a force to be reckoned with. He'd come a long way since the previous season. He and

I were being recruited by the same two schools, and I sort of hoped that we'd play a little college ball together.

The hardest part of the fall was that my time with Tia was limited. She worked; I worked. She and I saw each other at school, but that was about all the contact we were afforded during the week. After each win, no one went to Anderson Field to celebrate. The entire town was a soggy pit. It never flooded, but there were a few mudslides that closed roads.

A couple of times when she was babysitting, she took the Clarke boys to the theater, so I met her there with Jesse. Jason was able to bring her to the basement a couple of times, but after his car got stuck, and we had to spend the better part of an hour towing it back to the main highway, he refused to chance it again. Besides, he had his own stuff to deal with. He didn't want to spend time with Tia and me if it meant time away from Sherry. He also began the initiation process on the first full moon after his eighteenth birthday. He laughed about it at first.

"They wear these robes with all kinds of symbols on them. They take it seriously. It's so weird."

When the weather changed in November, there was no snow, just cold, deep, bleak cold that made your bones hurt. There were more gray, overcast skies and rain. It was depressing, and it took its toll on everyone, especially Mr. Roy.

I sensed his despondency, but I just thought it was the grief of losing Miss Grace. He missed her terribly. I saw him often, but we didn't talk much, and he didn't ask me if I'd made any progress in the books he'd given me. I brought him food and checked on his animals. He gave up any hope of a garden and let everything go. I wasn't sure how often he went to the house; he kept to himself and to his workshop.

I overheard him one evening while he worked on the Mustang. "God-forsaken, shit town," he muttered. "I should never have stayed. I only stayed for her. This town didn't need a Justice of the Peace; it needed a pastor. It needed God. First, Roy, Jr., now Grace. I could have saved her from a ton of heartache. She knew, but I didn't listen. There's nothing, here, now." He mumbled something else, but it was muffled by the hood and the engine. A tool clanked loudly as it fell. He cursed.

"Mr. Roy, are you okay?" I asked.

He looked out from under the hood. His eyes were bloodshot and rimmed with red. He was either drunk, or he'd been crying. He eyed me like he'd been speaking to me the entire time, not like I'd suddenly materialized before his eyes. "We thought it would work the last time, but it all blew up in our faces. I've never seen her so heartbroken as when Roy, Jr. died. It was devastating for all of us." He took a swig straight from a whisky bottle and closed the hood.

He handed me the bottle, walked into the party house, and let the door slam. I didn't follow him. I stood there admiring the Mustang and found my own relief in the bottle's contents.

Two days before the championship game, Mr. Roy followed me into the barn. It was the nastiest day yet. I looked up as he entered the stall. "I wanted to wish you luck in the big game. I'm sorry I haven't made any this season."

"It's okay; I understand." I nodded and accepted his apology.

"You won't need to be coming around so often to check on the animals, either."

"Why not?" I asked curiously.

"Got no use for 'em. Without Gracie, I've got no need to be milking goats, and the pig is big enough for smoking." I looked at him more closely. There was a change in him. "This cold will linger. It's all *her* doing," he said, and I could tell that he was referring to Tia.

"What do you mean?" I asked.

"She's strong." He smiled proudly. "She'll do it; I believe she can." Mr. Roy stroked down his beard that was now full and white. Wearing red coveralls and heavy, rubber boots, he looked a little like Santa Clause.

"Do what?" I asked. Before he answered, he turned and walked back toward the party house. I was stumped. Tia didn't have the power to control the weather. I finished with the goats and followed him, intending to ask him about some of the things I'd read, but before I could get back to the house, he pulled out onto the road in his old truck.

The final game was brutal. The rain fell steadily, yet we managed to pull out a win. Thanks to Coach, we'd been practicing in the stuff for months, so it wasn't like we didn't know how to manage it. Coach patted everyone on the shoulder and helmet during the game, keeping everyone's spirits up. He encouraged us with constant reminders about execution and form. It was the same words we'd heard from him all season, but that night they meant everything. When Jason threw the winning touchdown in the soaking rain, Coach lost himself, ran onto the field, and hugged Jason. The win was sealed, so he benched the kicker and decided to go for two. Our opponents were stunned as they watched Jason run through the defensive line and into the endzone. Puddles of water kicked up at his heels. It was a great night and an excellent way to finish out our final season. This would clinch our scholarships for sure.

The stadium erupted in celebration, and the fans rushed the field. We were all swept away in the revelry. My parents and Jesse were there;

heck, nearly the entire town was there. It was a great victory for all of us. The only disappointment was that Tia wasn't there to celebrate it with me. She rarely came to the games, and if she did, she left at half-time.

This year had been no different, but Mrs. Clarke had delivered another son over the summer, and Tia kept the two youngest ones so that they could bring the older four to the games. I would be sure to go by her house on the way home.

In the locker room, Coach gave an emotional speech. "Men, you did me proud, tonight. This season has been one of our toughest. You faced the challenges head-on, and you didn't once complain about the weather. That is, you didn't let me *hear* your complaints about the weather." There were chuckles and cheers from the team. We'd all done our fair share of complaining, but we knew we'd run if Coach got wind of it. He didn't tolerate dissension or mulligrubbing in the ranks.

He then turned his attention to the seniors. There was only a handful of us. "Take note," he said to the rest of the team. "Let these men be an example to you. They've forged through their own trials to get here. This is a great way to end your high school career. I couldn't be prouder." He pulled Jason over and then thanked each one of us individually. He put his hands on each of our shoulders and looked us in the eyes. "Good job.

Thank you," he said sincerely. "Best of luck to you." We all knew how much he meant it.

I showered and changed before I texted Tia. I drove by her house and knocked on the door. There was no answer. I texted her again and wondered if she was still babysitting. I drove by the Clarkes, but the house was dark. She replied to my third text.

With Catherine. See you tomorrow. Congrats on the win!

I wouldn't even try to hide it; her response disappointed me. I wanted to celebrate our championship win with her. I passed Catherine's, but the lights were off there, too. I cursed under my breath and drove home. My family was surprised to see me.

"No big celebration tonight?" Dad asked.

I shrugged. "Not that I know of. The field is too wet. No one is going to chance getting their vehicle stuck out there. It's not worth it. Championship or not, you couldn't pay me to go out there."

Dad agreed. Mom asked if I was hungry, but she didn't wait for an answer. She pulled out food from the fridge and made me a plate. I doubted college cafeterias were as accommodating. After I ate, I kissed Mom goodnight and accepted their congratulations and praise for an excellent season.

Although I was exhausted, I continued my habit of reading. I'd taken everything the books said in stride. After spending months reading the Bible, Miss Grace's book was a comparative breeze. I recognized family names. Some of the quotes were obscure and seemed taken out of context, but I continued to read. I'd pass it onto Tia when I saw her the next day.

CHAPTER 35

Miss Grace's book read like any other history book I'd ever been made to study, straightforward and detailed. It was mostly about a bunch of families and their obsession over our town. Its history began nearly two hundred years ago.

This book belongs to:

Grace Evelynne Carson Buchanan

Dedicated to Sally and Roy, Jr.

I begin this study on the town and county where I was born and raised. Much of the information comes from the residents through interviews. It is my sole intention to uncover the traditions and to shed some light for future generations.

There were eight founding families: Anderson, Andrews, Buchanan, Carson, Clarke, Moore, Reynolds, and Smith. The Reynolds were the first to settle, but the families all arrived within a year or so of one another. Each family was assigned a plot of land. The Reynolds and Carsons were the primary landowners. With them came indentured servants and slaves and a mixture of races and creeds.

The Carsons and Buchanans were deeply religious. The Carsons built Carson Chapel; they were devout believers. The Buchanans held the property, which later grew into Main Street. They erected the stone church in the center of town. Together their worship secured a sense of faith for the townspeople.

Over time, the families intermarried and had children and grew and filled the entire county. Less than thirty years after settlement, plight and devastation nearly took the town under. It became increasingly difficult to provide enough food to support everyone and their livestock. A second-generation Reynolds, Jedediah, was determined to find a way to secure the town's future. He went to the chapel and the church and prayed for a sign to guide him. He prayed fervently for deliverance from the fear and desperation. His wife had fallen ill, and she blamed him for not being able to provide for her and their children.

After her death, he went mad and fled from the house. He left his children with their servants and lived alone in the woods near their home. Reynolds told anyone who would listen that an old woman led him deeper into the woods. He called her an angel. He later confessed that she'd promised him the answers he sought.

He came across an ancient stone circle like the ones found in Europe. At the time, he was unaware, but it was later discovered that many of their slaves and servants had begun practicing their own rituals there.

When he found it, he was frustrated that he couldn't enter the circle. He accidentally injured his hand, trying to get into the stones. It was then that Jedediah realized he was allowed in with blood. Over time, he began placing offerings on the stone altar. Blood from small animals made the area around the altar lush and green.

With new clarity and purpose, Reynolds returned to his home and children. He studied the elements of fire, earth, water, and air, attributing the growth and fertility of the cycles of the seasons. He continued to make sacrifices in the circle, and he believed that if he collected the spilled blood and spread it all over his land, the power of the sacrifice would extend throughout his property.

Reynolds' land was the most fertile, and he became extremely wealthy in just a few harvests. He was obsessed and passionate, and even his family grew frightened of him and his visions. As long as blood was spilled on the altar in the circle, there was no worry. No one knew precisely when human sacrifice began, but Reynolds reasoned that humans had more blood than animals. He was convinced and gradually converted a few others in the prominent families.

Slaves' blood was used at first because they were expendable. As long as they were owned by Reynolds, they had his name. He couldn't afford to sacrifice a male because they were too valuable. It was documented that the women were all young, pure, and virgins yet mature enough to have children of their own. They were each listed by name and how long their blood nourished the land. I wonder if some of those early sacrifices were his own daughters.

Old Man Reynolds was meticulous in his research. He observed the weather and seasons. He believed that natural forces were behind the storms, rain, and snow. The Moores, Andersons, and Smiths were the first to participate, and together, they extended the sacrifices out toward the four corners. Their lands bordered the town on the south, east, and west. Reynold's property was at the northernmost tip. Blood from the sacrificed woman was taken to the four corners and scattered throughout.

After Reynold's death, the practice continued. Even after slavery was abolished, the elders continued to provide a blood sacrifice from the Reynolds lineage. Although they lived in town, the Clarke family soon joined the other four families.

At first, the Carsons, Buchanans, and Andrews would have nothing to do with the pagan rituals. They were too principled. Later, they were convinced that it was in their best interest. Duress and persuasion may have been involved, but regardless, all of the founding families were in some way affiliated. They may not have known all the details; Roy and I surely didn't, but once they were known, some of the families backed away.

Coincidentally, the Buchanans were run out of town, and the Carsons were left without a son to carry on the name. Ironic that Roy and I would be the two of those families to end up together. Roy, Jr. is the byproduct of two of the founding families.

Miss Grace had detailed numerous family lines. She had pages and pages from each and every person she interviewed. There were little notes and scraps of paper attached to the back of the book, too. I read each of those, but she'd included that information in the book itself. She detailed the blood covenant that was performed by the midwives and nurses at the birth of each child born in the family line. Given that, most children were treated the same way. Unless you weren't born there, each child was pretty much protected by it.

She explained her theory regarding Roy, Jr.'s being chosen as protector. He was initiated and passed whatever tests the elders gave him.

We were so proud. Roy, Jr.'s being chosen meant Roy had been accepted into the community and seen as an honorable leader. Roy, Jr. didn't mind the elder's attention or Sally's. He'd been attached to her long before his choosing. As a protector, he was given the freedom to be with Sally without anyone's speculation or ridicule.

We didn't see the change in time. Sally hid her pregnancy until the end. After graduation, she stayed at her momma's, so we didn't really know anything until the very end. Roy, Jr. couldn't keep away. His desperation led us all down difficult paths. I regret that we didn't know sooner and avoided heartache.

The final pages were written after Roy, Jr.'s death, and almost directed to Tiana. As I read, I suspected that they were written for me, too. It made me feel Miss Grace's absence even more. She was a strong and determined woman. I could see those same traits in Tia.

So much in the town changed after Roy, Jr. died. It became my unwavering belief that Sally Reynolds was Tiana Evelynne Reynolds' mother and that Roy, Jr. was her father. I confronted Gertrude (Trudy) Moore Reynolds, and she couldn't deny the truth. She told me everything she knew.

Roy, Jr. tried desperately to get Sally to leave town. The pull was too strong, and she delivered Tiana on Reynolds' property before they could get away. Trudy followed them and found the Mustang in the ditch.

"I found the baby clutched in Sally's arms. The tiny thing was screaming her fool head off. Roy, Jr. was dead, and Sally could hardly speak a word, but she did manage to tell me the child's name before she died. Tiana was the only survivor of the crash.

"I took the baby and drove back to the house. I called the elders, and they took care to remove Sally's body and dispose of it while I took care to find a suitable home for Tiana. I know I did wrong by keeping the baby from them; I just couldn't let them do her any harm. Still, it didn't matter in the end. When Sammy and Rebecca had no

children of their own, I knew it would all fall to Tiana in the end. She was the last Reynolds female," Trudy confessed through sobs.

The final entry was written in a fragile, shaky hand. It had been written recently.

Ways to protect Tiana:

Keep her away from the altar.

Loss of innocence.

Sally wasn't taken pregnant.

Refuse to follow the blood covenant.

Males have never been sacrificed.

Without another daughter, The Reynolds line ends. There are no more Reynolds females.

Everything Miss Grace wrote sounded like fantasy based on fiction, and I still didn't know how it would solve our problems.

Like the old church, our home was burned to the ground. No one confronted us, but we were all punished for Sally and Roy, Jr.'s disobedience.

I slammed the book closed.

CHAPTER 36

I had heard some speculation before the game. Everyone was hopeful that the championship win would somehow remove the melancholy of autumn. Sure enough, the next day, November rolled into December with no rain, blue skies, and a pristine sunrise. I almost didn't recognize the light that woke me the next morning – the *sun*!

My stomach growled, but I was too relaxed to care. It was the first morning after a game that I didn't have to rush out and watch film. I didn't have to relive the mistakes and make improvements. I checked my phone. It was a little after seven, too early to call Tia.

There was a knock, loud and insistent, on the carport door. I heard someone walking through the kitchen. It sounded like Mom's slippers scuffling across the tile.

"Jason? Jason Moore?" Mom asked with a note of surprise. In all the years I'd known him, he'd never come to my house.

"Good morning, Mrs. Andrews. Is Topher here?" His tone was pressing and impatient.

"Yes, but he's not up yet." Her tone was politely protective.

"Do you mind if I wake him up? I need to ask him something."

"Can't it wait until later?" she asked.

Jason's tone changed, then. "I'm sorry, Mrs. Andrews. I have to be at work in a little while, and I won't get off until late. Now that football is over, I need to catch up." It was the same tone he used with teachers and most adults. Mom would be wooed by it, too. He could get away with anything. "Please, I'd really appreciate it."

"Oh, alright," Mom sighed, and I heard the screen door open with its familiar creak. "I was about to make breakfast. Would you like some, too?"

I could almost hear Jason's mouth water. "Yes, ma'am. Thank you," he said with a smile.

"Chris's room is the first one on the right."

Jason was at my door in seconds. He knocked once and opened the door at the same time. "Topher, you awake?"

"What do you want? Why are you here?" I rolled over and sat up.

"Shit's going down, man. Big shit," he said low so that only I could hear. Jason appeared casual in jeans, a long-sleeved t-shirt, and a down vest, but he was fidgety and nervous.

I pulled on a pair of jeans and sniffed a hoodie before I pulled it over my head. “What kind of shit?”

“The kind that keeps you up all night. The kind that makes you realize that it’s all real. Your mom’s making breakfast. After that, we need to get that book and go.”

I didn’t ask any more questions. We ate while Mom plated servings of our food. Over breakfast, Dad and Jesse relived nearly every down of the final game. Jason appreciated the food and attention. They commented on the sudden change in the weather while Jason downed his second stack of pancakes.

“Thanks, Mr. and Mrs. Andrews. That was delicious,” Jason said before he guzzled the rest of his milk. He held in a burp before he continued. “Hey, Topher, do you mind going back to my house so we can finish that project for history?” he asked innocently.

I marveled at his ability to BS his way through most situations. “Sure, let me get my backpack.”

I followed him to the butcher’s shop. He parked around back and then stepped into my truck. “What’s this about?” I asked.

“You can drive; I don’t want to get my car stuck again. Go to Catherine’s. Tiana’s expecting us.”

“Where are we going?”

"Carson Chapel. I'll explain there." His eyes widened, and he cleared his throat. Throughout his initiation process, speaking to me had become increasingly awkward.

Tia was waiting for us at the curb. She smiled as I pulled up in front of Catherine's house. Jason got out and let her slide into the seat between us. She kissed my cheek in greeting.

"Good morning," she said.

"Good morning," I replied. She looked like she could have used a little more sleep.

Jason hopped back in, shut the door, and gave the nod for us to continue. Tia buckled her seatbelt and then curled her arm in the crook of my elbow. She rested her head on my shoulder as we rode in silence toward the chapel.

As soon as we were in the basement, Jason exhaled, relieved to be below ground. He sat on the bench and closed his eyes like it was the most peaceful place in the world. I sat next to him and pulled Tia down onto my lap.

Jason cleared his throat, testing his ability to speak. "Clayton's dad called my dad yesterday. He got a notice that his loans are being called in. The bad harvest took him under. Then, this morning, before daylight, the cops show up and ask my dad if they've seen Mr. Anderson,

Clayton's dad. They asked if we'd seen or heard anything. We're the nearest house to theirs. Mrs. Anderson called my mom right after that and said that Clayton and his dad got into a huge argument. He blamed Clayton, said it was all his fault for messing around with Catherine. Said none of this would have happened if he'd left to play ball like they'd planned. They've never approved of Catherine."

I watched Tia for her reaction. "Is that why you were with Catherine last night?" I asked.

"Yeah, after I got off from babysitting, she picked me up at the Clarkes, and I rode around with her for a little while looking for him. The police were actually the ones who found him; he was drunk and beaten up really badly. They took him to the hospital; he's in bad shape. Catherine and I went to see him. He's got a few broken ribs."

"What about his dad?" I asked. She shrugged.

"They haven't seen Mr. Anderson since," Jason said.

"Have either of you slept?"

"A little," T said.

Jason shook his head. "The real reason I didn't sleep last night wasn't because of Clayton. I got my summons last night after the game. The playoffs delayed my initiation. I was exhausted after the win, so my dad drove me to meet them, the elders. Anyway, man, they drove me out to the edge of the county. You won't believe where they took me." I listened intently and gestured with wide eyes for him to continue.

"It was still raining, and they'd covered my face, but I knew the exact dip in the road where it veers off toward Sherry's. You know, where the highway splits off at the county line." I nodded.

"I mapped it after I got home. I'm pretty sure it butts up against your Aunt Trudy's land, right on the edge of the county. The clincher, though…" Jason breathed, "is that…" He wasn't able to continue, and in the odd light, he looked green.

"What?" I asked, impatient for whatever he knew.

He stood and walked around the basement with a shocked expression. He wiped his mouth in disgust. "I saw where they do it. They plan to sacrifice her." His eyes glanced down toward Tia. I wrapped my arms around her protectively. "I'm sorry, Tiana. I'm so sorry." Tears welled in his eyes. He looked into my eyes, then, with increased intensity. He either couldn't stand to look at Tia, or he needed to convince me. "They take her blood and divide it, and then they scatter it all over the county."

I nodded, agreeing with what I'd read. "Yeah, I know."

"But there's more… They take her life, man. They're going to *kill* her. She *is* the sacrifice," Jason stated plainly. "They might have taken her at birth, but her parents were smart enough to seal the covenant before the elders could get to her. Good thing, except that when Sally died, they didn't know Tiana survived. They've been appeasing whatever they make the sacrifices to each summer. You were right, Topher, it was torturing her, taking bits of her, and allowing her to be *his* over the summer. He's been having his way with her for years!" Jason sounded disgusted and in awe at the same time. "Through her, everything will be completed," Jason said.

"But the final sacrifice," he hesitated, closing his eyes. What he had to confess next was either too restricted or too painful to speak even within the protection of the chapel's basement. "It's me. I have to do it. I had it all wrong. As the *protector*," he almost spat the word, "I have to protect the covenant. *I* have to do it. *I* have to…" His voice trailed off.

He collapsed down on the bench and held his face in his hands. He couldn't imagine it. Tia and I both stared at Jason. Some things I'd read in Miss Grace's book suddenly made sense. The weight of his words was too much to bear. I could only hold Tia at the moment because I didn't want to think beyond it. I held my breath, listening to his words. *No!*

After a few moments, he spoke through muffled hands, "Your dad couldn't do it, either. They never mention him by name, but I know that's who they're talking about. He loved your mom too much." Tia placed her hand on Jason's shoulder comfortingly. He looked up at her touch. He'd been crying.

"What have you found out?" he asked, surprising me with his ability to go from tears to determination so suddenly. "Give me the book," he demanded. I pulled my backpack across the floor and reached in for the book; I handed it to Jason, and he began skimming the pages. Tia sat on the bench between us and read over Jason's elbow, following his finger as it traced Miss Grace's elegant script. He and Tia read for several moments.

"This part. What's this?" He pointed to a scrap of paper. I shook my head. "What about this?" He pointed at another part.

"It's all more history. It's pretty boring at the beginning." I turned several pages over and tapped my finger over another bit. "This is where it gets interesting." Jason read for a minute or two before he cursed and stood, holding the book. He muttered something to himself and flipped the pages.

"Miss Grace wrote all of this? She was a freaking genius!" he exclaimed. I stood to look in the book, too. He was too animated to sit down. Tia stepped onto the bench and placed her hand on my shoulder to keep balance. Then, he flipped the page and continued to trace Miss Grace's fine script, concentrating on all the words.

"What does this part mean?" Tia asked curiously and pressed herself further over the book. Jason read it and then started back at the beginning. He read the opening paragraph aloud.

Tia and Jason sat on the bench, huddled over the book studying it from the beginning. Tia pulled out her phone and texted notes to herself. They went back and forth. The seasons, the solstices, and the equinoxes were all eluded to. Blood and oath and covenant were repeated too many times to count. Daughters and sons and lineages were important to the history, but they were essential to the blood covenant as well as the elements and cardinal directions: air, fire, water, earth, north, south, east, and west.

I had maintained my habit of reading every night. I made it through the entire Old Testament in a matter of months. I read it like a story, chapter by chapter, hoping that the more complicated parts would explain themselves as I continued. Like Miss Grace's book, some of it didn't make sense, and, yet, some of the later chapters sounded exactly like previous ones.

I didn't know how the birth of a son would make any real difference, except Abraham had been promised a *seed*. Everything in the Old Testament came through the sons. Most of the covenants included a mingling of blood. Through circumcision, an entire nation had been claimed. Even in marriage, *the two shall become one*. The land, the temple, the sins, everything was atoned through animal blood. The God of Abraham wasn't that much different from other gods in that regard. Blood was an atonement. Then came the blood of lineage of the family line.

I doubted any human son could make a difference until I remembered Isaac, and Abraham's willingness to sacrifice him. Through Isaac came Jacob, his twelve sons, and of course, Joseph. A woman named Hannah prayed and made a sacrifice of her son, Samuel. She didn't kill him but returned him to the temple to serve God. We were all sons and daughters in one way or another.

Returning to the present, I said, "According to this, it all passes through the Reynolds. Even before Roy, Jr.'s death, there was a separation in the town. The Carsons and Buchanans were broken off."

"It's a long-shot, but it just might work. Here," Jason said as he handed me the book. It was the most substantial book I'd ever held. It weighed at least twelve pounds, and now with its knowledge, it weighed even more. I slammed the book closed. I didn't want to read or listen to anything else.

"I want to go to Aunt Trudy's," Tia said. Jason and I both looked at her. "I want to talk to her. I want to hear it from her." When neither of us moved, Tia demanded, "Take me!"

"I can't; I have to work," Jason said. He hated not being able to do whatever she asked. She looked at me. I had nothing that couldn't wait, so I agreed.

CHAPTER 37

Tia was tired from her long night with Catherine. T put her head in my lap and slept the entire way. When I pulled off the highway onto the gravel road, we found Aunt Trudy's house run-down and in need of repair. Tia sat up when I put the truck in park. She rubbed her eyes and blinked to wake up, but she couldn't believe the difference, either. I got out and helped Tia down from the truck.

Aunt Trudy stepped out onto the porch, curious to greet her visitors. She looked frail like she was aging as rapidly as the house. She leaned on a cane and squinted her eyes, trying to see clearly. A mixture of joy and pain washed over her. She didn't know what to make of T's unexpected visit.

"Tiana, what brings you here?" she asked. Her smile was genuine, but her concern couldn't be concealed.

"I wanted to see you. We have some questions."

Tia took my hand before we stepped toward the house. Aunt Trudy was unable to muster her formidable presence from the summer. She looked at our clasped hands, and fear replaced her pleasant façade. Her eyes glanced over Tia and back to me. Recognition crossed her face; she grabbed at her blouse with her free hand and stumbled back in shock.

"Grace passed on the blessing, didn't she?" Aunt Trudy's voice squeaked.

Tia gripped my hand more securely at the woman's outburst. "Yes, ma'am."

"Fools! They're all damned fools!" Her eyes widened. The poor woman looked horrified. "What else?" she demanded through pursed lips.

Tia blinked in surprise at her aunt's tone. "Miss Grace said Christopher could free me," she stammered. "She said he needed to give me a son," Tia said timidly and looked at me with hopeful eyes. I felt my heart fall into the pit of my stomach at her words. "Is it true, Aunt Trudy? Does he have the power to free me?" I felt sick; my pulse quickened. My heart felt all sorts of wrong thudding in my stomach. Nervous sweat poured out over my entire body. It felt like an eternity before the old woman spoke.

Aunt Trudy found her way to the swing, and gingerly lowered herself. Still, the old swing creaked and moaned, or maybe those were the sounds in my mind. Tia released my hand, which did nothing to improve my own balance. I looked over my shoulder and felt the eerie chill I'd felt when I stood in the same spot over the summer. I shuddered and was cautious of potential threats.

Tia sat on the swing next to her grandmother. The familial resemblance was strong between them; I should have noticed it sooner. "Grandmother," Tia began, letting Aunt Trudy know she knew the truth. Tears welled in the old woman's eyes. She looked worn-out. Much like the weight of Mr. Roy's words, she, too, was weighed down by the truth. She patted Tia's hand tenderly. Her expression was pained, freed by the acknowledgment but filled with regret and shame. Tia wrapped her arms around Aunt Trudy. There was a claiming in their embrace, a knowing between grandmother and granddaughter.

After a moment, Aunt Trudy sat up and looked into Tia's eyes. She placed her hand on Tia's cheek affectionately. She didn't ask what we knew; she didn't or couldn't speak openly.

"You can't stay; you need to go," Aunt Trudy said. Her voice was stronger than I expected.

Tia nodded, embraced her grandmother, and then stood. Aunt Trudy looked away, out onto the front lawn of her property, avoiding my gaze. Tia took my hand and led me toward my truck.

"Wait! I want to know more. What does she know?"

Tia placed her other hand on my chest and forced me to look into her eyes. She shook her head, "No," she said flatly.

In frustration, I pulled my hand from hers. I glared at her. "Tia," I warned.

"Christopher, please." Tia's pleaded. "I need to go. I shouldn't be here."

The wind kicked up across the lawn, and clouds moved across the blue sky. Leaves rustled around the house. My fear from the summer returned, and Tia's resolve turned to apprehension. I grabbed her hand and pulled her into my side. I all but carried her to the truck and threw her forcibly into the cab. I was rough, but I wanted to get her as far away from that house as possible. She glanced back once to see Aunt Trudy on the swing. I watched the house shrink in the rearview mirror as I sped down the gravel road toward the highway. If I had any power at all, Tia would never set foot on that property again! She wasn't going back there after graduation; she wasn't ever!

Tia didn't say anything for a long time. I glanced over a couple of times, but she wasn't looking at me at all. I preferred her head resting on my thigh or on my shoulder, but she sensed my unease and stayed on the other side of the bench seat. I could reach her if I wanted, but emotionally she was a million miles away.

Once we were back on the highway, the sky showed a vibrant blue. The temperatures had been pleasant all day. I looked over at her again, and this time, she looked back at me. She reached her hand across the seat between us, offering it to me, palm up, open and receptive. I took it and kissed it.

"I'm sorry I lost my temper before," I said.

"It's understandable. I couldn't let you press her, though. She wasn't herself, and it might have been her undoing."

"She owes you an explanation. You deserve to know."

"I know what I need to know. Nothing she could say would make any difference. She's a victim in all of this, too."

I scoffed at that. "That's bullshit, and you know it. You're the only victim in all of this. They've lied to you, used you, and now they want to kill you. How can you have any sympathy for them?"

She lowered her gaze to our hands and rubbed her thumb over my knuckles. She didn't say anything, and I thought I'd offended or shamed her. The light changed to red before I turned onto Main Street. She looked down the road and smiled. She clasped my hand tighter before she spoke.

"I love this town. I love the people here, too. I can't explain it, but I can't hate them because I *love* them. Maybe that's why the idea of all of this isn't so overwhelming. It's like I'm supposed to protect this town no matter what."

The light changed to green, but I didn't proceed through the intersection. I just sat there, dumbfounded by her words. "You've been brainwashed for the past five summers. You've been sucked under. Whether or not they know, this entire town is guilty of taking advantage of you."

She didn't comment on that. I gunned the engine and headed into town. I didn't really know where she wanted to go. We passed the church ruins and the library. A block before I turned onto her street, she perked up. "Will you please take me to see Mr. Roy, now?" she asked, completely changing the subject. I really didn't want to take her home, so I agreed.

We found Mr. Roy in his shop. The door was wide open, and the sun was shining brightly. He was tinkering with his tools. The sound of my truck reverberated throughout the interior of his shop. He wiped his hands on a rag as he stepped out to greet me. He didn't even try to hide his pleasure at seeing Tia. His eyes twinkled, and he looked genuinely satisfied. She smiled and waved from the truck.

Tia greeted him with a hug, the sweetest, most affectionate embrace I'd ever witnessed. In a matter of hours, she'd been claimed by her two living grandparents. It was overwhelmingly sweet. She knew who she was for the first time in her life.

"Mr. Roy, Grandfather," she corrected. Mr. Roy beamed at the renaming. "This is all so ridiculously confusing. Am I the only one who didn't know? I'm not angry that you couldn't tell me, but when did you know?"

"I didn't have any idea until Gracie started noticing little things: the slant of your eyes, the shape of your nose, and that little dimple high in your cheek when you laugh. It doesn't show itself when you smile, only when you're full-out giggling. Am I right?" Tia nodded. "Your daddy, Roy, Jr., had all those same features. The more you came around, the more we noticed. I used to think that it was just wishful thinking, but then too many things fell into place for it all to be a coincidence. Gracie finally drove out and confronted Sally's momma."

"Trudy," Tia interjected.

Mr. Roy nodded. “Yep, none other than the proud Gertrude Reynolds. She’s been a thorn in my ass from the day I set foot in this town. She tried her darndest to get between Gracie and me. She tried even harder to break up Sally and Roy, but she interfered too late.

“Before I came along, Grace and Trudy were inseparable, two peas in a pod. It’s no wonder our children had such an attraction for one another; they’d practically been raised together. They fought like siblings their entire life, but then their friendship grew into love.” He paused, remembering. “But I’m just a foolish old romantic.”

Tia was amused by that. “What were they like? Do you have any pictures of them?” she asked.

“Most everything was lost in the fire. Luckily for Gracie, I kept all the negatives from my camera out here in the party house. How about we go inside and look around?”

Tia took Mr. Roy’s arm in the crook of his elbow. He walked proudly at her side. I followed them at a distance. This was their moment, and I didn’t want to intrude. Mr. Roy opened the door for Tia. I grabbed it above his head and held it open while he followed her inside.

The little house was dark and only held faint traces of Miss Grace’s presence. Mr. Roy opened the door to Roy, Jr.’s room and held out his hand to welcome us through. We'd seen that room before but felt like we were trespassing. This time, we were being introduced to Tia's father.

Mr. Roy opened a drawer and pulled out a photo album. He sat on the bed and patted the spot next to him for Tia. He looked around the room and sighed. "Roy, Jr.," he said, speaking out like his son was there. "I'm about to introduce you to your daughter, so I'd appreciate you being on your best behavior."

Tia's eyes widened, thinking the dead were about to speak to her. "Mr. Roy," I interrupted, "this is getting kind of weird."

He laughed, easing the tension. "No, no, we're not about to commune with the spirits. It was always a joke between us. Roy, Jr. was never shy, and he never met a stranger. His momma was shy, especially with strangers. When she was about to meet someone new, or they were out together, she'd always warn him to be on his best behavior because she didn't want him drawing unwanted attention. Roy's *best behavior* was usually a far cry from unwanted attention. He wanted all of it. He could draw every drop of it from a room, making everyone laugh and elevate a mood. You have that same gift, Tiana. You put everyone at ease."

Mr. Roy opened the photo album and began introducing Tia to the boy, the child, who would later become her father. She laughed with Mr.

Roy. She tapped photos and asked questions. After hours, I found myself staring at the framed pictures on the shelf. My eyes lingered over the ones of Roy and my dad. Then, I saw one I didn't remember. I stood and walked over and picked it up. I recognized my parents and Roy, Jr.

"Is this Sally?" I asked."

Tia looked up at the mention of her mother's name. The girl in the photo looked so much like Tia, the same brown hair and light brown eyes. The round face and dark lashes were her mother's too.

I passed the frame to Tia's outstretched hand, and she studied the picture. Mr. Roy didn't need to say anything. DNA samples weren't necessary; the similarities were too apparent.

Rebecca Reynolds, the woman who we all thought was Tia's mom, had jet black hair and blue eyes. What little hair Sam Reynolds had was blond, and his eyes were blue like his mom, Trudy. Tia's eyes and hair were both light brown. It was genetically impossible that her blue-eyed *parents* had produced a brown-eyed child. We'd learned that in eighth-grade science. I wonder if she'd wondered enough to ask them, or if they'd just explained it all away somehow.

"She's beautiful," Tia said wistfully.

"Indeed," Mr. Roy agreed. "Thanks to her, we have you."

"Thanks to me, neither of my parents are alive," she said remorsefully.

"Oh, child, you can't think like that. You didn't cause this. Your sweet momma wouldn't be here, regardless. They would have found a way to claim her, but Roy, Jr. wasn't as easily manipulated. Everyone always underestimates the power of love."

I put my arm around Tia comfortingly. I loved her too much not to fight for her. She'd said she loved this town. I wondered if she loved me more, or at least enough to fight for me, too.

"Be careful," Mr. Roy warned. His steely gaze held my attention. "Whether or not it was an accident, her mother and father died for their disobedience, much like your parents who were also punished. A generation was skipped, and that's why she's so protected. But you, Topher, you are causing a difference in her and in her protector." I thought about Jason's odd loyalty to me. It was all too much.

"You don't honestly believe all of this, do you?" I asked.

"I knew nothing of its ways before I sped into town in that car. You know that my Gracie was the only reason I stayed. The sooner you accept all of this, the better off you'll be." Like me, Mr. Roy was an outsider. Maybe that was part of the reason he'd taken such a liking to me. "I knew it would be hard for you your entire life. Then, to watch you fall in love with the wrong one." His gaze lowered back down onto Tia. "I can't blame you for that, though." He looked at her indulgently as if she had the same power over him. "Protect her."

The moment was intense, so of course, my stomach growled, breaking the silence. I hadn't eaten since breakfast, and it was already late afternoon. Tia chuckled. "I think that's our exit." She stood and looked down at Mr. Roy. "Thank you," she said.

"You're always welcome here. We're family, and this is your home, too." Tia bent down and kissed his cheek.

We left Mr. Roy in his son's room. Tia's steps were lighter as we made our way back to my truck. I opened the door for her, and she turned and hugged me. "Thank you, Christopher."

The entire day had been spent driving from one end of the county to the other, but more importantly, it had been spent with Tia, confirming everything we'd read and discovered. We picked up food and drove straight to the lake. The day had been so bright and beautiful.

Over three full-sized burgers, large shakes, and an extra-large order of onion rings, Tia and I talked about the day. In my arms, she didn't make any new revelations, but it was nice to just be with her. We let the day settle and watched the sunset. It, too, was breathtaking. Maybe she did have power over the weather, after all.

WINTER

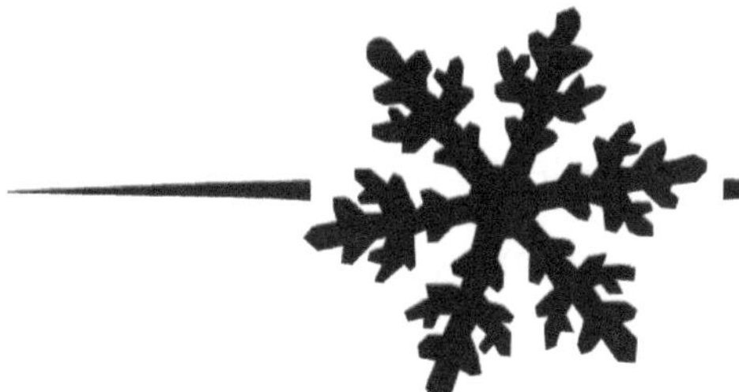

CHAPTER 38

The next couple of weeks went by in a blur. Jason was weighed down by all the knowledge he carried. His relationship with Sherry seemed to be more strained as well. Tia studied Miss Grace's book and read it in record time. She passed it along to Jason, but he kept it hidden in the church basement. He said his mom still cleaned his room and snooped through everything he owned. He didn't dare risk getting caught with it and provoke his dad or the elders.

Our senior class decided to follow the previous class's example and host another winter formal. To secure the gymnasium, the dance would be held the night following the actual solstice so that it would fall on the weekend. It just made it easier not to have things fall on a school night.

I picked up my tux for the dance before I met Tia at the Clarkes. They were out pretty late, but I helped her get everyone down, and then we had some time alone. I shivered, holding her while we kissed goodnight. We'd made out for an hour before I'd gone home. After leaving Tia, I fell asleep quickly and, of course, dreamed about her.

With the approach of winter, my dreams of Tia were lighter waves of color. If the pattern continued, she would be freer and more herself over the next few months. In the dream, I watched her follow the shadow toward the river, reliving what I'd observed during the summer. I was trying to get to her, but my feet wouldn't move. There had been a full moon overhead. The night was warm.

My dream transitioned from the summer to the winter. She was walking alone under the same full moon. She was wearing a long gown, similar to the one she'd worn in the summer, but it was too thin for the winter. She was barefooted and stumbled several times over the field. It was forecasted snow, but instead, it had only rained. The ground was soggy and made it difficult to walk. I recognized where she was; she was near my house. I called her in my dream and tried to get to her, but I couldn't.

Just like on the very same night the year before, she stood in my doorway. On the longest night of the year, she was furthest from the summer solstice and free from the power that possessed her during the summer. I pulled back the covers and got out of bed before I noticed her eyes. They were blank and unresponsive like they'd been the previous year and when she was sleepwalking into the forest.

"T?" I whispered. "T, can you hear me?" She gave no response.

I touched her then and knew she was real. I awakened fully and searched the room around us for any signs of the shadow. I didn't know to look for it before. She was barefoot, and her feet were covered in debris; her gown was soiled along the hem. She was wearing the gown I'd seen her wearing in my dream; I knew she'd fallen and stumbled.

I took her cold hand, sat her on the edge of the bed, and wrapped the blanket around her shoulders. A trail of mud and grass tracked down the hall toward my room. I grabbed a towel from my clothes basket and wiped her feet. I found some clean socks and placed them over her ice-cold toes. I used the same towel to wipe the trail from the hallway and then tossed the evidence into the laundry basket. I shut and locked my door as quietly as possible.

I laid Tia down on the bed and covered her with a blanket; her entire body was freezing. I pulled on some pajama pants and a t-shirt and lay down beside her. I stroked her face and kissed her lips. She closed her eyes. "You're safe, T. It's okay to sleep," I whispered. She settled herself closer to me.

Last year, I'd been a gentleman and gave her the entire bed; this year, I just wanted to hold her. Lying there with her felt right. We belonged together. What had drawn her to my room again? My mind raced, trying to think of a way to secure our future. I didn't want to give her up, but I didn't want to do what everyone thought was the best-case scenario. But what came after that? So what? I get her pregnant, and it's a boy. Then what? Does everything suddenly alter the course of the town? It couldn't be that simple, or someone else would have done it already. Mr. Roy, Miss Grace, and Aunt Trudy were all in agreement, but I desperately wanted another way. There had to be another way.

I reasoned that technically T wasn't a Reynolds. Her father was a Buchanan, but if they weren't married, then she never had his name. It was all too confusing to think about so late at night. At least my body had the privilege to hold Tia, even if my brain couldn't turn off long enough to appreciate it.

I only dozed for what remained of the night. I heard Mom get up and shower; Dad was out of town. I listened as my mom left for work; she'd be away until noon. Jesse thankfully had spent the night with a friend. Tia and I were alone to figure out what brought her to me in the night. I was concerned it might become a habit. I liked waking beside her; my body liked waking beside her, holding her in my arms. Knowing full-well that my body wanted to do more than hold her was challenging, too.

Tia wriggled beside me, and I knew she was waking. I anticipated her eyes opening. As soon as she realized I was lying next to her, I placed my finger over her lips so she wouldn't scream. Although we were alone, I didn't want to alarm anyone if they heard a girl screaming inside my house. Her eyes widened, and she went rigid.

"Shhh," I soothed. "It's okay. You're safe. You're at my house again." She swallowed and blinked nervously and then nodded. I released her mouth, confident she wouldn't scream.

"Did I walk here again?" she asked.

"I think so; your feet were covered in mud."

"How did I get in your bed?"

"Just like last year, I woke up, and you were standing in my room. I'm not sure how you get into the house. You were freezing, so I wanted to make you as warm as possible. I think you were sleepwalking." She closed her eyes and shook her head. "Can you remember anything?"

"I wasn't sleepwalking. I remember you calling me."

"I didn't call or text you last night; I went to bed as soon as I got home."

"No, not like that. I remember you calling my name, and I came to you. Why were you so insistent?" she asked like this was all my fault.

"I dreamed you were walking like you did in the summer. Then, it was winter. I was calling you in my dream, but I couldn't get to you. You were so far away and kept tripping in the mud."

I rolled away from her in the bed and discretely adjusted myself. She looked away and blushed. "Is that normal, or is that my doing?"

"Both. Probably worse because you're here." I chuckled nervously. "Can you give me a minute, I need to go to the bathroom."

She diverted her eyes. "If you don't mind, I'll stay here where it's warm." I couldn't tell if it embarrassed her or bothered her. I didn't have a sister, and she didn't have a brother, so figuring out this opposite sex thing was strange for both of us.

When I returned, she sat up from the bed and shivered. "It's freezing!" She crossed her arms and covered herself. Her gown was thin, and I did not need to see that, either. I opened my drawer and handed her a sweatshirt.

"Thanks," she said and pulled the hoodie over her head.

"Why aren't you sleeping in warmer clothes?" I asked. "Last year, you were wearing flannel pajamas."

"I wear flannels sometimes, but I prefer to sleep in a gown. I don't like the way the covers bunch up around my legs when I'm wearing pants."

"Me, either. Here, put these on. You still look cold," I said and handed her some fleece lounge pants." She smiled. "Want some breakfast?" I asked.

"Sure, but I should be home by eleven. My parents are both working twelve-hour shifts, midnight to noon. Can you give me a ride?" I nodded. She pulled up the pants under her gown and then rolled up the legs. "What time did I get here?"

"I don't know. It was probably two." Neither of us wanted to talk about it, but it was definitely on both of our minds. Tia followed me to the kitchen. "Cereal or eggs and toast?" I offered.

"If you don't mind cooking, I'd love some eggs. I'm pretty hungry."

I made our breakfast and served our plates before I sat down next to Tia. It felt comfortable to be eating breakfast with her. I marveled at her ability to be at ease, even in the oddest circumstances.

After we ate, I began, "Tia, we need to talk." She nodded. "How are you feeling now that the solstice has passed?" I asked.

"Fine." She looked fine; she looked better than *fine*.

"I don't understand what's going on. It's not safe to go trapesing across fields in the middle of the night."

"I didn't do it on purpose," she retorted. "Do you think I'm that stupid?"

"No, you're not stupid. I'm just worried, that's all. This is twice, on the same night of the year, that you've walked to my house in the middle of the night, not to mention what I saw last summer. You don't find that the least bit unsettling?"

"Of course, I find that *unsettling*. What kind of a person does that? I mean, really, I must be *possessed* or something," she said rhetorically. I reached to soothe her, but she moved away. She was upset. "You say I followed something into the woods after the summer solstice. You watched me, so why are you surprised that I'd do the same to get to you?"

"Oh, T," I sighed.

It didn't sound so out of the realm of possibilities when she said it like that. I loved her and was equally drawn to her. I hadn't wanted to leave her when I'd kissed her goodnight. Would it be possible to call to her in a dream? I stared into her eyes but didn't reach for her. She defiantly crossed her arms over her chest.

Impatiently, she stood and picked up our plates in one quick motion. She placed them in the sink and washed them. She put them over in the dish drainer and turned to face me.

"Break the spell, the curse; whatever you want to call it!" she demanded.

"I don't know how!" I groaned in frustration. I wished I could shake some sense into her.

"We're here alone. Have sex with me."

I blinked. "What?" I asked. I shook my head, disbelieving her words.

"Break the spell! If I'm not *pure*, then I can't atone anything. I don't want this, Christopher. I don't choose this." Her tone was no longer challenging; it was pleading. She suddenly clung to me, pulling me into her forcefully. She jumped up and into my arms and wrapped her legs around my waist and held me around the neck as she kissed me.

"No, Tia, this isn't right." I held her shoulders to push her away from me, but the intensity of her desire was too much. She kissed me again. What was I thinking? Why was I suddenly getting a conscience? The girl I loved and wanted was giving me the go-ahead, and I was the one backpedaling.

"Make love to me, Christopher. Take my virginity so they can't use it against me."

Her hands were on me, then. It didn't take me two seconds to know her intentions. Her hands were under my shirt, and I moaned. It felt so incredibly good to have her touching me and kissing me. I lifted her and carried her back to my bed. I fell over on top of her. Somehow, she squirmed out of my hoodie and sweatpants and lay there, under me, with nothing but that thin gown between us. Her hands were everywhere, enticing me to respond to her. I ripped off my own sweatshirt, and I could feel the shape of her against my chest. She pressed her hands against my waist and tugged at the waistband of my pajama pants. She was focused and determined.

I nearly gave in to her desires because they were the same as mine. I wanted her. I wanted to have her, all of her. Just as I was about to help her remove my pants, I stopped myself. She continued to pursue me. I took both of her hands and held her wrists.

"No!" I said, forcefully.

She squirmed and wiggled beneath me, trying desperately to coax me. I wrapped her hips with my legs like a wrestling move and pinned her to the bed. Our chests were heaving, and our hearts were racing. Her eyes glared at me for stopping her and holding her so that she couldn't reach me anymore.

"Take me! Break the curse!" she demanded again.

"I can't. I won't just take you and hope for the best. This is stupid!"

"Yeah, I know. Making love to me would be *so* stupid," she said with a petulant frown. "I thought you said you'd do anything," she scoffed. "I can't do this by myself, Christopher, and I'm sure I don't want to do it with anyone else."

I rolled over and released her. I grabbed my sweatshirt from the floor and put it on. I was suddenly cold and unsure. I ran my hands through my hair; I was desperately in need of a haircut.

She glared at me. She was right; I had said those exact words. When I didn't answer, she crossed her arms over herself and rolled over to face the wall. She reached for the blanket and covered her head so that I couldn't see her face. She shook, and I knew she was crying.

"Tia," I groaned. "Tia, please. Please, understand."

When she didn't reply, I stomped off to the bathroom in a huff. I needed to clear my head. I had just flushed the toilet and was washing my hands when I heard the kitchen door slam.

"Damn it!" I exclaimed.

CHAPTER 39

I grabbed my boots and ran after her. She looked ridiculous in my oversized clothes. She was half-way down the driveway before I reached her. "Tia, come on. Come back inside."

"No." She shook her head, angry and frustrated. She shivered and stormed off, quickening her pace. Her breaths puffed out white.

I didn't bother to get my truck but followed her at a slight distance. She stomped along the concrete in my socks. At least her feet were better protected than they had been in the middle of the night.

"Please, Tia," I pleaded.

She quickened her pace and was about to make a run for it. I saw the determination in her eyes when she glared back at me. "Maybe Jason will be more willing," she threatened and sprinted off down the street.

I cursed. That was a low blow, but I was afraid that maybe she'd take herself seriously. Running in boots was stupid; nevertheless, I took off after her. I tugged her elbow to stop her, but she pulled her arm away and ran toward Mr. Roy's. I had to jog a few more steps before I reached her. I scooped her up in my arms.

"Stop it! Put me down!" she protested. She fought me like a cat, but I held her hands forcibly.

"Topher! Tiana!" Mr. Roy bellowed from his driveway. "Put the girl down." I heard his booming voice loud and clear. Still, I didn't want to risk Tia running off. I dodged a blow from the back of her head, and it thudded solidly against my chest. Tia squirmed and wriggled against her restraints. Mr. Roy eyed me warily like he understood my predicament. "Never mind, bring her on in," Mr. Roy said. Tia calmed slightly, but I didn't let her go. I carried her into Mr. Roy's party house. "Set her down," he instructed.

I plopped her down onto the sofa, furthest away from the door. I stood back from her. Her hair was a mess, and her eyes were wet with tears. She glared at me. We were both breathing hard. I stood near the door to catch her if she tried to escape.

"Would either of you like a cup of coffee? I just made a fresh pot. Had no idea I'd have company this morning," Mr. Roy said casually, ignoring the tension between us. The smell of coffee filled the room, so I guessed *coffee*, this time, didn't mean scotch. When neither of us answered, Mr. Roy carried on. He refreshed his mug and sat down in his recliner. "Either one of you wants to tell me why I heard a young woman screaming, and why I find said young woman being accosted by a young man known for his impeccable character? Something just doesn't add up."

Tia crossed her arms, protectively, and looked away. A blush rose from her neck all the way to her ears. I felt hot all over, too, but for a different reason. My frustration surged.

"I'm sorry, Mr. Roy. Tia and I had a disagreement."

"Obviously. Care to give me a clue?" Mr. Roy took a sip from his mug.

I looked over at Tia and blushed, thinking about why I'd left her in my bed. "No, sir," I said firmly and looked away.

"He won't have sex with me," Tia said, breaking the awkward silence. I looked back at her, shocked at her candidness. My eyes widened, and I raised my hands in question. "It's true," she defended. It was true, but I didn't want it known. "Miss Grace said he was supposed to give me a son. That's kind of impossible if he won't do *it* with me. You and Aunt Trudy even agree with everything we've read." I may have been closest to the door, but I suddenly felt trapped with both sets of eyes on me.

"Hmmm, I see," Mr. Roy said and scratched his beard speculatively.

"It's not right, and you know it!" I said defensively.

"What would make it right, son?" Mr. Roy asked calmly.

"If we were older, done with school. If we were married," I blurted.

Mr. Roy nodded, considering my words. He pondered the topic before he answered, "Age is of little consequence. School is school. I've got little to say on that subject. As I see it, you're old enough to be consensual in the eyes of the law and nature. If it's marrying you need, then, I can fix that." I looked at Tia. She looked hopeful at the prospect.

"I didn't ask you to marry us," I sputtered, but instantly regretted it. Tia's hopeful gaze faded into rejection. She didn't think I wanted to marry *her*.

"But it would settle your mind if it were all legitimate. That's important to you; isn't it?" Mr. Roy asked.

I nodded. "Yes, sir."

"Would you?" Tia asked. "Would you actually marry us?" She stood and rushed Mr. Roy in her enthusiasm.

"It's within your rights, but I can't force *him* to do anything against his will."

What were they saying? *Marry her?* I felt all light-headed and sort of clammy. I shook my head but not because I didn't want to marry Tia.

Sure, I had always wanted to marry T, but not like that, not with everything else.

"What do you say, Topher?" I heard Mr. Roy's voice from a distance.

"What?" I asked, forcing myself back into the conversation.

"Tiana says you have a dance tonight. You'll already be all gussied up. We'll need a couple of witnesses." I swallowed hard. I couldn't believe what he was encouraging us to do.

"Tia, are you sure?" I asked. My mouth felt dry.

Her eyes held no doubt. "Yes, I am." She smiled for the first time all morning, and I didn't doubt her words were sincere. She wanted me, too.

I begrudgingly turned my attention back to Mr. Roy. "How is it possible?"

"Nature doesn't have ages or laws to protect itself. Nature only has levels of maturity. Birds, butterflies, bees, animals… they all attract and mate at the appropriate time of their development. Human females are ready between the ages of twelve and fourteen, and human males catch up about the age of fifteen. It's crazy, but we're *ready* way younger than society dictates. Sure, we aren't ready because we don't all have ways to support ourselves, but physically we are just fighting a losing battle against nature. It's so unfair!" Mr. Roy commiserated with me like he remembered all the angst of his teenaged self.

"But it's not legal," I argued.

"Ah, but it is," he countered.

"How? We aren't finished with school."

"Well, fortunately for you, there are no rules regarding whether a student is married or not. Enrollment and attendance have nothing to do with it. You two will have to figure out the logistics of marital bliss, but according to the law, the county has about a dozen contingencies for marriage. I've used a few of them in the past. There are some old laws on the books that make you of age."

"I want my grandmother to be there," Tia interjected like it was an actual thing to request.

"I can see to that," Mr. Roy offered. Could no one refuse her or make her see reason?

They both looked to me, then. "What?" I asked defensively. "What do you want from me?"

"I want you to agree to marry me and help me have a child, preferably a son." I rolled my eyes and shook my head. Obviously, I wouldn't be the one to refuse her, either.

"I thought the guy was supposed to do the proposing," I said, and she smiled at my words.

"I won't hold you to tradition, make you get down on one knee or anything." Her smile broadened, relieved that she would get her way in a matter of hours.

CHAPTER 40

I texted Jason while I waited for Tia to change; we met him briefly at the chapel. He was adamant that we act while Tia was furthest from the hold of the summer solstice. The winter solstice had passed; time was of the essence.

"I'll even be wearing white," Tia mused and shrugged.

Senior girls all wore white for dances; it was a tradition. That night, her white dress represented something very different for T and me.

"Mr. Roy's right. Tonight is perfect! She's ovulating; it's a full moon. What could be better?"

I looked at Jason dumfounded. "How do you know that?"

"It's about two weeks since her last period; her hair is all shiny, and she smells like honeysuckle. Just look at her."

I did look at her; I looked at her all the time. Her hair was always shiny, and she always smelled good. I didn't appreciate Jason knowing that much detail about the girl I was about to commit to loving forever.

Tia raised her eyebrows but didn't deny the truth of Jason's observations. *Shit!* We were playing with dynamite.

"This couldn't be more perfect! Sherry's got the flu and can't go to the dance. I don't have to divide myself tonight." He sounded so relieved. "Okay, so I've got a lot to do to make this place honeymoon worthy."

"*This* place?" I asked, looking around the chapel basement. I'd slept there briefly three months before, and it was not wedding night worthy.

"Of course, isn't it obvious? It's the best place for the two of you to be completely alone. Call Mr. Roy and tell him to meet us here at 8:30, and to bring some candles. We don't want to use the electricity upstairs."

Jason was trying to be everywhere at once. The plan was that he would escort Tia to the dance. Once she was walked through the gym and seen by enough people, he would drive her to the chapel to meet me.

I tried to remain calm while Mom took pictures like she'd done the year before. She straightened my tie and kissed my cheek. She and Dad had no idea what I was about to do. They wished me well and encouraged me to have a great night and to make plenty of memories. I told them that a bunch of us were going to be out late and that I'd probably end up crashing at Jason's again. I packed a bag with a change of clothes and a few essentials.

I was so nervous that I nearly lost my supper twice before I made it to the truck. I arrived at the chapel before everyone else. Mr. Roy and Aunt Trudy came next. Mr. Roy carried the candelabra and a bottle of wine. A loaf of bread and a bouquet of flowers lay cradled in Aunt Trudy's arms. I took the candelabra and wine so that Mr. Roy could hold the railing to steady himself. I ran to escort the old woman up the steps.

Mr. Roy placed the candelabra on the altar and pulled out candles from his jacket pocket. When he removed his coat, I realized for the first time that he was wearing a long tunic. I'd only ever seen him in coveralls or jeans. He looked very official in his priestly robes.

The strike of the match echoed in the old church, stirring it to life. The candlelight lent a beautiful glow to the old stone and wooden interior. Mr. Roy bowed his head and whispered words as he lit each candle. He gestured for me to bring him the wine. He poured some into a cup that he'd produced from underneath his robe. He then pointed toward Aunt Trudy.

"The bread," he said.

"Christian communion?" I asked.

"Yes," he cut his eyes toward Aunt Trudy, challenging. "If I'm going to marry my grandchildren, I'm going to do it the only way I know how and seal it properly." He recorked the wine. "Here, you might want this for later," he suggested. *Later?* I would definitely need it later.

Trudy and Roy were an odd couple with plenty of animosity and history between them. They were both Tia's grandparents, but they had a very different motivation for being there. Jason arrived just after I got the two of them situated.

Jason led Tia in through the chapel doors. She was wearing her coat over her white dress. They walked toward the altar to where we were all waiting. Upon seeing Tia, Trudy cried quietly and dabbed her eyes with a handkerchief. She offered Tia the bouquet of flowers. "Oh, Tiana, are you sure? Are you sure you're up to it?" Tia gazed fondly at the flowers and nodded solemnly. "My sweet child, I love you, always have. I've been proud to be your guardian; I'm sorry it has to be this way."

Tia kissed the old woman's cheek and hugged her fiercely. "Thank you, Aunt Trudy, Grandmother," she corrected. "I appreciate everything. We're going to make this right," she promised.

Mr. Roy cleared his throat. "Alright, Jason, you stand there next to Topher. Trudy, you can remain there. Topher, face your bride, and take her hand."

Tia removed her coat and handed it to her grandmother to hold. Her dress was long-sleeved, with sequins on the top and down the sleeves. The dress didn't reveal any cleavage but hugged her tightly. The skirt was long and flowy. I liked the way her hair was piled high on her head, and whisps fell loosely around her face. Last year she looked like pink cotton candy. This year, she looked like a sparkly snowflake.

Mr. Roy read traditional wedding vows but quoted words from the Bible that I had never heard spoken at a wedding before. I guessed they were the words he had been trained to say at a Christian ceremony.

Tia and I declared ourselves and then made promises to cherish and protect one another. We promised to love, to honor, and to be faithful for richer and poorer, in sickness and in health. I wondered if those vows also covered ritualistic sacrifice and demon possession.

I repeated the words, and although my tongue felt heavy and I was sweating bullets, I didn't stumble once. My hands were clammy, but I held Tia's hand firmly. I'd dreamed of marrying Tia ever since forever. It suddenly didn't matter that we were seventeen and marrying in secret. I loved her, and my wish was coming true. I looked into her eyes, and the words made it all real.

Mr. Roy then blessed the bread and the cup of wine. He told us the story of the last supper and how Jesus commanded his followers to share the bread and wine whenever they were together. "Christ said to them that they represented his body and blood that was broken and poured out for all." Mr. Roy pulled the loaf apart and offered a bit to me and then to Tia before he took a piece for himself.

"This is Christ's body, broken for you. Take and eat," he said before he placed the bread in his mouth. We followed his example. He then took the cup and lifted it. "This is Christ's blood, poured out for the forgiveness of our sins. Drink." He took a sip from the cup and then offered it to me. I took a sip and then gave the cup to Tia, who drank it and then licked the drops from her lips. Was everything connected to blood? Even our marriage communion made us drink wine that represented blood.

Mr. Roy asked us to kneel at the altar and bow our heads. He placed his hands on our shoulders and prayed a prayer aloud. He asked God to bless us and protect us and asked it all in Jesus's name. Before he said the *you may kiss your bride* part that I was anticipating, Aunt Trudy, interrupted," Now, I'll seal it the best way I know." She pulled a knife from her side. I stood and instinctively pulled Tia out of harm's way. Trudy held out her hand, palm up. "Give me your hands," she demanded. Tia put hers out trustingly. I cautiously did the same. "Blood protects blood." She took the dagger and made a two-inch cut in the palm of each of our hands. I winced when the sharp blade sliced my palm open. Blood pooled. I looked at the woman incredulously. "Blood protects blood," she repeated and placed our right palms together, forming a conduit with each heartbeat. It stung, and I could feel our hearts pulsing in my hand. She then removed a silk cord from around her shoulders, wrapped it around our hands, and continued to wrap the ends up toward our wrists. She whispered some words over us that sounded like a song.

Aunt Trudy lowered her head and released an aching sob. She whispered words over us that felt like the same warmth and blessing that Tia had received from Miss Grace.

"Grandmother," Tia began, but Aunt Trudy just shook her head. Tears ran down the old woman's face. Her shoulders slumped, and she sealed the blessing with a kiss over our clasped hands.

"You may kiss your bride," Mr. Roy said. I looked at Tia; she was my bride, and Mr. Roy and Aunt Trudy had just made it official. She was mine, and I was hers. Tia's eyes were expectant, and she smiled, waiting for her kiss. She didn't have to wait for a second longer. *Holy shit!*

I might describe the kiss differently from any other kiss, but that wouldn't be the truth. The kiss wasn't anything special; it was just a kiss. What the kiss represented was another thing entirely. I would need time to describe that, like maybe a lifetime before I knew for sure. After the kiss, I hugged Tia tightly, reassuring her, reassuring myself.

"We'll leave you to it," Jason said. He didn't make any crude comments or even crack a smile at the innuendo of *it*. Jason wrapped his arm around Aunt Trudy and escorted the tearful woman, making sure she made it safely outside. He looked back at us briefly and nodded once. "I'll get her home safely."

"Thank you, Jason," Tia said.

"Yeah, man, thanks."

Mr. Roy patted my shoulder encouragingly. "Goodnight, son." He turned to Tia. "Goodnight, Tiana. Congratulations," he said before he kissed her cheek. He took the candelabra and used its light to guide him from the sanctuary. He left us standing there together in the silence of a darkened chapel.

CHAPTER 41

Earlier in the day, Jason brought a camping mattress and some blankets and pillows and laid them out in a dark corner of the dank basement. He'd thought of everything: an ice chest, beer, water, and food. He'd even brought his family's small portable space heater. To be such an ass most of the time, he was okay, and I was glad he was my friend and no longer my enemy.

I thought long and hard about what came next. Tia and I would do this thing, and then we'd finish school and leave as fast as we could. We were escaping this stupid town and getting as far away as possible from the craziness we'd encountered for the past two years.

I was so nervous. The entire thing was insane; T and I were married. I'd imagined a million times what it might be like to be naked with Tia. I dreamed of making love to her all the time. Last summer, I'd awaked at least once a week in need of a cold shower.

"Christopher?" Tia asked, drawing my attention back to her. My thoughts were a million miles away.

"Yeah?" I replied, looking down into her eyes.

"How do you want to do this?" she asked.

I laughed humorously. "I have no idea." She put her arms around me and smothered her face into my chest. I could feel the heat of her blush through my shirt, and she laughed with me. I wrapped my arms around her and held her laughter close. She made everything easier. I kissed the top of her head and hugged her tightly.

"Tia, I love you. I want you to know that." She could feel my heartbeat and breathing change.

"I know that. I've never doubted it. I'm ready to give myself to you, but I'm afraid of the consequences. I'm afraid that my selfishness is going to ruin the lives of so many people."

"I'm only concerned about your well-being and your life. I don't give a rat's ass about anyone else but you."

At that proclamation, I suddenly felt brave. That was the entire reason I was there with her; it was my whole purpose. According to our research, I had the power to save her, releasing her from the curse. I hadn't been born there, but I was from one of the founding families.

"Christopher, I'm ready. We can do this, right?"

She needed reassurance and comfort; *I* needed to reassure her. "Yeah, T, we can do this. I've been ready for a long time; I'm glad you finally caught up." She laughed, and her eyes flashed from my flattery.

"You weren't all that ready this morning." She playfully pushed her hand against my chest and tossed her head back. I took advantage and pulled her in more closely. I kissed her neck and held her tightly against me.

"You know we won't be able to stay once this is all known. I'm not leaving you, especially if you're pregnant." She nodded. "This changes everything." She swallowed back the tears that threatened to spill over.

"I know. I've accepted that."

"You can still go to school, but you'll be with me. You can even start out part-time with the baby if you want. We can make it work."

"If I have a daughter, they'll take her just like they took me. It has to be a boy."

"I don't think so. She'll be an Andrews, not a Reynolds. We just made that official. I also don't think either of us has any control over that, but I'll do my best to give you a son if that's what you really want."

Tia smiled encouragingly, and I picked her up and carried her toward the blankets. I placed her gently down next to me. I turned on the camping heater, removed my jacket, and slipped off my shoes. Tia did the same. The small heater absorbed the dampness almost immediately. This might be more comfortable than I first imagined.

"It'll be easier to lie down without my pants. Do you mind if I go ahead and take them off?"

She shook her head. "I don't mind, but I'll need help with the zipper." She pointed toward the back of her dress.

We fumbled about and took turns figuring out the mechanics of lovemaking. It's a little awkward. No one tells you that in sex ed. No one tells you that sex is very different from what you see in movies. You don't kiss near the bed and then wake up under the covers, looking and feeling all content. The handsome male lead never gets his hands tangled in the female lead's hair or isn't able to smoothly lift her dress over her head, forgetting to unzip it all the way. There should also be lessons in bra removal.

They teach you how to secure a condom onto a banana and give you extras so that you can practice at home in private, but apparently, the bra hooks aren't as important. Thankfully, she was okay to remove that herself, and condoms weren't necessary. They also don't tell you how incredibly vulnerable you feel when you're naked next to the person you love the most in the world. She could see every flaw and every chink in my armor. I loved Tia; I had for a long time. Now, I got to show her with my body what my heart had helped me express for years: kindness, patience, strength, courage, boldness, acceptance, and forgiveness.

The glow of the heater was our only light, but we figured out all the critical parts just fine. That wasn't terribly hard. The last thing that I wish I'd known was how incredibly amazing it feels to become one flesh. I wasn't prepared for the intensity of the intimacy between us, but her laugh and her smile made it all worthwhile. Freeing her from this curse was the reason we'd married in secret and consummated our union under the safety of the church, in the only soil that wasn't tainted somehow.

The first time was because we had to. The second time was because we wanted to. How I wanted to, a million times, set it to repeat. I hoped she'd let me even after I knocked her up. After all, we were married. Isn't that what married people were supposed to do?

CHAPTER 42

On the one hand, we were like any other couple. Our school and work obligations set limits on the time we were able to spend together. I took every odd job I was offered and saved every penny I earned. Regardless of how this played out, I would have enough money to take Tia away. I needed to have enough money to support her and a baby. Every time I thought about the consequences of our lovemaking, sweat poured off of me, and I could feel tingles in my palm where Trudy had joined our blood. It also made me want to make love to her again. My *condition* had worsened, and now it wasn't just psychological; it was a physical addiction as well.

In the mornings, I met her at the bus stop or when she got out of Catherine's van. Jason was with me sometimes, and Catherine lingered, too. It wasn't like we were ever alone at school.

I didn't need the confirmation of the photo she texted me before daylight. My stomach growled noisily as I rolled over to retrieve my phone. A lead-filled balloon instantly consumed the deep hollowness, swallowing up my lungs simultaneously. My body's reaction was unnecessarily slow. My mind already knew.

The little lines on the pregnancy test were clear and defined. A single horizontal line, like a minus sign, meant negative. A second, vertical line formed a plus sign. *Positive*. But I already knew that. I didn't need the photo or the dreams that had haunted me for a week, dancing around me until Tia hovered over me and whispered, "It's a boy."

We'd gone to the chapel basement three times a week for the first month of our *marriage*. After his work at the butchers, Jason would drop Tia off to meet me and then take the back roads to Sherry's. He'd return a few hours later. I could hear the loud rumble of his car and the blast of music aboveground. He did it on purpose to warn us of his arrival. We'd dress, and I'd walk Tia to the top of the stairs. I hated letting her go.

By the end of the first month, I noticed a few subtle changes. Her breasts were fuller. That, and she fell asleep in my arms after we made love. She fell asleep in class almost every day. She said her lunch tasted bad and then ran to the girls' bathroom. She hurled what little she ate in the toilet. I could hear her through the door. I waited outside the bathroom for her, afraid of getting in trouble if I followed her inside.

When she came out, her eyes were wide. "You okay?" I asked. Her skin was pale with a light sheen of sweat across her upper lip. She took a deep breath and let it out slowly. Her eyes were bright, almost triumphant. Her radiant smile nearly knocked me over. *How could she be happy about any of it?*

A letter arrived before the end of winter. My hands shook a little, holding the envelope before I made myself open it. It felt heavy like maybe it was an acceptance and not a rejection. I'd been recruited, and Mom and I had submitted all the necessary paperwork and essays. I was impressed by the coaches and the facilities. It seemed like the best choice for me *and T*. My tuition and room and board would be covered.

"Congratulations," Tia said, smiling. "You've worked hard for this."

"We'll have to move right after graduation. We'll get an apartment near campus. I've got more than enough saved to get us through the fall. We'll be fine through the winter. This can work." I could feel myself getting excited at the prospects. "We are getting out of here!"

Tia didn't argue. "You really think this can work?" There was hope in her eyes and a smile in her voice. She was so beautiful! I kissed her full on the mouth.

"Yes, I do!"

SPRING

CHAPTER 43

So much happened in the spring. Tia said her *parents*, Sam and Rebecca, were surprisingly calm when they confronted her about the pregnancy. They, too, had noticed the changes. Being in the medical field, they were concerned that she needed to see a doctor right away. They also told her they'd take her out of town to get an abortion. Tia was appalled that they would even consider that. Still, she didn't tell them she knew they weren't her real parents.

"Why don't you tell them?" I asked.

"It's not time."

"Do they know your plans to leave?"

"No, but they will soon enough."

The Clarkes didn't say anything to her directly, but they no longer asked her to babysit every weekend. Mrs. Clarke gave Tia some lame excuse, but Mrs. Clarke had six sons. She knew all the signs of pregnancy. I think she may have suspected it before Sam and Rebecca. It wouldn't be long before everyone would take notice.

Since Miss Grace's passing, Mom made Mr. Roy's supper a few nights a week, and I typically stayed and ate with him. Now that Tia's evenings were her own, Jason took her to see him, too.

"I'm so glad you're eating with him, Chris," Mom said as she packed our suppers. "He seems lost without Miss Grace."

"Yeah, I know."

"He told me that he got rid of the goats. Miss Grace loved her animals," Mom remembered fondly.

"He says he's taking the pig to the butcher's soon, too."

Mom nodded. I think Mom's food was all he ate. By the end of winter, Mr. Roy drank every night. I didn't know until much later that we were witnessing a steady decline. On his more lucid evenings, we'd talk about our plans to leave for school. He'd ask after Tia until she started eating with us, and he was delighted by her presence.

When he first heard about Tia's pregnancy, Mr. Roy and I were alone. I thought it was only right to tell him before it was common knowledge. He received the news stoically but shook his head and took a deep breath. He stood and walked to the liquor cabinet and poured us each a drink. He raised his glass.

"To the future," he said with gusto.

"To the future," I repeated with less enthusiasm.

"You okay, Topher?" he asked.

"Yes, sir," I answered honestly.

"What are your plans?"

"Orientation is in a few weeks. I'll know my schedule then. Our plan is to leave after graduation and get settled in an apartment. We'll begin conditioning and practice in July. There are a few days of break, and then classes begin the first week of September."

"When's the baby due?" Mr. Roy asked curiously.

"The doctor said that the baby's due mid-to-late September, just as school is starting."

"Does it seem real yet?" he asked.

"No, sir. I mean, I've seen the ultrasound, and I see her belly growing, but everyone sees Tia, but they don't see me at all. I feel bad for what's coming, but she says she can handle it until graduation. She doesn't want it to be harder than it needs to be. Hearing the gossip is going to be harder on me than she knows."

"The Lord will get you through it."

"How?" I asked skeptically.

"By His grace and mercy. Ask Him for discernment. He will show you the way."

"No offense, Mr. Roy, I've read that Bible twice now. How is *God* supposed to help me? How is this god any different from any other deity? It's all a load of crap. It didn't help Roy, Jr.; how is it supposed to help me?"

"Roy, Jr. refused to accept any of it. The part of his heart that wasn't wrapped up in music and art leaned toward the town. I should have taught him from a younger age. For a time, I lost my own way and regret, but you and Tiana are different. I married you, and you received communion in the chapel in the presence of God."

"I want to believe that, but…"

"No *buts*, you do, or you don't, but I think you do, or you wouldn't bother to keep reading it through. I know life-long believers who haven't made it through as much as you've read in a matter of months."

Mr. Roy was right. I'd read it and couldn't stop reading it. Maybe there was something to it. "What do I have to do? I mean, to really believe, like you."

"You just pray." I looked at him, unsure what he meant. "Close your eyes and talk to God. You repent and ask Him to forgive your sins. Invite his spirit into your heart."

"Like now?" I asked.

"Now, or later, when you're alone."

"It doesn't have to be at an altar?" Altars seemed to make things more official in most stories and events.

"God doesn't need an altar. It's a matter of your heart and mind. Would you feel better if you prayed in the chapel?" he suggested.

I wouldn't be opposed to praying at the chapel or even at the altar in Mr. Roy's room, but I wasn't ready to commit myself to anyone but Tia, and I'd already done that.

CHAPTER 44

I'd been working all afternoon and had no idea what happened while I was at work. I came home and took a shower and scooped out servings of our supper from the crockpot Mom had started before she left for work.

Tia texted me. **Meet us at Mr. Roy's.**

We planned to eat with him, but she rarely texted me beforehand, and she never referred to *us*. When I pulled up to the house, I was surprised to see Jason lifting a suitcase from the trunk of his car. Tia stood next to him, holding her pillow like she was going on a sleepover. Tia's eyes looked determined, but also like she'd recently been crying.

"What's going on?" I asked.

"Tia's moving in," Mr. Roy said like he'd won the lottery.

As stoically as he'd received the news from me about the baby, he was equally as excited to congratulate Tia. He smiled and gushed and hugged her. He was happy for her, yet cautiously optimistic for me.

"What happened?" I asked, looking to Tia for an answer.

"Aunt Trudy's dead." She hadn't seen the old woman since our secret chapel ceremony.

"Oh, T, I'm sorry," I said.

She shook her head and waved her hand dismissively. "I was prepared for it; she's in a better place, but that's not why I'm here. *Sam* and *Rebecca* and I disagreed with how I was going to spend my summer."

Tia had received word that her Aunt Trudy was dead. Even after Trudy's death, her *parents* had the audacity to tell her that she would still be going to the old house for the summer. That's when everything exploded. When Tia refused to go, all shit hit the fan. After her parents left for work, Tia called Jason and packed a suitcase, her school backpack, and her pillow.

Jason cleared his throat. He furrowed his brow in consternation at everything Tia had said. He picked up the suitcase. "Where to?" he asked.

"She can have the house. I've readied our old room for her. Laid out some fresh linens and things. It's no bother since I keep mainly to the party house now." Jason and Mr. Roy followed Tia inside. I carried the food into the kitchen.

"What did they say when you refused them?" I asked.

"It wasn't just that. I told them I knew they weren't my parents. They were angry and denied everything. We argued. They went to work, so I left." Tia's tone was matter-of-fact.

"Thank you, Jason," she said, turning her attention toward him. He smiled. "Mr. Roy is my only *real* family, well, except for you, and he said I was always welcome. He made good on his offer." Mr. Roy nodded solemnly.

Tia's command faltered slightly, showing her vulnerability. Her lip quivered, and she blinked back tears that threatened. Her hand glided down her belly. She was strong, but how strong? I took her in my arms and held her close. I could be strong for her.

"I'm not going back. They can't make me." I looked at Jason and Mr. Roy for confirmation. Jason looked exhausted; Mr. Roy's eyes were steely gray.

One good thing about Tia staying at Mr. Roy's was that after school and work, we hung out there together. We helped Mr. Roy box up Miss Grace's things. He began the task after her death, but he said he wanted to make things more welcoming for Tia.

Tia didn't want to pack up everything. "We're going to be leaving soon. Don't clear everything away. Her things are beautiful."

On our four-month anniversary, Tia baked a cake and placed a porcelain bride and groom on top of it. "Since we didn't have a wedding cake, I thought we deserved one. These were Miss Grace and Mr. Roy's. Aren't they adorable?" The tiny bride and groom were smiling.

Mr. Roy and Jason appreciated the dessert. Now that Tia was staying in Miss Grace's house, Mom didn't have to feed Mr. Roy as often. Mom and Dad didn't have much to say about Tia staying at Mr. Roy's. They didn't know all the particulars, and it wasn't like they kept regular tabs on T, either. Mom was pressed with tax deadlines, and Dad was gearing up for spring planting and soil preparation.

The losses after the fall rains were quickly forgotten after a mild winter, an early spring, and hopes for a temperate summer. Somehow, I doubted anyone knew what was in store, even us. Selfishly, I liked Tia staying at Miss Grace's. Jason and Mr. Roy would clear out early and leave us a few hours alone. I helped her clean the kitchen and liked to imagine that it was getting us ready to live together, like playing house, except it wasn't just *playing.* I liked it when she took me by the hand and led me to her bedroom. It was different, too, making love to Tia in a real bed, in a real house. Lying next to her, I never fell asleep, though. I was too paranoid we'd be caught or found out, or I'd accidentally spend the night. I didn't want to be conspicuous.

At the beginning of May, Jason and I scheduled our college orientation. "We're leaving this weekend. I wish you could come with us."

"Me, too, but don't worry; I'll be fine. Will you be able to find us an apartment, too?" Tia asked.

"Hopefully. I'm really not sure what's available. Probably won't be as nice as you're used to."

"That doesn't matter. We'll be together and away from here. That's what matters."

"Once everyone knows, it's going to be rough until we leave." She sensed the changes already. I kissed her temple and left her sleeping soundly.

Jason and I headed out after school Friday afternoon. Welcomed by friendly students, we checked into the dorm for the night. I looked over the course catalog and wanted to get a jump-start and graduate as soon as possible so that Tia could begin taking classes, too. I wasn't going to let the baby limit her options if I could help it. We toured the campus, but with football and conditioning, I was only able to schedule two summer classes.

We filled out applications for housing and roommates. Freshmen were required to live on campus unless they lived close enough to commute or they were married. I was about to turn in my form unchecked when I noticed that there was a box for Married Student Housing. I spoke to the woman accepting our forms.

"Is this an option for freshmen housing?"

She adjusted her reading glasses and looked to the line I pointed to. She looked back up at me over her frames with dull eyes. "Are you married?" she asked wryly like I was playing some kind of joke.

"Yes, ma'am; I am." It was the first time I'd said it out loud.

She examined me but could tell I wasn't lying. "Then you're eligible. Be sure to mark the box. You'll receive a letter before the beginning of term. Fall start?" she asked.

"No, ma'am, summer, if that's available."

She pursed her lips. "Here, follow me."

I followed her to another desk, and she found a different form for me to fill out. I checked the box. "Is this included in a housing scholarship?" I asked.

"Yes. Will your wife be a student, also?" I shook my head, but then I reconsidered. Why couldn't Tia take some summer classes, too? She could totally do it.

"Is it too late for her to apply?" I asked. The woman handed me a piece of paper with all the college's deadlines.

"Scheduling might be a challenge, but it's not impossible," she said.

I thanked the woman and found Jason. We ate breakfast and stayed for half of the final orientation meeting. Jason was more impatient to get back than I was. He could hardly sit still. Now that Tia and I had an apartment, we didn't have to stick around.

"Will this be easier when she's with us?" I asked on the ride home.

"I hope so," Jason answered. "It's easier to leave Tiana when she's with you, but it's hard to just leave her alone. It's so weird. Sherry, too, though I miss her for different reasons." He smirked, and I shoved him playfully in the shoulder. "How fast do you think your truck can get us back to town?"

"Highways or backroads?" I asked, accepting the challenge on behalf of my truck.

"Doesn't matter to me, but the clock starts now." I would have never dared to drive like that with Tia or anyone else, but Jason liked the thrill.

The campus was a little over two hours away. It was barely noon when Jason and I made it back to town.

I dropped Jason off at his house and then drove straight to Mr. Roy's. I noticed that his truck was gone, and the Mustang was gone, too. Had he let Tia drive the car? I felt a pang of jealousy that he'd let her have a turn before me.

Since no one was there, I went home to shower and find something to eat. Mom and Dad were just getting in from Jesse's soccer game. Mom started making sandwiches and hit me with a million questions. I took it all in stride, and I could tell that Mom's excitement about college was bittersweet.

CHAPTER 45

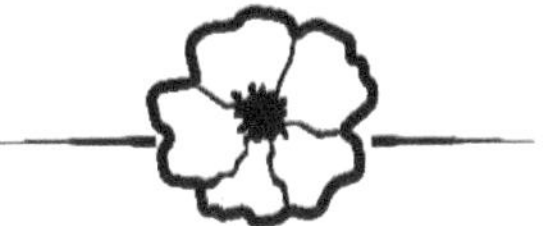

By the spring equinox, Tia wasn't quite showing, but she radiated a glow, a captivating power. She said she threw up some before school, but as long as she avoided certain foods, the morning sickness wasn't terrible.

When her skirts and tops became too small, she wore baggier clothes that concealed the early signs of pregnancy. Tia may have hidden her expanding belly, but the season couldn't hide anything. Spring came early as though Tia projected her own fertility out onto our entire community. Lush grass grew, and flowers bloomed where they had previously been none. All of nature approved, even if the townspeople didn't. Tia was naturally powerful and majestic.

By graduation, T wasn't just a little bit pregnant. Suddenly, she was pregnant all over! Her parents had known for months, but now everyone knew. It felt like such a cliché. In my own eyes, I was the jock who had knocked up his girlfriend, but in the townspeople's eyes, she was shamed and shunned, a complete disappointment. Tia refused to divulge the identity of the father, but everyone looked to Jason since they were most often seen together. He never said anything to the contrary, so the gossip began and carried considerable weight.

Jason was still torn about Sherry, but like with me, no one took much notice of her, either. None of it mattered to me; we planned to leave right after we received our diplomas.

Tia never let any of the negativity get the better of her. She went on as though it were nothing out of the ordinary. I marveled at her resilience. Jason never gave any hint that he would protect me like Tia, but by his silence, he did. We had such a bizarre friendship.

Soon after Tia moved into Miss Grace's house, the changes with Jason began. He looked like he'd taken up cage wrestling. Each morning, he appeared with a different bruise, a busted lip, or a black eye. One day, he came to school with his arm in a sling. Unseen forces in the night punished him repeatedly. Jason confessed that he never knew what new injury he'd discover each morning.

When he was absent, I went to his house after school. I was surprised to find Sherry there. She answered the door, and I followed her into the living room. Jason was lying on the sofa, propped up by several pillows. His sprained wrist lay over him in the sling. His chest rose and fell steadily, but his breaths were labored. He looked like he was asleep, but I wasn't sure because his eyes were blackened, and his face was layered in bruises. He looked rough.

"How is he?" I asked in a whisper.

Sherry shrugged. She looked worried, lowering herself onto the floor and sitting close to the sofa. She wrapped her arms around her knees like she was holding herself together. "His ribs are bruised. They gave him something to sleep, but I don't think it's helping his pain." Sherry brushed her curls back from her forehead and tucked them behind her ears. Her bright blue eyes were wide with exhaustion and rimmed in red. "Do you know why this is happening to him?" she asked. Her tone was so sweet and concerned that it hurt me. I looked around the room. She followed my gaze toward the kitchen. "No one else is home. His mom went to the store. She said I could stay with him."

"I don't know." My voice trailed off. I wasn't sure what she knew and what Jason was allowed to tell her. She bit her full bottom lip and cut her eyes back toward Jason.

"I wasn't asking you for an answer. I just wanted to know what you might already know." I nodded, understanding. "Don't worry; I haven't said anything. I'm not sure anyone in this stupid town would take notice of me anyway. I've moved a lot with my grandmother, and this place is the weirdest, yet." She rolled her eyes dismissively. "I know what everyone is saying, but I don't believe them." She shook her head slightly, and her curls bobbled. She smiled her sweet smile. "He didn't cheat on me. He acts all tough and full of himself, but he's really a marshmallow underneath all that. He told me that he was going to have to do something really hard. He told me that it would hurt me and that he regretted that fact more than anything. I believed him. I still do. They think Tiana's baby is his, but I know that's not true." Sherry's eyes were steely. To look so young and innocent, she knew more than I realized. I swallowed.

"She wouldn't cheat on you either. I know he's protecting her, and that's his *job.*" She dipped her head toward the sleeping Jason. "But don't you think *this* is a bit extreme?" Her long, blond lashes fluttered like she was trying to blink back tears. She couldn't stand to see him all beat up, knowing he was in pain.

I sat down on the floor next to her. "I'm sorry, Sherry. This is my fault. You're right; the baby's not Jason's. It was all to help Tia, but Jason took the fall. I didn't know they would do this to him. I'm so sorry," I repeated.

Sherry lowered her head down over her knees. The weight of her worry made her look fragile. I knew she wasn't, though. She was spunky and feisty, but the boy she loved was hurting, and she couldn't do anything to help him.

“Sherry,” Jason whispered. She bolted up onto her knees and took his hand.

“I'm here. Are you thirsty?” Jason's eyes fluttered, and it looked like he nodded. “Topher is here, too,” she said before she went to the kitchen to get him some water. Jason grunted an acknowledgment.

“Dude, you look like crap,” I said.

“Eat shit, Topher.”

“Same to you,” I said but didn’t mean it. I was thankful they hadn’t beaten his sense of humor out of him.

“Two more weeks, man. Two more weeks,” he groaned. We only had two more weeks until graduation. I hoped he could hang on that long.

CHAPTER 46

I left Jason's when he fell asleep again. I entered the house and overheard my parents talking in their bedroom. Mom sounded sad. "Poor Tiana. Her parents must be devastated. This comes as a terrible shock. Why is this happening?"

"It's not the end of the world, Clara," Dad argued.

"It could be," she whispered. "You know what happened last time. You know! Everyone suffered, some more than others." Mom's voice was muffled like she was speaking into Dad's chest. "We won't get another chance. There will be no mercy this time."

I stepped around and stood in their doorway, watching them. Mom was crying. The news of Tia's pregnancy was too much for her. I didn't think about how Sally and Roy, Jr.'s deaths had affected my parents, being best friends and their relationship. I didn't even consider how this might impact my parents. I naively thought that they'd be proud of me for making an effort to free Tia. The fear in Mom's tone and the way they clung to one another were intense.

"Poor, Chris. He must be so disappointed. He loves her; that's evident. She's his best friend. I can't believe she'd hurt him like that. What was she thinking?"

Mom's accusing tone broke my heart; I couldn't take it. This wasn't Tia's fault. I stepped into the room and cleared my throat. They jumped and released each other like I'd caught them doing something forbidden. Dad stood and faced me, but he kept his hand on Mom's shoulder.

"The baby's mine," I confessed to my parents without preamble. Their combined shock was evident; Mom covered her mouth and shook her head, denying the possibility. Dad sighed and shook his head.

"Tiana's parents said that it was Jason's," Dad argued. "Why would they lie?"

"That's the story, but it's not the truth."

"Are you sure she wasn't playing both of you?" Dad asked.

His words were a challenge, and I didn't appreciate his tone. It was like a punch in the gut. How could he say that about Tia? *Damn him! Damn them both!*

"You'd believe that, Dad?" I asked incredulously.

He stepped back, acknowledging the force of my protectiveness. At that moment, though, he sensed that I was a genuine threat. He stood a head shorter than me, and I outweighed him by a good fifty pounds. I wasn't thinking clearly, filled with fear for Jason and apprehension about my decision to claim Tia. I carried the weight of the consequences of creating this situation. The responsibility for Tia, the baby, my family, my friend, and the town all pressed in on me. I thought I was strong, but I didn't feel strong enough to carry it.

Besides Mr. Roy, there was no one else to talk to. My parents needed to know. “Jason claimed it to protect me. He's a good friend. He knew that he'd be punished, but he was willing to take it. He also knew there might be a risk to you and Jesse if we didn't play it this way. It's more believable, but I can't sit back and see him like this. I'm worried he's not going to pull through the next time he’s attacked.” I eyed them warily. “Did you know? Have you known all along?”

They looked balefully at one another, and then Mom nodded. “Go ahead, he needs to understand.” Her eyes looked sad, and she turned her gaze away.

“What do I need to understand?”

“Chris, Tiana is special. She’s been chosen for the greatest honor,” Dad explained like I was seven, not seventeen.

“The greatest honor?” I repeated. “That’s bullshit. She’s been chosen to be sacrificed. They want her blood.” Mom placed her hand over her mouth and held back a gasp. Dad’s eyes bugged out of his head. I wasn’t sure if they knew those details of the blood covenant.

“Do you know what you've done?” Mom asked. Her voice was unnaturally high and squeaky.

I nodded. “I know.”

“You two did this intentionally? You meant for this to happen?” Her voice was barely above a whisper, but it was heavy with fear and accusation.

“Yes, ma'am. We knew. We know everything; well, we know enough. Why didn't you tell me? Why did you make me figure this out on my own?” My tone was equally accusing.

“Please, understand. We wanted to protect you,” Mom said.

“We didn't know,” Dad said.

“You knew enough.” My voice raised. They may have had good intentions, but that didn't excuse them. “You knew they'd take her for good.”

“We didn't have a choice, son. We had to keep it from you.” My dad's voice was almost pleading. “We'd already lost too much.”

I couldn't believe what they were saying. “Why didn't you just stay away? Why did you have to come back here?”

Dad’s tone softened when he began, trying to appease me, “After my parents died, we knew we needed to return to town. We understood that we’d have to have another child. Jesse was a requirement of our return. It took us several attempts.” Mom squeezed Dad’s hand.

“I’d miscarried many times before, but it took three more times before we got Jesse. The miscarriages took a toll on my body differently than pregnancy; they also took a toll on my spirit. I was brought down, drained of hope, and felt like a failure. My body failed me with every loss. There was an emptiness that’s hard to fill,” Mom confessed.

“I’m sorry you had to go through that, Mom. I really am, but now my only concern is for Tia and the baby, our baby,” I corrected.

“We need her; the town needs her,” Dad said.

“What?” I asked.

“It’s been too long, Chris. The land needs recompense. Atonement will bring balance.” Dad said it like he was stating a scientific fact.

“Did you know that Roy, Jr. is Tia’s father?”

Dad’s eyes widened, and he stepped back like my words sent him reeling. He looked down and put his fingers on his forehead. He shook his head, not like he was refusing me, but like he denied the possibility of the truth.

"Robert?" Mom asked Dad, begging for an answer. "Sally? Tia is Sally's?" Her words were breathy with disbelief. She blanched and sat on the edge of the bed, bracing herself with the bedspread. Tears fell. "Robert!" Mom exclaimed.

He turned to her with a jerk, hearing her demand. Their eyes locked. "I didn't know," he said, almost pleading.

CHAPTER 47

The next couple of weeks were strained, to say the least. There were finals, working when I could, patiently biding my time until we got out of town, and finally helping Jason and Tia pack. Mom and Dad tiptoed around me, afraid that I might explode again. They didn't ask me much about my plans. They knew that Jason and I were leaving after graduation, but they didn't ask for any other details. I worked it all out on my own, and they seemed satisfied with that. It was probably safer for them if they didn't know. I said nothing about Tia's leaving. Jason and Mr. Roy were the only two people who knew that T and I were married and that she would be going with us.

As the days passed, Mom's eyes gave her away. She was sad to see me go, but she was heartbroken that there was a rift between us. She'd suffered for their rebellion. She'd suffered for Sally and Roy, Jr.'s disobedience. It was too late to save me from the consequences that lay ahead. Perhaps it was easier to carry her worry without words. I missed her hugs and her smile. I especially missed the look of pride and love in her eyes. All I could see was fear and disappointment. Once or twice, I suspected that she knew about our plan. She could read me well; she knew I would never leave Tia by choice.

Mr. Roy continued his habit of drinking every night, the pattern that began even before Miss Grace's death. I didn't know until it was too late that we were witnessing a steady decline; he was formulating his own plan. On the morning of graduation, I went to check on Mr. Roy and his pig before I drove Tia to the ceremony. I wanted to thank him and tell him goodbye. He wasn't in his party house, but he'd left an envelope with my name on it.

Dear Christopher, no need to check on the hog; she's at the butcher. I've already told your mom. I'm not good with goodbyes, so please don't hold that against me. I finally decided that I'd avoid it altogether. You two are going to be just fine. With you and Tiana leaving today, I realized that this town isn't worth it anymore, and it's time for me to be heading out. I put everything in Tiana Evelynne's name months ago. The papers are in the safe. The combination is her birthday. Do with it how you need to. Sell it; keep it. It makes no difference to me.

I will pray for you every day. You two have what it takes to make it through. Remember, Proverbs 3:5-6. Trust in the Lord with all your heart, and do not lean on your own understanding. In all your ways, acknowledge him, and he will make straight your paths.

Take care of our girl,

Mr. Roy

He was gone! He'd left everything; we were leaving everything. The weight of the day was suddenly too much. I sat down, holding Mr. Roy's letter in my hand, dumbfounded. I looked around the party house and then walked into the garage. The Mustang was still there. He'd taken his truck instead. I doubted he'd get far in that old thing, but what did I know?

I opened the door to the altar room and flicked on the light. The walls were cleared of all the papers and pictures which were stacked in file folders. The map was rolled up neatly and leaned against the corner. The candelabra, the Star of David, the piece of stained glass that hung overhead, and the padded kneeler remained. The drawing of the old stone church was gone, though. Mr. Roy's large Bible lay open, too. I wondered why he hadn't taken it with him, but it was a family Bible, and Tia was family.

I knelt down and read the scripture that was underlined. I wondered if Mr. Roy had left it open for me to find. **Proverbs 23:26: My son, give me thine heart and let thine eyes observe my ways.** I read the verse several times. I thumbed back a few pages to the scripture he'd quoted in his letter. *Trust in the Lord.* Now that Mr. Roy was gone, I had no one. Sure, I had Jason and Tia, but they didn't know any more than I did. Mom and Dad were worried; Mom and Dad were afraid.

I'd read, and I knew. I bowed my head, and for the first time, I prayed. I prayed because I didn't know what else to do. I fumbled in my mind for the words. "God, I don't know all the right, but I need your strength to get beyond all the wrong. Help me, if you can, to make this right for Tia. Please, help me protect her from whatever claims her. Amen."

"Christopher, what are you doing?" Tia asked.

I looked up and smiled, seeing her standing in the doorway. "He's gone," I said flatly but didn't answer her question.

"Yeah, I heard him leave this morning. We talked last night. He was good; he just couldn't stay."

"Where was he going?"

She shrugged. "He said he had a brother that he hadn't seen in a long time."

"He never mentioned a brother."

"He said I could keep the Mustang."

"He left you everything."

She nodded solemnly. "Are you packed?" she asked.

"Yeah."

"I'm ready, too. I packed up some more kitchen stuff and linens for the apartment."

I sighed, and she walked toward me. I was still kneeling. She placed her hands on my head and drew me closer. I rested my head against her belly and wrapped my arms around her. She stroked her hands over my short hair.

"Do we really have to go through with this?" she asked.

I pressed myself back to look at her. What was she asking? Of course, we had to. It was too late to get an abortion. I doubted her; I doubted myself.

"What are you asking?" I asked.

She sighed, and I waited for her answer. "I don't feel like going to graduation and have everyone gawk at me. Can we just go? I don't want to be here anymore."

"You're sure you won't regret that later?" I asked, relieved that I understood.

"Positive. I already texted Jason. He's not much up for it, either."

"My truck's loaded; I'm good to go."

Jason asked if he could see Sherry one last time. We agreed. I loaded up the Mustang for Tia and went back to my house to tell Jesse goodbye. The tension with my parents could be overlooked for a few minutes for his sake. They were loading into Dad's car to head to graduation. They turned when they heard my truck pull in behind them.

"Did you forget something?" Dad asked.

"No, sir. I'm not going. We've decided to leave early. I wanted to say goodbye before I left."

"You're leaving now?" Jesse asked. He looked at Mom and Dad and then back to me.

"Yeah, we're all packed. It'll be better if we go." Jesse ran to my side and hugged me.

"Jason's not going to graduation, either?" Mom asked in her I-do-not-approve voice.

"Chris, do you really think that's the best decision?" Dad finished Mom's strain.

"Yeah, it is. Tia doesn't need the attention, and Jason still looks like he got the worse end of a bat. Being there will only add to the gossip. She's ready, too."

"To what?" Mom asked. I didn't like her tone.

I looked down at Jesse and into his wide eyes. I smiled reassuringly at him, but my heart ached. Leaving him was hard. I squeezed him a little harder to my side.

I looked at my parents; I wanted them to understand without saying it out loud. "She's ready, too."

"Too?" Dad spoke the word slowly, and his expression darkened. His jaw tightened with understanding.

"Christopher," Mom whispered disapprovingly and rolled her eyes like I was a complete idiot. "No," she said flatly like I was a disobedient child.

"It's too late," I said.

"Too late for what?" Jesse asked innocently.

No one said anything to answer his question. I knelt down so that I was at eye level with him. "Hey, buddy, I'm going to miss you." He nodded, and I could see the tears welling up in his eyes. "Be good, okay?" He nodded again and hugged me tightly around the neck. I held him close and stood with him in my arms, lifting him up to my height.

"I'm going to miss you, too, Chris. Call me and tell me all about college and football." Jesse squeezed my neck tightly.

"I will," I promised.

I set him down. "Mom, Dad," I began but didn't have the words to thank them. Their disappointment and fear were too strong to overcome in a brief goodbye in the driveway. I turned and walked the few steps back to my truck.

"Chris," Mom called. I looked back, and she was coming toward me. Tears streamed down her face. "I can't just let you go like that. We love you, and we understand." Her voice broke. I stepped into her open arms and closed my eyes, surrendering myself to her hug.

"I'm sorry, Mom," I whispered. She nodded into my shoulder. When she released me, I saw that Dad was standing next to us, waiting for his turn to hug me. He held me in a firm embrace.

"Thanks, Dad," I said, and he squeezed me tighter.

I was so thankful that I had gone back to the house. It made leaving easier. We always planned that I'd go away for college, but we had no idea it would be like that.

I was ready. I had packed up my room days before and cashed out my savings account. College would be our way out. It had been mine for as long as I could remember, but now the plan included Jason and Tia, too.

I walked through Miss Grace's house one last time before we locked it up. I wasn't sure when we'd be back, but I knew it wouldn't be for a while. "Do you have everything?" I asked Tia. She walked out of the bathroom and looked around.

"Oh," she said as her eyes fell on the bride and groom figurines on the kitchen shelf. "I want to take these, too." She lifted them carefully and held one in each hand. "Aren't they cute?" she commented. She made the figurines touch faces and made a kissing sound like she was playing with dolls.

"Come on. Let's get out of here." Tia cut her eyes back at me, playfully and smiled.

"The bride likes to be kissed regularly, you know."

Tia was my bride. She was still my best friend, and I kissed her often, but with everything that was happening, I hadn't kissed her, really kissed her, in a while. The realization that we were starting a life together washed over me. The weight and responsibility of her and our baby were heavy, but I loved her, and that was all that mattered.

SUMMER

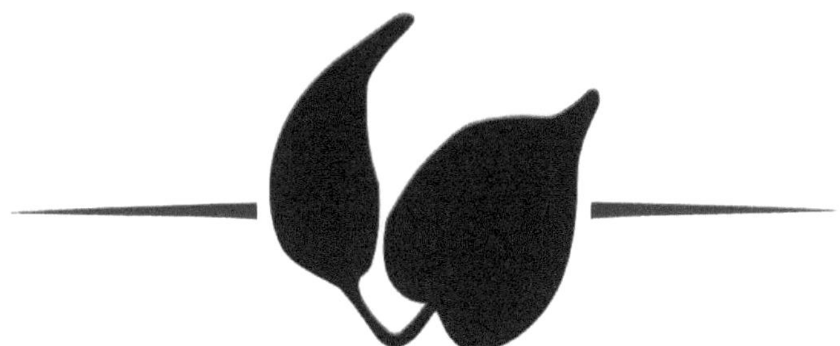

CHAPTER 48

When it was all said and done, we couldn't wait to get out of town. I pulled out of Mr. Roy's driveway and didn't bother to look back at either one of our houses. Tia followed, and as soon as we were on the highway, Jason pulled in behind the Mustang. We checked into a hotel near campus for a couple of days until our apartment was ready. Jason's dorm would open then, too. Tia thought to bring a deck of cards, and Jason was made comfortable in the second bed. He was missing Sherry and recovering from his attacks, so we left him in the room to sleep.

I had agreed to the apartment sight-unseen, but it wasn't all that bad for a cinderblock building with neutral-colored walls. I had driven past the complex during orientation, but we hadn't taken a tour or anything. From the outside, the landscaping and grounds looked well maintained. The one-bedroom apartment was furnished with a queen-sized bed, a double dresser, a vinyl sofa, and a small dining table with two chairs. There was also a little nook with a desk and third chair.

Next to the fridge in the kitchen was a stackable washer and dryer. I was glad we wouldn't have to be spending a bunch of time in a laundromat. The closet space was decent, but it wasn't like either one of us had a whole lot of clothes. Tia only had a few outfits that she wore over and over. She'd left her house with the bare essentials and clothes that would hopefully fit her again. We'd probably need baby things more than we'd need clothes for ourselves. Tia said she had cash from her own savings, and Mr. Roy had given her some money before he left, too.

Tia considered taking a class or two with us during the summer session. They would count toward any degree she pursued. She reasoned it would be a way to spend time together once practices began.

We spent the first couple of days unpacking our few items, shopping for the essentials, and attempting to register T for classes, but unfortunately, they were full.

"It's okay. I wasn't that interested, and we don't need to spend money on school right now," she conceded. "I'll be fine." She was fine, but she read my textbooks when she didn't have anything else to do. We found the library, and she checked out books on pregnancy and childbirth. She had her own agenda.

Learning to live together was our main task. I made an effort to pick up after myself and not leave stuff lying around. We shopped together and took turns cooking. Jason ate with us some, too. I think he would have moved in with us had we had a second bedroom. He regularly checked in on Tia. It was what he was used to.

"How's Sherry?" Tia asked one evening. We didn't have a TV, so we played games and cards. Jason had packed some board games. I didn't know he liked board games.

"She's okay. I haven't spoken to her much. She doesn't have a cellphone, so I can't text her, and her grandmother doesn't like her tying up her house phone. Sometimes, she calls me late at night after her grandma goes to bed. I'm so tired, though, that I'm not sure how good that is, either."

Tia frowned and stroked her finger over her belly. From the corner of my eye, I saw it move under her shirt. Jason saw it too. "What was that?" he asked.

Tia smiled. "The baby kicks a lot now. He's really active." Tia didn't want to have an ultrasound to see the sex of the baby. She believed it was a boy, and that was all that mattered. I didn't have the heart to press her.

Jason leaned forward and put his hand on Tia's belly. She looked at him and smiled, surprised at his curiosity. "Sorry," he said. "May I?" he asked but didn't remove his hand.

"Sure, but you can feel it better here." She moved his hand to the side of her belly. He stared and waited patiently for the baby to move. Nothing happened. Then, suddenly, Jason jumped back and looked at Tia with the goofiest smile. He laughed out loud and put his hand back in the same spot. Tia adjusted herself in the chair and moved his hand. It happened again with the same response from Jason.

"That's the coolest thing, ever!" he exclaimed. "I guess you get to do that all the time."

I shook my head. "No."

"Dude, you haven't felt your own baby move?" he asked like I was seriously slacking. He removed his hands and felt bad that he'd been the first besides Tia.

"No, it's okay. It just hasn't happened yet. I'm sure I'll get a chance," I reassured him. I honestly wasn't ready to feel the baby move. I mean, I was curious, but somehow it would make it real.

Later that night, Tia took my hand and rested it on her belly. "Talk to him," she said.

"That's weird, T."

"No, it isn't. The baby will be able to hear your voice and know you even before he's born."

I waited, but when nothing happened right away, I removed my hand. Later that night, though, while she slept, I stared at her belly. She wore a gown, covered only by the sheet. Curiosity got the better of me, and I placed my hand on her stomach, where Jason had touched her. I closed my eyes and relaxed, easing into sleep. I jumped awake when the baby's movement tapped my palm. I leaned up on my elbow and moved my hand to feel it again.

It thumped, and I smiled. I leaned up further and pressed my hand slightly to see if I could feel it again. Sure enough, the baby kicked. I chuckled.

"Hey," I whispered, not wanting to wake Tia. "How's it going in there?" I felt another little movement.

"See, it's not that weird," Tia whispered. I chuckled low. She'd caught me doing the very thing I'd refused to do earlier. Tia rolled over and faced me. She bit her bottom lip and smiled. "I love you, Christopher. Thank you. Thank you for everything."

She didn't have to thank me. I marveled at her ability to keep calm through everything. She was determined and strong. I felt strong for her and us.

"I love you, too, T." I kissed her, and before long, we were making love.

With everything going on, Jason and I were satisfied with being red-shirted. Our college coaches wanted some time to condition and groom us for their program. Jason's injuries were relatively healed when we reported for training, but I'm sure the coaches thought he'd been in an accident or that he was trouble.

Our days were full, but everything I did was merely a distraction. Class, football, studying, sex, cards, and Jason's presence were only temporary diversions from Tia's expanding belly. Tia made an appointment with a local midwife who would deliver the baby when the time came. Her due date fell at the autumnal equinox, which made perfect sense since she'd probably conceived at the winter equinox. As much as I'd enjoyed them, we didn't need all the other times we met in the basement for two months; she was most likely pregnant on the first or second try.

When the midwife suggested scheduling an ultrasound, Tia refused. We didn't know for sure whether it was a boy or a girl. Jason and I both wanted to know, but Tia was adamant that we not know. Surprisingly, Jason was the one who pressed her.

"Please, Tiana, we need to know."

"What difference does it make?" she asked. "Besides, we can't afford it."

Jason continued to press her until I stepped in. "Give it a rest, Jason. She's not going to change her mind." It was the first time Jason didn't do exactly what she wanted. It made me doubt him until he stopped mentioning it. I didn't always understand his motivation.

CHAPTER 49

As the summer solstice approached, Tia was restless and had trouble sleeping. It was the first time in years that Tia wouldn't be at Aunt Trudy's when the seasons changed from spring to summer. We thought our distance was enough to keep her safe, but we were sadly mistaken.

I hadn't spent a summer with Tia in five years. I didn't know how she would be. She spent her days reading and consuming knowledge. She read my textbooks and everything she could find of interest in the library – no wonder she was able to learn so much during her summers away.

As the days lengthened, she grew dark and introspective. Tia didn't want to talk about what was next. More and more, she was distant, and her thoughts were far away. Although she tried to hide it, we both knew she was being pulled in two different directions. Eventually, she even stopped trying to pretend anymore.

The night after the solstice, she pushed the covers back and left the bed. I thought she was getting up to go to the bathroom, but then I heard the front doorknob turn and felt the summer air enter the tiny apartment. I bolted from the bed to see where she'd gone. She walked down the sidewalk toward the parking lot.

I ran after her in my boxer shorts. "T," I called in a hoarse whisper. "T, where are you going?" I didn't want to wake the entire complex. I caught her elbow and turned her toward me. Her eyes were blank like when she'd appeared in my bedroom on the past two winter solstices.

"T?" I asked, but she didn't acknowledge me. I stood in front of her, and she kept moving her feet in the direction she was determined to go. I scooped her up and carried her back into the apartment. She didn't stir for the rest of the night.

The next morning, she didn't remember anything. "You walked out of the apartment last night. Were you dreaming?" I asked.

Her eyes were telling. "I heard its call," she confessed. "Now that the solstice has passed, I know it's calling me. I can feel it."

She read the anger in my expression. How was I supposed to fight and protect her from something I couldn't see? "You've got to fight it, T. You can't let it lure you back there." She nodded, but I didn't believe her.

During the day, Tia acted like herself. She entered her third trimester and was sleepy again, but at least the third trimester didn't include all the morning sickness. Her sleepwalking made her tired during the day, but as we read more about pregnancy and childbirth, I learned that sleepiness was typical.

I was less interested in pregnancy than I was in the actual childbirth parts. I kept a book with me all the time. At every opportunity, I read different scenarios and the most recommended ways to have a successful home birth. Boy or girl, Jason and I were paranoid of anyone getting to Tia or the baby. We worried that someone could snatch the baby if we went to the hospital.

Tia usually had something cooked for supper when I got home from practice and class. She wasn't, yet, as good a cook as my mom, but Mom had a couple of decades of experience over T. Together, though, we managed to feed ourselves. Some nights she could almost out eat me.

Tia's changes were most apparent in the evening. The sleepwalking was only the beginning. After the sunset, the real transformations began. She wanted to have sex every night.

We had been on a steady schedule since our wedding night, but I wasn't sure how this married sex thing was supposed to work. I could have had made love to her a couple of times a day, but I didn't want to seem like some kind of a pervert.

"So now that we're living together and married, and you're already pregnant, how do you think this sex thing will work?" I asked the day after we moved in.

She giggled and blushed and shrugged. Her ears turned pink when she looked down over her belly. I didn't mean to embarrass her, but I needed to know. She looked around the kitchen, and her eyes found the little bride and groom figurines. When we first walked into the apartment, she set the pair on the counter.

"Whenever they're kissing, you can be assured that I'd like to make love with you. I mean, it's not like I ever don't want to be with you, but just know when they're kissing, I won't need much convincing."

She slid the bride closer to the groom until their mouths touched, and she left them like that. "Like now? Does that count?" I asked half-joking. She didn't answer with words. Instead, she tucked her hair behind her blushing ear and smiled. I needed no other enticement. Since the solstice, the two were kissing every day. I didn't realize she used our intimacy as a way to escape.

At first, she didn't fight me when she was sleepwalking, but as the pull became stronger, she became more determined. I slept with her securely in my arms, but one night, she managed to escape my embrace.

I slept heavily after sex, and when I woke up just before daylight, she was in the Mustang. Thankfully, she didn't seem to have the wherewithal to start it. The next day, Jason and I installed a chain and door latch. Even at the top of the door, Tia could reach it in her sleep.

The lack of sleep was taking its toll on me. "Dude, you look like crap today," Jason said.

"Yeah, I can't sleep and keep up with her. Last night she fought me. I couldn't get in front of her, so I pressed the door with my foot and forced it closed. When she couldn't open it, she started beating on the door. I know the neighbors think we must be fighting, but I don't know how much longer I can contain her. I finally had to sleep in front of the door last night."

"I'll take a turn tonight so you can sleep," he offered. I appreciated it more than I could express.

Jason and I took turns sleeping in front of the door. Tia cried and sobbed and begged without words. When she was too exhausted to beat on the door or the person blocking the door, she would collapse in a fetal position and rock herself until daylight. We'd then get her settled in the bed, and she'd sleep until late morning. That routine continued for weeks.

CHAPTER 50

I returned to the apartment after practice, starving and exhausted, but the familiar aromas of supper weren't present. "T," I called. I walked through the small living room toward the bedroom. I expected to find her sleeping, but the covers were rumpled liked she'd been napping. I knocked on the bathroom door, but she didn't answer. I opened the door and found it empty

Breakfast dishes were still in the sink. I wondered if she'd stayed late at the library, but her backpack hung on the hook by the door, and her only pair of shoes were kicked off next to the sofa where she always left them. She had other shoes, but none of them fit.

I walked out to check and see if the Mustang was in the parking lot. When I didn't see it, I got a terrible feeling in the pit of my stomach. Before I freaked out, I called Jason.

"Hey, man," Jason said when he answered.

"Hey," I said absentmindedly, focused on finding the car. "Tia's not at the apartment."

"Have you checked the library?" he asked.

"It's doubtful; she left her backpack and shoes."

"I'll go to the library; you drive around and meet me there." His tone reflected the same feeling in my stomach.

Tia wasn't in the library or anywhere along the way. The Mustang was nowhere to be seen. The classic car stood out, so it wasn't like we'd overlook it. Jason was in the lobby; he'd already been to her regular spots.

"I'll start upstairs; go, check the basement," he commanded.

We met again on the main floor. "Come on, let's drive around some more and look for her."

After twenty minutes, we found the Mustang under a tree at the park near campus, but it took us another ten minutes to find Tia. We saw her from a distance and ran to her. She sat on a bench in her bare feet, watching the ducks in a pond.

"Hey, babe," I said, not wanting to startle her. She looked over at the two of us as we approached. She tried to smile, but her eyes filled with tears. I sat down next to her and put my arm around her shoulder. "You okay, T?" I asked. It was a stupid question. Obviously, she wasn't okay, or she would be wearing shoes, but it was all I had.

She shook her head. "No, but I had to get out of the apartment for a little while." I rubbed her shoulder. She leaned her head against my chest.

"It's okay. I wished you'd left a note. We've been looking for you for an hour."

"Do you have any water? I'm thirsty." She did something with her hand, and I noticed that she clutched something in her fist. "Sorry," she said, but I sensed something else in her voice.

"What's going on, T?" She shook her head, unwilling to say it aloud.

"Is it getting to you in the daylight now, too?" Jason guessed.

She looked over at him and nodded. "I fell asleep after breakfast, and when I woke up, I was in the Mustang. I managed to start and drive it." Jason and I shared a glance. "When I came to my senses, I found this clutched in my hand." The groom lay in her open palm. "I was confused, so I pulled over. I've been here ever since."

After that, Jason and I checked on her throughout the day. At every opportunity, we were with her. When my class let out early, I returned to the apartment. The covers were tossed around, and her shoes were next to the bed like she'd evaporated on the spot. She'd left without shoes, again.

"Damn it!" I exclaimed. I shouldn't have left her. Every time she slept, even in the daytime, the pull lured her back. I'd walked to class, so I didn't see whether or not the Mustang was gone.

When I walked back into the living room, The figurines weren't kissing. That was disappointing, and the bride stood alone. My stomach sank again. I was afraid she'd gone for good.

I called Jason. "Hello," Jason answered groggily. He'd been asleep.

"She's gone again!" The panic in my voice was evident.

"I'm on my way! Wait for me!"

I packed some water bottles and snacks in my backpack before I ran out to my truck and climbed in. She might be hungry and thirsty when we found her. Jason's tires squealed as he pulled into the parking lot beside me.

"Get in! Let's go!" I yelled over the roar of my engine.

"Let me drive," he argued and slammed his door.

"No!"

"You're not thinking clearly. Move over and let me drive!" Jason demanded.

The look on his face was determined, and my heart raced and throbbed behind my eyes. He looked calmer and more resolved. I eased over and let him behind the wheel. Taking off, the tires sped as he rounded onto the highway. He wasn't messing around.

"She's at Trudy's," I said.

"How can you be sure?"

"I can't, but I have a feeling. Last night was awful. I had to restrain her in bed all night. I don't know how much more of this either one of us can take. I'm afraid it's going to send her into labor. She pants, and her belly gets hard."

Jason, too, had noticed her weakened state. Together, we were doing the best we could, but the solstice and her approaching delivery tapped her strength. Whatever possessed her was draining her energy from a distance.

"She's only got a few more weeks to go. I know it's hard, but she can do this," Jason said confidently.

"The lure controls all of her impulses. Today is proof that we don't have any control at all. I can't stand to leave her, but I have to." I cursed, frustrated.

Trudy's property was closer than the town, but Jason made it in record time. The Mustang was abandoned in front of the house. The car door was open, and the keys were still in the ignition. The place was dark and quiet without any signs of habitation. Trudy had been dead for months, and it didn't look like anyone else had moved in. Jason ran up the porch steps and knocked on the front door.

"She's through there," I said, pointing through the tree line where I'd seen Tia go the summer before.

"Impossible," he argued.

"I know it; I feel it in my gut."

"Okay, but let's find something to take with us. There's no way I'm going in there without a weapon."

I agreed. There was a crowbar in my truck, so I grabbed that while Jason looked in the shed. He came out with an old ax and a couple of large hammers. He tossed the ball-peen hammer to me and weighed the ax and sledgehammer in his hands.

"I like these," he said. He looked like a barbarian readied for battle.

"Do you know where the altar is? Can you find it from here?" He nodded. A hot breeze kicked up as we ran, and leaves and debris blew around our feet. The trees rustled over our heads. It felt ominous like maybe it knew we were coming for Tia.

I didn't know what we'd find, but it was just a pile of wood and stones, encircled by jagged rocks. Tia lay next to the altar. She was cuddled around her belly, protecting herself and our child. Her breathing was barely detectable.

"Tia!" we called together. She didn't respond. "Tia! Wake up!"

The two tallest stones had a slight separation between them. It was the obvious entrance to the altar. There were symbols carved into the rocks, and fresh blood and a bloody handprint were smeared over the image of curved horns, or was it a crescent moon? She'd shed her blood to enter the circle.

Jason scraped his hand on the sharpest rock like maybe he'd done that before. He'd barely taken a step when he was knocked back about three feet, right on his ass. He was pissed and determined. He was still resentful about all the pain he'd endured through the spring when the elders thought the baby was his.

He jumped to his feet and ran back toward the circle. I took a step. Jason put his arm out and blocked me from entering the stone circle. He shook his head; fear and shock showed through his eyes. "You can't go in there."

"I have to try! That's my child! Her blood is mixed with mine. *Blood protects, blood*, remember?" Jason's huff was wary, but it made sense to him, too. I heard him let out a stream of curses. Clouds covered what remained of the sun. The clearing darkened.

I pulled out my pocket knife and placed the blade on my palm over the faint scar from our wedding night. "Blood protects blood," I repeated before I sliced my hand open and let the blood pool over the cut. Surprisingly, it didn't sting.

I dripped the blood on the same stone as Tia's. I placed my handprint over hers and stepped through, but nothing happened. I felt nothing strange or possessing.

Once I was through the stones, my arms went limp at the sight of her. I knelt and laid the weapons down beside her. Heat rushed through me, and I thought that she was dead. Her feet were bare and scraped and scratched from walking through the woods. The porcelain groom was clutched in her hand. "T?" I whispered before I touched her. I put my hand on her arm; she was freezing and pale.

I took her in my arms, and she stirred slightly. "Tia, baby, please; I'm here."

"Christopher," she panted. "The pull was too much; I had to come," she confessed.

"I know. I'm sorry. I'm getting you out of here."

Weakly, she shook her head. "Can't; my water broke when I passed through the circle."

"Shit!" I exclaimed.

"It won't be long," she panted, again.

"Jason, she's in labor!" I screamed.

The wind kicked up, and thunder roared in the distance. I saw a flash of lightning from the corner of my eye. I turned back to Tia. She panted and moaned in pain. "It won't be long," she repeated. "He knows I'm here. He'll take me as soon as I deliver. Don't let him take the baby, Christopher."

"No one is getting taken! Jason!"

Just then, lightning struck somewhere in the woods. The storm was getting closer. The wind whirled around us, lifting Tia's hair, but the worst of it was outside the circle.

Jason repeated what he'd done before and was knocked back again when he tried to pass through the circle. A new ferocity surged within him when he hefted the sledgehammer in his hand and swung. He struck the first stone with a resounding crack. The earth below us shuttered in protest. Jason staggered back but returned more determined. He smiled menacingly. He hit the same stone again; the earth rumbled, but it didn't break his resolve. He swung again, and the stone cracked under the force. His need to protect Tia remained strong. The lightning struck closer, and the third and fourth strikes hit their mark. Sparks flew from the metal on stone. The altar ignited into flames deep in the underside. The wind blew again, and like kindling in a campfire, the altar was ablaze.

Tia moaned and gripped my arm through a contraction. She screamed into the thunder. I had to get Tia out, but it would be too dangerous with the wind whipping around the circle and the threat of lightning.

"God!" I called, unsure of what else to do.

Suddenly everything I'd read in the Bible flooded my mind. Pagan altars had to be brought down; they had to be destroyed, dashed into pieces. The *Law of Moses* specifically dictated that the faithful were to remove the foreign altars and smash the sacred stones. Everything that was not of God was to be defiled and burned. *Hew* was a word that I'd had to look up, but it meant to chop down. I recalled the words from the Old Testament, "Hew down the graven images of their gods, and destroy their name out of that place."

I picked up the hammer and struck a stone from the inside. Without meaning to, mine and Jason's strokes connected on either side of the same stone. Jason approved with a nod. We synchronized our next swing and our next, crumbling the rock into fragments and slivers. Lightning flashed again, but the wind didn't impede our progress.

The flames on the altar were growing, spreading out across the top and down the sides. "Tia!" I screamed! She needed to roll or crawl away from the flames.

"Get her; I've got this!" Jason exclaimed. I ran back to Tia but didn't lay my weapons down this time. I picked her up and managed to carry her in one arm. Adrenaline, laced with terror, was my ally. I could feel the pull of the altar and the resistance from the stones. Jason attacked one of the entry-way stones with ferocity. I turned Tia away from the shards that sprayed across my back, and a piece caught my shoulder.

I bellowed a curse but held tightly to the hammer and even more tightly to the girl in my arms. She cried out again and stiffened. Her breaths were frantic now. "Go!" she screamed with determined eyes.

Jason's strikes were accurate, but I wasn't sure how much he could do alone. "Take her! I've got this!"

I didn't need to be told twice. I ran against the wind and threatening storm. Lightning struck again. I turned back at Jason's scream. The flames spread out toward the stones. He raised his arm to protect himself from the blaze of heat that threatened him.

"Go!" he screamed again. His thoughts were only for Tia.

CHAPTER 51

I carried Tia to the truck and lifted her inside the cab. The keys were nowhere to be found. Jason had taken them.

"Mustang," Tia panted. I exhaled in frustration, grabbed my backpack, and carried her to the car. "I need to lie down." I leaned Tia against the car so that I could move the front seat enough for her to step into the backseat.

I put the car in gear. It was insane that the first time I got to drive the Mustang was to save Mr. Roy's granddaughter. Roy, Jr. had been killed trying to do the same for Sally. He'd failed.

I could see Tia's pained expression in the rearview mirror and flames from behind. She panted and screamed in intervals. My palms were sweaty on the wheel of the car. I pressed the accelerator as far as it would go. The engine was the only thing that wasn't straining; it purred and maneuvered beautifully.

As soon as we passed the county line, Tia screamed like an animal, "Aaaaah!"

"Breathe, T. Try to relax," I encouraged. "We're almost there." I remembered from Mr. Roy's maps that the original boundary was another mile more. At our current speed, we'd be there in seconds.

"No! Stop! Help! The baby's dead!" Tia screamed from the backseat of the car. "He's dead!" she wailed. I skidded the car to a stop; gravel flew up around us.

I jumped out of the front seat and ran around the car. She'd been forced to deliver the baby alone in the back seat. Tears were streaming down her face, and her hands shook, offering him to me. Her eyes were dilated like she might be going into shock. I took the small, pale bundle in my hands and was overcome with fear.

The lifeless ball of flesh had so little color and wasn't breathing. She was right. The baby was dead, and I had no words to comfort her. The air was thick with disappointment and regret. I stroked his back gently and wiped the gooey damp from his tiny face so that I could examine him more closely. "Oh, T, I'm sorry," I whispered.

She cried out in agony between sobs. "We failed!"

At that, the tiny thing opened his eyes and let out a whimper. I exhaled in relief and surprise, and the tears I'd been holding back flowed down my cheeks.

Tia laughed out, releasing her fear, and reached for the bundle in my hands. "Give him to me!" she demanded through the sobs. I marveled at how quickly we had gone from sorrow to joy. I passed the baby to her, and his whimper turned into a scream; his lungs opened fully. He was much smaller than I expected, even being a few weeks early.

"Put him to the breast," I said, remembering what we'd read about home births in the likelihood we'd have to deliver the baby ourselves. I'd never studied so hard in my entire life, petrified that I'd be the one to be there with T when the time came.

She lifted her shirt and bra and rolled him into her breast instinctively. Just as naturally, he latched onto her exposed nipple and suckled voraciously. The panicked screams were replaced instantly with the suckling noises of a newborn. The sound reminded me of Mr. Roy's piglets. Tia gasped and then leaned her head against the window, sobbing with relief.

The evening was warm, but Tia looked cold. I opened the trunk and found a blanket and some old towels. I covered her and the baby the best

I could. The backseat was too damn small to hold the both of us, or I would have climbed back there and warmed them, myself.

The contractions came again, hard and fast. Tia gasped and lurched forward. I expected the afterbirth to follow, but instead, the crown of another head pressed down. Tia panted, holding our baby to her breast while a second one made efforts to show itself. I squatted down to get a better look.

"T, it's another one!" I exclaimed in surprise.

"What?" she panted and then groaned as her body worked to expel another baby. "It can't be," she said between waves. She shook her head, denying the possibility. When another contraction pressed, she was calmer but still focused.

I wiped the consternation from her brow. "Come on, T; you can do it." Her eyebrows shadowed her eyes, but she nodded and took a deep breath prepared for the next barrage on her body. With the next contraction, a crown of dark curls pressed through. With the next push, another baby slid into my hands. He was larger than the first one, more the size I had expected. I looked at the first baby that Tia still held to her breast. How had she managed to nurse one and give birth to a second? She was amazing! I looked down at the baby in my hands. His eyes were opened, and he wriggled and blinked. He didn't need rubbing and waking like his brother. I laid him to his mother's other breast. Tia gasped at the sensation of another little suckling mouth.

I could do nothing but stare at the three of them. I grabbed a bottle of water from my backpack and poured it over my hands to rinse them before I took a sip. I offered some to Tia. She nodded but didn't have a hand to take the bottle. I held it to her lips. She drank as fiercely as our sons. *Our sons*. I smiled, relieved, and exhaled.

"What?" Tia asked. She looked at me curiously. "Why are you smiling?"

"You are amazing! Look what you just did!"

"What *we* just did," she clarified. I nodded and agreed with her. I reached in and pulled her closer before I kissed her forehead and then her moistened lips. "Thank you, Christopher. Where's Jason?" she asked in a whisper.

I shook my head. "I don't know. I needed to get you out. The fire was too big."

"Go back. I need to know he's okay."

"No, Tia, it's not safe. I'm not taking you back there."

"It is, though. I don't feel anything anymore." She smiled at the realization that the pull was gone. Her expression was bright.

"I need to get you settled and call the midwife to check you out."

"No, I'm fine. Get Jason."

"Tia," I warned.

"Please, Christopher. I need to know he's okay."

CHAPTER 52

Against my better judgment, I drove back toward Aunt Trudy's. The billowing white smoke thickened as we approached the property. I slowed down, unsure of how to proceed. Breathing smoke wasn't healthy for any of us, especially newborn babies. Just then, lights showed through the smoke like glowing eyes. The smoke swirled around us as my truck passed us by at top speed.

I put the Mustang in reverse and sped around to follow Jason. I flashed my lights a few times to get his attention. He slowed when he realized that we were behind him. He was okay enough to drive, so I waved him on to follow us.

The sun set as we drove back onto campus. I called the midwife and asked her to meet us back at the apartment. She thoroughly checked Tia and the babies. She helped Tia get cleaned up and in bed where she could rest comfortably. The kind woman even managed to make us something to eat before she left. It wasn't in her job description, but I think she felt sorry for us.

"It's not that uncommon, you know, for babies to be born in a car. You'd be surprised how many times that happens. You were lucky to be so well prepared. They're a few weeks early, but they're fine. I'll be back tomorrow to check on you." She eyed Jason and me warily. "You need to get those looked at," she said regarding Jason's injuries.

"Yes, ma'am," he said, but I knew he wasn't as concerned for himself as he should be.

The midwife left me with instructions on how to make it through our first night. She hesitated but seemed to think we could manage until she returned.

Jason and I took turns getting cleaned up. When I came out of the shower, Jason was sitting in one of our chairs that he'd pulled into the bedroom. He stared at Tia and the twins. I quietly dug in my drawer for a pair of shorts and a t-shirt.

"How are you?" I asked. He quickly wiped his eyes; I'd caught him crying.

"Fine," he sniffed. Yep, I'd embarrassed him. He was having a moment. I didn't judge him; I knew exactly how he felt. "It feels different. I mean, I still care, and I think we'll always share a connection, but it's not the same." He exhaled and shook his head like he was trying to explain the unexplainable.

"I owe you, Jason. I may be in your debt forever."

"Yeah, you will be," he said in his asshole way.

AUTUMN

EPILOGUE

I now believe that God, as was His design, set the planets in motion at creation. Time passes, and seasons follow the natural order of the cycles of the earth. They are eternal and will continue without interruption, unlike the lifespan of a human, until God's plan for the world is fulfilled.

Tia and I survived a great deal, and with Jason's help, we were able to break Tia's curse. At the autumnal equinox, Jason and I returned to see what remained of the altar. We found Aunt Trudy's house burned to the ground. Together, we destroyed the altar's few remnants. It took us less than a day to burn the rest and demolish the stones. We'd taken sledgehammers. We didn't want to leave anything.

The next few years were full of a million new experiences. Without the distraction of his responsibility to protect Tia, Jason threw himself into football and had a memorable collegiate career. He broke all kinds of records and was hailed as the latest up-and-coming. He reveled in the attention. Sherry joined us the summer after she graduated, and they were inseparable, and for that matter, they still are.

Jason was the first to return home on weekends and holidays. He went back for Sherry, but he also went back to observe the changes to the town. At first, it didn't seem all that different, but when the harvest failed and families struggled to keep their land, we knew it was because of what we'd done. Many of the townspeople, like my parents, questioned the elders, and they renounced their affiliation. Financially, they were ruined and were forced to sell or foreclose on their properties.

Tia and I didn't go back for years. Mom and Dad came to visit us, plenty, though. They helped out where they could and brought us diapers and essentials with every visit. Mom stocked our freezer, too. College was a challenge with two little boys, but we managed it, and I even graduated early so that Tia could focus on her studies.

Football and grades were a priority so that I could make the best life possible for us. Although I'd studied finance and accounting, the semester before I graduated, I asked Tia if I might consider furthering my education. She didn't hesitate and encouraged me, and we moved together so that I could attend seminary.

Jason and Sherry married after they graduated and settled down back home. He began coaching at the high school the following fall. Coach retired the next year, and Jason was prepared to fill his shoes.

When the boys were five, we returned to Miss Grace's little house and made our home there. Soon, Tia had a garden planted and animals in the barn. She studied early childhood education, like she'd planned, and began teaching preschool when the boys started kindergarten.

When we returned, I spent my days as a farmhand. I worked hard and regained the trust of the town. I worked with Mom during tax season and took on clients of my own. After some research, I found out that the deed to Carson Chapel was held in Mr. Roy's name. Since Miss Grace's maiden name was Carson, maybe it had been in her family, or perhaps, he just wanted to have access to the only church in the county. Either way, it all belonged to Tia.

We began holding services there about a year after we moved back. Since then, the townspeople have opened their hearts to a new way. Gradually, our little congregation has grown. Sometimes, I wear Mr. Roy's robes, but they barely go past my knees. My faith and knowledge have grown exponentially over the years, but I don't presume to know everything. I'm still learning every day.

Robbie and Roy sit with their momma in the old wooden pew on Sundays. They're good boys, but I imagine they're more like their namesakes than my dad will ever admit. Along with Mom and Dad, Jason and Sherry attend services regularly. Our friendship is stronger than ever.

The change to the town is evident, and I'm thankful every day that we were successful in breaking the hold that cursed the county for a hundred years. My desire to make a life and family with Tia came true. It didn't happen the way I imagined, but it happened all the same. I still suffer the symptoms of my condition, but thankfully I have the remedy at my side.

WAIT…

As much as I would like to say that it all happened like that and that we all lived happily ever after, it's wrong to intentionally deceive others. I wish that it had happened like that. We all hoped it would, but every choice we made had a consequence. Every step we took, even the unintentional ones, significantly altered our course. In our case, the results were dire; the punishment severe.

Mostly, it happened as I described. Jason and I managed to get Tia away from the altar, but the damage to her and the baby was already done. The baby she delivered alone in the backseat never cried; he never opened his eyes. Tia's sobs were inconsolable. My heart ached at the waste and loss. All of our efforts had been in vain, a futile attempt to overcome something we had no power over. I removed my shirt and wrapped him up. I didn't force Tia to see our dead baby any longer than she had to.

She took the bundle lovingly, comforted to hold him in her arms. Nothing I could have done would have made a different outcome. When the next wave of contractions came, we were surprised by the arrival of another son. Much like his namesake, he was a fighter from the beginning. He had to be.

Tia held our living son to her breast and demanded that we go back and check on Jason, but as we approached Trudy's property, the lights that emerged though the smoke were being devoured by an all-consuming fire. My truck was blazing like it had been attacked by a fire-breathing dragon.

Tia and the baby screamed. I turned around and chased him down. We were helpless to watch as the truck weaved and careened out of control. Jason drove straight into a ditch at the side of the road. I slammed on the brakes and watched in shock as the entire thing was engulfed in flames. The explosion that followed sealed Jason's fate. Shock and disbelief absorbed me, depleting my limited reserves. I jumped out of the car and ran toward the blaze.

"No, Christopher, come back!" Tia pleaded. "It's too late!"

Tia's release came at a great cost. We lost a child and a friend. When it was all said and done, we lost even more than that.

Once Tia was settled and resting peacefully that night, I only imagined Jason was there. I needed to know I wasn't alone. How was I going to take care of them myself? Consequently, I believe he's there all the time. He's there when I'm working and playing with his namesake. He's there heckling me when I need some spurring. Even dead, he's still an asshole. Although he had to divide his time and loyalties, Jason never did things in halves. He committed to protecting Tia from the beginning, and he was willing to sacrifice himself to get the job done. He'd want me to do the same.

I studied and played football with renewed ferocity. I honored his memory with every play and every academic accomplishment. He wasn't just Tia's protector; he protected us all.

Mr. Roy wasn't heard from again. We tried to contact him about the baby, but we found no trace of a brother. I suspect he took a case of scotch out into a field and drank himself into oblivion, finally joining his Gracie. I could imagine him digging his own grave and lying down in it until his time came, or maybe he drove his truck off the road into a ravine and drowned. God wouldn't judge him for that; no one else would either.

The town was devastated by our choices, too. Trudy's house was demolished by fire, along with the acres of crops and outlining forests.

Nothing remained. The land was abandoned by Sam and Rebecca, who left town almost immediately. They didn't want to have anything to do with it, either.

It took years before things turned around. Surprisingly, it was Clayton and Catherine, who brought about the most amount of recovery. Jason's death didn't come as a surprise to Sherry. It's like she knew. After college, she married a farmer, and together, they manage their land.

All things considered, Tia and I are okay. We have a good life here. It's filled with love and hard work, and we don't take anything for granted. It took her a long time to come to terms with everything that transpired. Sometimes I wonder if naming our son Jason wasn't a mistake. Every time we say his name, we are reminded, and it's hard but good at the same time.

Melancholy often covers Tia during the summer. Some habits are hard to break, and I sometimes worry that she'll wake up and not know me again. Her distance continues until the season changes.

It's been a decade, but I'm compelled to drive out to Trudy's land every autumnal equinox and walk the field with a sledgehammer, bashing every stone I find. T and Jason Roy are too important, and I'm not taking any chances.

ABOUT THE AUTHOR

Kelda lives in South Louisiana with her beloved,
their children and dogs.
When she's not writing, she's knitting, crocheting, or quilting.
She loves music and literature
and mentoring young adults and teens.
Writing balances the hours she commits to tutoring math students.
To date, this has by far been the most challenging story to write.
Teen characters are as stubborn as their real counterparts.
Thankfully, patience won out.
It usually does.
Autumn's Captive is Kelda's fourth published work of fiction.
Her other work includes *IMPACT, Sweet Caroline,* and *DAWES: A Companion of Sweet Caroline.*
Her non-fictional work includes *Call Their Hearts Home* and
TWPH: Insights into Living with Teens.

Be Embraced.

www.ingramcontent.com/pod-product-compliance
Lightning Source LLC
Chambersburg PA
CBHW020353310726
48979CB00015B/2583/J

* 9 7 8 1 7 3 5 7 3 2 5 0 3 *